ANNE SCO
SHE FOUN
MOST GLA...

BRENDA
The chic New York woman. She ran away to Rome to forget a tragic love; now she was taking the first tentative step toward a hopeful new one.

COUNTESS ELENA BRISSON
The enchantress. Her incredible beauty and charisma still withstood the ravages of time—and the passionate depravities that were her tragic obsession.

GINO
The exploiter. He lived off the dark appetites of others. He had the coolness of a serpent and a primitive magnetism few could resist—or survive.

FREDERICO SEGRI
The rich Italian banker. A wise, compassionate survivor of his country's darkest hour. He could finally pay off a debt from the Fascist past, save a man's life—possibly a woman's love.

ALESSANDRO MASSINI
The dreamer . . . had it all—the charm, the looks, the title, the talent—until he risked everything in one foolish and near-fatal connection.

CARLO
The debonair playboy. He took his pleasures where he found them—until he found the one woman he couldn't just throw away.

THEY WERE ALL LIVING FOR
THE DAY AFTER TOMORROW

THE DAY AFTER TOMORROW

Sharleen Cooper Cohen

A DELL BOOK

To Jackie Farber . . .
And all my loved ones,
Especially Marty, Cami and Dalisa
And to Gary . . .

Published by
Dell Publishing Co., Inc.
1 Dag Hammarskjold Plaza
New York, New York 10017

Copyright © 1979 by Sharleen Cooper Cohen

All rights reserved. No part of this book may be reproduced
or transmitted in any form or by any means, electronic or
mechanical, including photocopying, recording or by any
information storage and retrieval system, without the written
permission of the Publisher, except where permitted by law.

Dell ® TM 681510, Dell Publishing Co., Inc.

ISBN: 0-440-12163-9

Printed in the United States of America
First printing—May 1979

CHAPTER 1

Anne hurried out of the parking lot squinting her eyes against the glare, and headed across Fountain Avenue only steps ahead of the oncoming traffic. The ancient hospital loomed before her, its hideous bridge connecting the original building to the more modern maternity wing. She detested coming here, even for a routine checkup. Shivers of nervousness ran through her as she entered the main lobby and made her way past the cafeteria and up the ramp to the bridge, and then the medicinal smell assailed her, triggering an immediate fear. For Anne, that smell would always mean pain and blood and tragedy, disinfectant to purify the most horrible experiences. The only good thing about coming here at all was that she could surprise Jeff and ask him to have lunch with her. I'll call and make a reservation at St. Michel, she thought, Jeff and I haven't been there in ages.

She pushed the elevator button, hoping that for once Dr. Kelsey would be on time. But she knew he wouldn't be. She always had to wait for "Big Deal Kelsey," the head of OB/GYN. He allowed her the privilege of being his patient, but he really did it as a favor to Jeff.

She remembered Kelsey, standing with Jeff at the foot of her bed after her miscarriage, while the memory of their tiny son born dead in the front seat of the car was still painfully new. The two of them consulted about her impersonally and it had bothered her that even her own husband was so clinical. They'd patted her on her empty womb and said, "Buck up, girl, be brave, better luck next time." Jill's casual get-well note had really hurt her, too. How could so close a friend be so stupidly unfeeling? Yet Jill's words echoed everyone's sentiments: What's a miscarriage?

Why expect sympathy from Jill? She never could understand why anyone wanted children anyway. Jill, with her size-five clothes from Theodore, her gold jewelry from Gucci, and her flair for the dramatic; she used her insensitivity to insure her success. Anne realized she was being disloyal, and a rush of guilt increased the hunch of her shoulders.

Dr. Kelsey's office was jammed as usual so she sat in the hall to wait. After a while, his nurse, Laura, stuck her head out of the exam room.

"Hello, Anne. You can put on a gown now, he'll be with you in a few minutes." As an afterthought she added, "How are you feeling? You do look better than the last time I saw you."

They had known each other in high school, but Laura had never paid much attention to Anne. And she still wouldn't, Anne thought, if I hadn't married Jeffrey Scott, the best-looking boy ever to graduate from John Burrows High. It must have amazed her, plain me catching the Big Man on Campus.

"Oh I'm fine, now, Laura," she answered. "More like myself every day."

"That's good!" Laura pronounced, the expert on miscarriages.

Why did I say that, Anne wondered when Laura had gone. I'm not more like myself. I should have told her the truth, that I ache inside for my dead child. And he is a dead child, not just a fetus like Jeffery says. A chilling sadness gripped her. *I will never have this child! This Brian Scott will never exist, never, never, never!* She pictured her dead son, a small version of Jeffery, taking his first steps, touching her hair with tiny fingers. She could almost feel the incredible softness of his skin. Oh Brian! I loved you.

7

The dressing-room bench was piled high with someone else's clothes. She pushed them aside and sat down, holding the gown together underneath her. Hospital gowns were demeaning. They exposed you no matter how you put them on.

She sighed, wishing Kelsey would hurry up. This was Jeffrey's morning at the clinic. If he were free for lunch today, she could justify taking the afternoon off from work.

"We're ready for you, Anne," Laura called.

Dr. Kelsey was writing at his desk with his back to her. She got up on the table and scooted down as Laura guided her. The table was still warm from the last patient. She put her feet up in the stirrups, and felt a twinge in her back. She never knew what to do with her knees, keep them open or closed.

The concavity of her stomach was accented by the position of her feet as Laura dropped a sheet unceremoniously over her knees. Her old doctor used to maintain courtesy with this ritual. Modesty was important to him. He'd cover her completely, first swathing her legs in side sheets, and exposing only the necessary areas as he examined them. One breast at a time, then her stomach, fleshy gap between separated sheets, and then the internal, with the top sheet folded so as to hide him from her view as if he were taking an old-fashioned photograph. Dr. Kelsey had no such ritual. There she was, all laid out, two peaks and a hollow, an orifice waiting for scrutiny.

Kelsey swung around on his little stool, and nodded her direction. "Morning," he said, as he reached for a speculum. He peered inside her and she visualized her cervix, newly scraped, doorway to her empty womb. Do all cervixes look alike? She held her breath and beads of sweat dotted her upper lip. Someone opened the door and stuck his head in for a moment and she almost clamped her knees together, catching Dr. Kelsey between her legs. It took all her control to keep from screaming, "Get out of here!" Why didn't they put locks on hospital doors?

"Everything's just fine," Kelsey said cheerfully, removing the speculum with a practiced twist. She exhaled. He never inquired how she was feeling, but he was the one who had helped her through her recent crisis, not her old doctor.

Laura helped her to sit up and face Kelsey. How could he ever make love to a woman after seeing this view of them day after day? He noticed her expression and winked at her. She felt her face burn with color.

"See you in six months, Anne." He smiled coolly.

"Are you going to get pregnant again?" Laura asked.

"Well, it depends on Jeffrey. Would it be all right?" She was avoiding Kelsey's eyes, enjoying her embarrassment.

Kelsey shrugged. "No reason not to. You're in good health. Just wait a few more weeks for your

9

body to resume its normal cycle and maybe next visit you'll come in for a urine test." He patted her knee patronizingly for someone who was only thirty-eight.

She climbed down off the table and clutched at the back of her gown, feeling falsely modest. The whole room reeked of intimate misery. Images of women lined the walls. The ghostly faces of those who received life-and-death news in this ancient office stared at her, while Dr. Kelsey's irreverence diminished them all. She forced a smile. "Thank you, Dr. Kelsey."

She was glad to be through, she really couldn't bear this place. If Jeff would agree to try again, she'd find another doctor. This first pregnancy had been her doing entirely, but after ten years of marriage she couldn't wait any longer and had "forgotten" to take her pills. As they wheeled her into surgery she'd had a fleeting thought that losing the baby was her punishment for tricking Jeff.

She dressed quickly.

There was a "Do Not Disturb" sign on Jeff's door, which meant he was with a patient, so she sat in the small waiting room across the hall. She loved to see his name on the door, "Jeffrey Scott, M.D." His degree had been a struggle for both of them. He'd had such a tough time getting into medical school and an even tougher time staying in, and she had tutored him through it all—high school, college, medical school. Sometimes she felt it was a miracle that he'd made it.

She glanced at her watch. It was 12:45.

She walked over to the door, thinking she'd knock and that perhaps Jeff's nurse would come out and tell him she was here. Odd sounds were coming from his office. Moaning, giggling, sighing sounds. The exam table creaked. She looked around to see if anyone else could hear it, but no one else was paying attention. She stood there, unable to leave and afraid to knock, indignant that someone else was surely using Jeffrey's office. Then she heard, "Oh, Jeff, yes, yes, oh, Jeff!"

Without thinking, she threw open the door.

There were two bodies on the exam table. The woman had her feet in the stirrups and Jeffrey's beautiful head was between her legs. He heard the door open and looked up, revealing a clear view of an exposed vagina. Anne stood there, white-faced and wide-eyed, while a picture of herself in the same position only moments before flashed in her brain.

Only it wasn't the same.

Jeff was on his hands and knees straddling the woman whose mouth was on his penis, and she was unaware of the interruption. But Jeffrey just squatted there letting her continue! He stared back at Anne with defiance and clenched his jaw as the tension mounted in his pelvis. She wanted to scream, "Stop it, stop it!" But she couldn't utter a sound. The woman stroked his buttocks, and his stomach until at last he came. But he never took his eyes from Anne's face. He hates me! she saw.

11

Carefully he extracted himself from the mouth that engulfed him and ducked his head under his arm to look behind him at the girl.

"Baby, that was brilliant."

"Yes, it was, wasn't it?" she said. Her view of the door was blocked by his body.

"We've got company," he said.

The girl's head shot up and an electrifying shock went through Anne as she recognized her friend Jill. All of her strength deserted her as she recoiled from that jolt.

"Oh God," Jill said. "How do we get out of this one?"

Suddenly, like an Arctic plunge, the electricity was shut off and Anne backed out of the room. She slammed the door but the awful vision wouldn't disappear. It repeated itself in a stroboscopic horror, flashing over and over, burning, etching, searing her. She turned and ran, sour bile choking her throat. Somehow her legs kept moving, somehow her lungs filled with air, somehow her heart kept beating. But she would have stopped them all, if only to destroy that image. Anything to stop that picture!

When she reached her car all the hurt and misery broke and she sobbed with amazement at her wound, wrenching, gasping, tearing sobs. "Oh God, oh God, ohGodohGodohGod!" Her friend and her husband. The oldest story in the book. She was torn with pain and disgust. Her trust, her faith, her work, he'd treated it all as if it were nothing. Jeff, whom she'd loved and cared for all these years—Jeff whom she had seen just now with a look of such hatred on his face.

A feeling of desolation swept over her. For ten years she had devoted herself to him, directed her whole life toward developing his career. And now, for what?

Anne heard the key in the lock and felt as if the door was opening directly inside of her. The apartment was dim, she hadn't turned on any lights. Jeff crossed to a chair and sat down opposite her, not bothering to take off his jacket. He was wearing the camel one with the lambskin lining she'd bought him last Christmas. It made him look like an ad for men's toiletries.

"Well," he said, "are you going to sit there staring at me all night?"

She felt the defiance and caught her breath, noticing the way his dark hair waved in that special place on his forehead, the angle of his chin with the cleft in it, his sculptured nose. But he was a stranger, this man, this husband, whom she thought she knew. She couldn't speak. His voice had stopped her. It was full of anger. He was angry with her! How could that be? Where was his apology?

"How long has it been going on?"

"Does it matter?"

"Yes, it matters. Was it while I was pregnant?"

13

Her words came out slow and disconnected, air gulped between the syllables.

"Before."

"When I was in the hospital, after the miscarriage, you were screwing Jill Marks."

"It had nothing to do with your pregnancy."

"It was our baby, Jeff. Not just *my* pregancy. Would you have felt differently if the baby had lived?" The pain was so strong she couldn't stand it. Please, she begged, please, God.

He shook his head. "No."

"Why didn't you tell me?"

"Well, you know now. Does it help?"

"Jeff, I love you." She sobbed. "What have I done? What did you want?"

"Don't, Anne, it only makes things worse."

She clutched at her stomach. "What could be worse than this? I just lost my child and now you. How can you do this to me?"

"Here we go again. Let's hear it for the little martyr."

She was stunned again, cut. "Is there no end to your cruelty?" She was still sobbing, her face sticky with mucus and misery. "Why? Jeff? Tell me why?"

"Because I never got what I needed from you."

She was incredulous. "You never got my help, my love, any of the things I did just for you?"

"I never got what I needed."

That was impossible! "But I have no more to

14

give." Her breath came in tiny pants, little gulps before the next blow.

"Jesus, you're something! Holier than thou, aren't you? Never make a mistake, never slip for one minute."

"Is that what you call it, a slip?" She had more control now. The first acid wash had slowed to a dull torture.

"I guess I really don't know what it was!"

"Am I supposed to accept that? I'm supposed to watch my life disintegrate before me and you tell me you don't know why?"

"How the hell do you expect me to know? Go talk to a shrink, ask your mother, look in the mirror." He stopped himself. "This isn't going to get us anywhere. Do you want me to leave? I'll leave. Just say so."

A scream of protest welled up inside her, pulsing in her throat, pounding at the roof of her mouth, trying to escape. Leave, he said leave, he's going to leave. No, he can't. He can't leave, he can't do it. No, *no*, NO. She saw herself at this moment as he saw her. Her gums too visible, her hips too wide, her eyes too round, her breasts too small, her looks too plain, her bearing too dull for mercurial Jeff Scott; and now her face streaked with tears and newfound terrors. She looked at him, her stranger, and ached for the past. Had it ever been? She would doubt it forever. How fast it was used up.

She stood up, a zombie in a plaid coat.

* * *

Outside, not even the chill of the November night penetrated. Somewhere it registered cold, winter, frosty breath, windy sparkling skies, billows of clouds, and in between black velvet, purple and silver. But she didn't feel it. Down the catwalk past the Goldbergs', down the stairs to the garage. She got into the car, stunned, keeping a tight lid on the well of hatred that boiled underneath, feeling it ignite and rev like the motor when she turned the key. She drove down the alley, wanting to smash the car into a tree because she saw Jeffrey's face in front of her.

The man she had just been with was not her husband. That wasn't Jeff. He didn't mean the things he'd said. He would want her back. Sooner or later. He'd come to his senses. And she'd wait it out. Until he realized how much he needed her!

CHAPTER 2

Elena jammed her passport and her ticket into the side pocket of her Fendi purse and buzzed for Pietro.

"Sì, *signora*." He was unfailingly prompt.

"I will be gone only one or two nights, Pietro, and I do not want you to inform the Count or my son where I am, but I will be at the Hôtel de Saumur."

He didn't show any reaction, but their eyes met.

He knows, she thought. He's the one who empties my trash basket. Involuntarily she glanced at it, lucite and chrome, sparklingly clean at the moment except for the one tissue she'd just deposited and some strands of her blond hair.

Her hands were beginning to shake as she pulled on her gloves. She detested flying, but these regular trips to Paris were unavoidable.

"I'm booked on the ten o'clock, so we'd better leave now. Tell Guillaume I'd like you to drive me. I know he gets fussy when you drive the car, but the fewer people who know where I've gone the better. Count Brisson was supposed to phone this morning. He probably couldn't get a line out of Porto Ercole, nothing works at this time of year. Ah, the civilization of the French is far superior to ours, *n'est-ce pas?*" She paused. "If my husband should call, tell him I'm out shopping or tell him anything at all." She hadn't spoken to Paolo in weeks, but she wouldn't delay her departure to wait for his call. I must stop calling him my husband, she thought.

Pietro picked up her suitcase and followed her down the staircase. She caught a glimpse of herself in the Venetian mirror on the landing, the narrow frame in the well-tailored suit, with the Russian lynx coat over her arm. Today she did not look her age.

The flight to Paris was crowded; even the first-class section was full. Elena hid behind her dark glasses and said no to the liquor and the vile-tasting wine. She could just imagine what they drank in the economy section, eau de toilette, no

18

doubt, only not the bottled kind. She thought of Gino and that damned apartment. How perverse of him to force her to meet him there, when he knew how much she hated it. And she hated Paris in the winter too. That bastard Gino didn't trust her any more. Well, she didn't trust him either, but God, how she needed him.

She closed her eyes and tried to relax. A man behind her was smoking a cigar, and the smoke annoyed her. Every now and then the plane would hit some turbulence and the jolt caused her heart to skip a beat. But she was still all right—for now. She squeezed her ankles together, holding her purse firmly between her feet. Her peace of mind was in that exquisitely styled bag. Thank God, there was no purse check on domestic flights; it was one of the reasons she lived in France most of he year.

The baggage-claim area at Orly was over-crowded and all of Paris was covered with gray clouds. It hardly made her feel gay.

But Madame Pene was happy to see her. "Welcome, Contessa Brisson. You are a little early. Check-in time is one o'clock. Would you care to have an aperitif in the lounge while we make up your room? The other occupants have already checked out."

"No thank you, I'll leave my luggage here and do some errands. I'm due at Van Cleef & Arpels this afternoon. Would you call me a taxi?"

Madame Pene nodded. "Right away, Contessa."

Her tone grated on Elena. She paced the small marble lobby until the taxi arrived.

As the taxi turned into the Rue de Rivoli, Elena noticed an abundance of police cars. There were even more parked in the Place Vendôme. "What is it?" she asked the driver.

"The Bank of Libya was bombed this morning, madame."

She glanced around the square. Half of the buildings had lost their windows from the ground up. Gaping holes stared back at her from the beautiful baroque structures. Proprietors of exclusive boutiques swept the streets in front of their shops, workmen placed large sheets of plywood over glassless fronts, covering the costly merchandise from view.

The taxi driver shrugged philosophically. "Yesterday it was a busload of Spanish tourists killed on the way to Versailles. The world is full of the crazy people."

André opened the electric gate at Van Cleef's for her and she stepped inside. After all the commotion, the quiet luxury of the shop immediately soothed her. André wore his usual finely tailored gray suit, but his broad face expressed the concern he felt.

"Excuse the confusion, Contessa Brisson." In spite of everything, his manner was charming as always. "You look as lovely today as ever. You have heard of the bombing, of course?"

"*Oui*, André. Have you had much damage?"

"Only a bit of broken glass in the upper offices. But the other buildings were much harder hit. Some of the glass in those windows was three hundred years old. It is irreplaceable." He shook his head. "I do not like all this fuss. It brings an undesirable element within our midst."

Elena's attention was caught by the diamonds and rubies that sparkled from small glass windows in the upholstered walls. Vibrant silks and velvets to enhance the beauty of their treasures. But the finely designed cases of glass and chrome on the floor were conspicuously empty today.

"We removed most of the jewelry to the safe this morning," André explained. "With everything that is going on," he indicated the workmen outside, "we wanted to be secure."

For a brief moment she realized how vulnerable one might feel working in an establishment with such priceless stock.

"If you will be seated a moment, Contessa, I shall bring you your pendant."

She perched on the edge of a tufted silk sofa until André returned and handed her the pendant with reverence.

"It is magnificent, André! Your people have enhanced a masterpiece." She kept her smile regal, cognizant of the line around her eyes.

The pendant was a glass sculpture of a ballat dancer by Pascal, the foot encased in a delicate gold ballat slipper, the body in an attitude of movement, hair piled high on the green-glass head, and around the neck of the piece a choker of emeralds and diamonds set in gold. She would wear it with her white silk caftan.

She wrote him a check for the balance owed, forcing the pen to move smoothly across the lines. Sixteen thousand francs—an expensive excuse to come to Paris. She glanced at her watch. It was time for her appointment with Gino.

André placed the pendant in a suede jewel box and she put it in her purse. She bid him good-bye and left the pleasant warmth of the shop, holding her white lynx coat about her, trying to keep the cold draft from seeping between the folds.

Workmen were busily repairing the damage of the morning, crowding the sidewalks with equipment, spilling their tools onto the curbs.

Just as she was halfway around the square approaching Cartier, someone pushed her from behind, very hard, propelling her forward. She barely caught her balance, before she felt an even harder push that knocked her into the arms of a swarthy-looking workman. But instead of assisting her, he shoved her backward, catching her under the chin, and she fell hard on the icy pavement. As she landed, the workman who had knocked her down grabbed her purse and ducked into an archway between two adjacent buildings.

She cried out to him, "Come back!" fighting the sense of instant terror that surged through her. She tried to see who had pushed her, but people crowded around asking if she was all right. Her body was as cold as the icy sidewalk underneath her, her heart pounded, and she felt as if someone had just torn out her insides. Thirty-two thousand francs worth of jewelry, her passport and her money—and it all meant nothing to her compared to what else was in her purse.

Someone helped her to her feet, someone else brushed her off. She was shaking from the effort of controlling her desire to scream for the police who were everywhere around her. But she couldn't tell them what had happened. She pushed aside the well-wishers and ducked into the archway after the thief.

It was no use. She'd never find him. There was a stone bench there, carved into the wall of the colonnade. She looked back, waiting until the curious had gone, and then she sat on the bench and wept, silent and motionless, trying to contain her despair and her fear. Her hands were shaking badly when she wrote that check at Van Cleef's. Now they were fluttering out of control. A sob broke loose from inside, releasing a torrent. "Oh God, no!" What will I do? she thought wildly, I must get to Gino. She couldn't go back to Van Cleef & Arpels. They would want to report the theft and she didn't have the time for that. She needed a handkerchief. Oh God, there was so much she needed right now.

She sat there for a while composing herself with great effort, trying to think of what to do. She couldn't walk all the way to the Rive Gauche and she had no money for a taxi, but she had to do something. She stepped back into the street and caught sight of a hotel where she had frequently stayed. They know me there, she thought, and she started back around the square, formulating a plan as she walked.

When she reached the hotel she hurried through the lobby and went directly into the gift shop. The salesgirl was typically French. No smile, black-red nail polish, three-quarter skirt, and pencil-thin body. Elena managed to appear calm as she browsed for a moment and then chose a leather purse similar to the one that had been stolen.

"Mademoiselle," she said to the girl, her chin raised, her body taut, "I am Contessa Elena Brisson. I wish to charge this purchase though I am not a guest in the hotel. I would also like you to cash a personal note for me. I need one hundred fifty francs, just enough to get me back to my friend's apartment."

The girl stared at her as if she were mad. "I'm not authorized to do such a thing, madame!" These crazy old crows, she thought.

Elena glared back at her, her heart pounding. "Call the concierge!" she demanded.

Monsieur Bonhomme was happy to extend the credit when Elena explained that she had been out walking without her purse and couldn't resist buying this one. "I'm staying with friends this time, Monsieur Bonhomme, but my next trip I shall be back in my usual suite on the eighth floor." She smiled at him, using every effort of will not to slap the smirking shopgirl. I'll never buy another thing from this little snit, she thought.

Armed with her empty purse and the money, she grabbed a taxi in front of the hotel, telling the driver to take her to 22 Rue du Bac. I can't be late, she thought. What if Gino has left without waiting for me? That was too horrible to imagine! Her skin was beginning to burn and yet she was still freezing cold. She would have to report her passport and her credit cards stolen. But I'll do it later, she thought, as she sat back in the taxi, and I will also stop payment on my check to Van Cleef's. Let their insurance company pay for the theft of the jewel.

The taxi crawled through the midafternoon traffic across the Pont Alexandre and past the Hôtel des Invalides. She felt as if she might jump out of her skin. *Hurry up, hurry up!* The sky was still a drab gray and it was beginning to snow. After I meet Gino, she thought, I will walk directly back to my hotel. It is only a few blocks away, and then I will have the rest of the afternoon to feel human again. Her nerves had worn paper thin. Her skin was beginning to itch and her teeth were chattering from the cold. She had that same sick feeling of death in the pit of her stomach.

The Rue du Bac was a fashionable street, with

antiques shops, boutiques and an abundance of coiffeurs. The French must have their hair done twice a day to keep so many salons in business, she thought as she hurried by. Number 22 was between a florist and a patisserie. She rang the bell and waited. No one answered, so she tried the door. It swung open and she stepped into a narrow hallway leading to a courtyard of apartments. Someone had converted this old building by adding a wooden staircase and catwalks across the front and then cutting doors into the outside stone to form separate entrances. It was ugly, she thought, noticing that Apartment D was on the third landing.

Her footsteps echoed on the flimsy wooden staircase. It shook beneath her weight, as if any moment it would give away and she would fall to the cement below. She was still shaking and her nose was running inelegantly. She dug into an inside coat pocket and found a handmade lace handkerchief. I must buy more of these in Portofino, she thought crazily.

There was music coming from one of the apartments. A radio, she guessed. She knocked on the door of Apartment D.

"Who is it?" a man's voice asked.

"Elena!" she answered defiantly. She heard the bolt slide open and she stepped inside.

The apartment was horrible. It smelled like boiled broccoli. There was an unmade bed and a portable kitchen unit littered with open containers of food and boxes of crackers. A plastic laminate table and two chairs sat in one corner and near the bathroom door was an upholstered chair with a torn green covering. A whore's room.

Someone grabbed her by the hair and twisted her arm behind her. She winced, but she didn't cry out.

"I don't like to be kept waiting," Gino hissed in her ear.

"And I don't like to be made to come here, like a common whore," she answered.

He shoved her hard and she fell against the table, bruising her hip.

She turned around to face him. He was smiling that half-crooked smile she knew so well. Even in February he had a suntan. She could see the white lines left by his ski goggles. His usual open-necked silk shirt had been replaced by a turtleneck. With his curly hair and slanted eyes he looks satanic, she thought. But that's because she knew him so well.

"Where is it, Gino? I've come a long way and I've had a dreadful time getting here." Her last reserve of strength was slipping away. She wanted nothing more than to cry on his shoulder and appeal to his sympathy, have him take care of her. But she knew him too well for that. He was the kind who kicked you when you were down. And she'd been down on him before, she thought ruefully. The events of the day had chewed up her control. At first they were tiny bites stealing a mouthful here and there, but for the last hour she had felt as if some voracious parasite were eating her soul bit by bit so that only the shell of her remained. Any moment she would fall into a spineless heap.

She heard the sound of a toilet flush and a woman stepped out of the bathroom. She was large and doughy, about twenty years old with fat upper arms and breasts. She was wearing a chemise that covered her just to the tops of her fleshy legs.

Elena hung onto the formica table behind her, or her knees would not have held her up. Why did he do this to her, she couldn't afford witnesses!

As she looked at him fury began to give her a rush of new energy.

"Tell her to leave, you bastard!" she said.

"Ah now, princess, it's freezing outside. You want to spoil my afternoon? Margareth won't see anything."

Elena looked at the girl. She was glassy-eyed and grinning stupidly as she shuffled to the bed and sat down on it in slow motion. She caught sight of her own exposed crotch and began to play with the hair—pulling it and smoothing it. Slowly she lay back against the wall and closed her eyes, continuing to fondle herself while they watched her.

Elena felt her freezing feet come to life inside her boots and warm surges flowed from her calves to her groin in spite of her anxiety.

28

She tore her eyes away from the girl and implored Gino with her expression. "Give me my packet."

He walked over to the chair in the corner and picked up a man's leather bag. He undid the double buckles and reached inside, then tossed her a plastic bag full of white powder. She caught it between her fingers, feeling its weight with glorious relief. It was enough to last for a while.

"I need a fit, Gino!"

"You can use hers," he said.

"No." She quivered with tension. "I don't know what she's got in her veins!"

"Then sterilize it. There's a stove." He indicated the kitchen unit.

I'm running out of time, she thought. In a minute I'll have to ask him to inject me.

The girl was moaning softly, rolling her head back and forth against the wall. The fingers of one hand had disappeared inside her.

Oh God, Elena thought as she moved to find a pot in which to boil water. I am no better than this whore.

Gino came up behind her and ran his hands over the silky luxury of her fur coat, sending the warm surge up to her shoulders.

He didn't try to excite her, knowing she couldn't feel anything more than the need for the drug at the moment. But as soon as she was mellow she would be begging for him. She would be begging for both of them.

He helped her off with her coat just as the water boiled. The hypodermic looked official lying in the chipped enamel pan. This new stuff he gave her hadn't been cut yet. She was one of his better customers. It wouldn't do to lose her too fast.

CHAPTER 3

It was after five when Brenda arrived at White Memorial. Her legs ached. It had been a long, intense day overshadowed by the knowledge that this was the only place she wanted to be. She cradled her bag of food, protecting it from the snow, and went through the revolving doors.

They were bringing dinner to the wards. The acrid, rotting odor of food mixed with damp clothing and steaming radiators assailed her.

She hesitated outside the door of 502. How would he be today? Could she make her news exciting enough so that he would share it with her and not feel apart from her? Should I play it down, or build it up, she wondered. That was one of the side effects of dying. She couldn't go with him and he couldn't stay with her.

She pushed open the door and went in. There he was. That dear familiar face so wasted and thin. Every time she saw him her heart lurched. His profile was outlined by the dim evening light. He looked terrible. His skin was a yellowish color and his brown eyes and natural grin were constantly distorted by pain now, even when he looked at her with love. He seemed to be asleep. At least he wasn't suffering at the moment. She tiptoed across the room and sat down quietly in the vinyl chair. She had sat in that chair so much lately she'd begun to dream about it at night. Her paper bag rattled.

"Is that a Wetson's jumbo burger I smell?" he said.

"Ratso. I thought you were asleep."

"Well, is it?"

"I've got onion rings, and jumbo cheeseburgers and chocolate shakes and cherry turnovers."

"Who would ever have thought a Jew from the Bronx could be so happy at the prospect of such *chazerie*?" he joked.

God, she loved him! "How did it go today?"

"About the same. I've had some bladder pain. They irrigated my catheter three times because of blockage. But I just had a shot so I'll be good for a while. But I couldn't eat lunch. Creamed beef on English muffin. It looked like vomit."

Brenda unwrapped the food and set it all out on the paper bag on his side table. She removed her coat and her muffler and her boots, and stepped over to the sink to wash her hands. As soon as she entered a room she overpowered it. It was not just her boisterousness but her general expansiveness. In fact, everything about her was larger than life except her height. She supposed that she looked ethnic, but Barry insisted she looked exotic. She had large blue eyes, a large full mouth, and an even larger smile. Her breasts were a bit too full for a woman her size and she wore her curly blond hair in a natural. She was usually eight or ten pounds overweight. But right now her weight was down eight pounds due to the permanence of the tight knot in her stomach. A tight knot she was loath to define as grief. Whatever it was, it had killed her appetite.

"Is it still snowing?" he asked.

"Yeah." She took a breath. "Guess where I was all afternoon?"

"Making love to Marcello Mastroianni?"

"No!"

"Marty Feldman?"

"Be serious."

"O.K. Where were you?"

"Being wooed away from B B C & R by the prestigious firm of McNaughton and McBride!"

"Honey, that's great! Now I can retire at thirty

and let my wife support me." He looked away from her. Her curly blond hair reminded him of a dandelion in a summer field.

"You should have seen me in those hallowed halls of Wall Street. They don't know what to make of me—a naturally talented, brilliant and clever stockbroker who looks like a slightly *zaftig* Streisand. Those gray-suited Wasps are so austere they're almost clerical." She tried to keep it light.

But Barry was solemn. "Speaking of clerical, Brenda," he said, "I've definitely decided against our getting married until I'm out of the hospital. I don't want to get married in this stinking hospital and I don't want a marriage that I can't consummate."

"But we've already consummated it. I don't want to wait."

"The answer is no!"

"O.K., O.K.! So I won't get the insurance," she teased, to hide her desperation. They both knew he didn't have any insurance. Damn, he was stubborn. He might never get out of the hospital. This might be their only chance to be married. She wanted to be his wife if it meant only having this much of him. "Anybody call today?"

"Yeah. My dad dropped in and your brother Bernie called and your mother too."

"That was nice." She bit into the burger, not tasting it at all.

"Dr. Otashi says the tumor in the groin is a bit smaller. So the chemotherapy might be having some effect." He started to cough. He seemed weaker today.

Otashi had told her they feared lung involvement. She'd wanted to kick Otashi in the balls.

He picked up his sandwich. "This hamburger is great! God, I wish we were at the Paramount Theatre right now, with this bag of food, watching a double feature of science-fiction movies. That's the one thing I can't wait to do. Go to the movies."

"What are they bringing you for dinner?"

"You filled out the menu. I don't remember."

"Oh yeah, tonight is lasagna. My favorite," she added lamely.

"You can have it all. This hamburger is enough for me." He hadn't eaten more than one bite. He put it down on the wrapper and shifted his weight, trying to appear cheerful, but she could see the pain was beginning again. He had told her that his legs from his hips to his knees felt as if they were being stuck by needles, while his lower back was being twisted on a rack, first one direction and then another. He tensed his body to fight off the spasm that clutched him, but it was no use. He sank back on the pillows and closed his eyes. "Oh shit," he said. "Tell me about all those assholes at B B C & R who are not dying of cancer. Tell me you want this pathetic, hairless, impotent skeleton of a man!"

Brenda jumped out of her chair. "Shut up, you ingrate!"

He looked at her in shock and tears came to his eyes. Usually she soothed him and cried over him when he talked like that.

"I'd love you and I'd want you if they cut you off at the waist and had bottles attached to every draining pustule! I'd love you if we made love with a dildo for the rest of our lives. I'd love you if you were so bald an eagle fought me for your affections. And I want you to live just as much as you do." She put her head on his lap and sobbed.

"I'm sorry, honey." It was hard for him to believe she could love him looking the way he did. "It's tough on you too. I know! I couldn't make it without you. You're the only reason I keep going. Otherwise I wouldn't want to go on." Her head was pressing in all the wrong places, but he didn't want to tell her. He just held her there wishing he could hug her without suffering for it.

She raised her head and smiled at him. "Did we miss the *Star Trek* rerun?"

"It's on in fifteen minutes."

"Want an onion ring?"

He nodded. "Brenda. About the wedding. I'll think about it some more, O.K.?"

"O.K." Maybe I'm pushing him too hard, she thought. It's his ego at stake. What would I get out of it after all? A bittersweet tragic ceremony where the groom can't stand on his feet for more than seven minutes. Two sets of hysterical parents, especially his mother, who thinks he should go to a faith healer in South America. His mother doesn't think I'm good enough for her brilliant son. Well, maybe I'm a little overweight. But if he went into remission I'd lose five more pounds so fast she wouldn't know what hit her.

"What are you thinking about?"

"Your mother . . . and *They Came From Outer Space.*"

He laughed.

It was so good to hear a moment of painless laughter.

"You know something, Brenda, you make me feel like a winner."

"You're a winner, all right." She sighed. "Second prize in a Polish raffle."

She didn't know how long she'd sat there staring at the grating on his window, but it had blended with the cells of her retina, forming a jail-like pattern on her brain, while the snow drifting down outside the window was obscured by her tears. Would he really be gone? The thought never failed to stab her, no matter how many times she tested herself with its potency. Barry dead? Stab! He's going to die. Stab! The pain of it radiated through her. Don't think about it! Think about the moments of joy, the meetings, and the loving and the promises. But the taste of tragedy made her choke while the knot inside expanded, enlarging, pressing on her diaphragm, hardly leaving room for air. Or was it her heart that hurt? He stirred and moaned. She realized that most of the time she felt sick.

"What time is it?"

She was shocked to find it was 9:30.

"Is it time for another shot?" His voice sounded anguished at needing it, at wanting it, at not wanting it.

She remembered the first time she'd heard that voice. . . . She was sitting in an empty row at the back of the lecture hall in Professor Weilhaussen's Advanced Accounting, and someone said, "Is this seat taken?"

It was a smart-ass question because there were only sixty students in this huge lecture hall. "Whatsamatta you don't got eyes?" she wise-cracked, and looked into his. They were brown, and smiling and teasing. He slipped into the seat next to her and lifted up the writing desk.

"What are *you* doing here?" he asked.

"I was born with brains!" she teased, thinking he was definitely cute—and he knew it.

Insolently he eyed her chest. "Brawn too?"

She stared at his lap. "I see you're well endowed also!" She was usually at ease with this kind of banter, but for some dumb reason she blushed then, and when she looked at him he was blushing too.

"I'm sorry," he said, extending his hand. "My name's Barry Cohen."

"And I'm Brenda Greenstein," she replied, reaching out to shake his hand.

The lecture was beginning and she tried to concentrate, but she was acutely aware of him, and
all the empty seats around her, and his jacket,
wool plaid, rubbing against her arm. Brenda the
sensualist, she thought, feeling electrical exten-
sions from her toes to her curls reach out to him,
lightly exploring him. And though they both appeared to be concentrating on the lecture, their
auras were having an electrical storm.

I should have made him show me a medical history back then, she thought. A pledge I could have
held him to: "I promise never to get cancer, Brenda,
so we can live happily ever after."

The nurse came in and gave him his shot. She
watched the needle go in. Don't be bitter. Think
about the good! About the time he met my parents and he and Dad talked sports all night, Barry
the baseball fanatic and Dad the football fiend.
She had been afraid someone would commit mur-
der that night. When he left, her father turned to
her and said, "I like that young man. He knows
what he's talking about!"

She knew him well before he kissed her. They'd
had lunch together twice, and coffee once. Then
she ran into him at the student union and they
went to the library together. She had excellent
discipline when it came to studying. Learning and
religion were revered in her household, and she
observed all the traditions. But that afternoon, the
history of Tudor England, the symptoms of para-

noia, the future growth potential of Company A based on its acquisitions, the rate of inflation, and a public stock offering, all swam before her eyes. Her hands perspired and her knees tingled and her right ear itched every time Barry looked at her. She was so unnerved that she jumped when he closed his book with a sudden thump that bounced off the vaulted ceiling of the business library.

"Let's get out of here!"

They were Tracy and Hepburn as he held her hand. Her books were like concrete blocks in her right arm. She clutched them, enduring the strained muscles rather than let go of his hand.

Snow had fallen during the night and continued for most of the morning. But when they came out of the library it had stopped and the sun was shining on a sparkling white blanket that covered humps of cars and roofs of buildings, making this gray section of New York clean and pure. The sun edged the billowy clouds overhead with touches of gold, and she felt almost religious.

Barry had an old Chevrolet, rubbed-out blue. It was rusted, worn, and freezing inside. He took her books solemnly and placed them on the back seat and she slid in, wondering where they were going. Her mind raced; I know he likes me or he wouldn't be bothering, but I'm not his type. I don't appeal to the slender, athletic fraternity guys, though he doesn't belong to a house.

"I'm an individual," he told her, "though I live

within the pack. I like to observe, and sometimes I participate with the rest. But I'm not interested in their games."

She thought how wise he was, and cursed herself for ever wanting, even for a moment, to belong.

He got into the car on the driver's side and she noticed how his short reddish-brown hair, curled at the hairline. He looked at her with a serious, questioning look. "Brenda, Brenda, what am I going to do with you?"

Her line reminded her of Cary Grant, "Kiss me, you fool!"

But he didn't laugh. Instead he leaned forward and touched his lips to hers. She had a sudden wish that she lived in her own apartment and could stop necking with boys in cars.

His mouth was warm in contrast to the cold air. The tip of her nose warmed against his cheek. He held her face with his hands as he kissed her and she knew she could love him. Everything solid inside of her melted as he kissed her, liquefying her mouth and her eyes and between her legs. She was trembling as he slid closer and continued to kiss her, reaching behind her hips to press her against him. It was a long kiss. A lovely kiss. And each of them found that it answered the question they'd both been asking: was there really a chemistry? God, yes.

Chemistry then and chemotherapy now.

When the kiss was over, Brenda knew she

would lose her virginity to him, at long last. Though she'd told herself that same thing many times before and it hadn't happened yet. She had never trusted anyone enough, never wanted anyone enough to allow it. Not that she didn't love to pet, but sex held too much of a promise to practice it with an acquaintance or a conquest, and not a lover.

After the kiss he asked her, "What do you want out of life?" His timing lent a special meaning to the question.

"Everything!" she answered. She was swept away with an overwhelming love of life, of old Chevies, of snow-covered campuses, and advanced accounting professors. "I want to make a fortune in business, and I want to get married, and have kids, and live in Manhattan in a gorgeous remodeled apartment with French paneled walls and modern Italian furniture, and I want to wear designer clothes, and maybe have a cottage somewhere for the summer at the beach or on a lake or in the mountains."

He was studying her carefully, measuring her investment in this dream. Her face lit up when she talked about life, always had.

"How many kids?"

She shrugged. "I come from a family of five, so three or four wouldn't throw me. Of course I want to get established in my career first, and I've got to travel!"

"Of course," he said gently. And then she saw

tears in his eyes. Real tears, from a man, from him. This self-assured, kind-of cocky guy who was certain to make Phi Bete, and seemed to know everyone wherever they went—"Hiya Barry," "Howyadoin' guy," "What's happenin'," "What's new," "How 'dyouliketo"—was shedding tears for her.

She touched her finger to his face and smiled inquisitively. "What is it?"

"Do you think you could ever be a baseball fan?"

The shot they gave him had relieved him, because he fell back to sleep. It was time to go. Back to her apartment alone, back to the knot, and the sick feeling inside and the dreams of sadness. She gathered up her belongings and tiptoed out into the hall to put on her coat. She told Mrs. Mason at the nurse's station she was leaving and headed for the elevator.

"Brendaaaa!"

His scream caught her halfway down the hall. Heart pounding, dear God, dead God, she raced back to his room. He was sitting up in bed, round eyes filled with terror, thin and balding, a refugee from Dachau, and he said, "I thought you had disappeared!"

Knives again. How about another stab, Brenda? Here and here and here! All the wind was knocked out of her. She rushed to his bed and put her arms around him, hugging him to her.

"I'm here," she soothed. "Don't worry! I'm

here! I'll sleep on old vinyl tonight! Don't worry!"

After a while his trembling subsided. "I'm all right now. I just wanted to see you, that's all."

"Can't get enough of me, huh?" She sat down again, and he relaxed.

"You can go now," he insisted. "I'll be all right. The medications make you feel so weird."

"Naw, I'll stick around and make sure." She held onto his hand until he was asleep again, and then she curled up and dozed in the vinyl torture chamber.

She was the only one who woke up in the morning.

CHAPTER 4

Alone! Anne plugged in her earphones and tuned in a music channel. An hour more until the movie. The earphones were uncomfortable. They irritated the tender inside rim of her ear, but the music shut out the passengers on either side. She hated to be hemmed in in the middle seat. The story of her life! she thought. But, it was going to be different now. She wanted it to be different. She wasn't going to live her life for anyone else ever again.

The stewardess in the next aisle reminded her of

Jill. They all looked like Jill. Sexy, glamorous, long-haired, young. She felt drab, lacking in style, without flair. But she didn't look much different at twenty-nine than she had at twenty-five. A few more lines around the eyes, maybe, and next year she'd have a few more.

The divorce had been bitter but at least that had helped put Jeff out of her mind, she hoped, once and for all. Now she felt free, and somewhat proud, having made the decision to take this trip to Europe by herself. The settlement from Jeffrey had helped, of course. Sixty-five thousand dollars and twelve hundred dollars a month for two years. With the twenty-five thousand dollars she'd inherited from her father's insurance policy last year and her half of their savings account she had almost one hundred thousand dollars. It was amazing how free she felt. Her attorney had been right, her friend Nancy had been right, her mother had been right: having money felt good.

And she would see Paris!

All her life, Paris had meant love and adventure and now she was going to find those things for herself. Romantic love, not deceit and failure. This was her chance to change, to break out of the old mold. She was desperate to be different. No more plain Anne. No more devotion to anyone else. Just me me me. Psychotherapy had not been the answer, though she had tried it those first few months after losing Jeff. But getting away, having capital of her own, these might make the difference. Ah, Paris. If it were only the first city on her itinerary.

In spite of the jet lag, Anne's excitement carried through to her arrival. She hadn't slept on the plane. The seats were too uncomfortable, the anticipation too great. She arrived at the Royal Angus Hotel around noon London time.

Her room had only one window and it faced a nudie movie house. There was a sign on the roof of the theater that flashed on and off all day. The hallways of the hotel had a nauseating odor of dusty cooked cabbage. But when she opened her window to get some air, the traffic below was so noisy she closed it again. The exhilaration of adventure beeped beeped its horns beneath her window.

"Welcome to England, Anne," she said aloud, and crawled under the bedspread and fell asleep.

When the phone rang at 6:30 she thought it was the middle of the night. The tour group director was calling to invite her for cocktails in the dining room, "our get-acquainted hour before dinner, Dear. We want everyone to meet their fellow tour members. Oh yes, and casual attire."

Well, here it is, Anne thought, replacing the receiver. Tonight I will be witty, I will be adorable! Tonight is a new start.

The tour director was Frances Whiteside, English, about forty, with glasses and buck teeth. She handed Anne a gummed-label name tag and turned her over to her son, Buckley, nineteen years old, with glasses and buck teeth.

"Take Miss Scott around, dear, and introduce her to some of the others since she is traveling single. Although now that you're with Uni-Spec Tours you need never be alone," she grinned. Anne grinned back, her sense of promise growing.

Anne glanced at Buckley, not a remote possibility.

Buckley led her to a group of four white-haired ladies in their sixties, wearing polyester pantsuits. "Hello, lovelies," he emphasized his accent, and they all simpered. "This is Anne Scott. Anne, meet the girls from Salt Lake City." They all nodded, their white heads bobbing like a field of overripe cotton.

"Where are you from?" a lady named Tessie asked.

"Los Angeles," she answered.

The one labeled Mary asked, "Isn't London exciting?"

And the one tagged Lorraine nodded. "The pulse of the city is really beating here."

"Well, I've really not had time to take it yet," Anne said.

"What, dear?" the one labeled Maggie said.

"The city's pulse," Anne quipped, and the ladies giggled appreciatively.

"Excuse me," Anne said, feeling she'd better make an exit while she was ahead. Polyester-and-cotton was not her blend.

"She's a clever girl," she heard Tessie say as she walked away.

Sharp as a tack, Anne thought.

A young woman with a blond natural approached her and they stared at each other's chests and then both of them laughed.

"It's awkward, isn't it?" Anne asked. "We should put our name tags on our foreheads."

"That's what God said to Moses about His commandments. 'Thou shalt wear them as frontlets between thine eyes. . . .'" She stuck out her hand. "I'm Brenda Greenstein from New York."

"Anne Scott, L.A."

Mrs. Whiteside announced dinner.

"Shall we?" Brenda said, and they joined the crowd inching into the next room.

There were three tables set up for the tour. Anne and Brenda were seated at the same table separated by a professor of botany from Whittier, California, traveling with his mother. Brenda deftly switched the place cards so that she and Anne were next to each other.

On Anne's right was a fourteen-year-old girl. Next to her was her brother, twelve, and their parents, the Wilsons, from Wisconsin. Ted Wilson was a high school English teacher and his wife taught piano. Then came two couples from Scotland whe were traveling together. The women both used dark eye makeup and wore heavy gold pendants around their necks; the men affected gold bracelets and drank a lot. The two Scottish women were involved in conversation with each other while their husbands talked. The professor from Whittier talked to the teacher from Wisconsin, the Wilsons' children talked to their mother, and that left Anne and Brenda to get acquainted.

"Your first trip to Europe?"

Anne nodded. "Yours too?"

"I thought a tour would be the best way to see the most places in the shortest time. I have this fear that I'm going to miss something. I want to see everything, museums and castles, and even the cities that aren't on this tour. Greedy, aren't I?"

Her breathy enthusiasm interested Anne. Brenda seemed free and unconcerned about what anyone else thought. Even the way she called herself greedy, as if that were an admirable trait. Her large features blended into a rich expression when she talked, and her openness drew Anne, made her feel comfortable. "You know what I mean?" she asked, as if Anne's understanding was crucial.

Anne nodded. "That's exactly why I took this trip. It offers an overview of all the major places; then I'll come back and see them in depth another time." If I ever get married again, she thought.

"It's going to be frustrating to see only the top layers of a city! You know, not getting to know the traffic patterns and the best restaurants and the latest boutiques!" Brenda's long slender fingers and expressive hands moved as she talked, carrying her words to the listener, catching every wan-

dering glance and bringing it back to her. Anne
had never met a young woman like her.

"Are you divorced?" Anne asked, during the
meal of well-done roast beef and Yorkshire pud-
ding. Brenda's openness gave her the confidence
to ask a personal question.

"No," Brenda laughed. "Just worn out." But she
noticed that Anne was the one who looked worn
out. Anne hunched her shoulders as she sat, as if
she were protecting herself from a blow she expected at any moment. Uptight lady, Brenda
thought.

"I'll bet you're divorced," Brenda said, noticing
that Anne winced at the question. She thought
Anne was beautiful. Not with the kind of beauty
that would grab you the minute she walked into
the room, but with a kind of feminine vulnerabil-
ity that had a definite appeal. Except to her husband.

"Divorces are boring!" Anne said, denying her
own interest in the subject.

"Well, you must tell me about yours sometime,"
Brenda said. "I don't mind being bored."

Anne smiled, and her tension eased.

Brenda helped herself to generous portions of
food as the waiters passed by. And in spite of the
fact that she was slightly overweight, she was
unquestionably chic.

"What do you do?" Brenda inquired between
mouthfuls of trifle.

"Grapic Designing . . . but I wanted to be a teacher," she added. Something in Brenda's raised eyebrow made her defensive. "My firm does Commerical advertising."

"Why didn't you teach?"

"I quit school when I got married. I was lucky to get my job. My husband was studying to be a doctor and he couldn't work and go to school."

"Couldn't?"

A flash of loyalty erupted from somewhere underneath all the hard feelings. "Premed and medical school are very tough!"

"There's always night school." Brenda didn't know why she was pushing. Let the girl alone. Don't be a one-woman crusader.

"I couldn't go to night school because I tutored my husband in the evenings," Anne answered, suddenly feeling sorrier for herself than she ever had during her marriage.

"And now he's got the M.D.!" Brenda couldn't resist.

"I know, I've got a lot to learn," Anne said. "That's why I'm here. But what about you, Brenda? What do you do?"

"Well, I completed an apprentice program for stockbrokers in Manhattan and I've been working there since November."

"A lady stockbroker! Is there much discrimination in the brokerage business?"

"It's like anything else run by men. A woman

has to be ahead all the time . . . as well as give it."

Anne laughed.

"Before that I went to Bayside High School and graduated in accounting from NYU. I figured I'd be sure to meet some guy majoring in bus-ad. I mean, there are so many more men than women. Well, I did. I met Barry. Barry Cohen from the Bronx. We went together for two years. We were engaged when he discovered a lump in his groin. They operated and removed his testicles, but he died a year and a half later, just last fall." She paused. "Watching someone die has a sobering effect, you know." She hated these explanations, they were so stupidly inadequate. How could she tell anyone about his smile! Her eyes filled with tears.

"Oh, I'm sorry," Anne said. "What a horrible thing to have happened. It makes my story petty by comparison."

Brenda nodded. Anne had understood. "Every time one of my friends says to me, 'I feel terrible,' I say to them, 'What's so terrible? If you got a stomachache or if your boyfriend is cheating, that's bad; but if you're dying of cancer, *that's* terrible.'"

"How did you get over it?" Anne asked.

"What makes you think I'm over it?"

"Because you seem able to talk about it easily."

"That's just my act," Brenda said, moved by

Anne's sincerity. "I cried every day at first. You think it won't end, the pain and the crying. Maybe I'll always cry when I picture him suffering like that. But after a while it becomes less and less, it gets easier."

"I know what you mean. I'm still crying about my divorce, but not as much as I did."

"Divorce can be harder in many ways," Brenda answered. "Your ex-husband is still around to torment you with his escapades."

They both smiled, comforted by the depth of their mutual understanding. Anne felt a small part of the knot inside her begin to loosen. She had a feeling of well-being that she had not experienced in a long time.

But Brenda, who did not want to continue such a serious conversation, said, "I never knew cherry pie could taste like my flouride toothpaste!" and they both laughed.

They spent their days touring London, the museums and the churches and the parks and the changing of the guard. They went antiquing and on a tour of the nightclubs, all the while enjoying each other's company, though Anne couldn't help but wish that something exciting would happen.

It was cold in England and cold in Holland and only slightly warmer in Germany. Forty degrees in June, who would have believed it? And then it was time for Paris. Magic city on the Seine. The couturiers, the boutiques, the magnificence and voluptuousness that was Paris. Lady of the afternoon, lying lazily on her side. Boulevards and bridges, chapels and churches. Breathtaking, enormous Paris.

The unrealized dreams of an American girl were waiting in every corner café. Never mind that she wasn't fluent in the language; magic had its own words, a wave of the wand, a sleight of the hand and, presto, transformation.

Paris was warm. It was early July, summer had arrived, and lovers actually walked with their arms around each other. Paris was all it had been touted. Barkers at a carnival promising the wonders of Little Egypt had actually provided it—the most beautiful city in the world. Things were going to be different from now on, there was no doubt about it.

CHAPTER 5

Anne and Brenda sat at the Café Deux Magots sipping wine and watching the passing parade. "If I see another Louis Vuitton purse I'm going to scream!" Brenda said.

"I think it's divine. I'll bet that girl over there is a model, and the dark-skinned man with her must be an Arabian prince."

"It's against my principles to drool over Arabian princes, Anne. That's what we call *traif*. My tree in Israel would shrivel and die! . . . Don't look now," she said out of the corner of her mouth, "but that gorgeous guy with the dimples and the hairy chest is giving you the eye!"

"Where?"

"Over there, don't look now! He's coming this way."

Anne turned and looked at him. He was wearing tight jeans and a body shirt open to the waist, an assortment of charms dangled from the heavy gold chains around his neck, and he swaggered with a cocky confidence. He nodded and waved to several people seated at the tables. Anne waited for him to approach her. This was it! Her romantic interlude, about to begin. He walked directly toward her. Their eyes met. But just as he got to her table, he turned and sat down next to a blond directly in front of her.

Anne recoiled in surprise, certain that he had been looking at her.

"Well!" Brenda exclaimed.

"Shhh," Anne cautioned.

"But he was flirting with you, I saw him."

"No, it was the girl in front of me. We only saw what we wanted to see."

The blonde turned slightly, glancing over her shoulder, and gave them a sly grin that said they didn't have a chance with her around. She was hanging all over him, smiling at him, leaning into him as she spoke. They were speaking German, or rather the girl was German. He was French or Italian. From the easy way they spoke it was difficult to tell if they knew each other or not. The girl

had pale skin, a delicate face, and a beautiful figure. The man put his arm around her, leaned back
in his chair, glancing over his shoulder at the people behind him. He had a strong square jaw. Anne
wanted to reach out and run her fingers along
it, tracing the sinews that jumped in and out on
his cheeks as he talked, but she never came close
to doing it.

Everyone's attention was drawn to the street
entertainment that began without an overture.
The expert beggars of Paris. Out of the crowded
street a pantomimist appeared in black tights and
a clown face. He began his act by trying to work
his way out of an imaginary box, a citizen of the
street captured in front of them. Bending and
pleading silently to be let out of captivity, he
placed his hands on imaginary flat surfaces that
surrounded him, feeling the area, defining it, all
the while he was locked up inside. Up and down
he searched, knocking on walls, high and low,
searching the corners until at last, with great cau-
tion and then increasing delight, he discovered a
niche high above his head. He jumped up to catch
the edge, his fingers hooked there tightly; he
glanced down in terror lest he fall, and then with
strength etched in every muscle, he laboriously
chinned himself over the top, his feet slipping on
the inside surface. Pulling himself to a straight-
arm position, with his toes, up and over, at last he
jumped out. The café broke into applause. Glad to
be free, the mime passed his hat, and everyone

contributed. The pantomimist's act was followed by a man who walked up to the seated audience, took out a stick with a blunt wrapped end, doused it with liquid from a tank in front of him, and set the stick on fire. Before the startled audience he swallowed the burning torch and exhaled a sheet of flame from his mouth, spitting a shot of fiery liquid into the street. With one bold move he wiped his mouth clean of the fire and began to ask the spectators for money. It was a spectacular moment.

The blonde and the handsome man paid their check and left the café, walking slowly up the Boulevard St. Germain.

Gino had seen the street show hundreds of times. He walked away from the café nonchalantly, the German girl beside him. She had a bad smell about her, and no innocence to recommend her. She was obviously looking for a place to hang onto. They were all alike, these busty Nordics in Paris, looking for a lover. He wouldn't have spoken to her if she hadn't been sitting at "his" table.

He'd made the drop quite smoothly during the fire-eater's show. The envelope stuck easily to the underside of the table. The two American girls sitting behind him, now they were the kind he liked. Untouched except for a husband, perhaps a few boyfriends. They'd seen nothing of the life he had to offer; wonderful birds to hold in his palm, petting their quivering feathers before he wrung their necks.

He gave the German girl a hard pinch on her ass and pushed her off in another direction. "Hey," she said, smiling, until she saw the look in his eyes. She took the hint and kept going, bewildered by his sudden change and his disgust. "*Cochon*," she said.

Dumb cunt, he thought. He wanted to go back to Deux Magots and talk to the two American girls, the one he'd been flirting with, though plain, was especially appealing, but he couldn't go near the café until Elena picked up her stash. He glanced at his watch, a diamond-studded Piaget, nothing but the best. This latest shipment of heroin from Hassan was also the best, nearly 90-percent pure. Hassan, his new supplier, was a find. He had a perfect cover, and traveled with diplomatic immunity because of his job with the Emir of Bhitamin.

Hassan insisted that the sheikh knew nothing about this narcotics business, but Gino doubted that. There was too much at risk if the sheikh didn't give his approval. Those guys didn't just kill you, they did things to you first. Who was Hassan kidding? Of course the sheikh knew; these Arabs never had enough money. Well, neither did he. And if he could increase his buying power with Hassan, there was no telling how far this connection could go!

Gino seldom made drops himself anymore except to a few personal clients like Elena. He felt a certain responsibility toward her. She brought him the better clientele, the ones who didn't have to steal or sell themselves to support their habits. And he had nearly lost her business six months ago when he made her come to Margareth's place to make her buy. But with all Elena's threats, she was still hanging around. He smiled. The man who said the rich are different from you and me, was wrong. But still, servicing elite individuals like Elena would never get him into their league. And that's where he belonged. Not just as someone they tolerated for stud service or drug supplies, but as an accepted member of their society. It galled him to be on the fringes. Even his friendship with Carlo, Elena's son, wasn't enough to insure his acceptance. Carlo and Elena had given him a taste but it wasn't enough. Not nearly enough.

He had walked up St. Germain as far as Ted Lapidus, where he stopped to glance at the clothes, and to check his hair and arrange his shirt collar in front of the glass window.

Everything hinged on Hassan, he thought. So far their relationship was good, Hassan trusted him. And once he was sure of Hassan he would put his real scheme to work. He had it all worked out, a way to be noticed by someone who could really help him up the ladder, the big man himself, Vincenzo Visconte. If he could impress a man like Visconte, he would be *in* anywhere he

61

wanted. Everyone would notice him, everyone would seek his friendship. And then he'd let them all have it! But he had to be very careful. The underworld connections of his youth in Naples were small-time compared to the power of a man like Visconte.

A charcoal vested suit in the window caught his eye. He pushed open the heavy door and entered the shop.

From her vantage point at the corner of the building Elena could see when Gino left his table. Quickly she pushed her way through the jumble of tables, anxious to occupy the spot first. She tried to appear unhurried, but she was tense. Her narrow hips maneuvered this way and that. She held her head high, regal profile belying her intentions. "Let it go well!" she prayed.

Anne noticed her as she sat down, a tall glamorous woman in her fifties, wearing a wide-brimmed sun-hat, silk scarf, and dark glasses. Her skin was evenly tanned, a bit leathery. She ordered a vermouth cassis.

Brenda stood up suddenly. "I'm going to the john, I think I've got a case of the Parisian parasites."

As she left, Anne saw the woman reach under her table and pull out an envelope that had been stuck there. She was about to put it in her purse, but she dropped it.

Anne reached down and picked it up.

It wasn't a letter, Anne could feel something heavy sliding around inside. The envelope was sticky from the tape that was wrapped around it, and it clung to Anne's hand.

The woman gave the envelope a swift yank, pulling it out of Anne's hands, avoiding her curious look.

"*Grazie*," she said, and her hand with its long red-lacquered nails shook as she took possession of the envelope.

Then she got up from the table as Anne watched, and went into the interior of the café.

That was strange, Anne thought, wondering what was in that envelope. Her imagination had been captivated.

She sat impatiently now, thinking about the woman and watching the people in the café watching her. She'd been here long enough for their faces to look familiar.

Fifteen minutes went by and Brenda had not returned. Where is she, Anne wondered. She might really be sick! She signaled the waiter for the check.

The interior of the café was not as crowded as the sidewalk tables. A counter faced the entrance, resplendent with pastries, hard-boiled eggs, liquors, and candy. Anne paid her check, amazed that half a litre of *vin ordinaire* could cost thirty-eight francs. Then she asked directions to the toilette and descended the stairs to the lower level, passing the kitchen and the banquet rooms on her way.

There was an attendant at a small table at the foot of the stairs with a plate of money in front of her and a roll of toilet paper. The attendant held up her fingers to indicate the cost of going to the bathroom and handed Anne the roll of paper. But the bathroom door wouldn't open. Anne pushed on it, but it was stuck. Something was blocking it from the inside.

"Brenda," she called, "are you in there?" There was no response. Anne gave the door a hard shove and called in. "Brenda!" She turned and motioned for the attendant and together they managed to open the door enough for Anne to get a hand and shoulder through. The lady with the sunhat and glasses was lying in back of the door, unconscious, and Brenda was sprawled underneath her!

"Oh my God, Brenda!" Anne cried, pushing her way into the room. She pulled the woman away from the door and off Brenda, who was also unconscious. There was no blood; no one had been shot or stabbed. A rush of fear shot through her. Frantically she shouted to the attendant, "*Un médecin. Vite! Vite!* Emergency! *Très rapidement!*"

It was then that she noticed the hypodermic needle on the floor next to the woman. Her sleeve was rolled up and her arm was covered with a mass of scars. The woman had obviously overdosed, but what had happened to Brenda?

She examined her friend quickly, looking for

wounds or injuries, but she couldn't find any. She checked Brenda's heart; it was beating steadily. Anne's thoughts were racing. Horrible visions of Brenda being attacked by a hypodermic-wielding maniac flashed into her mind. She made certain Brenda was breathing and opened her mouth to clear the trachea. Brenda seemed all right except that she was unconscious.

Quickly Anne turned her attention to the other woman. Her skin color was gray and her pulse difficult to find.

"I have telephoned for an ambulance, mademoiselle," the manager told her as he peered into the tiny bathroom, crowded by the two prostrate women. *"Qu'est-ce que c'est?"*

She shook her head. *"Je ne sais pas. Je les ai trouvé ici."*

"Narcotiques!"

"Non," she said indignantly, *"diabetiques!"*

"Les deux?" he asked incredulously. Both of them?

"Oui!" she answered. It was obviously heroin, but the manager seemed so smug.

Anne turned back to the woman. She had stopped breathing. Frantically she felt for her pulse. It was barely beating. She wanted to shake the breath back into her. She crawled in closer between the two bodies and stared from one to the other. Compulsively she checked Brenda again, but she was all right. Only the woman was in serious jeopardy. She hoped to God she was wrong.

But no, the woman still wasn't breathing. There was no time to waste.

Quickly she leaned over the prone body, trying to ignore her revulsion, hoping she'd remember the rudiments of her Red Cross training. I'm breathing into death, she thought as she cupped her mouth over this stranger's. The air she breathed out came rushing back to her. She did it again and again while the woman exhaled death sighs. There seemed to be no change. Why doesn't somebody help me, she prayed. *Keep going, don't stop.* Her knees hurt from kneeling, she was practically sitting on Brenda. Inhale—one, two, three—exhale. Please breathe! It went on forever. What if she dies with her mouth on mine? Oh please don't die.

She kept it up until finally the ambulance arrived, with two stretchers and two attendants. Mercifully they relieved her with oxygen and expertise, and the woman was breathing again.

I saved her, Anne thought. I saved her life!

CHAPTER 6

The corridors of the Hôpital du Sacre Coeur were ancient, lined with office doors of opaque glass like an old office building on Hollywood Boulevard Anne had once seen. All the beds had hand cranks with iron bars for the head and feet. And there were nurses and attendants everywhere, rapidly speaking a medical jargon that defied translation.

They rushed Brenda and the unconscious woman into intensive care while Anne waited, and paced and stared at unfamiliar faces. Finally, after hours of X-rays and lab tests they took Brenda to a ward and told Anne she could see her. As Anne approached the ward she was suddenly overcome with exhaustion. Her legs felt like rubber.

Brenda was in an iron bed in the middle of a large room of iron bedsteads. Each bed was next to a metal nightstand and a wooden chair and surrounded by a white privacy curtain on a ceiling rod that closed with a single pull. Blenda smiled weakly.

"Are you all right? What did they find?"

"Concussion and some bruises."

"I've been so worried! Do you know what happened?"

"Not really. I went downstairs to the bathroom. It was very small. And when I came out of the toilet there was this woman standing there. She had her back to me, and she was injecting something into her arm. I couldn't believe it! And then she just collapsed, knocking me against the sink. I lost my balance. It all happened so fast! And I remember thinking as I fell, Damn these platform shoes . . . Oh, my head hurts! I must have hit it on the way down. I don't remember anything else."

"When I found you lying there unconcious, I was afraid you'd been attacked. The other woman had stopped breathing. I gave her mouth-to-mouth resuscitation and then she started breathing again."

Brenda squeezed her hand. "How is she now?"

"I don't know, I'll find out later. Did they tell you anything else?"

"I have a hairline skull fracture."

"Does that mean you have to stay in the hospital?"

"Well, at least for a few days. Do you feel like a heroine?"

"I feel drained. You know, all the time I was doing it, I kept thinking, I don't want to be doing this! But there wasn't anybody else."

"That's what every hero says!"

They were both silent, and then Anne spoke, "The tour leaves for the wine country in the morning."

"That's all I've been thinking about. I want you to go on ahead and I'll catch up with you in the South of France."

"No!" Anne said. "I'm staying with you. There's nothing worse than being alone and sick in a strange city."

"Yes there is, overdosing in a Paris toilette. Who is she?"

Anne had never asked. "I don't know, I'll go find out."

"Not yet." Brenda held onto her hand, remembering other hospitals, and other times. "Stay with me for a while."

Anne nodded, grateful for the chance to rest. She sat there until Brenda started to doze and then went to find out about the woman. It is difficult to obtain information about someone whose name you don't know in a French hospital when you are not French. Finally Anne learned that the woman's name was Elena Brisson, Contessa Elena Brisson. But they would only reveal details of her condition to a relative.

Anne felt entitled to information about someone whose life she had saved. So she told the attending physician that she was Contessa Brisson's niece from America and he believed her, though she was nervous about lying.

"I shall take you to see her, mademoiselle," he said. "Her condition is *très grave.*"

The woman, who had looked so beautifully tanned only a few hours before, now had a yellowish pallor and her breathing was shallow. There were EKG monitors hooked up to her and tubes down her nose and throat. Without muscle tone to support the flesh, she looked terribly old and worn.

"Aunt Elena," Anne whispered, for the doctor's benefit, afraid that the woman would awaken and declare her an impostor. She didn't realize that speech was impossible with the tracheal tube. The doctor left them alone, and Anne sat and watched her labored breathing. How difficult it had been to breathe life into her. A feeling of sadness swept over her and she felt like crying.

Elena opened her eyes and looked at Anne. They stared at each other, one from despair, the other from compassion.

"You're all right!" Anne said.

The woman stared uncomprehendingly.

"*Vous allez bien!*" she repeated, and held the limp hand.

The eyes were blank at first and then a glint of gratitude flashed before they closed again.

Anne's heart wrenched. The woman seemed hardly able to sustain her life, that fragile thread that Anne had willed into her gaunt body. Had the overdose been an accident? Anyone who shot heroin into her veins must want to die! She wondered, watching Elena Brisson sleep, if this woman would listen to her, if there was any knowledge of life Anne had acquired that she could impart to a contessa. She asked the nurses to keep her informed of Contessa Brisson's progress and went back to her hotel. She felt strangely committed to helping this woman. Perhaps she could get through to her!

The next morning Anne stopped off to see the Contessa before visiting Branda. She was awake and the trachea tube had been removed, but the IV was still in place. There was a man sitting by her bedside.

Anne come toward the bed, a tentative smile on her face. "You don't know me, Contessa, but my name is Anne Scott."

The Contessa held out a slender hand, brown skin over bones, the IV taped to the outer wrist. Her nails were still perfectly polished except for one finger they'd cleaned off to check her color. "So, my niece from America!" Her voice was low and controlled, with rolled consonants. Italian, Anne decided. "How brave you were!" The Contessa smiled back at her.

Anne's eyes moved to the man sitting by the bed. He wore a gray pinstripe suit. An official? She might be in trouble for impersonating someone's relative. Ridiculous, she'd saved the woman's life.

He rose from his chair and offered his hand. "I am Elena's cousin, Alessandro Massini. We owe you a tremendous debt of gratitude. I know that my cousin will do her best to repay you for your courage." He handed Anne his card. "If you are ever in Rome, I should like to be allowed to do my part as well!"

"Thank you," she said, noticing how handsome he was.

He turned back to his cousin and took her other hand in his, bringing it to his lips. They conversed together in Italian while Anne studied him.

He spoke earnestly, as if he were the Contessa's lover, stroking her hand as he talked. He seemed gentle and kind. The kindness softened his strong features, the straight Italian nose, the graying temples, and dark eyebrows over green eyes. Yes, Anne decided as she saw him smile at Elena, he was very kind. He had a way of tilting his head as he listened, that showed his concern. And as he spoke to his cousin, he would glance politely at Anne from time to time as if to include her. It made her feel quite special.

As he got up to leave, he took Anne's hand again. "Thank you so much, Miss Scott." A red handkerchief peeked out of his breast pocket and she detected the scent of fresh lemons. "I trust we shall meet again."

He gave her a firm handshake. "I hope we do," she replied. He was so impeccably turned out she became aware of her plain Levi skirt and T-shirt, wishing they were more. If his cousin is a contessa, does that make him nobility too? she wondered.

When he had gone, the Contessa motioned for her to take his chair. "I'm afraid I'm very tired," she whispered. "It's difficult for me to stay awake. But as soon as I'm stronger, promise me that you will come and visit."

Anne wondered again if the overdose had been an accident. There was a certain wistfulness about the Contessa. "When I was a young girl," Anne said, "I was terrified of dying. I had terrible dreams and nighttime fears. But now that I am older I know it takes more courage to live than it does to die!" The Contessa nodded. Anne had never spoken like this to anyone before and she didn't want to overstep the bounds of propriety. "Whatever has happened to you, I'm glad you are recovering!"

"It's good of you to say so," Elena replied. This girl had more compassion than most of the people she knew. She couldn't help herself and she started to cry.

"It's all right!" Anne soothed, remembering how the Contessa had been yesterday, sweeping through the café as if she owned it. "I'll let you rest now, and come to see you later. . . . I hope you don't mind that I told them we were related." She wanted to explain further, but the woman was falling asleep. So she left the room and went to visit with Brenda.

CHAPTER 7

Brenda was grateful to Anne for remaining in Paris. Her accident had frightened her more than she would admit. It was horrible to be a patient, even a temporary one. She lay in the noisy ward and stared at the transomed windows, thinking of Elena Brisson with increasing resentment. It depressed her to be bedridden, she'd already spent so much time in hospitals. But even after her headache subsided she continued to feel depressed. The precious days of her European tour were slipping by, and all because of some rich

sickie. As much as she tried, she couldn't dredge
up any sympathy for the woman. It was one thing
to be an addict in the ghetto, quite another to
have a gold-plated hypodermic.

Anne spent the next few days at the hosiptal,
but she also managed to take in a few museums.
She even went back to the Café Deux Magots and
sat there alone, feeling self-conscious. The waiter
recognized her and was solicitous, inquiring after
her friend. But still she didn't feel comfortable. A
woman alone wore an obvious sign: *approach me*.
She studied her Michelin and avoided looking at
the available men, annoyed with herself for her
shyness. She might look self-assured, but it covered a tight insecurity.

Out of the corner of her eye she saw him the
minute he approached the café—Elena's connection, wearing a new outfit and his gold jewelry.
She half smiled at him and at the same time
ducked down into her chair and out of sight. Her
heart was pounding. Dear Lord, he excited her!
But how could he? He was a drug pusher! He was
responsible for Elena Brisson's overdose. And yet
she reacted to his presence. She watched him eye-
ing the passing girls and suddenly she realized she
could identify him. She had seen him make a
drop. What if he recognized her? What if he knew
she'd seen him? She slumped farther down in her
chair, glad to be invisible, not daring to take more
than a glance at him now and then. Once, he
turned and stared at her and she trembled, look-

ing away, menaced by his confidence. His handsome exterior covered an infestation of decay, and she knew it. Yet her pulse would not subside. He did not recognize her! Finally when no one interested him he turned and sauntered away. She sighed with relief and a touch of disappointment, resisting an impulse to peer after him, in case he turned and came back. He reminded her of Jeffrey, they shared a look of self-importance and a lack of interest in an ordinary woman. And that's exactly what she was, ordinary, not the kind who could catch their attention. Or anyone's.

She sat sipping her coffee for a while, waiting, but Elena's friend did not come back. It was late. She paid the check and found a taxi to take her back to the hospital, wondering how much longer Brenda would have to be there.

Elena's rapid recovery surprised everyone. Ironically, she improved more rapidly than Brenda. But for all her bright appearance she was shaken by her brush with death. She clung to Anne's visits with a selfish desperation. No matter how much time Anne spent with her, it was never enough; she would have liked Anne never to leave the room. It was only Anne's encouragement that kept her going. No one had ever been so concerned about her before. Everything about Anne put Elena at ease. Anne affected a kind of respectful timidity mixed with bravado that Elena found charming. Especially when Anne became officious and insisted that Elena follow all instructions. Anne might be indignant about Elena's addiction, yet she was sincerely compassionate about her situation. Elena was buoyed by Anne's enthusiasm, but she had no answer when Anne asked her, "Why, Elena?" Her self-searches uncovered only self-pity. She was thankful to be alive only because someone cared. And when Anne wasn't there, Elena felt she didn't deserve to live.

"I am so grateful to you, Anne. I cannot tell you what you do for me."

"Did you do it on purpose, Contessa?"

"No! It was an accident." She inhaled sharply, remembering that day, caught in her pain. Her supply had been low. She'd been shooting less to make it last longer until she connected. She had been strung out. Only the heroin would help. That was all she had any more. Gino had been horrible. Every day tore off more of the wasted cells of her youth. Long ago she had given up her dreams. Even the brilliant Brazilian Ivo Pitanguay who remolded her body hadn't given her enough youth to make a difference. The moment he saw her he recognized the signs of addiction and refused to take her as his patient unless she quit. She went through the tortures of withdrawal to be a candidate for his surgery, to regain herself. He had promised her wonders. During the recovery she held on, waiting for the transformation. But the smoother skin was a terrible disappointment. She looked better but she hadn't felt any different. She wanted to scream at him, to strangle him, but he was in Brazil and she was in France. Three months later she had been hooked again.

Now she was off drugs without having planned it and Anne's devotion was giving her determination. I will stay in the hospital for a complete detoxification, she thought. This time it will work. I will not go back to the blackness.

But the fear of death hung over her.

Anne would reach out and touch her arm, showing her understanding that pain and suffering knew no bounds or limits of wealth. And Elena would clutch the smooth hand, squeezing its youthful pads in her own dieted palm.

"You are a dear girl," she'd said.

And whenever Anne couldn't be with her, Elena longed for Alessandro to come back from Rome to sit with her. He was the only one she could tolerate when she was down. What a dear man he was, and how she hated herself for using him the way she did. But he was so chivalrous and easy to use. It was wrong of her to invite him only to her lesser functions, but he made everyone of substance uncomfortable. He was so unlucky, though he'd had many chances to make good. She couldn't even remember half the businesses he'd been involved in. But he was a good influence on Carlo. Even at thirty-two, Carlo could be such a baby.

It wouldn't do her any good to think about Carlo, now, she decided. She only hoped he wouldn't find out about this latest "accident" of hers. Dear Lord, she felt old. She hadn't known what to do when she had begun to age. She had thought it would never happen to her, she wouldn't let it! And then she became forty-five, and then forty-nine, and she couldn't face the mirror any more and she couldn't stand to be a puffed-up, tightly drawn image of her former self. Life seemed to fall apart then; maybe it had been happening all along and she hadn't noticed. She'd been married to Paolo for so many years; he had always been a comfort to her. He had an average intelligence, but he was beautiful, and his title and his money enabled her to do what she did best, socialize. But Paolo had an Italian ego and sense of values. Over the years he had several mistresses and many lovers, some of whom she knew. Only when she turned forty-five and his girl-friends were twenty-five, did she begin to mind.

She had been in love once herself, really in love, with an American army officer. But he went home to his wife in Ohio and she went back to Paolo. At fifty she had begun to find young men attractive, fiercely so, and Paolo was no longer appealing to her.

They had lived a life of social encounters not even broken any more by an occasional intimacy; both survived the death of their relationship and accepted it for their son Carlo's sake until Paolo had discovered her in bed with a young prostitute she had picked up in the Piazza Navona. The girl was only sixteen, so delicate. Elena had never thought of making love to a woman before. It had simply happened. The girl's appeal was something more than sexual. It was a desperate grasp at life. A recapturing of her own lost youth.

But Paolo had been compromised beyond the point of return. His ego was damaged and he was horrified by his wife's choice of a lover. He'd had no option but to dissolve the marriage, no easy task for a Catholic.

Elena was shocked to reality by the turn of events. She hadn't wanted this, hadn't expected it, and became repelled by her own behavior. For a while after the divorce she wouldn't get out of bed. When she finally did, it was to turn the tables and denounce Paolo as a cheat and an adulterer. Her friends gathered around her, thrilled to be privy to Elena's near-fatal mistake. Speculation was rampant, but no one could actually find out anything. Eventually it died down and she and Paolo retained much the same relationship they'd always had, in separate houses.

Then she met Gino. He was compelling and brutal. She told him about the girl and he used it against her, threatened her with it, taunted her with it, excited her with it. He took her rebuilt façade and whatever was left of her self-respect and stripped her bare, leaving her battered and addicted. She was deathly afraid of him.

But after this overdose, she would never see Gino again. Even if she went back on drugs she would find another source. *He may have tried to kill her!* He should never have given her such pure stuff, unless he hadn't checked his own powder. Thank God he hadn't tried to contact her in the hospital. If he ever showed up at the villa again, she'd call the police. It might be the only brave thing she'd ever do! She could just hear him: "You'll regret this, Elena," he'd shout, as they escorted him off the grounds. Yes, she would regret it. She already did.

But now there was something she regretted even more. Anne was actually leaving! The doctors discharged Brenda and the girls stopped in to say good-bye. Even Brenda made an effort to be civil. Her resentment of Elena had cooled somewhat because of Anne's propaganda.

Elena tried to fortify herself against Anne's departure, but her panic was just under the surface. She smiled shakily. "Well, where are you off to?"

"We're meeting our tour group in Venice," Brenda said. "We'll have to see the wine country and the French Riviera another time."

The tears in Elena's eyes were not for their lost tour, but for the loss of Anne. "Oh, you have missed this wonderful country because of me. How terrible."

"Terrible," Brenda agreed, put off by what she saw as Elena's fake pathos.

Elena caught the annoyance. "You will not see St. Tropez, or the villas in the South or Aix-en-Provence."

"They weren't on our list, Elena," Anne assured her.

"No, we've only missed a wine-tasting tour of the French version of Brookside Wineries and a trip around Cannes and Nice. So don't fret about it, and feel better real soon." Brenda's sarcasm bit. "Come on, Anne," she said, tugging on her purse. It did no good to bemoan their loss.

"Brenda," Anne hissed, "there's no need to be rude."

"I'm not being rude," Brenda said sweetly. "I haven't any hostility toward her!" Just because she cracked my head open, Brenda thought.

"Oh, but of course you do, Brenda, and I do not blame you in the least." Elena was on familiar ground with Brenda's kind of anger and jealousy. Her need for Anne's support overshadowed her pride.

"My, your English is excellent when you want it to be!" Brenda observed, wondering how Anne could be taken in by such a phony. Elena was not the poor unfortunate Anne had painted her to be.

Elena couldn't let them go. She smiled bravely. "I have a wonderful idea. When you have completed your tour, why don't you come and stay with me at my villa in Cap Ferrat? Both of you," she added. "I shall delight in taking you to all the enchanting villages in my neighborhood. You might enjoy to see how the other half lives."

Brenda was certain Elena didn't want her along. And she wasn't interested in an introduction to the world of heroin users. But Anne seemed to like the idea. "I don't think we ought to impose!" Brenda said, giving Anne a look.

"Oh you wouldn't be," Elena insisted.

"How generous of you," Anne exclaimed. The possibility of such a visit thrilled her.

"Anne," Brenda cautioned, "don't forget that Elena's *friends* and Elena's *life* are nothing like what you're used to!"

Elena got her meaning, and held her annoyance. Brenda could ruin everything. "I assure you that no one I associate with is in my situation." She turned to Anne, trying to keep the desperation out of her voice. "I . . . will be better soon."

"Of course you will," Anne assured her. "Brenda didn't mean anything. . . ."

Elena continued. "I *am* on a program here, you know. If I have your visit to look forward to it would help me so much. I would be inspired to get well. Is it possible for you to stay on an extra week or two and visit with me? I must be allowed to do something to repay you."

Anne looked at Brenda expectantly. "I don't have to return for any particular reason. There's no one waiting for me. How about you?"

Brenda shrugged. Anne was not her personal property. "I have to be back in New York on the sixteenth, but you don't need me. You can go on your own, when you've finished with the tour in Greece."

They both waited for Anne's decision.

Anne smiled at Elena. Her villa in the South of France! She didn't dream of saying no. "I would love to come and be with you."

"That's wonderful," Elena said, and wrote down her address on a slip of paper. She was relieved. "I shall expect you in Nice on the fourteenth of August. Wire me what flight you will be on and I'll have the car meet you. You can fly Air France from Athens to Nice in three hours or so."

Anne nodded and took the paper. "Take care of yourself now," she said, "and good luck with your cure." She embraced Elena, who returned her show of affection in spite of Brenda's raised eyebrow.

Only a few weeks to go until I have her back again, Elena thought. I can make it until then.

"Venice is more beautiful than I ever imagined!" Brenda said as their water taxi pulled up to St. Mark's Square.

But for the first time in her life Anne began to realize what middle class meant. The realities of the economy tour with its ordinary travelers were a bleak contrast to the life Elena represented, even with her misery. The two touring couples from Scotland, wives with makeup, husbands with jewelry, seemed different from the rest. The more Anne noticed their clothes and their style the more they appealed to her. Not their characters necessarily, but their overall effect. The two couples kept to themselves and only toured on the bus during the day. They spent their free time shopping in the best stores and dining in the best restaurants, often in formal dress. Anne hadn't even brought any evening clothes. In London she had heard them talking about their gambling losses; and she knew they had dined in private clubs; in Paris they had been to Regine's and New Jimmy's. Brenda told her how exclusive those places were.

Anne wondered how Brenda knew so much about status symbols. Brenda's sense of style was quite subtle, understated. Her clothes were mostly beige or brown. She wore expensive leather shoes and, though she carried a plain tan leather purse, her passport holder was Louis Vuitton, which she pulled out only when it counted. She was unobtrusive in her use of the Michelin and always knew how to ferret out the newest accessories in small unpretentious boutiques. Anne's discontent with herself grew in proportion to her exposure to the other life. And now her images were specific. Wanting to be different was no longer some vague feeling. She could point to them and say, "I want to be like that."

The tour group rode in horse-drawn carriages clopping along the streets of the Lido, while Mrs. Whiteside's supercilious, nasal twang echoed out of her megaphone, describing the architecture, telling stories of people who had lived there, dropping names like Dante, Mann and Shakespeare. It annoyed Anne when Mrs. Whiteside pointed to Don Juan's home without so much as a drum roll or a fanfare. The woman had no romance in her soul, while Anne was filled with the gloriousness of the day.

Soft air caressed her skin, fanned by the movement of the carriage; the sunlight laced through huge jacaranda trees. Families walked in groups along the tree-shaded sidewalk, three generations, each carrying beach paraphernalia. Vendors sold *gelati* on the corners, and cafés overflowed with groups of people enjoying leisurely midday meals under Rossi and Cinzano umbrellas.

And there was the Adriatic, spread out before them, calm and green. The perfume of tuberoses and orange blossoms misted the warm air, while Hibiscus grew around wrought-iron gates surrounding flower gardens.

Anne sighed with pleasure, caught in the peacefulness of an opulent world. Every pore drew in the environment.

They passed the Excelsior Palace Hotel, an enormous spiraled pink castle, nestled among green mossy trees and weeping willows. Flowers and topiaries lined the huge marble verandas, carved railings separated large expanses of grass, and striped awnings covered the walkways.

Along the beach, grouped in a large semicircle, were rows of white canvas cabanas shining in the sun, topped by round glass domes. Each one befitted a separate sheikh; each cabana hid, Anne was certain, Valentino on a bed of pillows, nubians fanning with peacock feathers, and exotic women undulating to music wafting through incensed air. In front of the cabanas bikini-clad men and women lounged on chaises in the sun, while others sat in beach chairs, baking behind their Dior sunglasses.

She glanced at Brenda's wistful smile. "You feel it too, don't you?"

Brenda nodded. "I've always been a romantic at heart. But my practical side says that forty dollars a day for a cabana to lie in the sun is a lot of money and there's more museums and buildings to see, and my skin burns easily and, what the hell—" Exasperation hung in the air. "What good does it do to press your nose against the window of a candy store, expecting the owner to give you a free bagful? No way!"

The glimpse of heaven had also ruined Anne's day. The beauty of the place was marred by its unattainability. How can I have it? she wondered. What are the initiation fees into that club? She was surprised at herself, even embarrassed. She had always been impervious to the charms of that other life. And now her throat tightened at the thought of it.

CHAPTER 8

All the way from Venice to Rome, Anne kept her nose pressed against that candy-store window. Even in Florence the contrasts were obvious on each stop of the tour. Every monument was next door to an expensive boutique. Every museum had once been a palace or a castle. The *other life* was all around her.

The tour bus lumbered past fields of mushroom-shaped trees, forms of cypress peculiar to Italy. Trees and ruins, evidence of decayed opulence, and glories of ancient civilization didn't make her grateful to be modern, only enhanced her new-found desire for wealth and position. The tour group ate in tourist cafés, while across the piazzas Anne watched others dine in elegant restaurants, envy bubbling inside her.

Their first night in Rome Anne couldn't sleep. Thoughts of her life in California, of failures, of new desires, and of Rome and its unkept promise spun round and round. After Rome came Greece and then the tour would be over. She would go on to Elena's villa in France for two weeks, and then what? None of her problems were solved. She hadn't changed at all. What have I learned? she thought. To pay a taxi driver in a foreign currency, to quote any number of travel guides. I know the Uffizi and the Murano glass factory and the Louvre, but I don't know why Jeffrey stopped loving me. She thought about holding Jeffrey, making love to him. Her body ached to be held by someone. She saw faces of other men. The two husbands from Scotland, the handsome Italian who'd made the drop at the Deux Magots—even the nineteen-year-old Buckley Whiteside. And there were two lesbians in the group, Terry and Marion. They were nice when you got to know them, but they kept to themselves. Still there was a fascination about them. She wondered what they did when they made love. She remembered her mouth on Elena's, breathing into her. I could never do it with a woman, she thought.

She became aware of a noise, a steady move-

ment from Brenda's bed. It had been going on for
a while but she hadn't noticed before. Back and
forth, back and forth, a scratching sound, like rubbing. Brenda's breathing was audible. It height-
ened as Anne listened. Something stopped her
from calling Brenda's name, arrested the question
in her throat, "What are you doing?" The rubbing
sound continued firmer, limb against sheet. She
looked over at Brenda. Her body was barely outlined in the dark, knees up, raising the covers into
a tent.

Brenda inhaled sharp jerky bursts of air, and
then exhaled in a deep sigh. The bed was totally
quiet. Brenda reached over to the bedside table
and took a Kleenex. She put her hand under the
covers and wiped herself.

Anne's face burned and tears ran down the side
of her face. She was consumed by embarrassment—
how could Brenda be that uninhibited? She was
revolted by the whole idea. But why should I feel
revulsion? she wondered. I'm not a child. Brenda's
not a child. She hated herself for her embarrassment and for her prudishness. Maybe Jeff had been
right—she was just an uptight, unsexy, unreceptive
woman.

She lay there for several minutes, trying to sort
out her thoughts, feeling an odd tingling in her
body. And carefully, timidly, she slid her hand
down her chest, resting it lightly between her legs,
finding the touch of her own fingers almost too
exquisite to bear.

The taxi driver let them out on a deserted street in the middle of the block and pointed to an open archway. They had been driving up and down old narrow Roman streets for fifteen minutes, trying to find this place. Their excitement was high. They were going to have a good time tonight!

The street was dark except for a ring of light above the archway. A brass plaque on the wall said: CLUB VOODOO. They went inside and down the stairs. The music grew louder as they descended. Purple lights lit their way. African hieroglyphs lined the walls in fluorescent colors. The hand railing was simulated animal bones.

Brenda glanced around. "It looks like there's been a fire sale on tank watches at Cartier," she shouted.

The club was crowded. Pulsing noise—only sounds until you tried to talk above it. They paid the cover charge and were left to find a spot for themselves among the overflowing banquettes and tiny tables. Groups of girls sat expectantly, sipping and smoking. Dancers intertwined and uncoiled, hips thrust, arms raised, vacant expressions that transmitted ego, ego. They found a corner where someone was not using the table at the moment and ordered two drinks, shouting into the waitress's ear.

Brenda loved it! She was at home, moving to the beat of Smokey Robinson. She danced on the sidelines in movements exactly like those of the other dancers. Universal language. She moved onto the floor with a nearby man, dark-skinned and mustached. Their arms moved in a back stroke, heads thrust forward, nodding to the music, their mouths forming the words to the song "I Heard It Through the Grapevine . . ." and they smiled at their mutual involvement.

Eventually they returned to the corner table where Anne sat, wiping their necks and their brows, fanning their flushed faces. The man, Nicky, had a friend, Larry Conley from Oklahoma. Larry asked Anne if she would like another drink. She nodded. She had finished her first gimlet quickly. The second had all the vodka on the top. She watched the green lime mix with it, sweet and sour.

Larry was in retail menswear. He came to Italy regularly, usually to Milan, to buy for his stores. But now he was here on vacation, visiting with friends. Oklahomans wore lots of Italian knits. The music was slow now, Diana Ross. "This place only plays American music?" Anne asked in his ear as they danced. He held her tightly. They perspired against each other though the air conditioning was chilly. Voodoo masks, fluorescent faces leered from the walls. The ceiling was covered in a straw dome, like the inside of a chieftain's hut. Purple velvet covered the side sofas. Pillows in prints and horn pedestal tables were scattered here and there. Occasionally a spear and drum caught the light, and over the bar a skeleton was suspended in a reclin-

ing position, arm jauntily supporting his head as
he grinned at the dancers.

Larry was shorter than she with wide shoulders
and sandy blond hair, Italian sport shirt and French
slacks. Brenda raised an approving eyebrow at
Anne over Nicky's shoulder. Nicky was wearing
jeans. With all the available girls around they were
lucky to find two presentable men.

Larry danced well, holding her back firmly, not
put off by her height. She decided she liked him.
His cologne was pleasant. Jeff never wore cologne. Jeff danced slowly, ploddingly, not like this
high stepper from Oklahoma.

They had another drink.

She told him she was divorced. He said he was
too. He talked about his three boys. His home in
Willow Creek. He pronounced it "Wila Crik."

His ex-wife Patty had opened a needlepoint
shop in the same shopping center where he had
one of his stores. He liked his ex-wife but she was
dating his best friend. He'd gotten divorced because he wanted to be single. He traveled a lot
and worked for the Democratic Party. He supported Fred Harris who was a real leader and a
good friend. He pronounced it "gud freeund."

He ordered two more. Anne's limit was always
two drinks. They danced a few more times. The
girls without partners eyed them warily.

Brenda and Nicky were very cozy on the dance
floor and in the booth. Brenda leaned over and
said to Anne, "We're going to his place. You can

use Larry's if you want, or else Larry will take you to our hotel. I'll knock before I come in. O.K.?" And she left.

Anne couldn't believe it. Brenda got up and walked out with Nicky, leaving her alone with Larry. She was on her own and shaking. How could she get out of this without embarrassing herself and him?

He paid the check. What had Brenda told them, that she was part of an arrangement? She didn't know this man at all. What if he hurt her, or killed her? They would find her body floating somewhere in the Tiber.

Larry helped her to her feet. The drinks had made her dizzy; she didn't realize it until she stood up. The stairs didn't offer any resistance. There were several cabs outside. He approached the first one and hesitated.

"I have to meet someone for a drink, for business. How'd you like to come with me?" He saw her reluctance. "I'll take ya home if ya want, but it's a nice place, really!"

It was silly of her to be so frightened. He seemed sincere and harmless, at least for the moment. She agreed and got into the cab.

The club he took her to *was* nice! A polished brass sign on the outside of the building was engraved with the words, LEGATUM DI ROMA, PRIVATE. It was completely different from the disco where they'd met. Legatum di Roma had a sleek and modern interior in contrast to its antique

stone and marble façade. As they passed through
the two-story entry, Anne noticed charcoal-gray
carpets and leather banquettes in the first-floor
discotheque. A small velvet-upholstered elevator
with smoked mirrors and gilt moldings carried
them to the dining room, which was decorated
with eighteenth-century furniture. Inlaid marble
walls and Corinthian columns served as a background for a raised dais where a twenty-piece
string orchestra played dinner music. All the dinner guests wore formal clothes and Anne had
never seen such jewelry. The place dripped with
opulence; just to be here was a thrill, she thought,
and a delighted smile played on her lips. She was
finally a guest, not a spectator. She turned to
Larry, who was following closely behind her, and
tried to communicate her pleasure. He smiled
back at her, seeming quite at ease here. Not one of
the many guests raised his head as the maître d'
led them through the dining room. Anne began to
feel distinctly out of place with her blue Banlon
dress and was relieved to reach the table, set for
eight but with only three men occupying it. It was
obvious from the empty seats next to them that
their dates were somewhere else—probably in the
ladies' room. The men stood as she approached
and Larry made the introductions. Two of them
were in their sixties, neither one attractive, and
Anne barely heard their names. The third man was
tall and slender and he was wearing a navy
double-breasted jacket with a tangerine silk hand-

kerchief in the breast pocket. He looked familiar.

"Alex Massini," Larry drawled as she shook hands with him. He came around the table to escort her to a chair next to him.

"I can see that you don't remember me, *signorina*," he smiled. And suddenly she did remember him. He was Elena's cousin, whom she had met in the hospital in Paris. Now she was even more conscious of the way she was dressed.

"You two know each other?" Larry was amazed. "Well, I'll be damned!"

"We met only once, in Paris," Alessandro replied. "Mrs. Scott was a great help to a member of my family."

Larry preened with pleasure. What luck to pick up a girl who might do him some good in his dealings with Massini. Not that he didn't have the upper hand: Massini probably needed him more than he'd let on. Hell, they needed each other.

"Signorina, you promised to tell me the moment you arrived in Rome!" Alessandro said.

"We're only here for a few days," Anne said, "and I didn't want to bother you."

"It is no bother, I assure you. Are you enjoying Rome?" he asked, and she nodded. "And have you been to Ostia? It's the one place I recommend without reservation, and yet so many travelers to our city pass it by."

"We go there tomorrow," she answered.

A waiter came by and Larry ordered her another vodka gimlet. The two Italian businessmen excused themselves and bade Alessandro a warm good-bye.

"Alex is in the same business as me," Larry explained. "But I'm tryin' to convince him to go into mass pro-duce. I can sell him big in Oklahoma City. That town is cryin' for the Eyetalian look."

"Ah, Larry, we should not bore this lovely lady with talk of business." It was obvious that Alessandro Massini did not like to do business on social occasions. But Larry didn't seem to notice. Business was something he discussed no matter where he was.

She touched Alessandro's arm. "Really, I don't mind."

"There's no money in custom clothes, Alex," Larry insisted. "You gotta diversify, expand your fact'ry, send me orders! I'll sell 'em! We could be partners, you manufacture and I'll do the rest!" Larry put a possessive arm around Anne's shoulder.

"Would you be willing to invest any capital?" Alessandro asked quietly.

"Hell, you don't need my money, you're rollin' in it. Besides, I got restrictions. My government discourages us folks from spendin' our profits abroad. But if we do make a deal, you gotta send me knits. That's what they want back home." He enlisted Anne's corroboration with a dip of his head.

She had no idea what they wanted in Oklahoma, but she had heard that Italian knits were popular, though not particularly stylish. From Alessandro's expression, he thought so too; his distaste for Larry's preference was evident.

"Why should guys like Car-dan and Saint Laurent make all the profits? They've got menswear so sewn up it's a joke. But I tell you, there's a market for the other stuff. I know half a dozen stores I deal with that can't sell the Car-dan look." Larry nodded his head wisely.

Anne finished her gimlet and another one was brought to her. She had stopped counting long ago and sipped this one, enjoying the company of two such attractive men.

"You know the cost of wool has doubled recently," Larry continued, "and synthetics are even worse. So cheaper labor has got to be the answer. I know a few companies who got fact'ries in Yugoslavia. One's makin' raincoats, and the other's makin' suede jackets. They make a good product, but not like the Eyetalian stylin'. Now that's sharp!"

Anne stifled a yawn, which Alessandro was quick to notice.

"I'm sorry for keeping you both here with me," he said. "I've enjoyed our conversation so much, but I'm afraid I must go now."

Larry was a bit startled by the change in conversation, until he realized that Alessandro was hinting for him to take Anne home.

"Oh sure," he said, rising along with Alessandro. They both reached to help Anne, who discovered she was quite unsteady on her feet. How much had she drunk? she wondered.

It was Larry who put a steadying arm around her, while Alessandro remained discreetly apart. "I have a wonderful idea," Alessandro said. "I should like both of you to have lunch with me to-morrow."

"Fine with me," Larry said before Anne could answer.

She turned her head too quickly toward Alessandro and the room swam; she almost fell, but reached out and clutched the table to catch herself. Oh, how awful, she thought. How did I let this happen? She smiled in the general direction of Alessandro. "I'm afraid I won't be back from Ostia in time for lunch." Her stomach felt so funny she might never be hungry again. "And I don't want to miss the catacombs."

"But they are in the opposite direction from Ostia," he said.

"Oh!"

"But don't worry. Join us for lunch, I will take you to the catacombs myself."

"Where should we meetcha?" Larry asked.

Alessandro hesitated for a moment. "I know a perfect place. It's a favorite tourist restaurant, but the owners are friends of mine and their chef can be extraordinary when he wants to be. It's called Meo Petacca." He reached into his jacket and wrote the name on two of his cards, handing one to each of them. "The restaurant is near the river, and I'd suggest that you hire a horse and carriage at the Piazza d' Espagna to take you there. It's a lovely ride."

His enthusiasm was contagious and Anne smiled back, promising to join him tomorrow as soon as she returned from the tour. She liked the idea of being escorted to the catacombs by Alessandro. The two couples from Scotland would certainly be impressed.

And then she and Larry were in a taxi and she found her head on his shoulder. It had been a long time since a man had his arm around her. He moved his hand up and down her arm and kissed the top of her head, breathing warm air into her hair. She was grateful to him for showing her such a good time, but now she just wanted to get back to her hotel without any fuss, without the embarrassment of refusing a proposition. The best way was not to give him any reason to hope. She tried to pull away, but he held her tightly.

"I'll drop you at your hotel first," he said, "and hold the cab till I see you in. It's hard to get a cab this time of night."

Anne sighed with relief. He did have nice Southern manners.

He reached down to lift up her chin. She knew the kiss was coming, smelled his breath, thought her own must reek, and kissed him back. It felt good. She was safe after all. He was taking her home. He leaned her back on the seat. The taxi turned a corner and they slid down a bit. She remembered kissing Jeffrey in a car. Larry ran his hand along her thigh, kissing her moistly, thickly. He was different from Jeff. His size was different and his smell was different. Her back was pressed against the armrest on the door. The liquor made his every touch, every advance seem less than it was and more than it was. She didn't care about protecting herself as she usually did. She felt soft, warm, and accepting. Everything blended into one kiss: his body, his hands, his chest against hers. He put his hand inside her dress and under her bra, cupping her breast. His hand was warm and somehow comforting. She sighed with pleasure. At last something is happening to me, she thought.

At the hotel he took her to her room. The hallway was not carpeted and the floorboards creaked. Two sets of guilty footsteps in an Italian hotel. He opened her door and stood there. Wasn't he leaving? "Your taxi's waiting!"

But so were the twin beds.

He leaned over to kiss her and she turned her head sideways to accommodate him, knowing that it was a gesture of acquiescence. But she felt like a young girl again. His mouth on hers did not arouse now. But she felt him hard against her thigh and pulled her hips back as he ran his hands up and down her back, bringing her to him, moving her body against his. She wanted to stop, but it was too difficult to resist. Might as well get it over with, his taxi was waiting.

He unzipped her dress and pushed it off her shoulders. It fell to the floor. He pulled off her slip and unhooked her bra. Then with one swift, surprisingly adept move he freed her body of the bra. She shivered and stood waiting in her underpants with her scarf around her neck while he undressed.

He stepped out of his pants and left his shorts on, reaching for her, kissing her neck, touching her arms and back and waist. He took the scarf from around her neck and bent to kiss her bare chest and her stomach. She looked at the top of his head, feeling nothing but his arms around her waist and his mouth at the top of her panties. She stepped back out of reach and pulled down the covers. The move was daring and deliberate; it did more to excite her than all his movements. She climbed under the covers and removed her panties. He took off his shorts and got in beside her, grabbing her immediately—no subtlety, no build-up, she had had that part already. He was hard against her thigh and bigger than she imagined. Or was it just that it had been such a long time? There was the familiar movement of leg over leg, of penis pressing insistently against vagina, the softness of her insides, compliantly opening as he thrust into her. God, he was big! He pulled back, little moves to wet himself, and in again. Relax Anne, relax, she told herself as he kissed her mouth. She enjoyed the feeling of his back, smooth and rippled. I'm having an affair, she thought, and waited for his buildup to begin.

He moved in and out of her, kissing her face and her shoulder, her ear, pulling back to look at her. She kept her eyes closed, her face averted. He lifted her legs up high and she gasped as he penetrated deeper. It was all so different! She didn't like him watching her! She reached up and pulled him down so he would stop looking at her. What is he waiting for? she thought.

"Tell me what you want," he said. "What do you like?"

She held him close so he wouldn't look at her.

"What makes you come?"

Her eyes shot open and she swallowed. The bed was too small to roll over, though he kept trying to do it.

"Tell me," he asked her.

"Anything you do," she finally whispered, hoping that was enough, as he began thrusting into her again and again. She moaned softly in his ear—Jeffrey's ear—and moved her hips in agreement. His body was soon covered with sweat. She could hear the embarrassing sound of sucking where their bellies slapped together. She wished it were over. What was taking so long? If they could only stop!

He grabbed her breast in his mouth and sucked on it, missing the nipple, getting the side. He was hard, and hard pressed to perform. She didn't know what to do, how to help him. He kept going and going, trying it faster and then slower, lifting her legs, and putting them down. He leaned back, his hips pumping furiously, his breath coming in gasps and his brow dripping with perspiration, and he said, "I'm sorry!" but he didn't stop. He continued pumping, falling back on her, sweating into her pillow, until she couldn't relax any more, until she wanted to cry with the shame of it, the disappointment, the raw hurt, the soreness inside. Still she allowed him to continue. She endured this onslaught for what seemed forever, until he became aware that his time was up, that she was rigid beneath him, that she had stopped moaning and moving and welcoming him. He tensed all over, clenching his muscles above her. Then, mildly, after all that effort, he vibrated into her and then lay there exhausted.

Thank God it's over, she thought.

As he got dressed to leave, he said, "I guess I identified you with my wife. It was hard for her to have orgasms, too."

"It's all right," she said, but it wasn't and they both knew it.

He kept his eyes on the floor. "About tomorrow. I don't think I can make it. You tell Alessandro I'll be in touch, O.K.? An' you be sure to look me up if you're ever in Oklahoma, hear?"

It wasn't until he was gone that she realized she would have to call Alessandro in the morning and break the date. The thought of Alessandro with his kind gentleness in contrast to the grossness of Larry filled her with sadness. Her control broke and she started to cry, sobbing with an anguish she thought had ended long ago. She was tormented by her ineffectuality and she touched herself gently, finding the soreness and the ache were inside as well as out.

I will never be used like that again, she vowed. And finally she fell asleep.

CHAPTER 9

Alessandro sat calmly in the waiting room, one black pant leg crossed over the other, his white linen jacket over a black silk shirt open at the throat. He had decided against wearing a tie today, hoping that the casual look of the open collar would give him an air of confidence. He smiled at the secretary, appearing unconcerned, but it cost him great effort. Last night's dinner was pleasant enough, but through the entire evening Enzo had said nothing definitive about the loan. He was too polite to bring it up himself, though he had been sorely tempted. It had been a strange night of sore temptations. First Lisl kept putting her hand on his thigh, and then Larry turned up with Anne Scott. He found Anne appealing; she had an inner strength and an outward fragility, very feminine, but since Larry had brought her, he stayed his distance. And then Larry had called this morning to tell him about taking her to bed. How tasteless these Americans could be, he thought. It was none of his business what Larry did with his girls, or what they did for him. Anne especially. He felt a responsibility toward Anne; she had been wonderful to Elena in Paris.

Since Larry wasn't coming to lunch he had expected Anne to cancel their date too, but when he left the house at 10:30 she hadn't called, so perhaps she would be there after all. I shall have a special nosegay sent to the restaurant for her, he thought. She might need some cheering up.

The office door opened, interrupting his thoughts, and Enzo stood there, his usual stern expression unchanged by green-tinted glasses. He came forward and embraced Alessandro cordially, leading him into the office.

"Thank you again for last night," he began, "though I've had a terrible morning. Indigestion the moment I awoke. Perhaps it was something I ate at the club."

Alessandro felt a cold chill down his back. Enzo was a notorious complainer about his gastronomical condition, but to blame his upset on the food at Legatum di Roma where the cuisine was superb meant he had bad news.

"Sit down, Alex," he said, indicating the maroon leather chair facing his desk. He perched on the front of the desk where he would be in a position of height, forcing Alessandro to look up at him. Alessandro realized he had been outmaneuvered.

Enzo reached across the desk to pick up a file, and turned back to Alessandro. "How long have we known each other?" he asked. "Too many years! I remember you when you were a young boy right after the war, idealistic, and so full of purpose. You and I have been involved many times in each other's successes and failures." Alessandro leaned forward to get up out of the chair, but Enzo held up his hands. "No, no, let me finish."

Alessandro sat back, a fixed smile on his face.

"All those deals, Alex!" His tone was patronizing. "I remember the Egyptian oil search we financed for you. Nothing ever came of that one. And the export car franchise in England? And then there was the art gallery back in the sixties. Where does the time go?" He shook his head. "And then we didn't see you for a while, you took your business elsewhere for those other ventures. What were they?" He didn't wait for Alessandro to answer. "Well, no matter. The point is that in a business community such as ours that is so closely knit, you are a poor risk. I'm sorry to have to be so blunt, but it's the truth." He closed his mouth firmly, shaking his jowly face like a bowl full of madrilene. He didn't look sorry at all.

"I've always made good my losses, Enzo."

"By borrowing from Peter to pay Paul. The intricacies of your financial maneuverings are a lesson in confusion."

"Enzo," Alessandro chided, forcing a lightness into his voice, "don't lecture me like a small schoolboy. I deserve better than that. Just tell me yes or no."

Enzo smiled. "All right, I'll be frank. The answer is no. I'm sorry, Alex, but your financial report cannot support another loan. You have no collateral that isn't pledged in more than one instance. It is interesting to me how none of my other colleagues have discovered that. But it would be foolish to lend money to you under the circumstances, especially in this inflated market."

"Inflation has nothing to do with it. I must expand to meet the demands of my business. You can see that it has the potential to grow."

"Your business isn't worth anything on the loan market, Alex. And you're personally overextended, so you'd have trouble getting State insurance to cover you. The clothing industry is one of the toughest businesses in the world. It's the most competitive, and its success is dependent on so many uncontrollable factors. But you're not even in the clothing business. You can hardly glorify a custom tailor shop with the title "clothing manufacturer.""

And you are naive to think you can establish yourself at your age."

"Is forty-two so old?" Alessandro asked.

"You're hardly a child, need I remind you? And you're not Pucci or Fendi, or Valentino. Leave the international markets to them, and to the Guccis and the Spagnolis, and stick to your personal clientele. Believe me, you can't go wrong by taking my advice."

"But I would be unable to expand if I listen to you."

"Be satisfied for once without taking a risk. Pay back some of your other debts. You won't be able to find anyone to cover for you any more. I happen to know that you've been everywhere for money or you wouldn't have come to us, would you? We were hardly your first choice!"

"Personal preferences have nothing to do with business."

"Yes they do, my dear Alex. I remember how hard you worked to save the Massini estate and its lands, and it was always my regret that we were made responsible for assuming its ownership. But we were only acting in the government's favor. Banco di Venezia has other considerations that are more important than friendship. Which is why I'm talking to you like this today, as a friend. My best advice to you is to use your name. It has a value if you sell it to an international company for a royalty. Let some company capitalize on your image to promote their product. You could be an international celebrity, and well remunerated. In fact, I have a friend who manufactures farm-machinery products who would be most interested in talking to you about it. This is the day of commercial exploitation. Why not capitalize on it? It's not every fellow who can boast of being the Duke di Valdagno."

Alessandro bristled. A peacock put on display to sell tractors—never! He got out of his seat slowly, adjusting his jacket, giving off an air of civility. But inside he was seething. Enzo had committed an unforgivable breach of etiquette. To even think that he would stoop so low. "I'm not quite ready for that, my dear Enzo, but I would endorse my own product, one with high quality. A commodity with which I'm afraid you are unacquainted!" He turned and walked to the door, thinking, Well, that is that. But with one hand on the brass doorknob, he turned. "I almost forgot. You do have one aspect of quality in your life. Your lovely wife, Lisl. Please remember me to her." He closed the door softly behind him, satisfied that he had increased the state of Enzo's indigestion. It didn't hurt to remind Enzo just who Lisl had been in love with before she married him. And from her behavior last night, she still was.

By the time he reached the street he was sweating profusely. All the tension of the meeting, all the rude words prompted by Enzo's jealousy had upset him terribly. This was his last attempt to get a loan and it had failed. He knew it would fail, but he had defined his better judgment and allowed that man to belittle him. Now his fierce pride had been damaged and he didn't know who he was angrier at, himself or Enzo. Where could he turn? Perhaps to Larry, though last evening Larry had not seemed disposed to offer any financial aid. But there was no reason why he should. Alessandro had played the gentleman's game with the American, picking up every tab. Larry had no idea this spending was only a front. When one owes as much as I do, he thought, it hardly pays to save on restaurant charges.

He hailed a taxi and told the driver to take him to Larry's hotel.

Larry met him in the bar off the lobby. The men ordered Bloody Marys.

"What's up?" Larry asked. "You look like you lost your best friend."

Alessandro's frown deepened. "I'm sorry to come here without an appointment but I've just been to my bank and the news isn't good. Apparently there has been a tightening of money due to the fluctuation of the lira, and no one is granting any loans." He gestured with his hand. "Perhaps they will loan to industries of extreme need, but men's clothing does not fall into that category."

"Well, I'm sure that's only temporary!" Larry said.

"I don't think so. Nothing is going to happen with this present government that will bolster the lira. We both know that. And bank policies won't change. They haven't changed in months. That's the reason I can't go into business right now, I haven't the capital."

"Gawd, why didn't you say so!" Larry sat up. "That's no problem. I know guys who lend money all the time! They're buddies o' mine. They'll be glad to help you out, especially when I tell them what a sure thing this is!"

Alessandro looked at him skeptically. "It's not that easy. I tell you I've tried."

"Not with these guys you haven't. Look, you won't need much cash to start with—ten, twenty thousand, whatever that is in lira—and I'll give you a guaranteed sale for your first season, till you get your feet wet. Heck, I buy more numbers for my stores than ten manufacturers can supply. You've got a gol' mine, Alex. I saw retail prices in your store on your handmade suits that I'm payin' wholesale for here and back home. If you can duplicate those suits and send 'em to me, we'll both clean up. And anybody in the business of makin' loans knows a good deal when they see it. They'll loan you money or they're crazy."

Alessandro stared at him. He'd always known that being well connected was an advantage in business, but Larry seemed to belong to a special club of private back-scratchers. He couldn't believe it was as easy as it sounded. "I'd like to meet your friends, Larry. Would that be possible?"

Larry sat up and swung his legs over the side of his chair. "I'll go call 'em right now!"

"You mean they're here in Rome?"

"Sure. What did you think I've been sayin'?"

Alessandro sipped his drink while Larry went to the telephone. What if there was a chance? Menswear was the first business he'd ever tried in which he felt comfortable and didn't question his right to be there. He had an innate feeling for fabrics, for the cut of a coat, for the detailing necessary to make it special. All his life he'd taken great pride in the beautiful tailoring and quality of Italian goods. The Italian artisan was the real aristocrat of the country and Alessandro was democratic enough to want everyone, even the average man, to afford beautiful things. But fine products were expensive. And he catered to an exclusive clientele, mostly his personal friends, who came to him for their custom clothes. It would be nice to broaden his business to provide good fabrics and finely tailored clothes to retail chains who could sell them to many people, and spread his own brand of liberal-artistocratic excellence even to the masses.

Larry came back, a broad smile on his face. "It's all set. He'll see us this afternoon."

And Alessandro smiled at him. "Thank you so much, Larry. It's very kind of you."

Larry sat back down. "I told 'em all about you, and they asked me to ask you one question—are you good for the money?"

"Absolutely," Alessandro said firmly.

"Then you're in! We're supposed to meet at Harry's Bar at 4:30."

This is an exercise in futility, Anne told herself as the taxi sat idling in traffic. The hot afternoon sun beat in on her and she wanted to pound on the seat of the car for making her later than she already was.

What will we talk about, she wondered, wiping her neck with a Kleenex. It was a steamy day and even her shower hadn't refreshed her. She'd changed and dressed in record time, but by the time she got into the taxi it was nearly 2:30—the bus had been late in returning from Ostia.

When the taxi finally deposited her in front of the restaurant the back of her dress was sticking to her body and she was grateful for the slight breeze. The restaurant was on a cobblestoned street in a typical residential quarter, but it was a gay and festive addition to the area. A wrought-iron fence, overgrown with bougainvillea, surrounded a huge outdoor garden. There were picnic-like tables linked up in rows underneath Japanese lanterns, and even at this hour the shaded patio was crowded with luncheon guests.

"I'm here to meet Signore Massini," she told the maître d', expecting him to scold her for being so late. Alessandro had probably left hours ago. But when she saw him walking toward her, hands outstretched and smiling, she was at ease at once.

"I was certain you would come!" he said, taking

her hand. "From the way you cared for Elena, I knew you were a woman of integrity. Those tours can be unpredictable!"

They followed the maître d' to a table inside the softly lit restaurant and Anne relaxed. The cool air was redolent of pungent cheese and sauces and she suddenly realized she was starving.

They sat in a brick-enclosed alcove, hung with bottles of wine and baskets of fresh grapes. The maître d' handed her an enormous parchment scroll with colorful calligraphy announcing the specialties of the house. Alessandro let her study it for a while, but when she glanced at him in confusion he said, "I've taken the liberty of ordering for us."

She was relieved by his thoughtfulness and yet aware that they were really alone, on what could be called a date. She wanted to enjoy it, but her memories of last night still troubled her. She had worried all morning about getting here, and now that she was here she didn't know why she had come.

"You may keep the menu as a souvenir," he said, tucking it inside the zipper of her purse.

She thanked him.

"Anne, there is something I would like to say to you." He looked uncomfortable, and she felt her shoulders tighten. "Larry and I are not close friends, though we have some business dealings together. But I am relieved that he isn't here today."

She looked surprised.

"Please don't get the impression that I would show interest in the girlfriend of a friend. I merely wanted to repay you in some small way for your kindness to my cousin."

"That's not necessary," she said, confused by his words. What had Larry told him, that she was his girlfriend?

She felt on the verge of tears but somehow she managed to control herself. "Signore Massini, I want you to know that Larry hasn't any claim on me." She saw his expression. "I did not enjoy being with Larry. . . . I only met him last night. I've never . . . I was married for ten years . . . and Larry is the first man . . . besides my husband . . . I've ever been with. . . . Being with him was an unpleasant reminder of my marriage. . . . Today I feel terribly guilty, and used." She spoke barely above a whisper.

Alessandro's protective nature was aroused. Larry had lied to him about her! A girl of her character couldn't be wild, she was too vulnerable and inexperienced. He longed to take care of her.

"Signorina—Anne, if I knew you better I would give you some advice. But after the morning I've had, giving advice is as unpleasant to me as receiving it."

She caught the note of futility in his voice, and wanted to comfort him as he was comforting her. "Please go ahead," she said. "I don't mind."

He hesitated for a moment, collecting his

thoughts. "I'm not making any judgments, please understand."

She nodded.

"When you are with Larry, or with anyone for that matter, and it is something you have chosen to do, something you want to do, then no matter how it turns out you have not been used. But if you allow someone to override your wishes and you give yourself without making your feelings or preferences known, then yes, you have been used."

Her expression was solemn, thoughtful. He could see he had struck a responsive chord and he was worried about her reaction. "That doesn't diminish you," he assured her. "Unless you keep allowing it to happen. Take your marriage as an example; although I am not familiar with the circumstances, you may have allowed your husband to use you. But you entered that situation by choice. Your husband was unique in your life. In a marriage it is seldom clear which partner receives the greater benefit because each of you retains certain advantages in a reciprocal arrangement. But now you are not married, and you must recognize that you are entitled to make demands for yourself. Even more than that, you are required!"

Anne was visibly touched. "Thank you for the advice," she said. "But why did you assume it would be unpleasant?"

The waiter arrived with an hors d'oeuvres cart and began serving them portions from the various selections. Fish marinated in oil and capers, eggplant diced with tomatoes, garlic, and peppers, two kinds of pâté, assorted bean salads in wine vinegar, small pieces of pizza bread, baked clams, cheeses, olives, insalata, prosciutto, salamis, and this was only the antipasto.

Alessandro enjoyed her delight as she tasted the food.

"An old adversary of mine gave me some advice this morning for my own good and I'm still fighting the urge to challenge him to a duel."

"A duel?"

He laughed. "It's a complicated story, but it confirms my belief that some people born of lowly origins are very jealous of those born to nobility, though we may have nothing else but our names. They mistake a noble name for a noble motive, which are two entirely different matters. I have always tried to combine the two, and live by a code of ethics. It often works to my disadvantage, but I could not do otherwise. Being a success has never meant enough to me to sacrifice my principles."

"That *is* noble."

"And often foolish. I find myself at this point in my life scavenging for a living when I should be enjoying the fruits of twenty years of effort. I'm not bitter, just discouraged." He found it a relief to voice his feelings, though he was surprised at his willingness to share them with her. Perhaps it was her own candor in discussing her problems.

That, and the fact that they knew no one in common. After today, he would probably never see her again. He was sorry about that. She aroused something in him he hadn't felt in a very long time.

"What did you mean by a noble name?" she asked.

"I am heir to the title of Duke di Valdagno. My ancestors became members of the Venetian nobility in the seventeenth century."

"I thought one was born a nobleman," she said.

"Well, in our case we bought the title when the Republic of Venice voted to increase the number of noble families. You see, they needed to raise revenues to fight a war with the Turks over the island of Crete. There were very few times during the history of the country that aristocrats were invited to join the nobility, and so my title is considered new, though it is a few hundred years old."

Anne found it amusing that anything dating from the mid-1600s could be considered new.

"Valdagno is a small town nestled between Vicenza and Verona. And the name Massini was an old name even when my ancestor became the Duke. He was a tenacious man, fought for causes and so did his descendants. The first Duke distinguished himself in the war for Crete that went on for over twenty-five years. The Doge Contarini was in power then. And our family fought for the glory of Venice during a short campaign in 1715 when Venice lost its possession of the Morea.

Shortly after that, Venice was conquered and was no longer a republic."

"Tell me about Valdagno," she asked.

And he smiled. "The town is undistinguished by any famous monuments, but it was my home. The countryside is beautiful there. Someday perhaps you may see it."

"You don't live there any more?"

"No," he said, losing the touch of sentiment in his voice. "We lost our holdings and our land during World War Two. Land which had been in our family for eleven hundred years."

"What happened?"

He leaned forward. "Of all the nations who have controlled parts of our country—the Spanish, the French, the Austrians—none have had so devastating an effect on us as did the Germans under the Nazi regime. I was a small boy at the time, but I recall how it became suddenly unpopular to belong to a noble family. And even more than that, it was extremely unpopular to be sympathetic to the plight of persecuted people.

"You see, to an Italian of noble birth, no matter who rules the country one must always maintain one's inheritance. That is vital! Over the centuries, however, our family holdings had dwindled considerably and most of the family had died out. If you recall, the economic conditions prior to the war were hardly ideal, here as well as in your country."

She nodded, encouraging him to continue.

"My father was an idealist, and he abhorred the Fascists as well as the Nazis. As his own personal protest against them, he invited a family of Austrian refugees to stay with us. And when he had managed to smuggle them safely out of our district he found other, local Jewish families who needed his help. At one time we had five separate families staying with us. The last family we harbored was from Modena, a neighboring city with a large Jewish population. The father's name was Jacopo and the mother's name was Eva, wonderful people, full of laughter and compassion, in spite of their fear of the Nazis. They never made demands for themselves, only tried to show their gratitude to my father. They had four children. The oldest boy was just my age." He drained the last sip of wine from his glass and poured them each another. "Our town of Valdagno was smaller then than it is now. We thought whatever we were doing was unimportant to the Germans, but we were wrong. Nothing was unimportant to them if it meant they could bring torture and death to innocent lives." He sighed and looked away remembering how it had been. The fear and the anguish. Anne was struck by the look on his face.

"Someone in the village must have reported my father to an official," he continued. Our feelings about the government and its practices were not the commonly held view. Or perhaps it was merely fate that sent a garrison of German troops to be quartered on our land. The commandant was short and blond. He had thick lips and a mustache—I remember because he kept running one finger over it as though he enjoyed the sensation of touching it." His voice tightened as he described the man. "He arrested my father and captured Jacopo and his family. They were to be sent to a concentration camp. I remember not knowing whom to be more frightened for, them or my father. Jacopo and Eva and their children managed to escape from the local jail where the authorities were not as strident as the Germans. They were all killed on the road right near our estate—machine-gunned. I remember Alfaro's face, that was the eldest boy, when they carried him away. He looked at me in death as if to say, 'Why me, and not you?'" He shrugged. "I still don't know the answer."

"What happened after that?" Anne asked, nearly moved to tears.

"The Germans confiscated our lands and kept my father in prison for the remainder of the Occupation, in spite of our efforts to have him released. He died shortly after the war. I don't think he could stand to live any longer in a world where honor had died."

"Poor man!" she said, reaching for his hand.

"I tried to regain our property, but it was impossible for me to maintain." He shook his head. "There was nothing left but the land, and it hadn't been worked. The castle, too, was destroyed by the Germans, and when the government finally granted me the return of my lands, I couldn't raise the money to work it. I still needed to get my education, so I was forced to sell my inheritance for whatever I could get. It was difficult not to be bitter."

"But you are not bitter, are you?" she asked.

"No," he smiled.

"And you still have your title?"

"Yes, but it has very little importance now. Many people claim to have a title these days."

"But you have the consolation of knowing you are authentic." She smiled. She was still holding his hand.

"And you have the consolation of knowing you are a most kind and lovely lady."

She was happy to see he had recovered some of his good spirits. What a terribly sad story, she thought, yet she felt completely at ease with him. What a shame she wouldn't be seeing him again. She withdrew her hand. "Are you going to be in France when I'm visiting Elena?"

His smile was double-edged. "No, I'm afraid not. My cousin has her own friends and I have mine. I think she feels an obligation toward me, that I have never encouraged. She doesn't realize that I am perfectly content to remain where I am. But you will have a wonderful time. Elena is a perfect hostess. How long will you be staying?"

"Only two weeks, then I shall return home."

He was saddened by that thought. "Well, two weeks will be all right then. I wouldn't recommend any longer than that. I'll tell you what! I shall try to drop in on you during your visit, just to see how you are doing. Would you like that?"

"Yes, of course," she assured him, pleased that he cared enough to make such an effort. "But I wouldn't want to inconvenience you."

"Oh no! I may be needed to act as a counterbalance against all that richness. Like a mint after a full meal. But don't be surprised if my cousin doesn't welcome me. We are only close when we meet in my territory. In hers she is like a lioness protecting her hard-earned carcass, while her jackal guests feast."

His brutal description frightened her. "Speaking of feasts," she said, "I can't eat another bite!" The luncheon had consisted of a vegetable soufflé served in a pastry shell, a large portion of mozzarella marinara, and a delicately shaped pasta tossed with clams and butter. Topping off the meal was a freshly made cassata.

"I'm happy you enjoyed it," he said.

"It was wonderful, but what I've enjoyed most of all is your company."

"My dear girl, let me assure you that no matter what you have gotten out of this afternoon, I have gotten twice as much. I shall never forget you! I'm only sorry I am unable to accompany you to the catacombs as I had promised. Something concerning business demands my attention."

She covered her disappointment well; after all, the luncheon was more than she had expected.

Besides, she was still tired from last night. She assured him she didn't mind. "It will leave me something to see on my next visit to Rome."

He paid the check, and hailed a taxi for her, taking both her hands in his. "I hope your tour of Greece will be wonderful." He pulled her toward him and kissed her lightly on both cheeks. "*Arrivederci, signorina*," he whispered.

She felt a twinge of sadness to be leaving him. She got into the cab and waved to him as it pulled away. What a remarkable man, she thought. And so wise. She remembered his words, "If you *choose* to do something then you are not being used." From now on she would make her own choices.

Harry's Bar was crowded with the usual assortment of locals and expatriate regulars mixed with the tourists, both American and European, and Larry was waiting for him at the entrance.

The maître d' led them through the darkened bar, through the pub-like atmosphere of the dining room and into a private room, empty except for a side table arranged with cocktails and several platters of hors d'oeuvres. The room was paneled in dark woods with forest-green leather booths, exactly like the public rooms. One of the tables was set with service for ten, indicating that a party was expected.

"I guess we're early," Larry said. But just then Vincenzo Visconte and his entourage arrived.

Alessandro studied Visconte briefly, pleased with what he saw. He wore a light-gray summer suit, and a blue shirt. He was tall and dark, and seemed in command of the room as soon as he entered.

"Duke di Valdagno, I am most pleased to meet you." He turned to the woman next to him. "May I present Signorina Claudia Luchino, and my son-in-law, Signore Flavio Rinaldi." The Luchino woman was blond, around twenty-five years old, and German, Alessandro guessed, in spite of her name. She looked well paid. The son-in-law didn't smile, just nodded his acknowledgment. Something about all of them made Alessandro suddenly apprehensive.

"Signore Visconte," Larry began, "I've told Alex somethin' about your willin'ness to loan him money, but he was a bit skeptical."

Visconte raised an eyebrow. "Then we shall reassure him! Would you gentlemen like a drink?" A waiter entered through a side door and began to mix a pitcher of martinis.

"Sit down, my dear," Visconte said to the woman. "I'll have something brought to you." She obeyed with a bored expression, crossing the room to slide into a booth at the opposite end. Rinaldi joined her after a look from Visconte.

Visconte took a drink from the waiter and slid into a nearby booth. Alessandro and Larry followed him. Alessandro could feel the cool of the leather through his trousers. A single candle decorated the table, pristine in the middle of the white cloth. Alessandro had a sudden premonition that this meeting would evolve into another dead end. Visconte was obviously a well-established businessman, who knew the risks of lending money.

Alessandro took a sip of his cocktail, but his throat was dry and he wanted a drink of water. If he asked for one it might be a show of weakness.

"I don't wish to belabor our discussion," Visconte said. "I know how difficult it is for a man of your stature to borrow from private lenders. But there are advantages. I know, for instance, that you have been turned down by my austere associates at various banks, and that is unfortunate. I, however, lend on a handshake, not a financial statement."

"You mean that I might qualify for a loan?" he asked.

"A man of your background? Of course. How much money would you need to borrow to begin your enterprise?"

Alessandro hesitated. He'd need between twenty-six and twenty-seven million lire for the entire project, according to his cost projections. He had slightly over two and a half million lire of his own, and if Larry advanced him another two and a half million, he would need to borrow twenty-one million, twenty-four thousand. He had calculated it all very carefully.

"Has Larry told you what I plan to do with the money?"

"That is not my affair, signore, I only ask you how much."

"Twenty-one million, twenty-four thousand lire. That's twenty-four thousand dollars at the current rate of exchange," he said, for Larry's benefit.

"And for how long?"

"Approximately three months."

"I do not lend money for approximate amounts of time. Three months is my maximum."

Alessandro was surprised. "That is all right," he said slowly.

"It's expensive, you know. I'm not in this as a charity."

"What is your rate?"

"One-third, for the duration of the loan." The dark eyes showed no expression.

Alessandro withheld his reaction, trying to assess what he'd heard. He couldn't believe it! It was staggering. "That's awfully steep," he said finally. "I'm not certain it would be profitable for me under the circumstances, but I would have to look at my figures."

Visconte glanced at Larry, and back to Alessandro, looking displeased. "I believed you were informed of these details, but apparently not. You have come to *me*, signore, and I do not bargain, *ever*!" He emphasized his last word but his voice remained calm. "If you are concerned about the advisability, or perhaps about a risk, then you'd better reconsider."

"No, not about a risk. I plan to carry a variety of insurance policies in case of contingencies, and with Larry's guarantee of purchase there is virtually no risk involved."

"I'm certain of it." Visconte smiled for the first time, but only with his lips. "When would you need the loan?"

"Not immediately. I'd want some time to prepare for production. Perhaps late September, so that I may be ready for the October market."

Visconte nodded, and handed him a card. There was only a name and number on it. "Anytime you are ready, give me a call. You'll have the cash in an hour's time."

The interview was over, and Visconte stood while Alessandro and Larry slid out of the booth. "Have a pleasant evening, gentlemen," Visconte said, and shook hands with both of them.

Alessandro reached the door and turned to wait for Larry, but Visconte had detained him.

"Are you certain he knows who we are?" Visconte asked when Alessandro left the room.

Larry smiled broadly. "I told him everything. Of course!"

"Good. I wouldn't want him to have any surprises." His look was direct. "You'd better make sure he knows that we collect our debts immediately."

"I'll tell him," Larry promised. "But he already knows." He hesitated. "My usual finder's fee?"

"Of course!" Visconte nodded and waved him away, crossing the room to sit with the blonde. Larry left and joined Alessandro.

"Well, what'd I tell ya?"

"I'm really very grateful for what you've tried to do. But I just don't know if this is the best way to go. My profit would be a third of what I expected. Those are really outrageous charges!"

"Got any other choice?" Larry asked.

"No," he admitted.

"Then don't worry," Larry insisted, patting him on the back. "You an' me are gonna make money, Alex. And this is only the beginning."

Like every other European, Alessandro had always shut down his operation in August and gone to a resort; this August he would stay in the city and work. Rome was hot and overflowing with tourists, but that didn't bother him. His main concern was whether or not to accept the loan from Visconte. He couldn't fool himself that any man who held his business meetings in a restaurant and who charged usurious interest rates was not someone to be wary of. But as Larry so aptly put it, he didn't have any other choice. There was no one in Rome from whom he could seek advice about such a matter. The fewer people who knew he had any dealings with Visconte, the better. Anyone of substance in the financial community would tell him to stay clear. But this was his opportunity. He couldn't let this chance go by without trying. And if he made his deadline on the loan, he shouldn't have any trouble with Visconte.

While he was trying to come to a decision he received a call from his cousin Carlo, one of his favorite people. There was a deep affection between the two of them.

"What are you doing here this time of year?" Alessandro asked him, over dinner at Legatum di Roma.

"I'm passing through on my way to Lago di Como."

"Rather indirect route, isn't it?" Alessandro asked.

Carlo smiled his white perfect smile. He had his father's features and Elena's beauty. "I wanted to see you. I have something to discuss."

Alessandro noticed Enzo walking across the dance floor and he was reminded of his own predicament. "You came at the right time; I too have a problem with my new business."

"What is it?" Carlo asked.

"No, you first!" Alessandro insisted.

Carlo shook his head. "Business before pleasure."

"I might have known." Alessandro laughed. He signaled to the waiter for another bottle of wine. "I am trying to decide whether or not to accept the offer of a high-interest loan. It would leave me with very little profit after a great deal of work. It is *private* money," he added.

Carlo understood. "Why would you consider it?"

"For several reasons. Even though my profit would only be about six million lire instead of a possible ten million if I borrowed from the bank, the money isn't the issue. It would give me the start I need." He omitted the fact that every bank had turned him down, and Carlo didn't ask.

"What kind of business is it?"

"Wholesale clothing."

"You're certainly equipped to do that."

"That's what I thought." Alessandro felt his enthusiasm rising. "And I have a guarantee of purchase from an associate in America for the production of my entire first line, so I won't be left with any merchandise. It's a great opportunity to open up the U.S. market and test my product without any risk. Then, too, I'd get to know the business of subcontracting and judge if I wanted to open my own factory.

"Subcontracting is where the difficulties lie! That's especially true in our shipbuilding firm."

Alessandro agreed. "But it is a great challenge for me. I want to show a few people who have been skeptical of my ability that I can do it."

"Like my mother?" Carlo asked.

"Elena is the least of my critics."

"It seems as if you have made your decision," Carlo replied.

Alessandro twisted the stem of his glass. "But there is one aspect that truly bothers me. The time limit of the loan. . . . It is very short. Only three months."

Carlo sat back in his chair thoughtfully. "Is it possible to accomplish all that you must do, given such a deadline?"

"Yes," Alessandro answered slowly. "I believe so. But it will not allow me time for contingencies, and when one depends on others for production and shipment of goods, anything can happen."

"Don't I know it," Carlo said.

"The manufactured goods have to be shipped to the retailer in time to be sold during the first rush of the season. With today's cost of overhead, retailers can't afford to miss a single buyer, and without merchandise they have nothing to sell."

Carlo nodded. "In a business such as mine, where we build our ships to order, we run into different kinds of problems, unless I accept an order with a deadline. And then, of course, everything goes wrong."

"Isn't that the truth," Alessandro commented. "You know, Carlo, it makes me feel better to discuss it with you."

Carlo smiled.

"So tell me, what is the pleasurable problem troubling you?"

"I've been having a romance with a woman quite a bit older than myself. It's certainly not the first time, but there are complications."

"Her husband?"

"Not so much that, as the fact that she's mother's closest friend."

Alessandro had a suspicion of who it was, but he would never have asked. "Are you happy?"

"I'm always happy," Carlo laughed. "Especially when I'm in love! She's interesting, and witty, and very beautiful. I find her fascinating, for the moment. I know it will not be permanent. But there is always that chance. I should like to settle down someday."

"And you want me to talk to Elena."

"Only if it becomes necessary."

"She doesn't listen to me, you know."

"But it would help to have you on my side."

"Of course," Alessandro agreed. He could just imagine Elena's reaction.

"Do you think you'll go ahead with the business venture?"

"I don't see why not. Compared to the hornet's nest you're in, my problem seems quite simple." And the more he thought about it, the more certain he was of success.

He began by making tentative arrangements to sublet space in a men's sportswear showroom in Milan's clothing mart. His line would not conflict with the others, in fact they might complement each other. But he had trouble getting representation with a buying office. He consoled himself with the thought that his first season was a guaranteed sale. Once his clothes were bought and shipped, he could use that accomplishment to gain acceptance. Next year they would be soliciting him.

To go into production in the fall meant he would be producing a spring and summer line, and that had its advantages. Cotton duck and linen and silk blends were not as costly as gabardines, cashmeres, and tweeds, so his initial outlay for fabric would be less than in January when he would buy wools for the following year. The spring market showing was in October, so he must have his designs and samples ready by then, and have purchased all his stock materials. The purchase of fabrics was the primary gamble of a manufacturer who depended on orders by sample. But it was necessary to have the fabric to cut the goods once the orders were placed, and that was costly. His line would consist of five sportcoats, three different styles of slacks, and four suits, all made in various combinations of fabrics. In order to produce it he would need to purchase a great deal of material. Fortunately he had that built-in order with Larry guaranteeing him at least a break-even point.

He and Rudy, his assistant, went to work altering the designs of his custom samples to appeal to a mass market and still retain their special styling and elegance. It was then that he began to believe his dream could be a reality.

CHAPTER 10

Anne and Brenda sat in an enormous Greek café opposite the yacht basin in Piraeus, both desperately wishing they had more time. The memory of the Parthenon was still as alive as the sore muscles in their legs. Of all the wondrous monuments they had seen so far, the Acropolis of Athens had been the most magnificent. The sky was cobalt blue and the sun shone white on the modern stucco buildings that climbed the hills around the bay, piled one upon the other, somehow temporary after the agelessness of Pericles' achievement.

Now and then a bee would buzz over to nibble at their fruit, its hum blending with the pleasant buzz of conversation around them. Across the street the yachts were moored side by side in their watery places, sporting registries—Panama, Yugoslavia, France, Italy—that spoke of a more leisurely life. Private passengers met their chartered yachts in Piraeus for cruises around the Greek islands, and Brenda kept thinking that she was going home in two days.

"Well, we've seen the major sights. Next time we won't be tourists."

"Next trip, or next life?" Anne asked.

"A toast." She raised her glass. "To group tours—a long life without me! I'm so tired of buses. 'The Jostle and the Bounce' makes a good title for a tourist guide. Did you ever feel like a schlep compared to all the elite we saw? Remember that gorgeous hotel with the private cabanas in Venice?"

"The Excelsior Palace?"

"Yes, and that restaurant in Florence with all the chauffeurs in front."

"Sabbatini's?"

"And the street with all the boutiques below the Spanish Steps in Rome where the shopgirls were more elegant than the customers?"

"Via Condotti!"

"And these yachts." She swept her arm to include a few huge ones complete with smokestacks and two launches each. "That's the way to see Europe. That's the way to live—Tour d'Argent, Laserre, Laperouse, not Maxim's by night."

"And Legatum di Roma," Anne said, remembering. "All it takes is money." Brenda had voiced her own sentiments, her own longings.

"That's what you think. Money can get you dinner or a hotel room, but it won't get you into the exclusive arena of name or title."

Anne recalled her discussion with Alessandro. Titles weren't so exclusive. "It's not the title," he'd said. "It's the nobility of your life." Easy to say if you speak from a position of security. "Would you want to live like that?" she asked now.

"I have no chance anyway, so it's a moot point." Brenda sighed. "But I sure don't want to go back to work. I feel as if I haven't had a vacation at all! I've lived it up, but I haven't really lived."

Anne sympathized. "Why don't you come with me to Cap Ferrat? Elena invited you."

"An invitation to Elena's villa isn't the same as being accepted on their terms. You'll still be ignored by the svelte. I would only go there if I had money or chic."

"What do you mean?"

"Anne, you're a sweet kid from Burbank who doesn't know a Gucci from a Lamborghini, or a Bulgari from a Maserati. But I know every eighteen-carat-gold inch of them, and I may eat my heart out forever, but I won't wear them or buy them until they suit me, which they don't."

"It so happens that I do know the names of the

status symbols and a few you might not expect me to know. But what do you think would make you suitable?"

Brenda sighed. "Lose some weight, straighten my hair, fix my nose, change my religion, learn a few languages, inherit a fortune, and grow five inches."

Anne laughed. "You've given this a lot of thought, haven't you? How are you going to grow five inches and why would you want to be tall?"

"Because, everyone in the jet set is tall and willowy, with no hips, and their breasts are small perfections—sticking out jauntily above skinny flat stomachs."

"That's ridiculous! An entire class of people from different countries, of different nationalities, and not one of them is short or chubby or ordinary?" What am I defending, Anne thought with a sinking feeling. I've thought the same things myself! She too had loved the touch, the taste, the glimpse of *la dolce vita*.

"Now I know what you think of me—chubby, short, and ordinary. Thanks a lot!"

"I didn't mean that," Anne protested.

"Well, even if all that changed, I still wouldn't fit in. Being chic just isn't enough. You have to come from an exclusive background, and there's a certain mental attitude that's essential."

They stared at each other in the harsh light of comparisons, as if seeing themselves for the first time. "It seems as though we've both been thinking the same things."

Now Brenda was surprised. "You too?"

"I haven't been wearing blinders, you know."

"But *you* could really be glamorous if you wanted to. If you created a new image, people would believe it."

"You think so?" Anne was glad for Brenda's corroboration. She thought of herself as having that chance if she wanted to take it, and it must have been obvious from her expression, for Brenda felt a stab of resentment and couldn't resist.

"Of course, as you are now, you're definitely too blah."

Color rose in Anne's cheeks, making them blotchy. "I wasn't too blah for Alessandro."

"You look ghastly when you blush like that," Brenda countered.

"I don't need your stupid opinions!" Anne stood up. "I'm going for a walk."

"You'll pass out in this heat. Sit down." Brenda looked up at her. "I'm sorry, I didn't mean to hurt your feelings! . . . Oh hell, yes I did. But I'm sorry. Forgive me?"

Anne sat back down.

"I guess it bothers me that you have the potential to make something of yourself. Like Princess Pignatelli, now known as Luciana Avedon. She was awful to begin with, and now she's the glamor queen of the world!"

"Brenda, I'm not awful."

"I didn't say you were awful, just that you could do so much more with yourself. Look at your life. You married a louse and let him walk all over you. Your job isn't particularly challenging, you do it with your eyes closed. What's wrong with aspiring to something more? Wouldn't you love to be rich? I mean really rich, villas and yachts and designer clothes rich?"

"Brenda," Anne said quietly, "I am rich. I have one hundred thousand dollars of my own. I inherited some of it; the rest came from my divorce settlement."

Brenda's mouth fell open. She stared at Anne in amazement. "Do you mean to tell me that all this time I've been feeling sorry for poor plain Anne and you've had all that money? Good God, what an idiot I am. Why are you wasting your time on a miserable economy tour when you could go first class?"

"Because if I spend all my money on vacations, I won't have any left."

"Dummy, you don't have to spend it. You can invest it and live off the income."

"For your information, Brenda, the interest on one hundred thousand dollars is only about seven thousand dollars a year. I did invest it, it's in the bank in a C & D account paying about seven percent, but I have to leave it untouched for two years or it won't earn the seven-percent interest."

Brenda stared at her in shock. "You were just going to go on like this forever, weren't you? Taking an occasional tour with your yearly dividends, working away at that design firm, while your great potential goes unused and underdeveloped. This is the age of women's lib, why not invest in yourself?"

"How would I do that?"

"Do a complete reorganization of yourself. Find out who you are, what you could be."

"I know who I am!"

"No you don't, or you wouldn't have been such a pushover for a creep like Jeff and you wouldn't think working for a graphics firm is the be-all and end-all of professions and you would wear makeup and great clothes and be with interesting people."

"I think you're interesting."

"Thanks, but that's not what I mean. Our duchess Lady Brisson is a perfect example. Even though I can't stand her, she's offering the chance of a lifetime and you'll blow it."

"So what can I do to become glamorous and interesting in two days? She's expecting me the day after tomorrow."

"You could buy some new clothes," Brenda said, offering a Band-Aid for a fracture.

But Anne wasn't patched, she was inspired. She stared off into the distance, thinking about Brenda's enthusiastic suggestions. She had already been mulling them over for a long time.

* * *

Anne lay on the bed staring at the ceiling, not seeing the white plaster cracks here and there or the beams or the flies crawling between them. All she could see were columns of statistics, cost projections based on her capital, ideas to reject or accept, battle plans to be imposed or dismantled, and always at the end of the rainbow a pot of gold (French and Italian gold) with her sitting on top of the pile, a super-sophisticated Anne Scott, throwing kisses to the masses and tossing roses to hordes of counts and barons who all looked like Omar Sharif.

Her head was swimming. What would I have to do to change myself? What would I want to be? A model? An actress? Would plastic surgery help? She wrapped her arms around herself, and rocked back and forth on the bed, tingles beginning to emanate from her ideas to her limbs. Long nails, long legs, long lashes. Long life, Anne! A toast to a new you. You could learn to speak languages, and play tennis, and talk politics, and ski. She hugged herself tighter. Two days to be transformed. Maybe I should make a deal with the Devil. Or better yet, maybe Brenda could help.

But Brenda was asleep.

If a fairy godmother would wave her magic wand . . . that doesn't happen in real life. Put your nose to the grindstone; never mind that it's a surgeon's hands that reshape you and instructors who teach you, you do all the work. My figure is

O.K. I could do something with myself if I really tried. Look what I did with Jeffrey!

She was on the deck of a yacht waving to the shore. There stood Jeffrey, and Jill and Jill's husband Harvey, and all the Larrys in the world, staring at her, desiring her. She was gorgeous. Suddenly it all came clear. She leaped out of bed and shook Brenda awake. "Wake up! You have to hear this." Her voice trembled with excitement. "I'm not going back to California. I'm not going home. I'm not even going to visit Elena just now. But I'm going to live in Europe. Brenda! I'm going to redo myself."

Brenda was fully awake now, pulling up on her elbows. "What are you going to live on?" her practicality demanded.

"I have temporary support from Jeff because I supported him through school, and I have my capital. Certainly enough until I find what I want to do. Do you want to stay with me?"

Brenda hesitated. "I'd have to get a job."

"I've figured it all out. I can afford to hire you as my secretary-companion until you find something."

"If you're serious they're gonna hate me in New York!"

Anne clenched the sheets with her fists as tightly as if she were grasping her future. "Yes, I'm serious. I've never been so serious in my life, Bren. All last spring I felt as if my life were over. All summer I've been licking my wounds and waiting for a wire from Jeffrey, 'All is forgiven, come home and be my doormat.' I waited for something to happen to me in every city we've been to. I wanted an adventure, something that would change me! But we have to make things happen to us. I have to make it happen for me! I don't want to be used any more. I've got to do something about it, don't you think?"

Brenda grinned at her. "Don't ask me, tell me!"

"I'm going to, Brenda. I'm going to do it!"

Elena held the letter from Anne in her hand. That stupid, infuriating girl, she thought. "Forgive me, dear Elena, but I will be unable to join you this summer. Perhaps in a few months if things go according to my plans . . ." What plans could a girl like that possibly have? How many times a week to shave her legs? She didn't know the first thing about plans. But Elena did. She had planned that visit. Everything was geared toward Anne's arrival. On Anne she had pinned the completion of her recuperation, she was just holding on until then. And now she felt more alone than she had before they'd ever met. She was going to surprise Anne with a trip to Majorca and then on to Marbella. Oh, it would have been so calming to confide in someone. For she'd finally decided that that was what she needed, a confidante. She wanted someone who would sympathize with her when she was at her lowest point. Someone who would lock her in a closet when she was tempted to shoot up again. But Anne wasn't coming. And now here she was, craving a shot, not because of physiological dependency but because the very source of her strength had betrayed her. Life was too cruel to bear. She'd told everyone in her family of Anne's kindness and concern for her, built her up to be a demi-saint. And now the selfish little bitch had callously written this insensitive note with no return address. How to find her? Elena knew Anne lived in Los Angeles. She called Information but the phone was disconnected. No referral.

She felt boxed into a corner. Everything she'd banked on was gone. How would she get through it all now, with everyone expecting so much of her. The social season began in late September and she had to do her part. But her nights were worse now than they'd ever been.

Over the years she had become the arbiter of St. Jean Cap Ferrat society. Her name carried the key to many a difficult door. Everyone envied her. Her body was excellent, her ex-husband the most desirable, her avant-garde taste the envy of all. She never forgot a detail that would flatter, a point of information that would interest, and she was an expert at making everyone feel at ease— even the most insecure. She always knew exactly what she was doing, and in society that was a comfort. However, Anne's change of plan left her at a very loose end.

She called Françoise de Kergoly and invited her

to lunch at André's. Françoise would think of something to amuse her.

Halfway through their aperitif Françoise dropped her news. "How broad-minded of you to be so supportive of Carlo. I could never be so generous." Her tone implied that Elena knew what she was talking about, and she watched for Elena's reaction with innocent green eyes.

Bitch, Elena thought. "Thank you for the compliment. But having a narrow-minded viewpoint isn't your fault. Blame it on your parents."

"I don't have a narrow-minded viewpoint," Françoise said, caught in Elena's offensive.

"Oh? You just said I was broad-minded and you weren't."

"Still. One's closest friend and one's son! It does take fortitude."

The *coup de grâce*, Elena thought. God save me from close friends. And then the meaning of Françoise's statement etched its way into her consciousness and her knuckles turned white as she fisted her hands under the table. Oh, Carlo! She wanted to cry, What have you done? To give herself a moment to think, she signaled the waiter for another Campari and soda. "Triana is going through a difficult time right now, poor thing," Elena modulated her voice to appear concerned and still regal. "She hasn't accepted growing old as easily as you."

Imagine Carlo with Triana! She could barely restrain herself from squeezing the crystal glass in her hand until it shattered. Triana was forty-four if she was a day, and Carlo, her beautiful Carlo, was only thirty-one. She wondered if Paolo knew. He would be furious. Triana wasn't even Carlo's type! "You can't believe there's anything between them that would concern me, do you? Oh, Françoise!" She was succeeding with her act. She had obviously caught Françoise off guard.

"But I was certain . . ."

"Every young man must have an 'experience' like that. I'll bet you were sorry it wasn't you?" She was all innocence.

Françoise looked away. "Honestly, Elena. Don't be vulgar."

At last the soup arrived. "But just to please you, I shall warn them to be more discreet. If you know about this, then everyone else will find out!" She stared at Françoise, her meaning clear: Keep your mouth shut!

"That's what I thought," Françoise said, finally vindicated.

Wait until I get my hands on Triana, Elena thought, her need for Anne suddenly displaced by a more pressing problem.

CHAPTER 11

Anne had never had difficulty sleeping, but now she developed insomnia, waking at two or three every morning, and unable to get back to sleep. Her body was overextended from physical excesses of a new type—she had begun to jog, she was studying ballet, and she was dieting for the first time in her life. After the initial burst of enthusiasm, drudgery had set in. Reshaping a flabby stomach was a bloody bore. By three o'clock in the morning the hunger pains were intolerable and never assuaged by the yogurt or the piece of fruit she allowed herself. She would try to relax, knowing she needed her sleep. But she was too keyed up, aware that she was an ant trying to carve a goddess out of the sides of Carrara.

She and Brenda had rented an apartment in Rome, reasoning that it was cheaper to live there than in Paris, and they worked to learn Italian. Besides, where there were pampered women, there had to be means of learning their ways. She searched herself for new resources, inspirations to fill the hours of self-doubt, thinking about characters in books she'd read, and of movies she had loved and the stars who had played the characters she longed to be like. Movies produced a dream of a better life. Somewhere women wore those beautiful clothes and knew how to talk to men, and made their lives work for them instead of the other way around. She took her inspiration from old movies on T.V. For her exercises, she became Myrna Loy determined to keep her man; for her tennis lessons she became Jane Powell determined to find her man; for her language lessons she became Jane Russell determined to take her man. Ann Blyth and Kim Novak and Grace Kelly were there whenever inspiration or muscle failed. And somewhere, he lay in wait for her. Mister Right. The golden cock at the end of the trail. It was all a fantasy but she persevered. And it was beginning to pay off.

* * *

"Look at you!" Brenda exclaimed. "What a difference."

They had gone to a boutique on the Via Condotti to buy Anne's first bikini, three tiny pieces of material that just covered her pubis and her nipples. Anne turned around to inspect herself from all angles. Her waist was small, hip bones extending from her pelvis. Her legs were long, accentuated by the line of the bikini which rode high on her hips. She did a plié and watched in fascination as the muscles contracted and protruded as she bent and pulled her knees together. Her calves were rounded, her ankles were slim, her thighs were shapely. The only flaw was a dimpled lump on the outside of her thigh. She hit the offensive spot with her fist.

"This is where I have to concentrate."

"You could use a tan," Brenda offered. "And some breasts."

Anne looked at her sharply. "Do you know where they sell them?"

She nodded. "At the plastic surgeon's."

"Forget it, Brenda. I'll just be small, thank you."

"Small is a compliment for what you've got."

"That's enough, Brenda," she snapped, glancing at the salesgirl.

"She doesn't speak English," Brenda said.

Anne stood her ground. Bette Davis would never take that! "Don't ever insult me in public again. If you have a suggestion you can damn well be discreet about it!"

Brenda stared at her. Would wonders never cease? But she didn't let up. She waged a campaign for breast implants until Anne couldn't stand it any more. "I'll think about it," she said finally, and then she had another problem to keep her awake at night. Could breasts be that important? No! It was silly, beneath her.

She couldn't get used to the new way she looked. In her ballet tights her height was accentuated. Long, lean Anne, she thought to herself. But her thinness didn't give her grace. She was awkward and ungainly, and struggling with ballet lessons depressed her. Though she had no real interest in ballet she felt competitive with talented young women in her class.

"What do you think, Brenda? Should I switch to jazz dancing?"

"Why not? Ballet lessons at your age are only supposed to give you an appreciation of the art. You've got the basics now. Sure, try another form! Maybe you'll enjoy jazz dancing!"

Anne winced. It wasn't what she wanted to hear but Brenda was right, jazz was easier. She learned to do the latest dances. They went to the discotheques at night and practiced, observing the vivacious and decorated girls who frequented them, whose popularity seemed to be in direct relation to their looks and their availability. Still, it was educational, and Anne was a quick study.

When she wasn't exercising her body she was exercising her mind. She learned to converse, not apologetically, but with an air of determination and confidence. She read current history, politics, economics, and discussed them with Brenda over dinner each night. Brenda was amazed by the quality of Anne's intelligence. She grasped facts readily and understood their implications. Anne familiarized herself with names and faces in the social scene. She had hated *Women's Wear*, but she read it religiously and now she was beginning to enjoy it. She bought a riding crop and asked Brenda to tap her whenever she forgot her posture and began to slouch.

"You make me feel like a pony trainer, Anne. If I do this, you'll hate me!"

"I don't care! Don't listen to me no matter how much I complain. Just do it! I'll never learn otherwise!"

She spent hours in front of the mirror, tilting her head at the most flattering angle and transforming her grin—never her best feature—into a smile that did not bare her gums. When she grew frustrated at the inanity of this pastime and furious with herself every time she relapsed into her old horse grin, she would clench her fists and remind herself, "If Raquel Welch could learn to flare her nostrils, I can change my smile."

They kept to themselves, but not out of choice. Though the American colony in Rome was diverse, American executives didn't fraternize with tourists—nor did producers, directors, and actors. To get into a social life worthy of their aspirations they needed an invitation, an introduction, a sponsor. And their would-be sponsor was not in Rome, but in Paris for the fall and Gstaad for the holidays, so Elena's servants told them when they telephoned.

"I hope the invitation will still be open for that visit by the time I'm ready," Anne said.

And everywhere she went she now heard, "Oh, how beautiful!" The salesgirls said it, the shoppers said it, and children said it. "Isn't that beautiful, *che bella!*"

What is beautiful? Anne thought, watching an obese mother hand a triple gelato to her toddler and then order one for herself. Why do I want to be beautiful? *Because beautiful is better.* She felt obsessed with herself, obsessed by that unattainable vision. Everyone else was beautiful. Everywhere she looked, young women, older women, dressed-up women, undressed women. Were they all trying as hard as she was? Her mother was not beautiful, but her father loved her. *But Jeffrey didn't love me.*

What was the right look for her? Not the flash of the available and sexy young women she saw in the discotheques. Nor the elegance that suited Brenda. For Brenda it was easy. These were the clothes she adored and wore well: St. Laurent sportswear, Buccelatti chains, Gucci loafers, nothing cute or faddish; her tastes ran to the classic. But for Anne neither the latest in fad or an understated elegance seemed quite right. Everyone looked the same to her, both on the disco scene and among the Gucci set. She knew there was security in uniforms, but uniformity didn't suit her any more. She'd conformed all her life, and now she longed to be different. She wanted her clothes to reflect that difference and say something about her—not be flamboyant, just unique. Every garment she saw she knew she could improve upon. And she began to sketch her ideas, finding that her drawings expressed the way she felt. The more she drew, the more ideas she got. It seemed neverending. Brenda thought she was quite innovative.

"I didn't know you could draw."

Anne laughed. "I made a living at it. But I've never tried to translate these ideas on paper before." Her talent was something she'd always taken for granted: doesn't everybody draw?

"These clothes have real style," Brenda commented. "Why don't you have one of the sketches made up?" She pointed to a three-piece outfit Anne had drawn, colored with mauves and lavenders.

"That's a difficult design," Anne said. "I haven't got a pattern for it, and even if I did, choosing the proper fabric for a particular design is a profession in itself. My mother sewed—in fact she made a lot of my clothes. She spent hours in shops picking out the right fabrics. She'd pull on the different materials to test their bias, ravel the edges, ask questions, drape bolts of goods one on top of the other, and once she even burned the corner of a piece of material because she didn't believe it was correctly labeled. And you know what? She was right! Besides," Anne added, "I don't know any dressmakers in Rome."

She stopped, as Alessandro's face came into her mind. He was in the clothing business, and she'd been wanting to see him all this time but she hadn't had the nerve to call him. This was a perfect excuse! But what would he say when he realized she'd been living here for months and hadn't called him. After the way he'd extended himself for her he might be angry. She had planned to be different before she called him—all transformed. I'd better wait, she thought, give myself a little more time.

But one day in early October she found herself on Via Barberini, and there was his shop. The sign said: FABRIC DI MASSINI, in small unimposing letters, and there were outdated photos in the window of men wearing designs by Massini.

The store was small and carpeted in a bottle-green color; the walls were wood. Against one wall was a marble table covered with men's fashion magazines. Two wooden chairs and a table were opposite the door and next to them was a clothes rack hung with suits and jackets. Swatches of materials were pinned to the lapels. The place had a kind of run-down, old-time look to it.

A woman came out of a back room to greet her. Her wavy gray hair was pulled tightly back in a chignon, stretching the skin on her gaunt, lined face. Her expression was proprietary.

"*Buon giorno, signorina. Come sta?*"

"*Va bene,*" Anne replied. "*Grazie.*"

"*Che desidera?*"

"*Vorrei parlare con* Alessandro Massini."

"You are an American, aren't you?"

Anne smiled. "My accent is terrible."

"No! It is quite good. It is I who must practice English. I'm sorry but my son is not here at the moment. Were you looking for something in the way of a suit, perhaps?"

Over the whir of the sewing machines coming from the back room Anne could hear voices. One of them sounded like Alessandro's. She glanced in that direction and evidently Signora Massini noticed, for her proprietary look was now covering her embarrassment.

Alessandro must have girls throwing themselves at him, she thought, and reached into her bag to take out a pencil and paper.

"This is my name and telephone number." She wrote it down for the woman. "Please tell Signore Massini that I stopped in to see him."

The woman took the paper, but barely smiled as Anne left. Anne was halfway down the street when Alessandro caught up with her. He was out of breath from running. "Anne! You cannot leave so soon! What are you doing in Italy? How wonderful you look! *Meraviglioso!* It's lovely to see you."

He took her arm through his and walked her back to the shop, keeping up a steady conversation to hide his annoyance with his mother. Signora Massini did not seem overjoyed to have Anne back so soon!

Alessandro showed Anne around the shop and introduced her to Dominic, his tailor, and to Rudy, his patternmaker. The shop was even less than Anne had expected, but he looked happy, and seemed very proud of what he was doing.

"How is Elena?" she asked him over dinner at a trattoria near the Piazza Navona.

"I assume she is fine, I haven't seen her since Paris. When I heard you had canceled your trip to France, I too changed my plans."

"Oh, I should have told you. But everything happened after I left Rome for Greece. That's when I decided to come back here and live."

"You are living here? In Rome? Splendid! We shall see more of each other!" Alessandro was aware that the attraction he'd felt for her when they first met was as strong as ever.

Anne couldn't believe his enthusiasm. The fact that this charming man liked her was amazing to her. And now she would have another friend, someone besides Brenda in whom she could confide. There were so many things she wanted to ask him.

"How is your business thriving?"

He smiled. "Many things have changed. You remember Larry?"

"Of course." She wished she could forget.

"We have gone into a business arrangement together. I will be producing a line of men's clothes, and he will buy them and sell them in America. I have been making arrangements for factories, and working on my designs. I am extremely pleased with the way our samples look. At any moment I expect to hear from him, and then I shall begin production. It is something I have always wanted to do." His eyes glowed with excitement as he looked at her. "You know, at this moment you remind me of one of my ancestors in a painting by Titian. It is a religious theme, but he used her as a model."

"An authentic Titian? How I'd love to see it."

Alessandro laughed. "I would be honored to show you my etchings." He grabbed her hands across the table, aware of her embarrassment. "Don't be shy. I'm so delighted that you are here, and I am only teasing."

But as soon as she could, without offending him, she withdrew her hands from his. No one would ever accuse her of throwing herself at him.

"Do you still plan to open your own factory?"

He became more serious. "I've been trying to decide about that since last summer. I have custom orders for suits I cannot fill; the work is more than my tailor can handle. But my operating costs are such that it wouldn't pay to hire another tailor. Unfortunately, even with a demand for more merchandise, I am not making the profit I had projected with my custom designs. I had to let one of my workers go, and my bookkeeper too. That is why my mother is working for me. And why this experiment with Larry means so much to me. I will be able to judge if investing in my own machines and my own building would be warranted." His tone changed slightly, as if he were apologizing without saying so. "You know, my mother means well, but she doesn't belong in business. She insists that my customers all meet with her approval or she doesn't want me to sell them my clothes." He chuckled. "It is a difficult way to operate. Last week a man came to me for a suit. He was from Brindisi, and recommended to me by a cousin of his. When Mama found out he was from Southern Italy, she became like an icicle. Mama believes that any place south of Rome isn't really Italy, that a different class of people lives there. I'm afraid she's not the only one in Italy who believes that."

"She does seem formidable."

"She likes you," he said, though Anne felt Alessandro was not telling the truth. "Says you are a nice, simple girl."

"Well, I'm planning to complicate myself just a bit. That's exactly why I'm living in Rome. Haven't you noticed how much weight I've lost?"

"Yes," he admitted. "I did think you looked a bit drawn, but you are still the same lovely girl."

"Alessandro, I'll be thirty in the spring!"

"How wonderful! We shall celebrate with a party. You must tell me when, so I can prepare for it!"

She couldn't believe he was serious. He was either the most superficial man she'd ever met, or he wasn't listening to her. "You don't understand what I said. I am trying to change myself. I want to be more . . . more social."

"But whatever for?" he asked her. "You're delightful the way you are!"

"Perhaps then someone like your mother would be glad to meet me."

"But why would you care what my mother thinks?" He was truly puzzled.

"Never mind," she shrugged, toying with the stem of her glass. He was born to society and couldn't understand her needs as an outsider. But when she looked up at him, he was smiling at her in a way that made her feel he did understand. "I want to show you something," she said, and took one of her sketches out of her handbag. "What do you think of this?"

He studied it for a moment and then glanced up at her. "It's interesting," he said.

She felt her hopes fall. "Is that all you think of it?"

"Ungaro has always been one of my favorite designers."

"That's not Ungaro," she said. "It's mine. I sketched it."

"Yours?"

"Yes, mine. It's original! I designed it. And I wanted to ask you if you could make it for me!" She was bewildered by him. She would never copy another designer! She didn't like any one of them enough to copy.

"Do you have any more of these?" he asked her.

"Yes, a few."

"Then you must bring them to me, I should love to see them. You have a flair for design."

Her smile lit instantly across her face. "Do you really think so?" She hadn't dared to even hope.

"A great deal of flair," he said, with reserve in contrast to her eagerness. He did not want to encourage her prematurely. He recognized that what she had done might be unusual because it showed a high degree of originality. Of course, women's fashions weren't his forte, but over the years he'd had a great deal of experience with couture, if only from a buyer's viewpoint. Betsey had worn only couture. How different Anne was from his wife, so unspoiled and honest, compared to Betsey's English blondness and her aristocratic pretensions. He'd been so enchanted by everything about Betsey until her charm gave way to indifference and then bitterness. His mother had warned him, but he had been so in love with her. And in spite of the objections of Betsey's Anglican family to her marrying an Italian Catholic, they had gotten married anyway. His title was real, Betsey had liked that. He could still see how she looked in her Balenciagas, in her Chanels, in her Givenchys, outfitted and extravagant. He hated to deny her anything; it reflected on him as a man. But he was only a workingman then. He had the Maserati franchise in London's East End at the time and it hadn't gone well. Nothing about that marriage had gone well, especially the pain of losing her. So much pain that even now, eight years later, he shied away from any romantic involvements. He did not want to be hurt.

Anne was staring at him waiting for his reaction. "This is a complicated dress pattern, Anne. I'm afraid Rudy wouldn't know what to do with it. Why don't you see if you can find a ready-made pattern similar to yours, and we'll adapt it. Or perhaps the dress can be modified to fit an existing pattern."

She looked disappointed. "If I change any of the lines, it won't be the same dress."

"How do you know that?"

She looked at him in surprise. "It's obvious. "This dart," she pointed to a line under the bust, "is my own creation. I've never seen one done like this before, and it means that the bodice must be engineered specifically to include that factor. Just as the sleeve must be cut to fit into the bodice right here." She pointed to another spot.

He was startled by her knowledge. "Have you studied design?"

"No. But I watched my mother sew. She taught me a great deal."

He nodded. "We can all learn from our mothers." And then he winked. "Come by the shop sometime soon and we will talk to Rudy. He may be able to help."

CHAPTER 12

After her first frenetic efforts to find employment, Brenda was ensnared in a silken net of complacency. Normally active, the more she watched Anne pushing herself, running, exercising, dancing, and drawing, the less Brenda could manage to do. It was autumn in Rome, but she was gripped by a Polynesian paralysis.

At first she was enthusiastic, job hunting was a challenge. But after a while it became so exhausting to navigate the city that she went job hunting less and less.

"Have you heard from that American firm?" Anne asked.

Brenda sighed. "Another dead end! American companies hire their employees in the U.S. and then send them overseas. None of the companies I've interviewed are hiring overqualified women who can't speak Italian."

"But you're improving," Anne offered.

"Not enough! Speaking Italian doesn't mean giving instructions to a cabdriver. I should be able to converse about the commodities market, and selling short, and debentures and capital investments if I intend to work in my field."

"You're not thinking of going home, are you?"

"Only three times a day. But don't worry, I'm not giving up yet. There's another alternative besides selling my soul as an au-pair girl."

"What alternative?" Anne wanted to know.

"Wait and see," she said, lightly. Her alternative was something she was not eager to do.

It wasn't until December that Brenda burst into the apartment with good news. "I've got a job! I'm assistant to a loan officer at Banca Moderna Italia. My boss handles only English-speaking depositors who have Italian investments."

Anne was excited for her. "That's wonderful, Bren!" she said, hugging her. "But I thought you couldn't get a job without a work permit and you couldn't get a work permit without a job."

"It's amazing what you can do when you know

someone. I finally swallowed my pride and wrote to my training officer at B B C & R. After reading me the riot act for not coming back to New York, he sent me the name of someone in personnel at Banca Moderna Italia, along with a letter of recommendation. I went for an interview and they hired me. They seemed thrilled to get me!" She smiled slyly. "Of course the thing that cinched it was my fluent Italian." And they both laughed. She spoke Italian with her hands.

Brenda loved her job. After the first hectic days of orientation it was exciting to be around money again and the power it symbolized. She'd forgotten how comfortable she felt with the people who controlled it. Banking differed from the stock market in attitude more than actuality. The brokerage business was by nature frenzied, electric; banking was slow. People only hurried at closing time.

And Italians were different from Americans. The men noticed her as a woman, admired her for herself as well as her accomplishments. She suspected their attentions were chauvinistic but she decided to reserve judgment on that.

Banca Moderna Italia was a commercial bank that operated as a short-term credit institution but it was a huge organization with numerous branches all over Italy. The bank's center for foreign investments was located at the main building on the Via dei Corsi. Brenda's immediate supervisor had been with the bank for twelve years and he spoke about Frederico Segri, the bank's president, as a kind of god.

"He knows what is happening in all our departments. His word is law; a remarkable man!" he assured her.

The description reminded Brenda of a banking "Big Brother" who sees and knows all. She was sure she wouldn't be impressed.

She was wrong. Her first meeting with the famed Frederico Segri came one morning when she was in the vaults learning the bank's process of loan certification. An old woman with bent shoulders and white hair came hobbling into the steel room wearing the customary black dress of the widows of Italy. A well-dressed man in his late forties followed her in, helped her to unlock her safe-deposit box from its place, and carried it into a private booth for her.

Brenda's supervisor was flustered by the presence of the man, and then Brenda understood why.

"Signore Segri," her supervisor said. "May I introduce to you our newest employee, Miss Brenda Greenstein."

Segri extended his hand and Brenda was aware of his piercing stare, and a fluttering response somewhere inside of her. Nothing gets by this man, she thought, and stared right back at him. Why was the head of the bank providing a service that was the function of a lesser clerk? she wondered. Or did he run every department as well as oversee it?

Segri was medium height, with broad shoulders and strong features. His wavy graying hair was combed to perfection, just as his suit was beautifully tailored. He had the appearance of austerity, but it was softened by the touch of amusement in his eyes when he smiled. Brenda relaxed as they shook hands.

"Welcome to BMI, Miss Greenstein." His voice was warm with a hint of that underlying amusement. "I understand you have a certain expertise in investment counseling. Our government is most anxious to attract American dollars and I'm counting on you to be a valuable asset to our foreign-loan department."

So he knew who she was, and he remembered the details of her background. She was impressed with his memory, and she found him dynamic, wishing she could think of a more original way to describe him.

She couldn't help responding to him. "I know I shall enjoy working here!" Her enthusiasm seeped through her attempted cool.

"You know, Miss Greenstein, you are an exception in our organization. Very few of our women employees have your education or background. We are pleased to have you with us. And if there is anything I may do for you personally, I expect you to ask!"

Brenda thanked him graciously while Segri

studied her carefully. From her letter of introduction he'd expected her to be older and not as lush. She was a bit unorthodox for the banking profession, but he liked her appearance and her attitude. This young woman was definitely unique, he thought, and he was exceedingly sharp about the differences in people. She would have her supervisor's job in no time!

It was Segri's intimate knowledge of every aspect of banking that had gotten him where he was. He had a computerlike mind and the terminals of his awareness were hooked into every phase of the business. His sixth sense reinforced his reputation as a mind reader, and now he was reading Brenda Greenstein's mind, surprised to find that she liked him and that she wasn't the least intimidated by him. Well, good, he thought. That was a quality he seldom saw in anybody, especially women.

Over the next few weeks Brenda became more aware of Segri's ability to keep a finger on every department of the bank. He exuded power, and worked long hours, always there when she left for the day and when she arrived in the morning. She watched him stride purposefully from deal to deal, from department to department, not like a banker at all. He capitalized on every aspect of his ability and his considerable charm. His foreign connections were legendary; he was known as a "deal-maker," which allowed him to take a percentage from every group he brought together, and that, in turn, brought other short-term loans into the bank at a phenomenal rate. He was knowledgeable in the precious-metals markets, he sat on the board of directors of an oil company, and was instrumental in finding Eurodollars for an English offshore drilling lease, rumored to be one of the largest discoveries of oil ever made. Financial wizardry was his invention. Brenda was wildly attracted to him.

One morning she arrived at the bank at seven o'clock, determined to get there before him, laughing to herself at the idea that he would even notice she was there at all. What chance had a minor loan officer's assistant to gain the attention of a man of his stature, she wondered. She told herself that if she could only absorb a fraction of his knowledge of business, it would give her an advantage she could only dream about. And she was dying to get to know him better.

Dressed in a beige gabardine suit and a pale-blue shirt, she went to his office to ask him if he wanted a cup of coffee. A thin excuse but she didn't care. As she was about to knock, she heard voices coming from inside his office. She hesitated a moment and was astonished when she realized the language was Hebrew. They were the same words her grandfather chanted every morning and every evening when he said his prayers and wrapped his tefillin around his arm and

173

around his head. Segri was Jewish! At last they had something in common. She had found the perfect opening.

Later in the day she went back to his office. "You once told me if there was anything I need personally, to come and ask you."

He was sitting at his desk, and he stood and offered her a chair.

"I would be glad to help you with any problem you might have," he said formally.

She took a breath. "I would like to know if you could recommend a synagogue here in Rome where I might feel comfortable attending services. Most of the temples are orthodox in the old tradition, and I've found them quite different from what I'm used to in New York."

If he was surprised by her question, he didn't show it. "I can see how they might be different! I have attended services in the United States, and we have nothing here that is similar to the joyous participation of both men and women and boys and girls at your Friday-night services. However, if you would allow me, I should like to accompany you myself to my synagogue, on the Lungotavere Cenzci, where you would be allowed to join in the service. Would this Friday night be agreeable?"

All she could do was nod. It was much more than she'd expected.

"Fine," he said. "Leave your address with my secretary and I shall have the car pick you up at 6:30. Our services begin early in Rome."

As she was about to leave, she turned and smiled at him. "I can't thank you enough, Signore Segri. You don't know what this means to me." And she found she was telling the truth. Having someone to attend a religious service with was an experience she had long missed. Perhaps her anger with God over Barry's death would begin to subside now, as well as her feelings of being so alien in a foreign culture. It would be good to establish roots with her people again. Especially through Segri.

After the service he took her to dine at the Excelsior Hotel. She could hardly believe she was actually there with the president of Banca Moderna Italia. Of course she didn't fool herself that he was interested in her, but still she was flattered.

"Have you always lived in Italy?" she asked him.

"Yes. But not always in Rome. . . . But tell me, Miss Greenstein . . ."

"Please call me Brenda."

"All right, Brenda, how did you become interested in finance? It's unusual to find a woman of your intelligence and at your level in the business."

"I'll answer your question with a question," she replied, admiring the way his dark eyes appraised her. "Do you know what it is about you that thrives on the control of other people's lives? Or why it is easy for you to handle large sums of money and not be influenced by the tremendous pressures placed on you for the spending of that money? Can you tell me how you know *what* you know, or is it some innate ability that you couldn't manufacture even if you wanted to?"

He stared at her, watching the intensity of her expression, absorbing what she was telling him.

She leaned forward. "If someone asked you to explain what the command of a boardroom does for you, or how you know, in here," she placed her hand across her stomach, "when someone is trustworthy, or a poor risk, or how it is that you never forget the details of a new government regulation, or the vagaries of the law concerning foreign investments, could you tell them?" She sat back in satisfaction, as if resting her case. She saw him nod slightly, as if he were picking up more from her than her words.

"Those unknown qualities, those inner-directed attributes aren't easy for me to define either. We have a colloquial saying in my country, 'It turns me on!'"

He smiled. "I have heard that before, but only in reference to the use of drugs."

His clinical explanation of her statement made her laugh, and she reached across the table and squeezed his hand. He laughed with her, not certain why they were laughing. "Well, it's the same thing in banking, or stocks. They are a potent stimulus to the blood!" She detected a note of amusement in his eyes and something else she couldn't define. She withdrew her hand.

"I shall be eager to watch your career, Brenda." He stopped himself from recapturing her hand.

"I have every intention of earning promotions, Signore Segri," she said, and the moment passed.

"Please call me Frederico," he said, smiling. She smiled back, feeling a special bond of kinship with him.

A few days later he gave her some information about a fluctuation in the silver market which could be to her advantage. Some friends of his were very involved in the commodities market. She told Anne about it.

"What do you think? It's practically a guaranteed profit."

"Nothing is guaranteed, Brenda," Anne said.

"But I've watched him, Anne, the man's a genius. He's in a group that controls certain metals markets. If he told me to invest in Fratelli Pastores, I've got to listen."

"What did he say exactly?" Anne asked.

"He said, 'It's only a few days' wait, Signorina Brenda,'" she copied his accent, "and he didn't say go short. That means silver will go up, enough so that we can. get in and out, pay our fees and make a profit."

"How much money were you planning to invest?"

"Fifteen hundred dollars."

"When?"

"Tomorrow at the opening, we place a buy order with the bank's brokerage house."

Anne was silent, mulling it over. "If we each put up fifteen hundred dollars and make ten percent return, or even twenty, that's only six hundred dollars. Is it worth the risk for that amount?"

Brenda was impatient. This was an incredible deal and Anne was too unsophisticated to know or understand. "When one invests, it's not the amount of the profit earned that counts, it's the percentage earned. Very few investments ever make a profit of twenty percent. If we can do that well on a straight investment, we're doing O.K. But if we bought on margin, we'd make a killing!"

"What do you mean by a killing?"

"Buying on margin with three thousand dollars would give us thirty thousand dollars' worth of capital buying power. At a twenty-percent return, that's . . ." she calculated quickly, "six thousand dollars profit!"

"But buying on margin is much riskier, isn't it?" Anne questioned. "If Fratelli Pastores goes down we'd not only lose our three thousand dollars but we'd be liable to lose part if not all of the thirty thousand dollars, wouldn't we?"

"But it will go up!" Brenda insisted. "Segri is the president of the bank. He's worth a fortune because of deals like this."

"Will he guarantee our losses?" Anne asked sarcastically and then was sorry for her comment. "Look, Brenda, my friend Nancy worked for a bankruptcy attorney. And bankruptcies don't happen just from business failures, they happen when people gamble on stupid investments. You and I know nothing about the silver market."

Brenda shrugged; she was through convincing. "The man's doing us a favor, Anne. I'm going to invest my own money, if you want to join me, you're welcome."

"I suppose I can afford fifteen hundred dollars, but if it doesn't go up you must promise to sell. I'm not going to wait around and watch myself lose thirty thousand dollars."

"I agree. If it goes down, we sell out fast!"

"I'll even put in another five hundred for each of us. That will give us forty thousand dollars on margin. What is it selling for?"

"In lire?"

"Yes."

The figures tumbled from Brenda in a breathless rush. "Sixteen thousand, five hundred lire a share or about twenty-five dollars a share at the current rate of six hundred sixty lire to the dollar, which gives us sixteen hundred shares for an investment of forty thousand dollars on margin."

In two weeks they had each cleared eight thousand dollars profit. In three months, with Segri's help, they each had pocketed another fifteen thousand. Anne loved the power she felt from earning such profits by her own risk. Even though the risk was minimal, still it could have gone the other way. She didn't feel guilty about this gain at all. It had an unreality about it. It would be easy to lose one's perspective, she thought. But she wasn't about to let that happen.

And Brenda thoroughly enjoyed the increase in her bank account. But even more than the growing numbers, she was warmed by the growing friendship she felt toward Segri, and the smile he gave her whenever they met. Their Friday nights were becoming a habit for her. All very proper and religious, but she began to live for Friday nights.

CHAPTER 13

Gino reached behind his back and tugged at the bottom of his beige flannel jacket. It was already pencil smooth, but he wanted to make sure. Then he ran his finger inside the waistband of his slacks to see that the brown silk shirt was tucked in tightly. Satisfied that all was perfect, he did his customary touches to his hair and entered the restaurant. Feelings of both elation and apprehension clutched at him. It had taken him six months to get to this point and he didn't want anything to go wrong. Carefully and cleverly, he had ingratiated himself into the acquaintanceship of Angelo Luceri, one of Vincenzo Visconte's associates. Of his last three shipments of heroin from Hassan, half of his supply had been sold to Luceri, at cost. He wanted to prove to Visconte that he could be a steady, reliable, and valuable supplier. They must have begun to trust him or he wouldn't be invited to meet the big man himself. What a kick it was that Vincenzo Visconte held court in a place like Harry's Bar. Right under their noses he operated and no one was the wiser. It was real power when a man could thumb his nose at the officials and dine with the patricians. This meeting was something Gino had been anticipating for a long time.

So why the apprehension? he wondered. Because he'd told Luceri that he was selling them his entire supply. Very soon they would ask him directly for his source, and then they'd find out that he had been holding out on them. But what could he do? He had to live, didn't he? It was a damned tightrope. One slip and his guts would be splattered all over the pavement. He had to hold tight against their pressure, not let them back him into a bad place, then he could come out of this as his own man and still be part of their organization. That was the trick with people like this, you had to hold out for yourself.

He was led all the way through the restaurant to Visconte's table, in a room off the side. Luceri greeted him, and they shook hands, while four waiters hovered around the men seated at the table. The one in the middle was obviously Visconte. Three sets of muscle surrounded him, black suits, large shoulders, and tinted shades. Next to him on his right was the heir apparent, Flavio Rinaldi. Gino had heard about Rinaldi, a partially educated hothead who had been smart enough to marry the boss's daughter. Too bad she didn't see me first, Gino thought.

Luceri introduced him: "Gino Belmonte, this is Mario, Rocco, Flavio, and Signore Visconte." They shook hands. Visconte didn't rise, though all the other men did.

"It is a pleasure to meet you, sir," Gino began, noticing that Visconte was appraising him coldly. If they decided they wanted his whole setup he would not be able to refuse. Visconte's silence made Gino more nervous, as if the man knew what was in his mind and was waiting for him to say it. He tried again. "I am honored to be invited here."

"We always try and reward our loyal associates. And you have been proving yourself most valuable."

"Thank you," he said, formally. He was still apprehensive.

"Your merchandise, it has been purchased by us at cost?"

Gino nodded.

"Most generous. And we are pleased with the quality. So pleased that we should like to increase our purchase." Visconte waited.

"But I am buying now at full capacity from my

source." Gino explained. "If he could get me more goods we would all be richer . . . but," he shrugged, implying the impossibility.

"Perhaps if *we* have a talk with your source."

Gino glanced at Rinaldi who was staring at him from across the table, a crouched animal ready to strike. They were pushing him into a bad place; he didn't like it at all. What could he do? He had a sudden flash of inspiration. There was only one way to go and that was straight at them. He took a deep breath. "Signore Visconte, may I speak openly?"

Visconte nodded his gray coiffed head.

"You know how I make my living?"

Another nod.

"I have taken great pains to discover my sources and to build a clientele. When I approached Signore Luceri with my offer to sell quality, inexpensive merchandise, it was because I hoped it would bring me right where I am today, here, at this table with you." He paused. "I want to branch out into other areas, into legitimate business arrangements, once I have proven my abilities," he added. "I hope that is what I've been doing."

"You have," Visconte agreed. He still seemed to be waiting.

Gino took the plunge. "There's one other thing. I know that a man doesn't become a part of this organization merely because he wants to. He must develop trust." He stared directly at Visconte.

"That is why I'm telling you that I have been selling only half my supply to Signore Luceri. The other half I have kept for myself, to sell to my regular clients so I can keep on eating." He smiled but no one smiled back. His silk shirt was sticking to his armpits and to the small of his back. Silk stained so terribly when he was nervous.

The tightness in Visconte's shoulders began to ease and so did his expression. The coiled cobra might not strike this time. "I'm glad you told me this," he said. "But of course I knew. It is my policy to keep myself well informed in every area."

"You knew?" Gino covered his shock. "Then you have been the generous one." How close he had come to falling off that tightrope!

"I too believe that you are capable of branching out. We can make good use of your abilities. There is one job in particular that I have in mind, but it will not be available for a while. In the meantime you will begin small, doing various services for us, while we watch your performance. I understand you're from Naples. It's a good training ground," he commented. "You may continue to run your own organization provided it shows no more growth than what it has been for the last six months. We like to keep our associates happy. You will wait for word from me."

"May I ask what I'll be waiting for?"

"It is not my habit to reveal anything until the right moment, Belmonte! I shall let you know when I need you," Visconte finished, dismissing him.

Gino got up to leave, glad that it was over. Later he would enjoy his elation, now he just wanted to get out. These weren't his people, Rome wasn't his city, though he had many connections here. He felt uncomfortable away from his associates. He'd rather be in Paris.

"I'll be in touch," he said, as he reached the door.

"No!" Rinaldi said. "You are not to contact us. We will summon you when we want you."

Gino felt a surge of anger, but he fought it. Rinaldi was nothing but a punk. He wondered what Visconte's daughter looked like. I should fuck her, he thought, just to bring Rinaldi down a peg. But then, I'm too young to die.

He smiled as he walked up the Via Veneto. You're in, Gino, you're in! He checked out the action all around him. It was time to celebrate. The people in this city were crazy when it came to celebrations. And he knew exactly where to go to find that craziness. There was a Greek in the Piazza Barberini who could set him up with anything he wanted.

Now that Alessandro had complimented her and asked to see her other designs, Anne was afraid to show them to him. If she had his tailor make up one of her dresses and it turned out to be a disaster, then what? Don't be like that, she told herself. The most I can lose is the cost of the fabric and my time. And right now I could use a break from my routine of disciplined reorganization.

But if she were honest with herself, she had to admit that Alessandro's approval meant a great deal—and so did the fantasy that she could be a designer.

It was several weeks before she brought him her other sketches. Weeks in which she and Rudy spent time cutting and recutting the pattern for the lavender dress. She tried making it in challis wool, and in silk crêpe, but the wool fabric was by far the best. It fascinated her that the slightest change in the pattern altered the look of the dress. She spent hours calculating the differences before deciding on what she wanted. And Rudy knew exactly what he was doing whenever he advised her. She loved working with this master craftsman who was gracious and helpful to her.

Anne also loved being around Alessandro, who gave her tremendous encouragement and support. But his mother's attitude was another matter. Anne's acquaintance with Signora Massini had never progressed beyond the formal stage, and the Signora's presence in the shop made Anne uncomfortable.

She had other things on her mind, too. She worried about Alessandro's deal with Larry. The October market for menswear in Paris had come and gone and Larry's order had not come through.

Alex was so eager to begin, yet he was virtually tied to his exclusive agreement with Larry. As far as Anne could see, whatever advantage there might be to this arrangement, Alessandro should be able to approach other manufacturers with his samples and get their opinions, perhaps even their orders. But it wasn't her business, so she stayed out of it. Until finally Alessandro confided in her that he had talked to Larry.

"What did he say?" she asked.

"I explained that the samples were wonderful. I told him I wanted to show them in Paris, but he was adamant against that. You know how he talks." Alessandro imitated Larry's Oklahoma drawl. " 'I arranged yer loan fer you and I can put a stop to it jest as eas'ly'. . . . You know I will honor my commitment to him, Anne. I would never go back on my word! I tried to make him understand that it wouldn't jeopardize my arrangement with him if I sell to others, but he wouldn't hear of it."

"He arranged the financing for you?" Anne asked, surprised.

He nodded. "But the rate of the loan is very high." As well as the risk of taking it, he thought. If there was only some other way to go.

"Perhaps you should speak to someone at Brenda's bank. She might be able to help you."

"It's worth a try," he said. "I would like very much to have a better loan. Even if I only produce exclusively for Larry's company, a loan at several

188

points above prime instead of what I'm paying would increase my profit tremendously."

"I'll speak to her about it," Anne said. "Don't worry, something good will happen soon."

Brenda's bank said no. Even with Larry's commitment to purchase the entire order, Alessandro couldn't obtain commercial money.

"He's not a good risk, Anne," Brenda told her, omitting the information that Alessandro's creditors had attached his accounts twice in the past and he still owed them a great deal of money.

"But you should see his line of clothes," Anne insisted. "They're very good!"

Brenda shrugged. "Maybe so, but his talent does not insure his business acumen." She studied Anne. "Your defense of him is touching. Any ulterior motives?"

"No, we're just friends. Though I get the feeling he'd like it to be more than that. Yet he never oversteps the bounds of friendship. Perhaps I'm too plebeian for him, or not enough of something else. It's too bad, really. He's a wonderful friend, but that's all."

"I'm sorry," Brenda said. "You could use a little romance in your life. For that matter, so could I."

In spite of her protestations to Brenda, Anne was coming to depend on Alessandro more and more. She had never felt so at ease with a man before. There was nothing she couldn't tell him he wouldn't understand, not that she had many secrets. Their only area of disagreement concerned her need to raise herself on the social scale. Alessandro didn't verbalize his disapproval, but she'd noticed a certain look in his eyes and a tightening around his mouth when she spoke of exterior beauty, or social standing. That was one area of conversation she avoided with him. And oddly enough, no matter how many times he told her he preferred her the way she was, his behavior was one of the strongest incentives to keep her on her course. If he liked her so much, why then didn't he try to take their relationship further? When she flirted with him, he responded. He was thoughtful of her to excess and always complimentary. She was impressed by his restraint, and tantalized by it. A romance with him would be tender and enjoyable, but would it last? Perhaps he had his own doubts too. There was none of the fiery longing she had felt for Jeff, none of those palpitations and wild desires, but there was certainly an attraction! I shall keep it on a friendship basis with Alessandro, she decided. I'm not ready for a relationship. But she suspected that her readiness depended on the chemical attraction between them that was boiling just beneath the surface.

But in spite of their friendship, it was November before she worked up the courage to show him the rest of her designs. And then it turned out that she'd chosen the wrong moment.

She arrived at the store with her portfolio to

find the place in a turmoil. Samples were in piles on the chairs, tissue paper strewn about, and clothing bags open and ready to be stuffed with samples. Alessandro caught her by the waist and whirled her around, knocking her portfolio from under her arm.

"What's all this?" she asked.

"I got the order last night, from Larry!" he said, setting her free. "He wants delivery by March fifteenth, so I will be taking out a loan in the middle of December. That way I will not have to pay warehouse costs through the month of February if the goods are finished early, and I'll still have a full three months to produce them."

"Is it a good order?"

"Sizable enough, but he wants me to cut only summer fabrics, so that eliminates one of my problems. The spring supply of fabrics is certain to be picked over by now."

"What about the Christmas holidays? Won't they interfere with your schedule?"

"They shouldn't. My foreman assures me he will meet my deadline no matter when I activate my contract with him, unless it's during the month of August."

"Now what happens?" she asked, retrieving her portfolio.

"I'm off to Milan to place a deposit on the fabrics I've chosen. The deposit will hold them until I secure the loan. Then I'll deliver the samples to the factory and go over details of production with them. It's fortunate that I've had all this time to perfect my designs. Then while they are in production, I shall begin work on my designs for the fall and winter line."

"It's wonderful, Alessandro! I'm so happy for you." And she was. Not his fault, she thought, that she had waited so long to show him her drawings that he'd lost his enthusiasm.

"What's in the portfolio?" he asked.

"Just some sketches. I told you about them, remember?"

"I'll look at them when I return." He was barely concentrating on her.

"Shall I leave them here?" she asked.

"Yes, yes. I promise to study them, Anne. They will get my undivided attention. And I always keep my promises."

"I know, Alessandro." She hid her disappointment. "How long will you be gone?"

"Not long," he assured her. "I'll certainly be back before Christmas."

"I'll miss you," she said.

He looked at her and impulsively stepped toward her, taking her shoulders in his hands. She thought he was going to kiss her and she stiffened, not willing to commit such an irrevocable act. He hesitated for a moment, studying her, and then gave her his customary kiss on each cheek.

"I shall miss you, too, my dear," he said softly, and disappointment coursed through her. She shouldn't have stopped him, she thought. But in a moment he was jubilantly arranging his samples in tissue, and she helped him stuff the arms, and "neck-tie" the collars to prevent wrinkling. But every time his hand brushed hers, she was acutely aware of a lump in her throat.

While Alessandro was away, Anne worked at her reconditioning with renewed fervor, studying herself critically to see what more could be improved. She'd always been tall and filled out. Now she was just thin, giraffelike, she thought. Her recent loss of weight made her face more interesting, her eyes and nose had more definition than before, and her large teeth were more in proportion. Her jazz class had definitely helped with her dancing. She felt a sense of triumph the first time Brenda was impressed with her on the dance floor. She moved as she had been taught in class, experimenting with the hip thrusts and the bump-and-twists. She could find as many beautiful young men partners as she wanted, and when she caught a glimpse of herself, svelte body, turbaned head caught in a pose, for an arresting moment she thought she'd seen someone interesting.

Though she liked her silhouette, flat and sparse, she did feel something was missing. She didn't know what it was until one night she saw a young girl wearing a sheer embroidered peasant blouse. Her nippled breasts looked back at Anne like another pair of eyes, and overwhelmingly Anne wanted them. Two exactly like those! Not too small, not too large, just perfect.

"How much does it cost to have a breast implant?" she asked Brenda.

"I thought you'd never ask." Brenda handed her the name of a plastic surgeon. "I've done a lot of research on the subject. When you were dancing your head off the other night I asked some of the women in the ladies' room."

"What did they say?"

"Not one of them was sorry. No one had a complaint that they'd admit. They all recommended it highly."

"And pointedly?" she laughed. "I don't believe you. You just went up to some Helga and said, 'Pardon me, but are those real?'"

"Why not?" Brenda opened her eyes wide in mock innocence.

"Should I have it done?" Anne asked.

"I don't think you'd be sorry, Anne!" Brenda said. "Why don't you call this Dr. Tzaro tomorrow morning. He has an excellent reputation."

Two weeks later, Brenda went with her to the office of the famous plastic surgeon, Pygmalion to the rich.

Anne plied him with questions. "What about the scars? Do the breasts feel natural, Doctor? Do they feel soft. Will I lose any sensations, Doctor? Will I gain any . . . and what about the pain? How much pain is there?" Oh God, Doctor, make me beautiful, was what she meant.

Dr. Tzaro was a man in his late thirties, studious and tanned. "For the patient who considers all the consequences of this operation, it usually results in miraculous changes which they easily accept because of their psychological preparation. I want to stress that aspect of plastic surgery to you," he said. "As for the procedure, it's done under local anesthetic in my operatory which is right here in this building. You will be sleepy, or drowsy, because I will also administer a potent tranquilizer, and there is no pain during the operation. Though afterward there is a certain amount of soreness."

She remembered how sore her breasts were after the miscarriage when her body had provided milk for the baby she would never feed.

"As for scarring," Dr. Tzaro pointed to a diagram of a breast, "I prefer to make my incision either here," indicating a spot at the lower edge of the aureola, "or here at the center of the nipple."

"Why the center of the nipple?" Anne asked, shuddering at the thought.

"The breast is designed as a modified sweat gland," he explained. "Its one function is to secrete milk, which it does, through the nipple. Therefore all nerves and ducts are constructed to converge at this point. And if the surgeon incises at that particular point, there is less nerve damage and virtually no scar. It's rather like the principle of the calm at the eye of the hurricane." She nodded, still skeptical. "I've done this surgery so many times that I'm able to insert the silicone-jell

195

sac into this small opening," he drew a line through the center of the nipple, "and place the implant under the existing breast tissue against the wall of the chest. Therefore, the normal functions of the breast and its normal sensitivities are in no way compromised by the operation."

He got up from his desk and walked to a matching sideboard against the opposite wall. Glancing back at her, he asked, "How tall are you?"

"Five eight," she answered.

He opened the cupboard, revealing several rows of brassieres, each with the centers removed and a plastic breast inserted into the opening. "You may try these on, and determine what size you wish to be." He handed her three of them. "These are the sizes I would recommend."

She almost laughed at his bizarre version of Frederick's of Hollywood. She tried the brassieres on in the dressing room, wondering, Is this what I'll be, a plastic person augmented by modern techniques? Nevertheless, she chose a medium to small size.

"Please understand that this surgery is often reversible," he assured her when she came out. He noted her reluctant expression. "Many women repeat these procedures several times, though I don't recommend that."

"Is it because their breasts become too hard?" she asked. "I've heard breast implants are unpleasant to touch."

He grinned at her broadly. "Not any more! Several of my colleagues have found a way to change all that. You see, the body's natural defenses form a protective tissue around any foreign matter that's introduced into the body. This protective tissue encapsulates the implant completely and tries to reject it or repulse it from the body. Of course the body cannot reject the breast implant, too much normal tissue interferes. In the past we always instructed our patients to remain perfectly still during recovery and not to disturb the breasts. Now we know that constant manipulation almost immediately postsurgery is essential. This movement prevents encapsulation from occuring, and leaves the breast soft and normal, about as firm as, say, a pregnant woman's breast. I'll demonstrate the manipulation technique to you. It is quite simple, and it only takes thirty seconds once a day."

She made an appointment for the surgery.

CHAPTER 14

Alessandro arrived back in Rome on January third and went directly to his shop to pick up Anne's portfolio. He was well aware of how important it was to her, even while he had been hard at work in Milan, plagued with scores of petty business difficulties—setting up production, arranging for insurance, meetings with Visconte's man. But his neglect of her had caused him the most distress. She was very special to him and he felt an emotion very close to love. He knew Anne was not ready for him—he himself was not certain of the way he felt. His divorce had nearly destroyed him. He promised himself that no woman would ever be able to do that to him again. But then Betsey had been uniquely destructive. Right now he was happy with the way his relationship with Anne was growing. She too had been deeply hurt by her husband, and she came from a different culture than his. He often found her difficult to understand. But he sensed in her an excitement, a dormant quality about to waken. This quality showed in her designs, in the way she absorbed the life around her and learned to incorporate elements from it for her own benefit. The change in her over the past months was already remarkable. She was much less retiring and he could feel her outer layers peeling and melting away, revealing a lovely kernel of womanhood.

He wanted to do nothing to impede that growth, though her talk of changing herself unnerved him. He passed it off to her youth and her lack of experience. He wasn't fooled by the veneer of charm that a life of glamor offered.

Now that he was back in Rome he would give her drawings the attention they deserved.

He was amazed at what he found. The inner woman, the one she did not show to the world, was remarkable. Anne's designs were sensational! She'd used everything she'd seen, adapting it in her own way. Her own unique signature was in every line of her clothes. And yet he couldn't help but smile. She had clipped explanations, almost

199

apologies, to each picture, describing how she saw them and the manner in which they should be utilized, even to the size of the woman they would fit and the market for which they were suited, as if she had no confidence in the pure brilliance of the designs. The stance of the models she'd drawn as tentative, their posture demure. While the clothes blared in opposition. But they weren't gaudy, oh no, they were merely brilliant. He was excited. He couldn't help it. The possibilities of manufacturing these clothes fit exactly with his own goals. Incredible, he thought. God just handed her to me.

Without even pausing to rest from his trip, he hurried over to her apartment.

He rang the bell several times before he heard a movement inside the apartment. She came to the door dressed in a bathrobe. He thought she looked tired.

"Alessandro!" she smiled. "When did you get back?"

"Just now," he said, reaching out to embrace her, but she drew back.

"Don't do that!"

"Why not?" he asked. "Are you ill?"

She led him into the apartment and then turned to him. "No. It's just that I've had some minor surgery."

"My dear. Are you all right?"

"Yes," she said. "I had a breast augmentation."

She was proud of the phrase, it took one to know one.

All the color drained from his face and he stared at her. "My God, Anne. Why?" He couldn't believe she'd do such a thing, and he couldn't help thinking she'd changed them before he'd even seen them. Her pleasure disappeared and she stared at him with hostility. He wished with all his heart he'd been here to stop her.

He went over to her liquor cabinet and poured himself a whiskey, glaring at her. Whatever could induce a person to tamper with nature? A person wasn't a set of breasts or the wrinkles under her eyes. How could he make her see? Well, it was too late anyway.

He crossed the room to where she was standing, and took her hand, bringing it to his lips. "Anne, you are wonderful any way you are. Can you forgive me for not being here on the New Year? It was unavoidable, so many problems in Milan."

She looked as if she didn't believe it was unavoidable but she nodded just the same. He would have felt more relieved if she'd been angry at him, that would have meant she cared. No, he didn't understand her. He wondered briefly if her husband ever had.

"Do you have any pain? Would you like to sit down?" he asked.

She walked past him looking self-satisfied, and sat on the sofa. "There's still some soreness. It's only been a few days."

He wanted to shake her, he'd never seen her like this. "I came to tell you something!" He caught her wary expression and lightened his tone. "I came to tell you that you are a wonderful designer!"

"What do you mean?"

He indicated the portfolio. "They're marvelous, Anne! And I would like the honor of being your partner."

Her mouth fell open and he almost laughed. "What did you say?"

"You and I are going into business together! I should like to try to produce your designs, go into women's clothes along with my menswear. I want to aim for the April prêt-à-porter!"

Now it was her turn to be astonished. She jumped up from the sofa and threw her arms around him, pressing her face to his. "You are a brilliant, adorable man! Did you really like them? You don't think they're too simple or too complicated, or too impossible?"

"They're a little bit of all those things. That's why I like them."

"I can't believe it," she said, with a squeal of excitement. "Things don't happen just like this. Do they? Don't you have to sweat, and kill yourself, and pound the pavements with your designs before someone gives you a chance?"

He threw back his head and laughed. "We'll do plenty of that before we're through."

"Oh, Alex, I'm so glad you're back. I missed

you!" She wanted to kiss him, but she held back. "When do we get started?" she asked.

"Right now," he said, reaching for the portfolio, realizing that another opportunity had been missed. "There are a few changes I'd like you to think about, and a few clarifications."

"Certainly," she agreed. A few changes were nothing. To be expected. She almost pinched herself. I never knew life could be like this, she thought.

And her new breasts were incredible. She couldn't stop looking at them, touching them as soon as the bandages were removed. They were two marvelous playthings she could carry around with her everywhere she went, to be admired as much as a puppy or a baby in a carriage. Of course people wouldn't pet or coo, or chuck her under the chin, but her own reaction was worth all the doubts and the pain. Her heart sang, "Worth it, worth it, worth it!"

She stood before the mirror. The skin on her breasts was taut and tender, sending delicious tremors through her limbs as she ran her hands over them. They weren't too large, they were perfect. She examined the scars. Dr. Tzaro assured her that they would fade and so would the uncomfortable swelling. She took a blue silk blouse from the closet and slipped it on, leaving it unbuttoned to the waist. No matter how much she twisted and bent over, nothing slipped out. Then she tried on an embroidered white peasant blouse like the one she had seen on the girl in the discotheque. It was the first piece of clothing she'd bought after the implant. Is it really me? she wondered, staring at her breasts through the material. Colored flowers ringed her chest, making her breasts look like two soft hills in a field of daisies. Will I have the nerve to appear like this in public? With breasts like these I can't keep saying no.

It was weeks before she could sleep comfortably on her stomach, but she slept well nonetheless, always aware of the two mounds that rose and fell as she breathed.

Plastic surgeons were worth every lira they charged, she thought. And little by little she began to feel differently about herself. Her shyness began to fade. Her breasts weren't something to cover or hide, they were to display, and their existence affected everything she did. She loved them! And was frightened by them.

She tried explaining it to Brenda. "I keep thinking everyone will point to me and say, 'Those are fakes' or 'Why ever did you do it?' But I'm beginning not to care. Because of these," she pointed to herself, "I'm admired as if people were saying I'm damn lucky to have such a pair. I can't get used to it! I find myself feeling exactly the same about me as everyone else. Look at me, can you believe it?"

When the newness subsided and nothing drastic happened she became intrigued with what other possibilities there might be to alter her even further. The fatty deposits on either side of her legs that she had not gotten rid of came under scrutiny. Once she took that first step the next one would be easy.

What did I have against plastic surgery? she wondered. What was I defending against? Being like others? We're all alike anyway. She'd hung onto her self, her individuality, which was her way of settling for mediocrity. She'd been afraid to take the risk of competing in that other world, so she put it down. How could she have known it wasn't worth anything unless she tried it? Am I rationalizing? she wondered. Is it so terrible to be beautiful? Attractive people aren't any happier than unattractive people, but they were better off in certain ways. They didn't have to make the initial effort. They were accepted first, understood later. Why the debate? she asked herself. Because she'd tried the other way for nearly thirty years and it wasn't such a thrill. She felt as if she was on the brink of something. Of what? A better life? But there was no proof that it would be better simply because of beautiful breasts. What in God's name, she thought, had she begun?

Anne's agreement with Alessandro to "rethink" some of the designs turned out to be a major undertaking. She signed up for a course in patternmaking at Rome's Instituto Technica dell' Arti, and her Italian was forced to improve.

"I had no idea what I'd agreed to," she complained to Brenda after days at the drawing board with nothing to show for it. "My designs can't be rethought, they'll have to be scrapped. I've lost my expertise!"

"What did you expect!" Brenda asked. "You've had no real exposure, or training, and yet you think you can design for other women? You're not even devoted to clothes! To be a designer you've got to eat, sleep, and dream about clothes. I'm amazed you've gotten this far."

Anne stared at her in surprise. "There's no need to attack me! What's wrong with you?"

"Nothing!" Brenda exclaimed, dropping down on the sofa and closing her eyes. "Everything! I'm tired and I'm unhappy and I'm homesick!"

Anne was unprepared for this. Brenda was so dependable. "What is it?"

Brenda opened her eyes. "All my life I've loved clothes. I pride myself on my taste and my resourcefulness, and I guess I've always harbored a desire to pursue the field of fashion. But where I grew up intellect was stressed, the classics, the religion, the debate. I convinced myself that the clothing business was ignoble, a waste of my talents. Now here you are, designing up a storm, and damn good at it too." She sighed, "I guess I'm jealous as hell!"

Anne got up from the table and came over to sit by her. "It takes a real friend to be honest. Thank you. But I have a confession, too. I'm scared. I could use your help, but I've been embarrassed to bother you." They both stared at each other and Brenda laughed, until Anne joined her.

"You see what a dope I am? I'm dying to help you! . . . And my best advice would be to follow your instincts. They're sound!

"Do you think so?"

"Yes!"

"But I want to sell what I've designed. I want to appeal to a wide market."

"Commercialism versus the artist's integrity? You'll have to compromise, my dear," she said, doing a Groucho Marx.

Anne sobered a bit. "I hope not too much," she said.

CHAPTER 15

Frederico Segri was a self-made man, as self-made as any Jew with his heritage could be. His family came from Modena where his father owned a small grocery store and where the Segri family had lived for generations. But during the war when anti-Semitism became a reality and life changed, they had moved south and then after the war settled in Rome.

When he was eighteen years old, his father chose a bride for him, and he married the daughter of a family friend. The families arranged the marriage between Frederico and Elizabetta Gianni. Elizabetta was not the girl of his dreams. She was neither blond nor pretty, but he hoped that they would come to love each other. At first he was pleased by his marriage, by the way Elizabetta set up their home and by the way she deferred to him. He enjoyed being the man of his house, and was content. But with his growing contentment, Elizabetta became demanding and spoiled. She picked on him for his habits, and admonished him for his faults. She too had broken dreams.

Elizabetta separated her duties from his in their marriage and in their home. Soon there was no sharing of life with her and very little joy. She resented his parents for arranging their marriage and she wouldn't visit them. When Frederico went to see them, she would scold him about it for days. She complained of the housecleaning, but she wouldn't let him help her. She hated their tiny apartment, though they were fortunate to have it as Italy was recovering from the disastrous effects of the war. It was there in that apartment that she bore him two beautiful sons. Sons to carry on his name, and his religion. Sons who would listen to him and respond to his patient teaching and his enthusiasm, sons to work for, to build a life for, Angelo and Bernardo.

Before he was twenty-one Frederico knew that a life of selling groceries was not for him. He wanted more for himself than the meager income he could obtain as a storekeeper, though the Segri family was better off than many of their friends and relatives. At least they had survived. And with Frederico's great zest for living he began to pursue money, not for the things it would buy, but to give himself the means to attain a greater taste of life, to be able to revel in and enjoy life's pleasures. He was a sensualist in the true meaning of the word. And also devoted to his religion. The hours he spent in prayer brought him as much joy as his hours studying and his hours sitting in the park or lying on the beach. There was no freedom to practice Judaism when he was growing up in Fascist Italy. He never knew what it was like to worship openly until after the war when the temples reopened. Suddenly, after so many years of repression, to be a Jew was no longer a sin against the State, something that could cost him his life. The freedom of worship was so important to him, and his gratitude at liberation was so intense that he became zealous in his devotion to God. He also believed that God wanted him to be fulfilled and that is what he set out to do.

He was an expert gambler. When the stakes were high he was at his best, though he enjoyed superb control over his gambler's urge to go one more hand, one more throw of the dice, one more turn of the wheel, and, later, to make one more investment. He did what other men only spoke of doing, but were seldom able to accomplish: he accepted his losses. As much as he loved winning, as excited as it made him, when the dice were cold or the cards or the deal wasn't working, he would bow out. That was the secret of his success, that and an innate shrewdness and sense of fair play. Brenda had those same qualities; that was why she fascinated him so. She was the only person he had ever met who knew instinctively when to stop.

Frederico made his original stake in life because of his refusal to accept defeat. When he and Elizabetta were married just a few years he decided to better himself, to find another opportunity for advancement, even though postwar Italy was rebuilding itself and unemployment was a serious problem. The veterans returning from the war were given most of the available jobs, but one day Frederico heard of an opening for an apprentice clerk in a bank. Contrary to anti-Semitic propaganda, very few Jews were in the banking business in Italy, though one of the largest banks in Italy, Banca Commercia Italia, had been founded by two German Jews. Frederico applied for the job along with twenty-five other men. The testing and interviewing was long and tedious and by process of elimination the field was narrowed down to Frederico and one other man. As soon as the other remaining applicant informed the bank manager of Frederico's religion, the manager made his choice.

It was not supposed to be that way. Reparations were being made to survivors of the war, property returned, money paid, jobs offered. But anti-Semitism was a way of life not easy to suppress. Frederico lost the job. But before he left, he requested an appointment with the bank manager, Benito Ponti.

"Signore, I wish to have a brief word with you."

The manager indicated a chair.

Frederico declined. "It seems that I was highly placed in the competition for the job as an apprentice clerk," he began.

The man nodded. "You placed second, Segri. That is almost the best."

"My scores were very high?"

"Excellent!" Ponti exclaimed, bending over backward to be generous.

"My interviews went well?"

"You made a fine impression."

"I would have been an asset to your company?"

"Signore Segri," Ponti sighed, growing impatient with praising a Jew, "you made a fine showing, second only to our choice for the job."

"Then you will have no reason to refuse me a letter of recommendation?" Frederico asked.

Ponti's eyebrows shot up. "What for?"

"Why, to secure a job in another bank, or perhaps even here when there is an opening."

"But that it most unusual," Ponti sputtered.

Segri stared at him. "Do not give me excuses. Call your secretary and dictate to her the most complimentary letter about me that you can manage. I want it to say that only an arbitrary decision made you choose the other man over me and that you would employ me in a moment if there were a spot available."

"I can't say that," the manager said. "I refuse to do it!"

"You can do it, all right! You told me that my tests were excellent and that I made a brilliant showing and you and I both know why I wasn't hired. I happen to know that you have many Jewish accounts in this bank and I can get them all withdrawn. I can take my story to the American newspapers. I have a friend who is a reporter and I will even protest to the provincial government. Your attitude against my people is extremely unpopular at the moment."

"Stop!" Ponti stammered, caught in his own device. "I'll write your letter, but don't ever let me see you in this bank again."

Segri acknowledged his victory with a polite "thank you." But it was a sweet victory.

Armed with his letter of recommendation, he applied at Banca Moderna Italia and was given a job. After ten years he was a major stockholder at BMI and at Ponti's bank as well. Unfortunately, Ponti didn't live to see it.

And now here was Brenda, so bold and brash. She reminded him of himself. She was always prepared whatever the topic, she knew her quotes and her companies and when she didn't know, she listened. And always she looked at him admiringly. He didn't flatter himself that her devotion was anything more than hero-worship. At forty-eight he was not as handsome as he used to be, though his silver hair added a touch of distinction and women found him appealing. He kept his body in shape, for himself really, since most women didn't interest him. Occasionally he went to a prostitute, but in the last few years that happened less and less often. The beautiful young girls some of his colleagues kept as mistresses seemed like children to him. They were of another generation and he thought his friends were foolish for bothering with them.

Elizabetta hadn't improved with age. To the contrary, their wealth had brought out her tyrannical streak. She used her money as a weapon against their less wealthy relatives and basked in the glory of the attention paid to her by the women of their synagogue. Frederico had been president of the temple several times, so Elizabetta thought of herself as Signora la Presidenta. Frederico practiced extreme tolerance with his wife's behavior; she was part of him and he never imagined a life without her. Not until he met Brenda.

He began to contemplate what it would be like if he'd married a girl like Brenda. To him her blond curly hair and full bosom were beautiful. And he found excuses to have her near him.

Frederico, like most bankers, had a conservative approach to life, but he wasn't conservative with Brenda. She demanded openness and honesty from him because she knew no other way and he responded to her. They talked easily of their feelings; she was so candid that he held nothing back. She would come and sit in a chair in his office quietly observing him for a time while he worked, and then suddenly she would say, "I know you're going to approve that transaction," and he would approve it and wink at her and something intimate would pass between them.

One day they were alone in his office when he turned to her. "There is something I would like to discuss with you. I haven't shared this with anyone else because those whom I value would not give me an impartial opinion in this case. Will you listen?"

She nodded, wondering what he was going to say.

"I have been asked to do business with people whom I abhor. If I do not accept their request, someone else will. It is not uncommon for certain of my associates to enter into similar arrangements, but it goes against me, personally. I have spent many years building my financial position. I am not without certain connections, but this deal will place me in the league of companies like Lazard Frères, Warburg of Belgium and the Rothschilds. And yet it means I must go against everything I believe in."

Her eyes reflected her concern. "What is it?"

"The Emir of Bhitamin wants me to cofinance oil refineries in his country."

"An Arab?"

He nodded. "You see the implications."

She saw flashes of murdered Israelis, pictures of bombed kibbutzes, Zionists collecting money on the streets of New York after the '73 war. "Do you mean that Jewish bankers deal in joint ventures with Arabs? Financing projects in spite of politics?"

"Yes. The loyalties of money are multinational. Although these things are never publicized and there is always the risk that they could nationalize our refinery and our investment along with it."

"When must you decide?"

"In a few months. I'm meeting with the sheikh in August on the coast of Italy."

"You've already made up your mind, haven't you?"

He smiled. "I wanted you to know about it."

"Thank you for your trust," she replied. She knew she should have been appalled, but nothing this man did seemed wrong to her.

"I was just wondering, Brenda, if you'd consider accompanying me on that trip."

CHAPTER 16

"Californians are not fashion-conscious," Anne complained. "I have to make an effort to train myself to see what you notice naturally, Brenda. Perhaps it's because we don't have four real seasons, and no need for separate wardrobes. We wear the same old thing year after year and it still works. And if it doesn't work, who notices?" She laughed. "I think the only fashion craze that ever made it to L.A. was the miniskirt. And that's because it appealed to everyone's sexual fantasies rather than to their fashion sense."

"I hated minis," Brenda said.

"And I hate being so undercapitalized. If Alessandro had some money we could buy our fabrics before we design the clothes and I could use the textures and prints for my inspirations, instead of using muslin and lining materials to make samples. How can I tell what this is going to be?" She plucked a muslin sample from the chair next to her drawing board and tossed it to Brenda.

Brenda caught the dress and held it up, inspecting it front and back. She was worried about what Anne was going to say next. "This isn't so bad. At least you're not experimenting with expensive fabrics."

Anne sighed. "I know, but it's like working backward. If only Alessandro would listen to me. I've offered to invest my own money so we could buy the material now, before the patterns are completed, but he won't hear of it. He doesn't believe in taking money from a woman. Something about it being dishonorable. What antique chauvinism!"

"Thank heavens for small favors," Brenda said under her breath.

"I heard that."

"Why don't you have the clothes modeled? That might help you to visualize them."

"No money. And without models I can't get a proper perspective. There's got to be some way I can get some feedback."

"You could wear the clothes yourself," Brenda

suggested. "And I could photograph you in them."

Anne liked the idea. "It's worth a try. We'll use my Olympus, rent some indoor lights and a tripod."

At first she was only going to wear the clothes, and walk and turn and sit. But the more she planned for the photo session, the more she realized that the clothes demanded a total look, not just a body inside them. So she experimented with her hair, trying it in different ways, and using more makeup than she'd ever worn in her life, just for effect.

The session itself was exhausting, between the setting up and shooting, and posing and arguing, and pinning the clothes. But for the first time she had moments when she felt it was all coming together. And she waited anxiously for the prints to come back from the developer, as if they would not only provide the help she needed with her work, but would also show her the way she had fantasized herself during the session. She was looking forward to seeing one particular pose when she'd worn her own leather pants and a ruffled chiffon blouse. Her nipples were exposed through the sheer fabric, her head was lowered, and her eyes were gazing up from under her brow as she'd seen models do. She'd even *felt* sexy!

Brenda picked the prints up on her way home from work. She was all smiles. "I think they turned out wonderfully!" she announced. "Some of them especially."

The clothes did look beautiful but Anne was mortified. At a glance she could see how awful she looked. The muslin fabric and cheap acetates might be adequate to test the patterns, to illustrate what was working and what wasn't, but they did nothing for her at all. She could hardly look at herself. Her nose was too prominent for her thin face, even with the tailored smile and sultry expression. A wind machine wouldn't have helped. Her profile was a disaster. For the first time in her life she admitted it, she was a chinless wonder. And if she was not exactly chinless, her chin was definitely receding.

She was in despair. How could she have been so blind all her life, telling herself her looks didn't matter, that she was attractive enough? She'd always known she wasn't, and now it faced her in glossy color. The woman who stared back at her from the photographs was painfully imperfect.

She went to Dr. Tzaro for her checkup. "I've been thinking of having my nose done," she said, certain he would scoff at her, say that it was ridiculous and unnecessary. "What do you think?" she asked. "Could I be improved?"

"If you do the nose, Anne, you must consider your chin as well." He turned her head to the side, studying her briefly. "Yes, it would be a definite improvement."

She turned back and stared at him. He was only saying that because he was in the business. But she might never know that. "When do you have an opening?"

"Both? You're crazy, Anne!" Brenda wailed, panicky at the idea that she had started all this. "What if it turns out badly? What will Alessandro say?"

"'Badly' is better than being the same as I was. I don't want to be the same. Besides, look who's calling the kettle black. And we both know what Alessandro will say. But he'll get over it. A beautiful partner is good for business."

"Give yourself a chance," Brenda pleaded. "You haven't tried out your new body yet. Why don't you wait a while for a new face? You might change your mind."

"What's the matter, Brenda, are you jealous? Afraid I'll be really pretty?"

Brenda was surprised by the question. Perhaps she was a little jealous. "I just want you to be sure of what you're doing. I don't believe you've given it enough thought."

"It is what I want, Brenda. I'm as sure about this as I'll ever be."

But the morning she was to go into the hospital she felt terribly ill.

"You can still call it off!" Brenda insisted. This was a forewarning of disaster.

But Anne shook her head. "Let's get it over with, before Alessandro finds out."

"You didn't tell him?"

"It was hard enough to convince myself."

She was partially awake during the surgery. They administered local anesthetics and a sleep-inducing drug. The first shots pricked a little. The sound of scraping and the pressure of Dr. Tzaro's hand holding the instruments were painless. Her teeth stood exposed, lower lip drawn back. "I'm giving you a cleft in your chin, Anne." She waited for the moment when he would break the bone in her nose. She had been warned of it, heard various versions of what it sounded like, felt like, but she must have slept through it. He let her see herself for a brief second before he bandaged her. "Now don't move, don't smile. There, do you see?" Her mouth was dry and sticky and her lips were numb, immobile. She liked how she looked, noticing the surgical cap around her hair. Too quickly he covered her up, afraid of an emotional moment. The swelling and bruises hadn't begun yet. Later she couldn't remember how she had looked. Even though she tried. She knew that the lights had been bright, and witnesses, students and interns, had stood by, interested in the changing more than the change, their next procedure awaited in the wings.

Putting off her reaction was not as easy as she'd hoped. Dr. Tzaro's words nagged at her. "If you have a deviation in your septum, the surgery cannot correct it. In fact it will exaggerate it. Yours is very slight. Everyone has some irregularities. You may expect the swelling to remain for some time."

She was frightened of deviation. The bandages felt straight to her. Would it be straight? she wondered. *God, I hope so*—please *no deviations!*

I must have been crazy, she thought, plunging into this without hesitation, ashamed of her vanity and the need to look beautiful.

She had been harsh in her judgments of other women who'd had cosmetic surgery. How vain, how insipid, how much alike they all looked. Dr. Tzaro told her that a surgeon was not only limited by his ability and his vision of what would look best for the subject, but by the structure of the nose and face he had to work with. A chin could only be changed so much by an implant, a nose shortened only to the point where it didn't pull the upper lip out of shape. Oh great, she'd thought, I'll end up looking like a chipmunk.

But Dr. Tzaro was a master and he believed Anne's structure to be quite adaptable.

"We make a good team, Dr. Tzaro," she told him when she awoke in her room. Her voice assumed a hard-edged brittleness that was unlike her.

"You don't seem very happy. Are you all right?"

"I get lonely when I'm scared," she admitted. The taste of temporary blindness from her bandages frightened her right now.

"What are you afraid of?"

"Having it not matter, having it not make a difference."

"It will and it won't," he said.

"I don't understand what you mean."

"Anne, if you depend on exteriors, only a mirror will make you feel beautiful. How you feel about yourself, the image you project, is what counts. No matter how you look, you must accept yourself first, and forgive yourself for whatever you think you've done. Then your looks won't matter."

She was groggy from the medication, wafting in and out of sleep. She hadn't really understood what Dr. Tzaro was trying to say to her and she was sorry she hadn't told Alessandro. She wished he were here. She felt Brenda take Dr. Tzaro's place at her bedside.

"How did it go?"

"Not so bad. The worst part is not being able to see. And it hurts to talk."

"Then don't talk!"

"Brenda, are you afraid of anything?"

Brenda held her hand. "I'm afraid of cancer. Or some other lingering death. And of not being loved."

"Not being loved?"

"If nobody loves me, then I'm unlovable. That's something everyone suspects about himself, deep inside. Being loved is the most important thing in the world next to loving. Because if someone loves you, he accepts you for what you really are. My loving Barry is what gave him peace of mind before he died. The fact that I loved him and that I would mourn for him were his only consolations. He had no children to leave behind, he had no business success to point to. He hadn't made any great discoveries. But he had me. And I loved him."

Anne heard the tears in her voice. She didn't realize what hospitals meant to Brenda.

"I only pray that someone is there to love me when the times comes."

Everyone wants love, Anne thought. She realized for the first time how much she wanted it. She wondered if now she could find someone to love her, someone she could love as much as she had loved Jeffrey. No. I don't want to love anyone again the way I loved him. She was envious of Brenda's experience with love, however brief. It was more than she'd ever had.

She was told she could go home after the eye patches were removed. They had been on twenty-four hours and it was such a relief to see again! Her eyelids were purple and swollen, red eyes looked out through the wrapping. "No shampoos for a while," the doctor cautioned. It hurt to chew so she sipped protein malts, vegetable juices, broths. There was a throbbing in her face and head, but it subsided after a few days, responding well to aspirin and ice packs. What if I don't like myself? she worried. There's nothing I can do! The antibiotics nauseated her, but she took them as he directed to avoid any infections. "The chin is the most vulnerable area. Most prone to infection."

It was difficult to get comfortable. It hurt to lie on her chest, her face needed protection, and her behind was still sore from the injections. Ten days till the stitches came out. She took her pills, mashed-up melon, and liquefied cereal. Brenda went to work and left her every day. She'd never minded before! She told Alessandro she had the flu and forbade him to come over. He sent her flowers and fruit. But he was off to Milan again.

It hurt her eyes to read, but she read anyway, not wanting to wallow in self-pity or dwell on what she'd look like after. The Italian elections would be a farce, or at best controversial. The Communists had a good chance. There were three bombings in Italy in one day and a derailment in France. The Greek Cypriots were threatening to resume their aggression with the Turks. The U.S. Ambassador to Italy postponed his trip to Washington. There was an outbreak of cholera in Turkey, another strike, machinists this time, and everyone still discussed the Moro assassination.

She felt homesickness sweep over her. It had been nine months since she'd come to Europe and now she was forced to let down her pace. She couldn't push herself to excel while she was in a state of recuperation. She did isometrics so as not to lose muscle tone, but the inactivity weighed on her spirits. The loneliness muffled her, made her listless.

"You know this is only temporary, don't you?" Brenda assured her.

She nodded. "I can't find the phrases to bolster myself. I haven't felt so low since my divorce."

"It's only normal, you know."

"I know, but tell it to me so that I feel it. So that it changes me."

"You have to do that yourself."

Anne tried to smile, but it hurt her chin.

She awoke that morning with a lighter feeling. This was the day! She almost smiled at Dr. Tzaro's prune-faced nurse.

He didn't waste any time. He laid her back on his table and began to cut off the outer layers of gauze. The air on her face felt sharp, almost indecent. As if she needed the bandages to hold everything in place and now she might lose part of herself that would fall off without support. It hurt when he removed the stitches from her newly sewn nasal passages, worse than the surgery itself.

He gave her a mirror. "There!" he declared, as she sat up.

And she stared at two nostrils in the middle of her face. Her nose was pushed, ski-shaped, toward her forehead, her chin was witchlike, fit for a cackling crone over a kettle of frogs' ears.

"It will settle down," he said, watching her dismay.

She wanted to yell. She wanted to hit him. Oh my God, is that me! She couldn't trust him or believe him. He had made her a freak.

"There is always a great deal of drop in the nose as it sinks into the healing process. I've compensated for the natural gravitational readjustment. Don't judge it yet."

Don't judge it, she thought, choking on her disappointment. What else can he say? It will sink! She felt her heart sink through her abdomen.

"What about my chin?" she whispered through clenched teeth, wanting to cut off at least an inch of it all the way around.

"It's still swollen. You're having a mild reaction to the solution. It sometimes happens. You've had a lot of surgery lately, you know." He took her hand. "Calm down, Anne. It's always hard at first. You have to say good-bye to someone you've known all your life, someone you're used to. You're replacing the old you with one you don't know yet and don't even like. You'll get used to it."

Her hands shook, her nerve was gone, tossed into the receptacle along with the iodine-stained bandages. What did I do to myself? She cried very carefully. There was nothing she could do but trust him, this barbarian butcher.

But her nose did come down. The swelling receded and the bruises faded. It was difficult for her to notice the gradual changes. But Brenda could tell the difference. She was effusive with praise.

"Anne, you're beautiful!"

"Am I?" she asked, feeling the beginnings of her new life, a new package freshly unwrapped, gleaming with the shine of untouched glaze, unmarred finished, chrome trim, shiny and polished, no kicks, no scratches or touch marks.

Everything was different. Old men looked at her. Young men looked at her and women turned all the way around to stare. People looked at her everywhere she went, and it wasn't her retoned muscles. At first she was self-conscious, checked herself for an open fly, bare breasts. But she was intact. She tried to read their expressions. Was it interest? Curiosity? Admiration? No, it couldn't be admiration. But it was!

She experimented with makeup; what an amazing difference it made now! She shaded her cheeks, extended her lashes, put iridescent color on her lips, molded her temples, and then the final touch by Gambrelli of Rome himself, waves of blond streaks, shoulder-length hair skimming her throat.

She got an appointment with the famous stylist by mentioning Elena Brisson's name—Elena whom she would soon see. How would Elena react to the new me, Anne wondered. Gambrelli's services were expensive, but she wouldn't trust this important addition to some unknown crimper. She sat in the swivel chair, watching him work.

Was Eliza Doolittle happy at the Royal Ball or was she too busy thinking, How do I look? Is my gown all right? My hair? Will I remember what I've learned? What do they think of me? There was so much to keep in mind. Be careful with the profile, be careful with the stare, and especially the smile.

She stood outside Gambrelli's door still amazed by the reaction she'd gotten just walking through the salon. She took long, careful strides and waited unconsciously for recognition. She could see the look on every face: Who is that beautiful woman? she knew they were thinking, as every head turned. I'll tell you who she is, Anne thought, she's the elegant, desirable Anne Mayo Scott. She was beginning to fall in love with herself.

But most of all, best of all, wonder of all, she loved her designs. When she went back to work, it was so simple. She just hadn't seen it before. A sash, a dash, a tie and a twist made all the difference. For the first time the clothes she designed were really for her. Not just for others. They wouldn't make *her*, she would enhance *them!* Even Brenda had to admit to the difference.

"They're really good!" she announced.

"Yes, I know," Anne answered.

CHAPTER 17

Alessandro was having more difficulties in Milan. And as usual he was running out of money.

The April prêt-à-porter was slated for the twenty-second and he was expecting the large payment from Larry on the fifteenth of March, or at the latest by the eighteenth. After he paid back Vicsonte's loan and recouped his own capital he'd have enough to begin the new line. They might be able to raise some working capital based on Anne's finished samples. That would give them only four weeks to purchase their fabrics, and cut and finish her samples, provided she didn't need to do any more work on them. Too close. But if they had the fabrics now, these extra few weeks could mean the difference between being ready and missing the whole show. He wouldn't need much, and he could repay it right away.

There was only one place he could turn. And he prayed that Elena was still grateful to Anne for saving her life. One could never tell with Elena, she might have adjusted by now or she might be at peril's door. He hoped he could reach her by phone.

"Alessandro!" Elena said, with more enthusiasm than he'd expected. She was surprised at Alessandro's call. She was afraid he might be asking to come for a visit. "How are you, my darling? It's been too long!"

"Elena, I'm not calling to be invited to Villa Brisson." Alessandro believed in getting to the point. "I've another request."

She paused. "It's money again, isn't it, dear? I can hear it in your voice." She lapsed into her standard refusal speech. "Now you know I've such limited funds, Alessandro, my cash is totally unavailable at this time."

He interrupted her before she could shut out every possibility. "It's not for me, Elena. Do you remember Anne Scott? The young woman who befriended you last summer?"

Elena's voice changed subtly. "Of course I remember her. Have you heard from her?"

"Yes. She's living in Rome, and she's been studying to be a designer."

"In Rome?" Why hadn't anyone told her about this? "What kind of a designer?" Her curiosity was inflamed and her heart beat harshly at the mention of Anne's name. "How long have you known she was in Rome?" she asked sharply.

"Oh, not long," he replied, sensing her jealousy. Elena was always possessive. "But I have a feeling that she has talent. A great deal of talent, as a fashion designer."

Elena's laughter was shrill. "That child a designer! Oh, my sweet Lord, that's the most amusing thing you've ever said." A picture of Anne as she was in Paris came to mind, Anne in those Levi skirts and flowered prints. God, Alessandro must have lost his mind! "I'd suggest you ask someone whose opinion you respect, dear. Call Andrea Odicini, tell him I sent you over. He'll give you advice. And I'll bet he'll say to forget the whole thing. Better yet, send me her address and I'll invite her down. Though her ingratitude over my last invitation galls me. Does she think I invite just anyone to Villa Brisson?" And then the realization overwhelmed her that Anne was in Europe and that she could see her and she was filled with unreasonable joy. It was the first good news she'd had all winter.

"Elena, Anne needs backing. Not much, five or

ten million lire to get us started, and only for a very short time. That's not much considering what you owe her, now is it?" he asked. "I would gladly provide it myself if I could. But everything I've got is tied up right now. In fact, I will guarantee to pay you back in just a few weeks. I'm due to collect some money by the middle of March."

Elena thought for a moment. After all, it wouldn't hurt to have the obligation reversed. "Could you send me some of her work? Something I might see?"

"I told you she's good, Elena, but she would never allow you to help her. If she knew I'd asked you, she'd refuse. You'll have to take my word."

"That's not good enough. This is money we're talking about! If you'll show the designs to Odicini I'll accept his opinion, but only then."

"But I don't want another designer to see her work. These ideas are unique."

"Oh, don't be ridiculous. Andrea wouldn't want to copy anything Anne might do. If he says she's good, I'll send you some money."

"All right," Alessandro agreed. "It's very kind of you!"

"There's one small favor you can do for me in return."

"Anything!" he offered.

"Convince her to accept my invitation."

"But I can't spare her right now. We have so much to do before April, and then we'll begin our production."

"Then she can come in May, in time for Cannes."

"I'll do what I can," he agreed.

"Yes, do," she said. "We shall have a lovely time."

"And you'll wire the money right away?"

"As soon as I hear from Andrea, love!" she promised, feeling actually happy. Ah, there was some hope after all.

Anne was bringing the designs to Milan herself; she would not trust the mails with her precious cargo and Alessandro waited for her with anticipation. When she told him about her additional surgery he couldn't help trying to imagine what she might look like. But nothing could have prepared him for what he saw when she got off the train. This was not Anne, not the girl he knew. That soft doe-eyed woman had disappeared and in her place was a beauty! His heart was aching in his chest. He had waited too long! This beautiful woman would never love him. She came walking toward him and the closer she got the more she reminded him of *Betsey*. He felt that sudden rush of anxiety that the sight of Betsey used to cause in him.

But she was Anne after all. He held her away to look at her.

"It is wonderful, my dear," he assured her. "You are magnificent."

She seemed to be waiting for something but he

was too shaken to figure it out. "I'm so relieved to hear you say that. There is still some swelling, and . . ."

"Don't apologize!" He put his arms around her, feeling tenderly protective. But she pulled away.

"Tell me some good news," she joked. There was a high color in her cheeks, and he could sense her nervousness. He was nervous too, on unfamiliar ground. He never would have believed her appearance could have made this difference, caused this awkwardness. But they were still the same people.

"I do have wonderful news." He waved for a porter to take her bags. "I've raised enough money to buy fabrics. We can begin cutting the samples right away!"

"Oh, Alessandro, that's wonderful!" she exclaimed. "What a lovely surprise this has turned out to be. I can't wait to show them to you!"

"And I can't wait to see them," he said. "Why don't we drop off your things at the hotel and get right to work?"

In her hotel room, after she had relaxed a little, Alessandro sat her down on the sofa and took her hand in his. "Anne—you know how beautiful you look. And—I would never want you to think I only cared about you for your looks. But now, if I told you I cared, you might suspect my motives. . . . They are sincere, Anne, believe me." He tilted his head to the side and smiled, leaning toward her.

All his love was there for her to see and it almost hurt to look at him. She stiffened, praying, *Not yet*, but he stayed where he was.

She sat there trembling, ignoring the intimacy between them. His waiting seemed timeless and only inches separated them, but a chasm measured in those inches. What is it? she wondered. And finally she broke the moment and turned her head away. "I know you care for me, Alex—I'm just not ready yet."

Why, why? he thought, and realized that again their stars had refused to collide. He put out his hand and she turned back to him. "Partners?" he said.

"Partners," she replied, and they shook hands. But why did she feel so sad?

He picked up the sample bag and walked to the door while she followed him silently, thinking ahead to all their plans. There is time, she thought. And she felt closer to him than before, wishing he was more than her friend.

It was glorious to be in Rome in the spring, Brenda thought as she drove her new Fiat through the familiar streets on her way to work. Poets sang Rome's praises, writers wrote plays and books about it, and even bankers were susceptible to its charms. There was just a nip of coolness in the morning air but she knew the afternoon would be bright and balmy. The weather reminded her of home, but when she passed by the ancient ruin of the Forum, or one of the magnificent fountains of Rome, the similarity ended.

With Anne gone to Milan, Brenda felt wonderfully free. If only she could have Frederico Segri there with her in the empty apartment. She turned the car into the garage of Banca Moderna and made her way to her stall. Until the real thing comes along, she thought, my Friday nights with Segri will do just fine.

There was a note on her desk to report to Segri's office and her pulse quickened as it always did whenever he was around. She tried to remain calm, as she summoned all her extra abilities, gathered her scattered qualities, forced herself to be doubly alert.

He met her at the door of his office and kissed her on both cheeks, something he did whenever they were alone. She loved it, except that even in private he was so chaste. He looked at her admiringly and she was glad she had worn her new flowered chiffon blouse, and the mid-calf chamois skirt and matching boots. The outfit made her feel springified.

"What have you decided to do about DuMonde?" Segri asked. DuMonde was a Frenchman in financial difficulty due to a badly managed business. The bank was trying to decide whether to wait, or call in his loan.

"I have his accounts on my desk, if you'd like to see them. But I've decided to give him time," she said, steeling herself for his disapproval.

But he only raised an eyebrow. "Why have you made this decision?"

"Because DuMonde showed genuine concern in my interview with him, and he gave me every indication that he will make the payments on time if we allow him the full term of the note."

"Is that all? An emotional decision?"

She grinned impishly. "That, and his excellent collateral."

He laughed. "Your timing is perfect, Brenda. Much better than mine."

She beamed with his approval.

"Are you all prepared for today's presentation?" he asked.

She nodded. "Anything special I should know?"

"If you don't know it all by now, you haven't been earning your salary."

"Oh I'm prepared," she assured him. "I've spent weeks researching this loan application. I've become an expert on the restaurant business. This is a small-scale partial franchise, fast-food chain, Italian style. I've done my field work, and made a thorough investigation of my client's private finances as well as the corporation's. I know the language of the business and the economic projections, as well as the climate of the proposed expansion in this industry." She was enjoying herself as she rattled off her areas of knowledge. "But what I wanted to know from you is whether any members of the loan committee might give me trouble."

He gave her question some thought. "I'm the toughest one on that committee," he said.

"You? I didn't know you were sitting in today." Her heart gave an unauthorized thump. She didn't want to have to perform in front of him! Why hadn't he been there when she'd made her report on the Auriello Computer Programs for aerospace research? That had been a bear of a presentation to compile.

But Segri's presence in the meeting bolstered her more than unnerved her. She fielded all their questions with expertise, buoyed by the challenge of her work, ever conscious of his eyes on her. All the research really paid off. There was one thing she'd learned in this business: there was no such answer as "I don't know." If she wasn't totally prepared with every fact and piece of information on behalf of the applicant and if she didn't present it coherently to the committee, the client would be refused his loan. Banks are in the business of granting loans, that's how they make their money, so they are anxious to find investments. But every factor has to be considered, and it was up to her to search and uncover every possible contingency for success or failure. If Marco Venuti was granted a loan to open his own semi-franchised restaurant and then couldn't fulfill his obligations, her job, too, was at stake.

"You were very thorough, Brenda," Segri said to her afterward.

"Do you think it will be granted?"

He nodded. "I believe so. . . . Are you free for lunch today? There's something I wish to discuss with you."

She was dying to know what it was, but she controlled herself enough not to ask. If it was 10:30 now, lunch was only fifty years away.

"I wanted to take you someplace special," he said, as they drove south along the river and then veered east through the new residential district, past the Esso stations that lined the roadway, and through the smaller townships with their cafés and garages and fruit stalls, until the only visible buildings were farmhouses set in lush green fields.

They stopped at a roadside Pavesi market and marched up and down the immaculate over-stocked aisles buying an obscene variety of canned, bottled, waxed, and corked delicacies. Then they took the nearest road out into a grassy field where Frederico located a large butternut tree close by the road. He pulled off to the side and helped her out, and while Brenda watched in amazement, the President of Banca Moderna Italia spread a blanket from his Citroën underneath the tree, unfolded two back rests for them, and spread out their lunch.

He took off his jacket and folded it neatly over the branch of the tree, then he took off his tie and opened his collar. She caught a glimpse of salt-and-pepper body hair and her pulse quickened. Take it all off, she thought, longingly.

241

Frederico sighed with contentment. "This is so good for me! I have needed such a diversion for a long time. And there's no one I would rather share it with."

She was pleased with his attention. But after sampling all the delicious foods, Brenda finally said to him, "This is wonderfully delightful, Frederico, but what was it you wanted to talk about?"

That was one of the things he liked about her, she was never diverted from the point. "You know that I am pleased and impressed with your work." He saw her about to protest. "Now don't be falsely modest. You've done a remarkable job of learning the banking business in record time. All your apprenticeships have gone quickly and you have mastered them well. I knew you would advance, but I had no idea it would be this quickly. After watching you this morning, I am convinced that you can handle more responsibility. But there are other factors to consider. One, that you are a woman."

"And banking is a man's profession."

"It has been, but I believe that should change. And you might be one of the women to change it. Sometime in the near future, I shall have you transferred to the corporate division, where you will be under my direct supervision. With the plan in mind to make you my special assistant at some future date."

She would be near him every day. Be able to work with him directly. It was more than she'd ever hoped! "But how can you do this? Aren't there others better qualified than I, whose positions are in natural succession?"

"But they are not the ones I want." The look of rapture on her face was more than he could stand. There was no doubt in his mind that he had made the right choice. Neither was there any question that Brenda was a talent. And he was beginning to wonder if his admiration for the vivacious, curly-haired blonde was purely for her business acuity.

A torrent of appreciative words filled her throat, clamoring to be let out, but she swallowed them. Finally, she managed to say, "Thank you! I hope to be worthy of your trust."

Later, alone in her bed in the empty apartment, she hugged this special knowledge to herself, and relived every precious word, every unforgettable moment. She thought she had caught a feeling of something, a special something that was still unexpressed. And as she lay there and her hand wandered over her body, across her full breasts and lightly down to the soft mound, coming to rest between her legs, she found herself murmuring his name, "Frederico, Frederico, oh, Frederico!"

CHAPTER 18

Alessandro dropped Anne at the airport for her noon flight to Rome, and then drove to the Alitalia air-freight dock to meet the truck loaded with his order for Larry. It was done! Jackets, suits, slacks, and ensembles, neatly packed, marked, and invoiced. Sweet Jesus, he felt good. And he'd done it on time! Larry would have everything on the day he expected it.

Armed with his proof of shipment, and the receipts for the goods sent, he went directly to the Milan branch of Bank of America to receive his money. But the manager of the branch couldn't release it without a notarization from Rome.

"That's no problem," Alessandro replied. "I'll be in Rome tomorrow and I'll be able to transact everything with them."

The manager looked relieved. There seemed to be some discrepancy between what Signore Massini was requesting and the funds on deposit in the Oklahoma account. The manager didn't want to have to go through an interbranch, international investigation to see if the discrepancy was theirs or not. Especially if the customer could take the matter up directly with Rome.

That evening Alessandro put a call through to Oklahoma. Larry wasn't there and he left word for him to call back.

He was completely exhausted. He hadn't realized until now how getting everything done on time had drained him of his energies. He told the phone operator to try the call to Oklahoma again in an hour, but before he knew it it was the next morning and Larry had not called back.

His plane landed at ten, and it wasn't until close to noon that Alessandro appeared at the bank in Rome. He was immediately ushered into the assistant manager's office, but after forty-five minutes he was still waiting.

"Just a few more moments, please," Signore Fazio said. Three different pepole had checked his bills of lading, read and reread the cost sheets, shipping receipts, and every piece of paper in his file.

Alessandro looked at them in disbelief. "Signore Fazio," he said finally, "my patience is wearing thin. Could you please ask your superior to handle this transaction, or someone with the authority to issue me my payment. Your bank in Milan told me to take everything up with you here in Rome and that I wouldn't have any difficulty. All that is needed is a simple notarization.

"The papers are in order." Alessandro went on. "You've seen the export customs approval; here's the list of merchandise, witnessed and signed. The shipping agreements are here, along with the note from my associate in Oklahoma stating that I'm to be paid upon presentation of all receipts and proof of shipment. What seems to be the trouble?"

Signore Fazio gazed at him, his dark eyes hugely magnified by thick glasses. Someone had put him in an awkward position, very awkward indeed. "All your papers are in order, signore. But we cannot find an account under the name you have given us. Could your associate be listed under any other name, or business?"

"No! Of course not. His name is Larry Conley, and his store is Conley Limited, with three separate locations in the state of Oklahoma. Here is his signature and his letterhead." He pointed to the letter of credit for the third time.

Fazio nodded. "You see, signore, this letter is a personal note made out 'To whom it may concern.'

It is not an official letter of credit issued by this bank or any of its branches. If you can locate any bank where this gentleman has an account I'm certain they will honor your request."

Alessandro was beginning to feel a nervous twinge in the pit of his stomach. "Doesn't it say, right here in this letter, that Mr. Conley's account is at the Bank of America?"

"Yes it does," Fazio agreed. "But that account was closed last week. It may have been moved to some other bank," Fazio assured him, "and you were not informed. However, if that is the case, this letter you hold is of no use, as it only authorizes our bank to pay you and there is no account to draw from."

"I don't understand. When a letter of credit is issued, doesn't that mean that the bank is obligated to make it good, whether the holder of the account is solvent or not? Don't you verify the credit of a buyer before you issue the credit to him?"

"Yes, of course we do. But this is not our letter! It is only a letter between two people without bank sanction at all."

"But I must have the money." By this afternoon he would owe Visconte twenty-eight million, fifty-three thousand lire, including the interest on the loan. He had to pay that debt. He'd been duped by Larry. How could he have been so stupid as to trust him? Yet he couldn't believe that the man was a crook.

"May I use your phone?" he asked.

"Certainly," Fazio agreed.

He called New York Customs, charging the call to his phone, hoping that it wasn't too late to stop the shipment. But it had already cleared. The shipment wouldn't do him any good, it was money he needed, not the merchandise. But he wanted to prevent Larry from having it. He had to get that cash today. Mother of God! What would happen if he defaulted on a loan to Visconte?

"Is there anything I can do?" Fazio asked, realizing that Alessandro was in serious trouble. "Why don't you leave me a number where I may reach you. I'll make some inquiries on your behalf concerning Conley Limited, and this Larry Conley. Then I'll let you know what I've found out."

Alessandro nodded and gave Fazio his home phone number and the number of his insurance agent.

He went directly to his house and placed another call to Larry, but there was still no answer. He called his agent, Gimmo Pasquale.

"Calm down, Massini," Pasquale said. "I want you to write out an account of what's happened in your own words and bring it to me as soon as possible along with copies of all documents relating to the transaction to see if you're covered."

"But you issued the policy, Gimmo. Can't you tell me yes, or no?"

"There are some technical problems here, my friend. It depends on whether your letter of credit was approved by our company. Is our stamp on it anywhere? Or do you have any correspondence from us referring to Mr. Conley's agreement with you?"

"I'll be there soon!" he promised. "With all my papers." But he knew there was nothing in the file like what Pasquale mentioned.

By the time he had written out a history of the transaction and taken it to Pasquale's office, Fazio at the Bank of America had called with some information. He returned the call.

"It doesn't look good, I'm afraid," Fazio plunged ahead. "There are no accounts under any of his names, either business or private, in all of Italy. In order to check with the United States we will have to wait a few hours until they open for business."

Alessandro thanked Fazio for his help and turned to Pasquale anxiously, still unable to believe this was happening. "What do you think?"

Pasquale looked nervous. "I've known you a long time, Massini. But I must be honest. There will be an investigation to determine if there was collusion on your part."

Alessandro winced. "And then what?"

"Then we will determine the facts and either we will pay or recommend noncompliance with the policy."

"But credit insurance policies are difficult to obtain, and I've passed all your investigations. So did Larry Conley. You're obligated to pay!" His voice was rising.

"Calm down. As I said, there probably won't be any difficulty, but it will take a bit of time."

"I don't have any time!" he insisted. "My loan is due today."

"Then ask for an extension. We can't issue a check on the day a claim is made." He frowned at the absurdity. "Now if the goods had been lost or damaged, it might have been easier to make your claim on your maritime policy. But you say they arrived safely?"

"Yes," Alessandro said, "The goods cleared customs as soon as they arrived. Someone with proper identification and authorization was waiting there to receive them." He put his head in his hands. "I don't understand what happened. The man has three stores. He's been in the business for years, buying all over Italy. I know some of his suppliers. None of them ever had any trouble."

Pasquale looked through the file. "He seems to have checked out initially. He did give you an advance payment. He kept in contact during your entire transaction, but businesses have been known to fail in a short amount of time. It's difficult for us to judge, being so far away."

"But you had him checked," Alessandro repeated.

"That's because you didn't want to embarrass him by requesting an official letter of credit from his bank. He told you he was good for the money and you believed him."

"And he passed your inspection!" Alessandro insisted.

"Then you have nothing to worry about. When all the facts are in we will most likely pay the claim. Or better yet, he might still wire you the money himself."

Alessandro left the sympathetic Pasquale and went home. He dragged himself up the stairs and fell across his bed, staring up at the velvet canopy, feeling the trap closing in around him. Finally, an exhausted sleep overcame him, blessedly blotting out his consciousness.

The telephone awakened him from a druglike stupor an hour later. It was Visconte.

"Massini? It is nearly the end of our business day, and we haven't heard from you."

Alessandro was instantly awake. "I was about to call and make an appointment with you."

"To pay off the loan?"

"Not exactly."

"Harry's Bar in thirty minutes." The voice was steel through the telephone.

Alessandro's hands shook as he poured himself a brandy. He dialed Larry's number again. No answer. He called the Oklahoma City Police Department. At this time there was nothing they could do for him, but they agreed to try to locate Larry for him.

And there was nothing he could do but keep his appointment with Visconte.

The taxi pulled up to Harry's Bar and Alessandro had barely paid the driver when two very large men came up to him on either side. Each grabbed an elbow and escorted him roughly toward a black limousine parked at the entrance of Borghese Park. A clutch of intense fear gripped him. There was no one around to help him.

The two men shoved him unceremoniously into the back seat of the car and slammed the door behind him. Visconte sat inside. His son-in-law Rinaldi was on a jump seat facing him. Alessandro's two escorts got into the front seat and they drove into the park.

"Well?" Visconte asked, declining Alessandro's offered hand.

Alessandro used every ounce of will to appear composed. Any doubt he might have had as to who Visconte was had been savagely dispelled. Legitimate private lenders did not use these kinds of tactics. He couldn't believe that Larry was involved with gangsters. But he was learning lessons fast.

The two men stared at him, waiting.

He met their eyes. "Have you had any word from Larry Conley? Anything at all?" he asked.

"Not since the day he brought you to meet us," Visconte answered.

Alessandro's heart was pounding, but he

wouldn't let them know. "I have learned, only today, that Larry Conley has not fulfilled his business obligations with me, and therefore I am not
able to pay you the money back for my loan until
my insurance company makes good on my claim."

"Who do you think you're dealing with? A fucking Italian bank?" Rinaldi interrupted, and leaned
forward to grab his lapels. "My father-in-law
never waits for his money."

Visconte held up his hand, cautioning his son-
in-law to calm down. "Why don't you explain to
us the terms of your insurance coverage and the
amount which you expect to recover."

Alessandro told him the details, and Visconte
never missed a word.

"So ninety percent of your costs plus profits are
insured, and you had approximately ten percent of
the total of your own money invested. With Larry's ten-percent deposit and our interest calculated you'll be about eight hundred thousand lire
in the red after you have paid us back. Even for
the Duke di Valdagno I have no intention of becoming a creditor for any more time than is completely necessary."

"I say we do him now!" Rinaldi snapped.

Alessandro never took his eyes from Visconte's
face, trying to ignore Rinaldi. It was Visconte who
would make the decision, but Rinaldi would carry
it out. He shuddered slightly.

"If you were not the man you are," Visconte
stated, "this meeting would never have occured.

We would have recovered our loan from you in another manner." He narrowed his eyes. "But since you are a man of reputation, and you do not have a record with us of . . . improper behavior, and since you are covered for the repayment of our money to a degree, I will grant you an extension of thirty days, at an additional twenty percent."

Alessandro could not allow himself to feel relief, with Rinaldi's hostility and displeasure so evident. But he nodded to Visconte, thanking him. He knew without even figuring that the increase of interest would be devastating. But at least they were giving him a chance.

"Therefore," Visconte continued, "it will be up to you to make certain that your insurance company pays off your claim within the time period we have allotted." The car was slowing to a stop in a secluded area of the park, and Alessandro began to fear again for his safety. His moment of respite was gone.

Rinaldi leaned across Alessandro and opened the car door. Cool night air rushed in on his right. Visconte indicated that he could leave.

Alessandro was torn by the desire to escape the atmosphere of danger and by the fear of what he would encounter once he did get out of the car. "You'll be hearing from me," he said, and without any further hesitation he nodded to Visconte and Rinaldi and swung his legs out the door.

"After this, you will not have another chance!"

Rinaldi said and gave him a shove. At the same moment, the driver gunned the motor and the car leaped forward, peeling rubber and throwing Alessandro to the ground. Frantically he rolled away from the tires. He could feel a rush of air as the door of the car slammed closed over his body, just missing the top of his head. His heart was tearing around in his chest and the dust rose in his face to choke him as the car sped away. He jumped to his feet and ran for cover behind a nearby tree, feeling the agony of shame in every bone. A Massini forced to grovel in the dirt! Bastards!

He waited there until the taillights disappeared and he knew they were not coming back. Then he sank to his knees in gratitude. He was shaking all over. Was he doomed to a life of these defeats time after time? Why go on?

Because I must, came the answer.

And so he got up and brushed himself off and began to walk toward the Via Veneto.

CHAPTER 19

"What is bothering you, Alessandro?" Anne asked. "Ever since you came back from Milan you've been tense and moody." He looked at her sharply, but said nothing.

It was so unlike him, she thought, this ill humor, and it stirred a gnawing question that she'd refused to acknowledge before. Now she had to ask him. "Is it my designs, Alessandro? Are they not turning out as you'd hoped?"

"Anne, I assure you, it has nothing to do with

you." He attempted to smile, but his expression was forced.

Her heart was gripped more by his valiant attempt at lightness than by his shortness of temper. She'd never known him to lie before. If it wasn't her work, what was it? "I feel as though you're shutting me out. And I miss you. Is it anything I've done?" she asked. There was a sudden panic that it might all be over, her future along with his devotion.

He was touched by her concern. Under normal circumstances he would be elated that she'd noticed his problems, that she cared enough to want to discuss them. But she had no part in this mess. And it was a mess. His life was torn apart. Disbelief had given way to desperation. He had finally reached Larry's accountant in Oklahoma, who had spoken with sympathy, describing Larry's backslide to financial ruin, unaware that Larry had dragged Alessandro with him. "Larry's quite a gambler, you know!" Alessandro didn't know. "He's always lived on the edge of disaster, only this time he went too far and lost his business!" Alessandro wished the voice wasn't so clear in his ear, speaking truths on the transatlantic with an Oklahoma twang. "He must have picked up your order in New York himself and sold it right away, had somebody waitin' on him! Maybe even in Canada. He didn't have the money to pay you anyway . . . nobody's heard from him in weeks. There's a rumor he called his lawyers and filed bankruptcy. Everybody's lookin' for him. 'Specially his wife's lawyers." There was nothing Alessandro could say.

It was a sad tale of a man running scared, who had used his one last chance to bail himself out. Except that Alessandro was equally as desperate and had no bucket with which to bail. At least Larry hadn't planned to cheat me from the beginning, he thought. Small consolation!

And tomorrow was the fifteenth of April. The loan and the extension were due to Visconte, but the money hadn't come in yet from his insurance company. How many nights were there in a month? An eternity of cold sweats and palpitations. Nothing could dissipate the sickening terror that lay in the pit of his stomach, rubbing his nerves raw with every screech of a tire, every shout in the street as he walked.

At the insurance company he was known as the crazy man with dignity; cold, teeth chattering, muscles tight with tension, dignity. They had finally approved his claim, but until the debt was paid, his life was on the line. How many times had he thought of running? Constantly! He longed to hide somewhere until the check arrived, but cowardice was not a family trait. And every moment, no matter where he was, he imagined a bullet tearing into his brain, or a knife in his ribs, expected it to happen. There was no one in whom he could confide, it was too dangerous to involve any one else.

Gimmo Pasquale had promised to push every button and pull every string to secure him his money from the insurance, but he was terrified that it wouldn't happen on time. They'll have to give me a few days' extension, he thought. Visconte knows that I mean to pay him. But there was Rinaldi to consider. Rinaldi would never wait! Alessandro couldn't escape the reality of doom, nor could he be cavalier. They would kill him if he didn't pay them by the fifteenth of April. Finally he confided in Pasquale exactly how much he owed and why he needed the money on time. There was a terrible silence while Alessandro's stomach shot acid.

"You should have told me before," Pasquale said, frightened that somehow he would be blamed for this delay. "I'll get it for you, don't worry!"

"I can't help worrying," he said. His head was gripped by a vise, but for the first time in weeks there was hope that he might still be alive the day after tomorrow.

And if he was, he would make everything up to Anne. The prêt-à-porter was scheduled for next week in Paris, and he'd managed to get their line into one of the best buying offices, plus he'd secured a date for their showing right in the middle of the week, before the splash of the opening could overpower them, or the exhaustion of the week's end could bury them.

Anne's reaction was a delight to see and he

longed to share her excitement, but he was merely going through the motions until he was safe. Life had been a torment ever since that moment he'd been pushed out of Visconte's limousine last month. How could it be that all he had done should end like this? If he could only make it through this week and pay his debt—extricate himself from terror—he would be in paradise! He would soar with joy, he would be alive as he'd never been alive before! And he would finally declare his feelings to Anne. He had held off long enough; her concern indicated that she was ready for him too!

The harsh sound of the telephone awakened Anne, and she jumped out of bed. Good Lord, it was ten o'clock! She had slept so soundly she hadn't heard Brenda leave for work this morning, and Brenda was never quiet. It must be Alessandro calling to find out where she was. She grabbed for the phone.

"Hello," she said.

"Anne?" a man's voice asked, and her heart lurched. "How are you?"

She couldn't even talk, she couldn't believe it was he. She forced his name from her throat. "Jeff? Where are you calling from?" She sank down on the bed in disbelief. "How did you get my number?"

She heard his laugh—what a long time it had been. The sound vibrated deep inside of her. "I'll bet you're surprised to hear from me! But I decided what the hell, might as well call while I'm in Rome. There's a symposium on psychosomatic medicine. Thought I'd get in some skiing in Switzerland before I go back. But mid-April is a little late in the year even for Europe."

"Oh, you're skiing?"

"Yeah. Intermediate so far. It's my first year."

She hadn't imagined his even living without her. It was easier to think of him frozen in time. But his voice sounded alive. Too alive! He'd taken up skiing, the religion of the singles' world. "Hail Mountain Full of Snow, My Skis are With Me. Blessed Be My Date for the Evening."

Jeff's voice shot hot sparks through her. Get hold of yourself, Anne Scott, it's only your ex-husband come to town, your much-imagined, wondered-about, longed-for husband. She looked up and saw herself in the armoire mirror. For a moment she'd forgotten her own changes. But she too had been living all this time. And this was a moment she'd been waiting for! Without planning, it had happened, far more opportunely than any fantasy. She felt her confidence return. She knew what she wanted to do.

"Oh Jeff, forgive me for sounding so stupefied." She cast off her line. "I've been working such late hours, this morning I was catching up on my sleep."

"You're working?" He took the bait. "What have you been doing?"

She smiled as she set the hook and let him take enough line. "Oh, I'll tell you all about it when I see you. Are you free for dinner?" She ran down a list of what she'd have to do today to get ready to see him. She had a dinner date with Alessandro, but she'd beg off, just have a drink with him instead, before Jeff . . . and then . . . oh God, shivers of anticipation coursed through her.

Jeff hesitated. "Tonight? Well, I did have a tentative date."

Her catch was beginning to tire. "Oh, can't you break it?" She added just the right touch of disappointment. "I'm dying to see you." She began to reel in the line.

"I'd like to see you too. Unless you know someone to introduce me to," he asked. Same old Jeff. A barracuda!

"I'll have to check you out myself first," she teased. "See if you pass inspection for one of my friends."

"You know any good places?"

"Do I? This is my town!" She pulled her catch up to the boat. And wondered if she sounded any different to him.

"Sure," he conceded. "Dinner is fine."

With one big pull she hauled him on board. He'll make a beautiful banquet, she thought. "Where are you staying, Jeff?"

"The Hassler."

"Wonderful!" she exclaimed. "I'll meet you in the lobby at eight-thirty."

"Don't you want me to pick you up?"

"Oh no," she said. "I have an earlier date, so this will be fine!"

"O.K., see you then."

"I'll make the reservation," she announced. "They require a tie."

He sounded surprised as he said, "All right, good-bye."

"Bye-bye!" She smiled as she depressed the phone and then dialed immediately for a hair appointment. What to wear? Everything great was in the collection. The three-piece ensemble? No, too covered up. It's got to be sexy, whatever it is. The black! she thought. I'll get Dominic to finish it today. I'll do the hem myself.

She called the shop. "Alessandro? I'm sorry. I overslept." She sounded as if she had drunk champagne for breakfast. "I won't be in till later today."

"We need you now, Anne!" He was exhausted. "We've been holding off on three different decisions until you try them on yourself."

She knew what he meant. "I'll take care of them all, but something's come up." She hesitated, hating to do this when he sounded so disturbed. "I can't make dinner tonight, Alex. An old friend is here from California and we have so much to catch up on." Why not the truth? No, it wouldn't help to add to his worries. "But I can still meet you for a drink. About seven o'clock?"

"I don't know, Anne. It may not be possible."

"Oh, please, Alessandro. We must talk. Have you been home since last night?"

"Only for a few hours."

"I can hear it in your voice. I want you to promise me you'll get some rest today. You can't keep pushing yourself like this."

"I have a lot to do today."

"What about our date?"

"I'm expecting a call from my insurance agent. If it comes in before noon with good news, I can make it. If not, then I won't be able to. What time will you be in the shop?"

"Midafternoon." That would give her time for her hair, a new pair of shoes to go with the dress, a facial, and a leg wax.

"All right," he said. "I'll know by then."

When Anne arrived at the shop at three there was a note from Alessandro:

> Wonderful news! *All is well.* Meet you at "our" place, seven o'clock. Gone home to sleep.
>
> A.

What wonderful news? she wondered. She had been well aware that Alessandro had been troubled lately, but whenever she had asked him what was bothering him he had evaded her. Perhaps it was all resolved. That would be wonderful! In fact, today was a thoroughly wonderful day! Nothing could go wrong!

She took the black dress out of the closet. Long and elegantly draped black silk jersey, slit from throat to waist, with multicolored cords that wrapped and tied around the body. It was perfect on her. But there were some adjustments to be made in the facing, so that it would lie flat across the bust and not gape open as she moved. Dominic and Rudy had worked it several different ways, none of them right. She had an idea of not using standard facing material, but using the jersey itself, as a kind of self-face. That might work better.

Before she knew it, the afternoon was gone, but the dress was finished. Just as she was about to leave, the phone rang.

"I'll get it," she called out. *"Pronto!"*

"Alessandro Massini, *per favore.*"

"Chi parla?"

"Gimmo Pasquale, Insurance Corporation of Italy. I am sorry to bother you but his office said he might be with you, signorina."

"He's not here, Signore Pasquale. But I will be seeing him in a short while. May I give him a message?"

"Yes. Tell him the check I expected to arrive tomorrow has arrived today! I am holding it in my hands right now. I know he has been anxious about it and he could come to pick it up right now."

"I'll tell him. You're very kind."

"Signorina, it's very important to him to have the money. I don't think he can wait until you find him. I know he has an account at the Banca Commerciale Italia. Could you tell him I'm going to deposit it in his account directly. It's very important."

"Of course. Thank you, Signore Pasquale."

Poor Alessandro. So that's the strain he's been under lately. Anne added, "Signore Pasquale, I thought the shipment went to America and Mr. Conley paid Alessandro. Didn't Larry receive the goods?"

"Signorina, you must ask Signore Massini about all this. I'm not at liberty to tell. But it is of the utmost importance that you tell him I've deposited the money in his account. *Grazie, signorina.*"

"*Prego.*"

By the time the taxi pulled up at the Hassler Anne was in a fever of anticipation. But a drink with Alessandro should take the edge off her nervousness and put her in exactly the right frame of mind for Jeff. It was coincidental that she and Alessandro came here often enough to call it their special place. Even if Jeff wasn't staying in this hotel she would have chosen the rooftop restaurant for dinner—it was a perfect setting. She was only sorry that Brenda couldn't have met him. It was difficult to discuss an ex-husband with a friend when they'd never met.

"You're crazy to see him," Brenda told her when she got home from work and found Anne dressed and ready to go.

"I'd be crazy not to. I can't wait to see his face when he sees me." She laughed and ran her fingers through her expensive hairdo. "This is one chance I wouldn't miss!"

"Are you still in love with him?" Brenda asked.

That stopped her. "I don't think so. After everything that's gone on between us, and besides there's Alessandro now."

"Do you love him?"

Anne nodded and then shrugged.

"What kind of an answer is that? Either you're in love or you're not!"

"It's not that simple and you know it! I have a score to settle with Jeff. And my relationship with Alessandro is still 'undefined.'"

"Don't you think that's strange?"

"Not necessarily." But she did. She blamed her own reluctance for Alessandro's lack of commitment.

"I think you're playing with fire by seeing Jeff."

"Do you mean to tell me that you wouldn't do exactly the same thing if you were in my position?"

"No," Brenda laughed. "I sure as hell would!"

Alessandro was sitting at a table in the corner of the bar and as he rose to greet her his face came

267

alive. He was so dear to her, so much of her life was involved with him. Why isn't all of me, she wondered. She wanted it to be. Perhaps tonight would be the final test. Perhaps, after seeing Jeff, that unknown element that held her back would be gone and the way would be clear for them.

Alessandro kissed her lightly on the lips and it surprised her. Cheeks were his province. "You look beautiful!" he exclaimed. "That dress is marvelous on you. But how did you finish it so quickly?" He reached out to feel the facing on the front of the dress, knowing this was the area with which she'd had problems. But the facing felt soft and pliable. He forgot for a moment that she was inside the dress and his hand touched the warm skin of her breast.

"Alessandro!" she exclaimed, and he looked at her with surprise. She laughed, and so did he.

"I'm sorry," he said. The feeling of her breast under the thin cloth had caught him off guard, filling him with desire for her, and he was shaken by it. So was she. He had never touched her before.

"You feel beautiful, Anne. Just as I knew you would. Just as you've always been to me."

She looked away, but her heart was pounding. She slid into the chair, afraid to meet his gaze. The waiter brought her a drink. People were staring at her. They usually did nowadays. Was Jeff one of them? She hesitated to look around but she couldn't help but hope so. "You must have had

some good news!" she said. "Tell me, please. What
has been going on?"

"I couldn't tell you before," he said, "because I
didn't want to involve you or worry you unneces-
sarily, but Larry never paid me for the order I
sent him. I only learned yesterday that he'd gone
out of business. For weeks I thought he was an
out-and-out crook."

"You poor man. How you must have been suffering. Why didn't you tell me? Oh, Alessandro."

He took her hands and stroked them as he
talked. He told her about Elena, and the harrow-
ing month he'd spent trying to get the insurance
company to come through, and a little bit about
Visconte. He didn't tell her all about Visconte.
There was no need for that.

But the more he talked, the more incredulous
she became. Finally, she pulled her hand away
from his, her fury rising. "How naive I've been! I
thought we were close, I thought we confided in
each other, and now I find that you've been going
through hell for weeks and you never told me
about it." Her eyes flashed gray anger at him.
"Did you think I had to be spared? That I'm not
mature enough to know the truth? That I'm just a
child? Is that what you think? You had no right to
go to Elena behind my back." She was wild with
anger.

"Anne," Alessandro tried to interrupt, but to no
avail.

"You know, if you'd asked me, I would have

backed myself. I offered enough times. What did you think I was doing? Kidding you? Pretending to have money when I didn't? Partners confide in each other. I feel as though I've been cheated. As though I can't trust you because you've kept me in the dark. You told me your problems didn't have anything to do with me, and I believed you, but that's not true!" She had not been this angry in a long time—not since that terrible day she saw Jeff and Jill together in his examining room. It was as if Jeff's presence nearby was enough to cause her life to fall apart again.

Alessandro watched her with disbelief. "I shouldn't have told you about Elena. But I knew when you saw her she would be sure to mention it."

"That's not the point!" she shouted. "You shouldn't have asked her in the first place! I can take care of myself. And besides," she added, "I haven't decided to accept her invitation. I thought we would be too busy in May for me to get away. But maybe it is a good idea for us to be apart for a while." Here she'd thought she was ready for a relationship with him, and now this! His expression was too painful to look at.

"This isn't the way I imagined this evening would be," he said softly. "What time is your dinner?"

"Eight-thirty," she told him.

"Then we'd better go," he said. "It's nearly that now."

Alessandro signed the check and they left the bar.

Just as they came into the lobby the elevator door opened across the room and Jeff stepped out. She faced him for one heart-stopping second before she turned back to Alessandro. She'd seen Jeff look at her without recognition, but she saw his expression of instant lust! Oh, it was better than she could have dreamed!

Without planning, without hesitation, she looked up at Alessandro and put her arms around him and then she kissed him full on the mouth, catching them both by surprise. But the effect on the man behind her was what she wanted. She pressed her body against Alessandro's, feeling his muscular frame tighten around her. His spontaneous reaction was complete, and with part of her she realized that he was wonderful to kiss, and that he cared about her very much. But another part of her was painfully aware of the curve of her back as she kissed him, of the way her hair fell across her shoulders, of the rounded bareness of the dress, and of Jeff's eyes as they bore into her.

She pulled away from Alessandro and stared into his eyes, wanting to give back to him what he had just given to her. I'll make it up to him later, she thought. The prospect of leaving Jeff and going to make love with Alessandro excited her. Even without Jeff she would have been excited.

If Alessandro was surprised by her abrupt change of mood, he said nothing, just gazed at her with a mixture of tenderness and apology, hoping her kiss had been a gesture of forgiveness.

"I'll see you later," she whispered, and he nodded turning to go.

All eyes in the lobby were on her as she walked toward the man who had been staring at her.

"Why Jeff, I didn't know you were there!" she said, smiling at his stupefied expression.

"Anne?" he said. "I didn't recognize you!"

I'll bet you didn't, she thought. She would relish his expression till her dying day. Taking his arm, she led him into the elevator. "We're dining right here," she said. "It's so convenient." She knew at that moment that she had accomplished all she wanted. Showing off to him any further would almost be a waste of time, but not quite. She deserved her turn, and she would take it.

She swept him into the restaurant, speaking Italian to her friend Claude the maître d', who delightedly led her to their table. The captain hovered around her as if she were some royal peacock, and indeed she was.

"Who was that man?" Jeff couldn't resist asking.

"Oh, that was my business associate, Alessandro Massini, Duke di Valdagno."

She crossed her legs carefully, leaned on her elbow conspiratorially, and winked. "Your mouth is still open, Jeff."

"My God, what happened to you? You look terrific."

"I had a few things done," she said offhandedly. It was so simple to carry off when you knew you looked great. And she did look magnificent in her ankle-strap sandals, clinging silk jersey, Deco diamond clips and ivory bracelets, her hair pulled to one side. The stares of everyone in the dining room attested to that.

"How's your practice?"

He was too amazed to question her. But how could a sow's ear turn into a goddess? He sat across from her tongue-tied. She not only had mind-fucking beauty, she had drama, and poise, and class. More than anyone he'd ever seen. This was out of his league and he didn't even know there had been a race.

She recognized the look. How vulnerable I was then, she thought, flashing on the moment when she'd opened that door to his office.

"Would you like to go dancing?" he asked after the pasta al forno.

She was tempted but she declined. Enough of Jeff was enough. She didn't want him any more. She'd suspected it for a long time but now she knew it. He didn't make her tingle in the least. Shudder was more like it. She was free, free at last, free for Alessandro. She thought of Alessandro and she couldn't wait to see him. And then she remembered: she'd forgotten to give him the message from Gimmo Pasquale. How stupid of me to have forgotten, she thought, but I've been so wrapped up in Jeff.

She looked at Jeff across the table, feeling nothing. Halleluia, nothing!

"No Jeff, I can't go dancing," she said. "I've got a late date."

"You know, there have been many times I've thought about the way we ended it, and I've been sorry. I just wanted you to know that."

"Don't be," she said. "You did me the biggest favor of my life."

When they reached the lobby she couldn't resist a long lingering kiss on his cheek, she leaned into him and ended the embrace with her hand trailing from under his chin. And then she turned on her heel and walked out, knowing he was watching. She was not the same Anne who had turned and walked away from that terrible scene in his hospital office eons before. This time she did not look back.

I'm ready, she sang, yes, I'm definitely ready. And she gave the driver Alessandro's address.

CHAPTER 20

Anne kept the taxi waiting as she rang the outer bell at Alessandro's home. The night watchman appeared at the huge carved doors in his soiled trousers and old coat.

"He's not here, Signorina Scott. Only the Signora is home tonight." He saw her disappointment. "Some other men were looking for him too. I told them to try his club."

She thanked the old man and climbed back into the cab. Alessandro could be at the club, but he was most likely at the shop. She told the driver to take her to Via Barberini.

She was in luck; there was a light coming from the back room. She went around to the back door and knocked. "Alessandro?"

"Anne?" She heard his voice faintly through the thick wooden door.

"Yes," she replied. There was the sound of a bolt being drawn back and a shaft of light from the open door revealed discarded scraps of fabrics and waxed paper with the remains of his dinner in a box in the alley. She waved to the taxi and stepped inside.

"I thought you might be here," she said. It was right that they should be here alone at this moment, in this place which had such meaning for both of them. Her samples hung on a rack in the corner. There were patterns and sketches in the front office along with all her hopes and dreams. But the look on his face shattered her bouyant mood.

"Who was the old friend from California?"

He must have seen her with Jeff. "That was my ex-husband. I should have told you, but I didn't want you to worry." Her lie sounded familiar, he had said the same thing to her. But she had felt guilty about seeing Jeff, as if she were cheating on him.

"Then we are even," he said sharply, "I didn't tell you about my financial problems because I didn't want to worry *you*."

"I don't like being angry with you, Alessandro," she pleaded.

"Nor I with you. But I am furious with you for using me that way, to make an ex-husband jealous. It is unworthy of you!"

"But I didn't use you! I wanted to kiss you. Why do you think I'm here?"

"You chose a public place, and the presence of your ex-husband to do what I've longed for you to do all these past months. . . . Do you know what I was feeling when you kissed me?"

She shook her head.

". . . And what I felt when I saw you take his arm only a moment later? I've never seen you so . . . self-involved. I trusted you. I thought you were different, but you're not!"

"I'm sorry," she added again. "I didn't mean to hurt you. It was selfish of me."

He took a step toward her, but he didn't soften. "And how did it work, your little scheme? Was he sufficiently impressed? Is this the reason you have gone to so much trouble to change yourself? Was it worth it?"

He was hurting and his pain cried out to her from every part of him.

"My husband was my whole life . . . but he didn't want me." It sounded weak, yesterday's news. "It was worth it to me," she said. "But not at the expense of hurting you. I'm so sorry, Alex."

She reached out for his hand, wanting him but stopped by his severity. He stared at her unbending

. . . it seemed like forever, and then she was in his arms and he was kissing her, pressing her to him fiercely, murmuring her name over and over. And she was coming awake! A part of her that had been dormant, all this time, stirred and stretched and reached for him in spite of her reserve.

"Anne, Anne," he murmured. "I've been sick with jealousy."

"I want you to make love to me," she whispered as he held her and rocked her back and forth as if she were a treasure he'd just found.

"Not here," he said. "I'll take you home with me."

"What about your mother?"

"I have my own wing, and separate entrance. Don't worry."

Of course, she thought, too aware of how many times he must have used that separate entrance.

Suddenly the sound of breaking glass shattered the stillness and he jerked away from her as she froze in his arms. The front door of the shop burst open, with a loud splintering sound, and two men in work clothes came hurtling toward them. One grabbed her and threw her roughly aside. She landed on the floor in the corner, bruising her hip. The other man unlocked the back door, letting in two more men. Alessandro rushed to help her, but they threw him back against the worktable, holding him there.

"Get out of here, Anne!" he cried out to her, as one of the men pulled back his fist and slammed it into Alessandro's stomach. Alessandro groaned and doubled over, while Anne watched in horror. One of the men held him from behind while another began to beat him over and over again, across the face and body. Blow after blow smashed into him, until his nose ran red and his mouth bled all over the front of his clothes; the thud of each blow mingled with Anne's sobbing, but they paid no attention to her pleas.

She scrambled out of the way as they kicked and stomped their way through the shop, systematically wrecking everything in sight. Bolts of fabric were ripped in half, and furniture was smashed. Her samples torn to shreds.

When they'd beaten Alessandro almost to unconsciousness, she saw one man nod to the other. And then each of them grabbed one of his arms and twisted them both until his shoulder sockets made a popping noise. Two screams rent the air, Alessandro's in agony, and hers in horror. In the middle of her scream one of the men grabbed her by the head, lifting her off the floor until her neck felt as if it would separate from her body.

"Not a sound from you!" he growled at her. And he let her fall back down. She moved back into the corner away from him.

They're going to kill me, she realized, as soon as they're through, because I've seen their faces.

It was suddenly very quiet. She wasn't even aware that they'd gone or how long she'd sat there, until the cold night air blowing in through the back door made her teeth chatter. There was a sound of dripping water coming from the toilet, and Alessandro's labored breathing, death rattling in his chest.

She crawled out of the corner expecting a blow at any moment. She almost welcomed it. Anything to keep from finding out if Alessandro was dead. She made her way through the debris toward him, unaware of sharp slivers that cut her hands and knees. She touched his chest, but she could hardly see him. There was blood pouring into her eyes from a cut in her forehead. She crawled toward the front of the shop, praying, crying, pleading with God to let the phone be intact. It was! She called the police.

It was two days before they knew if Alessandro would live. Two days in which she suffered the tortures of the damned. His lungs were filled with blood and he was in a coma. His injuries would take months to heal, if he did survive. They feared possible brain damage from one of the blows to his head.

A priest paced the corridor, comforting Signora Massini with whispered prayers and rosary beads. Anne was questioned again and again, but she couldn't remember anything except the size of a shoulder when its muscles bunched up to deliver a blow and the twist of a mouth as it leered in plea- sure at Alessandro's pain, inflicting, hurting, pounding. She never left the hospital, sleeping on a chair in the lobby. Brenda brought her some clothes and a letter in a blue envelope that had no return address. It had been slipped under their door sometime during the night. All the note contained was a phone number.

Her hands were trembling as she dialed. A man's voice answered. "Who is this?" he asked.

"Anne Scott."

"If we do not get our money in one week's time, Massini will be dead!"

She jammed her fist into her mouth to keep from screaming. "Where can I meet you?" she said, but the phone went dead.

She called back again and again, but the number was busy. And within hours it was disconnected. Now she was terrified. They were going to kill him! She didn't understand what could have happened. Alessandro had received his money from the insurance. He was going to pay his debt. Why had they beaten him like this? Why were they still threatening him? How much did he owe? Had he lied to her? She couldn't ask him, he was too sick, and she didn't know where to turn.

She called his insurance agent, Gimmo Pasquale. "Did your company make that payment to Alessandro that you told me about?"

"Of course," he said, with genuine surprise. "Why?"

"Alessandro is in the hospital. He's been beaten very badly."

"Please give me a number where I can reach

you," Pasquale said. "I'll make some inquiries and call you back." She gave him the number of the corridor phone, and waited there for over an hour. Finally Pasquale called her back.

"Mrs. Scott, I checked with my supervisors and with our main division. The money from the claim was paid by check to Signore Massini and was, as you know, placed directly into his account. That is where, perhaps, we made an error."

"What?" she asked, afraid to hear the rest of his news.

"It is difficult to determine the exact events that surrounded this unfortunate incident, except to explain to you a bit about Signore Massini. You see, he has incurred various debts over the years, in several different ventures. This last deal was only one of many financial losses. And his creditors have been waiting for such a time when they might recover some of their capital. They picked this as their moment. Evidently Signore Massini has not been depositing funds in any of his checking accounts to keep his creditors away.

"He has been transacting his business dealings recently all in cash to avoid any payments to former creditors and he was cautious for good reason," Pasquale explained. "For as soon as his insurance claim was paid directly into the bank, his former creditors were notified and a closure was placed on the account pending attachment proceedings. He would have been served with notification of attachment on the day following the deposit of our check, except that by then he was already in the hospital.

"I'm afraid that you and I made an error in not giving him that check directly," Pasquale announced.

"Oh, God!" Anne said. "I forgot to tell him." She had been so preoccupied with herself and her feelings about Jeff and Alessandro that she had inadvertently caused him terrible harm.

"Yes, and the people who made the Duke his most recent loan learned of the attachment and knew that he would not be paying them as promised."

"How can I reach these people, Signore Pasquale?" she asked. "I can do something!"

"I wouldn't advise that," he insisted. "They are not reasonable men."

"Could you just tell me how much Alessandro owes them."

"Thirty-three million, six hundred thirty-eighty thousand, four hundred lire."

"How much is that in dollars?"

"Thirty-eight thousand, four hundred dollars."

My God! The amount was staggering. So much money! And yet what could she do? She couldn't let him die! He had helped her, and believed in her, and now he needed her help. She thanked Pasquale for his assistance, and called Brenda at the bank.

"I'm leaving the hospital now," she explained. "And I'm coming over to the bank right away. I want you to draw a cash draft for thirty-three million, six hundred thirty-eight thousand, four hundred lire."

Brenda couldn't help but ask, "What for?"

"Brenda, please. Trust me," Anne said.

"All right, all right," she agreed. "I just don't want you to do something crazy."

The moment she arrived at the Banca Moderna, Brenda met her and took her directly to Segri's office. Segri was kind, in the same way that Alessandro was kind, and he cared. Anne noticed the way Brenda looked at him and her heart went out to her friend. Segri was soft-spoken, but he was a hard man to argue with.

"Both Brenda and I are afraid you'll never get this money back, Anne. Signore Massini is insolvent. He's not a good risk and I find it personally abhorrent that he would borrow money from you."

"He didn't ask me. He doesn't know anything about this!" And she explained to them what had happened.

Segri listened to her story. He admired this young woman's devotion. How could he advise her not to save the life of a man who needed her? Money was not important in itself, but in what it could do for others. "Issue her the check, Brenda," he said. Brenda opened her mouth in surprise, but he shook his head.

"I'm glad you see it my way," Anne said, "because I have no alternative. And I want you both to promise me that you will never tell the Duke di Valdagno who paid his debt. I do not want him to know."

Segri looked startled. "I'm certain you don't," he said. "Did I hear you correctly, Signore Massini is Duke di Valdagno?"

"Yes," she said. "And he would not want me to be the one to help him."

"I understand," Segri agreed. Brenda left with Anne, but he knew she would be back, wanting an explanation. And he would give her a logical reason, not exposing the fact that he was a romantic at heart. A romantic who liked to clear up old debts.

Anne went back to her apartment and waited by the phone. Finally the call came. "Do you have the money?" a man's voice asked.

"Who is this" she asked.

"Flavio Rinaldi. I've been informed that you made a withdrawal from your bank today."

These people found out everything. "Yes, I did. Where can I meet you? I want to settle this as quickly as possible."

"So do we, Mrs. Scott," he answered. "Come to Harry's Bar this evening, about five o'clock."

The payment went quite smoothly, but she took no pleasure in the impression she made on Flavio Rinaldi. As she was leaving she asked him, "Does this free Duke di Valdagno from any obligations to you people?"

Even his smile was crooked, she thought. "Yes, this clears it up. We won't bother him again."

She went directly to the hospital. But Alessandro had been moved to a different room, and the nurse at the desk wouldn't tell her where he was.

"No visitors, signorina. No one is to see him!"

"Please check the list!" Anne insisted. "I know my name must be there."

The woman shook her head. "We have our instructions. You will have to speak to his doctor or Signora Massini."

Anne didn't understand why they were doing this, but it didn't matter. She would cover every floor in the hospital until she found him. As the third-floor elevator opened, she came face to face with Signora Massini. The woman was waiting for her, arms crossed, a mixture of triumph and hatred showing in her face. The nurse at that desk must have warned her.

"Where are *you* going, signorina?" Signora Massini asked. "They told you he wouldn't see you. My son has given me full control. He will see no one. Especially not *you!*"

Anne was stung by her words and the hatred in them. "Signora Massini, I am his friend. I care for him very much. Please, may I see him?"

"He does not wish to see you! Here! She thrust a paper in front of Anne. It was a request from

286

Alessandro that no visitors be admitted, and it named her in particular. This must be a mistake!

Anne went back down to the lobby, and tried using the house phone. But the operator told her the same thing, his phone was blocked.

"Could you please tell him Mrs. Anne Scott is calling?" she pleaded with the operator.

"*Sì, signora*, he will get the message."

Finally, she left the hospital, not knowing what to think, not understanding what in the world had caused this sudden change in Alessandro. The expression of triumph on his mother's face burned in her brain.

When she heard Brenda's key in the lock she burst into tears, unable to stop the outpouring of her disappointment. Brenda was stunned by the news of Alessandro's behavior. "What will you do?" she asked; the anguish of her friend was almost too much to bear. What kind of monster was this man? She wanted to march past all those nuns and priests at Ospedale d'Celio and shake some sense into him.

Anne's self-loathing was horrible to see. "You've got to get away from here for a while," Brenda insisted.

Anne didn't seem to hear. "If I could only talk to him," she sobbed.

"What about Elena's invitation? Why don't you accept?"

"I don't want to go alone."

"So, I'll take a week off and go with you."

"Would you?" Anne's face brightened for a moment. At least someone in her life had remained constant.

"I'll try," Brenda agreed. "The bank can spare me for a few days."

"As soon as Alessandro is well enough to see me," Anne announced. "Then, I'll decide."

"What are you waiting for?" Brenda insisted. "He's not worth another second of your concern. I don't know how you find such winners." But Brenda's wisdom didn't help.

Anne wrote to Elena and received a cool reply. There was an obvious indifference now that Anne's career was dead—dead along with all her dreams of happiness with Alessandro—and Elena's money badly spent, as if Anne had engendered the loss herself. Elena would allow her to come merely to comply with a past obligation. "We could fit you in for a short visit sometime next month . . . before the cruise."

It doesn't matter, Anne thought. I'll go anyway. Anything's better than staying here.

Ten days went by and still Alessandro wouldn't see her, until she wrote him a note:

> I'm going away for a while and I'd like to say good-bye. I promise not to tire you. Won't you give me five minutes. Please?
>
> Anne

She couldn't trust herself to say more or sign more.

She came to the hospital prepared with a self-righteous speech. She would tell him what she'd done for him, ask him why he'd treated her like this even if it meant humbling herself. But when she saw him she couldn't say a word. He was terribly bruised and swollen. His touch with death had taken all his spark. Casts and traction covered most of him that wasn't purple or bandaged, and she saw that he couldn't withstand any discussion at all, much less an emotional one. She longed to hold him and stroke him and cry over him, but she kept the appearance of gaiety and smiled fixedly. "Thank you for seeing me," she said. His cheeks were drawn with discomfort; hollow areas she'd always thought of as crevices, deepened and marched their way across his face. Why hadn't he let her see him before? But even his eyes didn't smile, and she knew by that that he didn't want her. Once again someone she loved had been completely transformed. Was there poison in goodness that murdered a relationship?

His jaw was wired and he spoke through his teeth. "I didn't want you to see me like this, but I'm going to be here for a long time . . . and I wanted to wish you farewell."

It sounded so final. She promised herself she wouldn't cry so she kept smiling her new smile over her new chin, as she thrust her new chest

289

against the blue silk. A second time, a second rejection. She didn't want to go through it again.

"I'll write you from France. If you need me, please let me know." He wouldn't need her, and if he did he wouldn't tell her. She was more bewildered than hurt at the moment. The hurt was sure to come later. The route was familiar, but this time there was no marriage, no miscarriage, only an unformed relationship and an aborted business.

Just as she was leaving he called to her. "Anne!"

"Yes?" She turned.

"Thank you for coming."

She didn't hear him add, "my love." She was too busy wiping away the tears as she ran down the hall.

In his hospital bed Alessandro watched helplessly as Anne ran out. He cried out with torment, shouting until his voice cracked into severed pieces like his heart. Her lack of concern for him was more painful than all the injuries he had suffered. For if she had cared even the smallest amount, she would have come to see him before this. She was the only person whose name he had put on his list of allowed visitors except for his mother and Father Santino.

It had taken all his courage to let her come and see him so broken, so ashamed and so low. He knew what she thought of him. He'd known it that night in the lobby of the Hassler, when she'd turned from his embrace and taken another man's arm. If she felt contempt for him then, what she must feel now to see him humbled like this. He'd been unable to defend himself that night, responsible for her safety and failing miserably to protect her. Failing in every way, as her partner, as her sponsor, and as her lover. He thanked the Lord that he had never tried to really love her. That failure he could not have endured. And as a testimony to her he was proud that she hadn't berated him, as he deserved, as his mother had been doing. It wasn't Anne's fault that any of this had come about. He knew that, no matter what his mother said. Anne had been a dream nearly realized, more painful to lose than he could have imagined. And when he had healed and paid back Visconte he would pick up the pieces of his life. But no more dreams. He was through with them. He was past the point of being able to fight back against what life had dealt him. He had brought this all on himself.

The pain in his shoulders was excruciating, but he twisted in his casing to increase it. He wanted these tortures to hurt him, until they surpassed the pain of what he had lost. He pulled on his jaw, screaming again as the wires were stretched to endurance. He yanked on his ankle, strung from a trapeze, feeling all of his injured parts burning. But none of it shut out the sight of Anne's retreating form that he had been powerless to stop, that he would have killed for, now that it was too late.

The nurses came running, their skirts rustling along the tile floors. "Now, now," they soothed, alarmed at his frenzy, summoning a young doctor who sedated him, numbing the pain in his limbs but not in his heart.

CHAPTER 21

Numbness was a blessing, keeping Anne insulated as she prepared for her trip to the Côte d'Azur. Methodically she shopped and packed. She took mostly her own designs, the things she'd made for herself, all of them classic, understated, as opposed to the collection of delicately wrapped and layered things she'd designed to be shown, now dead and buried shreds of material. How she'd worked on them, all for nothing!

She kept in contact with the hospital, checking on Alessandro's progress without leaving her name. And when Brenda commented that she had been taken, she cried, "It was in my power to give! Should I have denied him his life? And I'm telling you again, I want you to swear you will never reveal to him who paid his debt! I want you to ask Frederico to swear never to tell him either."

"You're crazy, Anne," Brenda said, "but I'll do what you request."

But when Anne and Brenda finally left, Frederico decided to pay Alessandro Massini a visit. It was about time he and the Duke became acquainted. He told himself he would keep his promise of secrecy only if it proved to be advisable. Massini was certainly entitled to know that someone had bailed him out, and that he was no longer in danger.

Alessandro was surprised to have a visit from Frederico Segri and he studied the illustrious banker as he approached the bed.

"I'm afraid you've caught me at a disadvantage," Alessandro said after Segri had introduced himself. They smiled at each other, recognizing their similarities, their differences, and the oddity of their common ground.

"I understand you've had some bad luck."

Of course he would know, Alessandro realized, and looked away in embarrassment. He couldn't blame Anne if she confided in her roommate. Probably the whole world knew about him.

"I haven't come here to upset you," Frederico

assured him. "But to inform you that you are no longer in any danger."

Alessandro's head snapped back to Segri, upsetting every sore part of his upper body. He winced. "What do you mean?"

"Your financial debt has been paid by a good friend of yours." He hastened to add, "No, it wasn't I."

"Are you certain of this?" Alessandro was afraid to allow the relief to flow through him, afraid to direct the signals from his brain to his broken and injured parts that it was all right for them to mend now. And who could have done this for me, he wondered. Elena? Unlikely! Paolo Brisson? His nephew Carlo? No, none of them would risk their money for his life. To whom was he indebted for the light of day, for the comforts of medicine, for the right to breathe?

"I cannot reveal the name," Frederico said in response to his expression. "I have promised not to . . . but I will not deny it if you guessed."

And of course Alessandro knew. "Was it Anne?" he whispered, and Segri nodded. The answer was too much for him; tears came to his eyes. He had ruined her hopes and lost her forever, and yet in an unselfish act of charity she had saved him. She did care! He owed her so much!

Segri waited until Alessandro composed himself. "I understand Anne is a very talented designer."

"Yes. She's extraordinary. She could be one of

the biggest!" he said. "She must be encouraged not to give it up . . . simply because of what happened, or because of my failures."

Segri took his seat again. "What will you do now?"

"I don't know," Massini replied.

He's very hard on himself, Segri thought. "Would you want to continue as a couturier?" he asked casually, one acquaintance to another.

"Not for myself," Alessandro said. "But for Anne's sake. There's nothing I care about anymore."

"That's understandable," Segri commented.

"Everything I have was ruined when those men destroyed my shop. All the samples, the materials, the machines, everything!" He saw Anne crouched in the corner, heard her cries all over again. Everything he touched turned sour.

"How much would it take you to start again?" Segri asked quietly.

Alessandro looked at him in surprise. "More than I've ever been able to raise before, even when I was in a position of strength, and not lying here helpless!" He knew he sounded bitter. "But I haven't the heart to try again, to turn myself loose on another innocent victim. And besides, Anne would never trust me again."

"That's too bad," Segri replied, "because I was about to offer you money. Not a loan, but money as an investing partner. If Anne's as good as you say, I'd like to be in on her success."

"Just like that?" Alessandro said.

"I'd like to help," Frederico said.

"But everything was ruined . . . and Anne . . ." He tried to shrug, but the bandages prevented it.

"What became of the patterns to the designs and the drawings?"

"I still have them," he said. "But there were so many changes, so many alterations in the finished products . . . impossible. . . . But my pattern-maker and my tailor will remember what the changes were. There might be a possibility."

"Good!" Segri said. "When you're feeling better come and see me, and we'll work out the details. It might be just as well if you could surprise Anne with a re-creation of what you lost. She'd listen to you then!"

Before Alessandro could respond Segri told him, "I have some friends and acquaintances in the retail end of the business. I might be able to help you in that aspect also."

"I cannot express to you how I feel, signore," Alessandro began. "I'm afraid I'm still too shocked to be coherent."

"I'll be in touch," Segri said, getting up to leave. "And I'll send you a letter of intent spelling out my wishes in this matter, just in case anything should happen to me." He always put in writing whatever his future plans might be.

As he reached the door he turned back. "One question?"

"Yes?"

"Are you any relation to the Arturo Massini family of Valdagno?"

"That was my father."

"I thought so," Segri replied.

"Did you know him?" Alessandro asked.

"No. Only by reputation. He was a fine and compassionate human being." And then he left, secure in the knowledge that this had been an easy debt to repay. His Uncle Jacopo and his Aunt Eva and his four cousins would have been pleased with him.

The Brisson chauffeur met Anne and Brenda at the Aeroport de Nice–Côte d'Azur. He took care of their luggage, seated them in the gunmetal-and-black Rolls sedan and drove toward Cap Ferrat through Nice—past the Negresco Hotel, the shops and the beaches and the bay of Nice dotted with industrial ships and private yachts. The signs pointed in the directions of Villefranche, Eze-sur-Mer, Monte Carlo. Magic names! Finally they left the road and wound down into the exclusive area of St. Jean Cap Ferrat that lay beside the Mediterranean. The streets were tree-lined borders of huge estates, set back from the road, most of them hidden from view. They breathed expensive air with every breath.

The car turned in between two ornate iron gates topped with gold finials, and then followed the approach to the house which carved a path through a thicket of trees. The driveway seemed to climb forever until it reached the villa perched on top of a hill, a salmon-colored jewel, with bombe windows and carved balustrades, and turrets, flags, and flowers.

"This isn't exactly a Polish garden!" Brenda said, almost leaning out of the window to get a better view.

"It's a genuine castle," Anne said in a hushed voice. It was all she hoped it would be.

"Don't blow your cool, cookie. This kind of place is supposed to be old hat to you. Chances are that Elena won't remember what you were like in Paris. She'll see you as you are now and think you've never been déclassée."

But Brenda was wrong. Elena recalled perfectly well what Anne had been like in Paris and she nearly fell over when she saw her. She didn't recognize her at first, until Anne embraced her and spoke to her.

"I never would have known you! What have you done to yourself?"

"Do you like it?" Anne asked, fluffing her hair.

"Like it? My God, not just your hair. All of you is different. You look wonderful! I can't find the words to describe it."

"You look better than the last time we saw you, too," Brenda interjected.

"Oh, hello Brenda," Elena answered coolly. Brenda was like a bad penny, always turning up.

Anne sensed the tension and gave Brenda a look saying, *Don't start!* "We are so grateful for your

hospitality, Elena. Aren't we?" she asked pointedly.

Brenda squelched a reply. After all, Anne really
needed this diversion. "Yes, Elena. We really do
thank you."

Elena was amazed at Anne's display of strength
and influence. She smiled and extended her hand
to Brenda. "Shall we call it off?"

Brenda shrugged. "Why not?"

"Now, let me show you around," Elena said,
and led them into the morning salon, washed in
yellow silks and damasks, Louis XIV furniture,
Gobelin tapestries, and an Aubusson rug that
would be outstanding even at the Trianon. The
afternoon salon was dominated by rusts and golds,
velvets and heavier brocades, Louis XV antiques,
dark oak inlaid floors, and a carved fireplace. The
dining room, enormous and formal, was in English
Tudor. "*Très amusant* for the South of France,
don't you think?" Elena asked. "But then, I've always believed that certain styles of furnishing
were conducive to certain rooms. For instance,"
she said as she led them through treasure-filled
room after room, "the game room is in Empire,
the bar is cozier as an English pub, and the bed-
rooms alternate between Victorian, Louis XVI,
and Art Nouveau." The discotheque in the base-
ment was ultramodern, with a glass dance floor
that lit up from within and neon sculptures over
mirrored walls.

The girls were speechless at the opulence of

their hostess's domain, and they recognized the museum quality of the furnishings.

"We have an amusing group here," Elena said, putting her arms around them. "The film festival is occupying everyone's attention, but then the summer season will be upon us followed by the Croix Rouge Gala in August. You couldn't have picked a better time, girls. But tell me, Anne, how is it that you have changed so much? And why did you hide all this excellence under that mousy demeanor?"

Anne smiled. "Let's just say that I've come of age, Elena. I was trying to get away from myself when I met you, denying myself, covering up. You see, you really knew very little about me when we met."

Elena looked at her for a moment, remembering the devotion Anne had displayed. The hours Anne had spent listening to her, comforting her. She was disappointed by what appeared to be the loss of that ingenuousness, but her interest was renewed in another way. This visit might prove to be more than she'd expected. Wait until Carlo met her! "We'll have plenty of time to get reacquainted, my dear!" She rang for a servant.

"Pietro, please take Mrs. Scott and Miss Greenstein to their rooms." She turned to them. "After you've settled yourselves, I should like you to meet my guests. We'll be gathering in the afternoon salon at seven for cocktails."

* * *

At 6:55, when Brenda knocked at her door, Anne was ready. She wore a white crêpe dress, cut on the bias, showing just enough cleavage, set off by a jeweled head piece.

Brenda whistled. "You look great!"

Anne smiled. She noticed Brenda's dress, a black silk, tailored, simple, and flattering. Her tan was as even as Anne's; her blue eyes shone with happiness for her friend.

"You know, Brenda, as you say, with a little plastic surgery, a few more inches in height, maybe a religious conversion and some speech lessons, you could be gorgeous too." They both laughed.

Brenda descended the staircase slowly with Anne while her mind calculated all the angles, all the odds as she approached the glittering group below. Her thoughts were not here. . . . She was thinking about Rome and Frederico.

But Anne was on the brink of a new life and she felt it in every nerve in her body. She was determined to put Rome behind her. She was ready for adventure. She floated into the salon and every head turned to look at her.

"Everyone," Elena announced, "I want you to meet Anne Scott from California and Brenda Greenstein from New York." And then she steered them from group to group.

"Darlings, this is Baron and Baroness Philippe de Marcos of Rome."

"Elena, must you use titles, you're simply terrible," the Baroness said. She was a tall, auburn-haired woman with a classic Roman profile and slender, magnificent hands. "We are Triana and Philippe," she said, extending her hands to both girls.

"They're Americans, darling, they love titles. Don't you, dears?" Elena asked them, unaware if they were impressed or embarrassed by the exchange.

"Why don't you use your title, Elena?" Triana asked. "Just because you've chosen to ignore it!"

"I divorced my title with my husband."

"How unfortunate," Triana said, and Philippe, a gray-haired, handsome man in his early fifties, winked at Anne who almost winked back, but caught herself in time.

Elena ushered them to the next group. "And I'm certain you've seen Lilli Touveau in one of her marvelous roles."

The small actress with the smoky blonde hair and soft green eyes was standing next to a short and wiry man with a crazy, inappropriate grin on his face. "And this is John Martine," Elena continued. "He makes brilliant movies. Lilli and John have just completed a film together. We know it's going to sweep the festival!" Elena said, patting his cheek. He continued to smile menacingly, like a psychopathic killer, Anne thought.

"Meet Bill and Lorraine Burton. Bill produced the film." The Burtons nodded to them. Americans with money, Anne decided.

"And over here," she interrupted another small circle of people, "is Allan Ornstein from California. He's just been appointed president of CAM-Zenith Records and we're delighted for him." She turned to a good-looking tanned young man standing with the Ornsteins. "Anne Scott, Brenda Greenstein, meet Norm Martinson, he's in real estate in Beverly Hills." Elena winked at him and he kissed her on the neck in a proprietary way. They were about to move on when Elena realized she had forgotten to introduce Allan Ornstein's wife. "And this is Mrs. Ornstein." She hesitated over the name.

"Mindy," the woman supplied.

"Of course! Mindy. You three should have a lot in common, being from California."

"I'm from New York," Brenda said.

Allan Ornstein had premature silver hair, a dimpled face, and a nice smile. His wife, Mindy, was about thirty-two, with large blue eyes, thin curly hair, and a California dress off the rack. Her nails were embarrassingly bitten and she wore Gucci jewelry. She looked timid and out of place with the titles and the money in this room.

That's me when I was married to Jeff, Anne thought, as Mindy Ornstein let go of her husband's arm just long enough to shake their hands. Anne looked from Mindy to her husband who stared back with obvious interest. You creep, she thought, and gave him her most sophisticated, dazzling glance. "How thrilled you both must be," she said. "Congratulations." And she took his face in both her hands and kissed him lightly on the mouth. "A new European custom I just invented to honor newly appointed record-company presidents." And she turned and walked to the next group, leaving Elena and Brenda quite impressed by her.

The next two women were well past their sixties, silver-haired and plainly dressed—with an Old World grace. "May I present my mother-in-law, the Contessa Brisson," Elena said of the woman on her right. "And her sister, Madame Cevantes, who will bury us all." She hugged the other woman. "This is Anne, to whom I am so indebted."

The Contessa smiled. "Elena, have your young friends met Carlo?"

"Not yet, darling," Elena answered. "I'm saving him for last."

"Elena's told us so much about you two. How fond she is of you," Madame Cevantes said to Anne. "We are very grateful to you for your assistance, in a most delicate matter. Your influence on her was most positive!"

It was the first time anyone had mentioned Elena's addiction. Anne nodded. "Elena and I were drawn to each other in some strange way that only the two of us understood," she answered, smiling at Elena. "I'm only glad I was there at the right time."

They were interrupted by a deep male voice.

"Do not monopolize these beautiful women, ladies." Anne turned toward the voice.

"Oh, Armand and Françoise," Elena said. "Let me introduce Anne Scott from California and Brenda Greenstein from New York. Duc Armand and Duchesse Françoise de Kergoly."

A duke and a duchess, a baron and a baroness, Anne thought. I wonder if there's a prince hiding in the wings somewhere—in search of a princess!

Triana de Marcos joined them. "I understand you have been living in Rome," she said to Anne.

"Yes, and I adore it," Anne said in Italian.

And then she turned and saw him. Prince Charming.

"Anne," Elena said, "this is my son, Carlo. Isn't he beautiful?" To Brenda she said, "He looks just like his father."

He was beautiful! And tan, with a flashing smile that crinkled the corners of his eyes. Tight and slender in his beautifully tailored black silk tuxedo and French batiste ruffled shirt. The shirt was open, revealing gold chains on a brown body. His black tie hung untied around his collar.

He stared at Anne, taking her two hands in his as if holding her open for inspection. His eyes teased but his expression was rapt sincerity. He was amazed at his mother. The young women she thought suitable for him were usually unbearable. Now this was a different story.

"Aren't you going to wish me happy birthday?"

he said, speaking impeccable English with a beautiful Italian accent.

"Is it your birthday?" she asked him.

"It is now," he said. "And Christmas and Easter and St. Carlo's day, my patron saint."

She laughed and had the craziest feeling that she should check to see if she were wearing glass slippers.

"Are we all ready?" Elena asked. "Anton has been holding my table against terrible pressure, I'm sure, so we had better go and relieve him of his burden."

"Where is your table, Elena?" Brenda asked.

"On the terrace of the Carlton, my dear. Where else, on opening night of the festival?"

"Where else?" Brenda said, raising an eyebrow at Anne.

They all trooped out to the limousines, with the exception of Contessa Brisson and Madame Cevantes, who declined, and the Duc and Duchesse de Kergoly, who were dining elsewhere.

The Carlton was a madhouse of excitement, glamor, and absurdity. A tall woman in a leopard bikini sporting rhinestone collar and a cheetah sat with a short, fat, prosperous-looking old man— probably a producer. The paparazzi were everywhere—swarming, snapping, pushing their way. Everyone was either chic or sexy or both. Blue jeans of every decoration—embroidered, patched, leathered, studded, tie-dyed, and jeweled. Lothars, Mic Mac, and T-shirts, gowns and caftans, see-through and see-under and see-over were there. Frizzy hair, straight hair, bouffant hair, and sculptured hair, enormous sunglasses, and lorgnettes and binoculars and opera glasses; even an ostrich-plumed fan with feathered tail to match walked by. Anne was dazzled.

Brenda said, "I've heard of the human zoo, but this is ridiculous."

And each one of the paraders had some specially equipped antennae reaching out to the producer, the film star, the director, the playboy. All eyes flitted and all seemed to settle back to Carlo and Anne.

"You've got it now, baby," they transmitted, "but watch out, hold on while you can until the glue fails on your Juliette manicures and then see how fast you fall and we grab your slot."

"Don't fool yourselves," Anne replied by the code of the Corniche, a tilt of the cleft chin, a dip of the cleft chest. "I'm prepared for all of you."

"The distribution in America will be helped enormously by our placing in Cannes," Bill Burton was saying. "Lilli is certain to win best actress. No other film offers such scope for growth for an actress."

"Perhaps the Swedish film will offer some competition," John Martine added. Lilli yawned; she was used to uproars and fusses and only came alive on the set.

Norm Martinson was nuzzling Elena, who

didn't mind at all. Eighteen years was the appropriate age difference here.

Mindy Ornstein sat between Triana de Marcos and her husband, Allan, listening to their conversation like someone watching a tennis match. Finally unable to contribute more than a blue-eyed sigh, she fluttered and sank back in her chair.

Why do I give a damn about her, poor thing, Anne thought, observing Mindy's wide-eyed expressions. The old Anne Scott personified. She was too close a reminder for comfort.

Carlo breathed in her ear. "*Cara mia,* come back to me." She turned and looked at him, hazel eyes with flecks of brown, large and enticing. She was flooded with a warmth that spread from her toes to her ears. Whatever he had, it made her feel wonderful.

"The wine is delicious," she said.

"You are delicious! Where did you come from? Who has made you; you are perfection," he said.

She wrinkled her nose. "From the foam of the seas and the powder on the snow, the nectar of the flower and the scent on the air. All for you, darling Carlo, all for you. And we shall be lovers and you shall adore me, *c'est tout!*" My God, was she crazy?

He stared at her, mesmerized. As were the others. Who is she, what is she, how did she, they all thought, all speculated, all wondered. Philippe de Marcos and Allan Ornstein and even Norm Martinson came up for air long enough to contemplate her, and she smiled. If they only knew!

And Elena couldn't help but wonder. She had expected an entirely different girl from the one who had arrived. Though this one was certainly interesting. If she had only known! Carlo was so vulnerable right now after his "thing" with Triana. And so anxious to please her. He would think Anne was invited just for him.

CHAPTER 22

Brenda's reasons for accompanying Anne to Cap Ferrat were not strictly altruistic. She had been working at a fever pitch for eight months and she desperately needed some time off. But more than that she needed to put some distance between herself and Frederico. Wanting to be with him was becoming an obsession. She thought of nothing else eighteen hours a day. And though her thoughts of him were directed in terms of work, she still felt intimately tied to him.

She was determined to make the most of her vacation. She would find someone—anyone—to take her mind off Segri. She'd have marvelous adventures which she could use to impress him when she returned. Perhaps he would become jealous and (hopeless though it seemed) make a declaration of his passion for her. It was a crummy plan, she thought. Underhanded, and dishonest, and desperate. She'd never felt like this before in her life, so attuned to someone, and yet forbidden to sing about it.

Why am I playing a game like this? she wondered as she sat on the terrace of Elena's villa, so far away from him. And the answer roared in her head—because I love him. There, she had finally admitted it. In love with a married man! No hope for a relationship. He was so moral, and so tied to his wife, if not for love then from duty. I'm more stupid than Anne, she thought, at least she chooses single men. She thought of Frederico's smile, and his strength, and his tremendous power over people, and she almost wept for leaving him.

Everyone in France, at least everyone Brenda met, paled by comparison to him. The young Frenchmen were no more dynamic than the young Italians, and she longed for Frederico. She wrote him witty one-liners on picture postcards, telling herself that he only thought of her as one of his kids, who had gone off to summer camp. When she could stand it no longer, she decided to cut her vacation short and fly back to Rome. She simply had to do something! She couldn't sit any longer with a winning sweepstakes ticket in her hand and not try to collect on it.

Anne was dismayed at the idea. "What will I do here alone, without you?"

"You don't need a chaperone, you hardly know I'm here. Besides, Elena doesn't want me on her cruise."

Anne couldn't argue the point, but Brenda represented more than just a friend or someone from home. She stood as a needed reminder of Anne's meager beginnings—something Anne tended to overlook when she was surrounded by the glitter of Elena's life-style.

"I'll really miss you, Bren," she said, "but I do understand your need to go back."

When Brenda arrived in Rome, her second thoughts were having second thoughts. She didn't know how to approach Frederico. What if he wasn't glad to see her? What if there was absolutely no chance for her at all?

She went home to the apartment and stared at the walls. Textured stucco, chipped tile in the bathroom. It was hardly a place he'd feel comfortable in. It smelled dusty from being closed up and it had no romance. But what could she do, this was all she had. Time after time she went to the phone to call him, but lost her nerve. He'd never come here, and she couldn't blame him. She needed neutral territory.

Summoning her nerve again, she checked into

the Excelsior Hotel and ordered champagne sent to her room. She took a luxurious bath and then got dressed again. It still wasn't the right time to call him. She waited until his work day was over and then finally called him at the bank, explaining that she had suddenly decided to come home and that she was at the Excelsior. Would he come to see her, she asked, assuring him that nothing was wrong.

Still, when he arrived at her room he was concerned.

Seeing him standing there, briefcase in hand, she started to shake, and all the color drained from her face. She asked him to sit down.

"For God's sake, Brenda, what is wrong? Did something happen in Cap Ferrat?"

"Yes, something happened. I'll tell you after we have some champagne. Would you like some champagne?"

"In a while," he replied. But she handed him the bottle anyway, and two glasses.

What could it be that she was afraid to tell him? That she was pregnant, that she was getting married, that she was broke, that she was dying? He waited.

"Frederico, I needed to talk to you."

"I am listening."

"It's hard for me to say. I don't want to lose your friendship; it is very important to me."

"Brenda, for heaven's sake, what is it? Why don't you look at me when you talk?"

She shook her head. "It's too hard." She took a deep breath. "Frederico, I love you." And then she looked at him. "I adore you, I worship you, and I want you." She stared at him full force, the look on her face full of emotion.

He was flooded with amazement and shock. She loved him! This endearing girl, who wanted to conquer the world for breakfast, loved him! An ageing Jew with a mind for business and no knowledge of love. He'd been so afraid of what she was going to say.

He shook his head in wonder. "I don't know how to love," he said.

She touched him on his cheek, on his lips, on his chest, on his groin. "You can learn," she said. And she picked up his hand, kissing his palm, and placed it on her breast. "Oh, God, Frederico, I love you so!"

And she kissed him when he realized that he did know how to love.

CHAPTER 23

Anne awoke with a feeling of giddiness and nearly leaped out of bed. Ahead of her stretched more days like those she had already spent with Carlo. Could she really have known him for just this little while? It felt as if they'd been together forever. His smile was as brilliant as the sun filtering through the shutters onto the dark-green carpet. He made her feel wonderful! His voice, his touch, were gentle and soothing, but beneath the surface she sensed a torrent of unreleased passion. Ah, there was nothing like a beautiful man to help one forget.

She crossed from the Louis XV bed to the armoire and studied her brown body, turning to see if the scars were visible. She used touches of makeup to hide them. "If I were Catholic I'd light a candle to Dr. Tzaro," she thought. Her breasts were brown from topless bathing and her bottom was brown from nude bathing. No one in their crowd wore suits, and only wrapped a sarong around themselves to eat luncheon. And I've got the best tits and ass of them all, she thought.

She had found the community nakedness a little hard to handle. She wanted to show off her beautiful body, but she did have a natural modesty. In the beginning she had undressed gradually, rubbing her body with oil as she uncovered a part at a time, lying on her mat, never looking at anyone else. She kept her eyes closed most of the time, and refused to get off her mat. But lately it was becoming easier. It had been strange to see Carlo nude before they'd even been to bed together. Bed. That was their only problem. She would tie up in knots when he tried to make love to her. Even that dreadful night with Larry she had not felt as inhibited. Carlo was so enthusiastic, as soon as he came near her he was all over her, never giving her a chance to react.

She opened the armoire door and chose an outfit for the day, carrying it with her into the bathroom. Carlo's enthusiasm wasn't the problem, she thought, hanging the gauze pantsuit on the back of the door. It's me. I don't like sex that much. I'm not one of those girls who can allow anyone to make love to them. But if I don't want Carlo, what do I want?

She did want him; at a safe distance, as a prince on a white horse should be. Not expecting anything more from her but that she be beautiful and attentive. He had the potential to hurt her, as others had. She stared at the blue and white tiles of the bathroom. I don't want to be hurt again.

The day was glorious. They drove to the Colombe d'Or, had a delicious lunch, very good wine, and took a lazy stroll around the countryside. That evening, after dinner at the villa with all of Elena's friends, they went off alone to a discotheque in Beaulieu and afterward walked back along a footpath to Elena's estate. Anne had kept him at arm's length all day, but suddenly Carlo turned her toward him and kissed her. He gently touched her breasts, then massaged her nipples as he held her to him, his groin pressed against her. She tilted away from him as usual and gently deflected her chest so that he lost his grip, but she didn't pull away from his mouth.

Suddenly he grabbed her between her legs and held her tight. "Don't do this to me, *cara* Anne, why do I not please you? Why do you not desire me? I want you so much, I am consumed with it, I feel myself here every moment that I am away from you!" He pressed his penis against her. "Just the thought of you makes me come. I taste you in my dreams, and smell you with my meals; I can think of nothing but you." He held her. "And you, you are lukewarm. Never before has a woman not desired me as you do. What is wrong? Do you not love me? I love you, my darling!"

"You speak of love so lightly, Carlo. It is not a word you can give away as you do the keys to your car. Love is not what you are feeling. You don't love me. It's too soon for love."

He looked at her in surprise. To him, love was the easiest thing in the world to feel when a woman was beautiful and desirable. It was true he did not love every woman he was with, only the special ones. He needed to love, and be loved, but his requirements for it were not as stringent as his American inamorata's. "Don't say that, my darling. Do you not feel the blood in me, the heat in me?" He took her hands, placing them on his erect penis. She could feel the heat from him, the ardor.

"When we make love, you act as though you are playing a part. You move in the right places, and you sigh in the right places, but your lovemaking has not the same excitement as when we dance, or when we swim, or even when we eat caviar," he said.

A shiver coursed through her body. Naked on the beach, she was bewitching; clothed and coiffed in the clubs, she was enchanting; but snuggled under her perspiring lover who was desperate to get a response from her, who was used to pleasing his women, she was a wet rag. There had to be something wrong with her.

She couldn't let go, even with him. He was too perfect, too loving. And if she did let go she wouldn't know what to do. He really doesn't love me, she told herself. If he saw what I really was, if he knew me as I really am, not this glamorous, educated fraud, he wouldn't give me a second glance.

"Am I too mild for you, darling?" he asked her. "Do you want someone else? A woman perhaps? Was Brenda your lover? I don't mind. I understand. It's all right."

She pulled away from him. "You filthy man," she said, and ran back to the house. By the time she reached her room she was crying bitterly. So there it was again. The picture of Jill and Jeffrey, on that table, in that position. Only this time she saw herself and Carlo and Brenda. She was out of her element with Carlo. She didn't know what he expected. She had tried hard. She had done all the right things—what did he want?

She looked in the mirror. Her small nose and cleft chin caught the light. She turned her head, her loosely flowing hair moved over her tanned skin, she was beautiful! Wasn't that enough? She remembered those hours in the hospital when she felt the same as now, worthless and alone and unloved. What am I doing? she wondered, staring at herself. Why do I make myself feel guilty? Just because Alessandro and Jeffrey hurt me doesn't mean Carlo will too.

She would not lose Carlo as she had lost Jeffrey and Alessandro. But she knew that to retain the upper hand was essential. If she ran after him and apologized, she would be relinquishing a position that she wasn't secure enough to abandon. Her sexual education would have to develop slowly. She would try to be more open with him, and less guarded, try to learn from him. And who could be a better teacher than Carlo?

Carlo was relieved that Anne was not a lesbian. But he was puzzled about her. Maybe she was frigid, but that didn't jibe with her sensual demeanor or the carefree attitude she seemed to have about life. She was refreshingly enthusiastic, after the blasé women he knew, unaware of her beauty, as if it were new. He liked that! And she listened to him. There were times when they had begun to make love that he sensed a spark, a response in her. But it died as soon as it appeared. He hoped to fire that spark, but he was frustrated with every encounter.

Perhaps she didn't know how to make love! As crazy as it seemed for anyone as beautiful as she to have missed an education with the number of lovers she must have had!

He asked her questions, indirectly, when they were talking of other aspects of her life—how old she was when she was married, had she been a virgin, faithful to her husband, how long had she been divorced? In the year since her divorce, there could have been a different lover every week, he thought. But when he asked her how many men she had dated, she shrugged and said, "Only you." He wasn't fooled by her answer. They all said he was the only one.

Anne knew what Carlo was getting at and she was grateful to him for his discretion. That night when he took her in his arms, she could feel the difference. He approached her with a tenderness; she responded with confidence.

He was eager and excited, as if he were initiating a virgin into the glories of sex. Every one of his partners, who, when he was young, had taught him and when he was older were his equal, had been experienced. Now his beautiful Anne was presenting him with the greatest challenge of his thirty-two years. He only hoped he could awaken her sufficiently and overcome her reluctance.

He was patient, he was gentle, and he was very determined. He touched her until she drew away and he could find exactly how far to go before she stopped him, then he'd retreat until she trusted him again, until he could go an inch further, a curve further without feeling her withdraw. He marveled at the walls she had built around herself; she was nude on the beach all day, but at night she insisted on pajamas. He lay in bed each night after she had fallen asleep and satisfied himself with a few quick strokes. He thrilled with the anticipation of what she would be like when he finally unpeeled her, got to the center of the real Anne. He taught her to touch him, to taste him, to watch him respond as well. He kissed her mouth, touching her lips, her tongue, showing her what a sensuous area it could be. He tested what gave her the most pleasure, until in a spirit of experimentation, she allowed him to try his penis there, briefly, teasingly, which he withdrew immediately before she could decide against it, before she could form negativity.

And, strangely enough, she liked it—the size and feel of it on her lips—and she explored him timidly with her tongue. She never questioned the slowness of their journey, as he played with her and fondled her and waited. She began to anticipate small changes in his movements, the tiny step further he took each time, his knowledge about just where to stop. His technique was working. She found herself in a fever of excitement. Every new area he included became her favorite. She began to love his touch—to think about the next thing they would do.

When he finally included her nipples in his caresses, touching her with fingertips he had moistened by placing them in her mouth, she uttered her first sigh of real pleasure and felt her first surge of sexual juices. Her nipples became like two buttons that opened the doors to pleasure. He need only press them, touch them, look at them, and she would sigh and moisten without hesitation.

And still he waited, knowing that he was close, certain of victory. The more he gave of himself, the more he loved her.

She lay before him with her arms and legs apart while he touched her body. "Tell me what you think. I know you are going to touch my vagina and I need to know what you think about it," Anne asked.

"What do you think when you touch my penis? When you taste me?"

"I like it!" The realization was incredible to her. "I like it, Carlo. I like the shape of you and the firmness and the smell, everything about you I like. And especially I like the way you touch me."

He smiled. "I feel the same about you."

"But I am different from you," she said.

"Thank the Lord for that," he laughed.

"Don't laugh at me. Please."

"I'm not laughing," he said. "I think that every part of you is beautiful and I want to touch you and taste you and be inside you!"

She shivered at his directness, wanting to hear it but frightened all the same. "I've always thought it was wrong to touch. But it can't be any more wrong to touch me than it is to touch you!"

"That's right!"

"And those feelings that you have when you climax, those are good feelings for you, aren't they?"

"The best ones," he said.

"Then they can't be bad for me, can they?"

He shook his head.

She looked at him sitting above her. His body was smooth and lean in the filtered light, the muscles in his abdomen were outlined by the tension of his position. "Oh God, Carlo, I've been afraid of it for so long."

"I know," he said.

"Show me, please show me how," she begged him.

He began exciting her in the way he had trained her, watching as he brought her to reactions she had never allowed, only this time he told her how beautiful she was and how much he loved to touch her and how good she felt to him and how natural it was to do what he was doing. And she came, the first time in many years; she came and, as it happened, stared at him in gratitude and trust and pleasure. And he said, "Again." And she nodded and he started over, only this time he entered her and moved gently against her until she came under him in a definite and deliberate response. And the next time he placed her on top of him and guided her to pleasure, and the next time he showed her how to tighten her muscles and thrust against him while he held himself exactly right for her, and enjoyed her fascination, and she learned and learned, and then when she had done it all, when she had learned to control her every angle, her every muscle, her every portion and yell with every convulsion, he came with her, a soaring, tearing, giving of pleasure that culminated his devotion and his extraordinary ability.

CHAPTER 24

Anne lay on the deck of the *Brisson* feeling the gentle movement of the sea beneath her, the cooling ocean breeze on her tanned skin. She didn't know which was more wonderful, this idyllic voyage or her sexual awakening. A dark closet, she thought, that's where I've been living all my life.

She wondered how Brenda was doing in Rome and hoped everything was all right with her. She missed Brenda and her pragmatic way of finding reality in an unreal setting. This sleek, pearl-colored yacht, with its slender, brown-skinned guests, provided endless luxury just as the superb food and sunshine and lovemaking had an over-ripening effect. Sometimes Anne wished for the firmness of hard mouthfuls after all the cream puffs, and more clarity in discerning the difference between appearances and reality. Lately she had lost that ability and didn't know why she loved making love with Carlo, yet wasn't certain that she loved him.

She opened her eyes to watch Elena and Norm Martinson playing backgammon on the pad next to her. Elena was a brilliant player. She never made an error and her guesses were always lucky, but she wasn't getting the dice today.

Anne marveled at Elena's ability to concentrate and her bright-eyed appearance this morning. After last night's session, Anne was exhausted. I've got to do something about these nighttime ordeals, she thought. I'm not helping her and she's getting to me.

Elena had sworn she was clean, off the junk, as she called heroin. But last night she had awakened Anne again in near hysteria. It was the same panic, she said, that she had prior to her addiction to drugs. She begged Anne to talk her down, to help her over the crisis so that she could "make it."

And Anne sat with her all night as she had many other nights before, knowing that Elena's increased dependence on her was not benefiting either one of them. Elena had manipulated her into a role of surrogate everything—therapist, mother, daughter, and friend. She was drained by Elena's need to be supported and loved and if she tried to stay away, Elena engineered a situation where Anne would be trapped into listening while Elena cried, complained, bemoaned, and vilified everyone in her life. Her hysteria was loosely based on fact, primarily based on self-indulgence. She demanded immediate gratification and Anne couldn't say no to her. More and more it was apparent that psychotherapy, no matter how much Elena denounced it as quackery, status crap, and uselessness, was the only way.

But at the moment they were all captives on this floating hotel, only putting in to small ports where no help could possibly be found. By day Elena was supercalm superhostess. Most nights by 2 A.M. she was sniveling and hysterical.

"You don't know what it's like," she had told Anne the night before for the hundredth time. "You can't imagine what pain this is. I can't sleep, I can't eat. I can't stay calm without drugs. There are nettles in my blood scratching from inside. You're young and beautiful; I'm ageing and miserable."

"Elena," Anne sighed, repeating the same sentences, "you are elegant. Everyone looks at you wherever we go. You have boyfriends who admire you. You're at a wonderful time in your life."

"Oh, what do you know!" Elena snapped. "Your taste is in your ass!" But she regretted her remark and clung to Anne, weeping, "Oh, forgive me, I'm such a shrew. You're right. What should I do? Oh, dear girl, why don't you brush my hair for me. Massage my temples. It always relaxes me. Perhaps I'll be able to sleep if you do it."

So Anne brushed her hair and massaged her head and her temples until she noticed that Elena was masturbating. Anne pushed her away, horrified. "I don't care what you do, Elena, but not right now! How could you do such a thing in front of me?"

"Well, what do you expect me to do to relax? I do this so much my poor clitoris is almost raw!"

"Elena, honestly! What's wrong with Norm?"

"Oh, come off your high horse, darling. Don't tell me you didn't find that a little bit sexy?"

Anne got up to leave. "No, I don't! I don't understand you, Elena." But her repulsion was mixed with the slightest bit of curiosity. Why do I put myself through this, she wondered. Why do I let her affect me?

"It is wonderful to want sex again," Elena said. "That was the only bad thing about using junk. After a while sex became a bore, even with Gino."

"I should think that overdosing wasn't too pleasant, either! Who is Gino?"

"Never mind," Elena said. "He's not important."

"Elena, you need professional help. Someone should be taking care of you who knows what he's doing. I'm not helping you at all."

Elena's eyes filled with tears. "Darling, you are so sweet, so lovely. You don't know how helpful you are, how much I depend on you. Only you make my life bearable lately."

Anne sighed. "But it's wearing me out. I'm tired, Elena. These all-night sessions are more than I can take, and they don't help you! We talk for hours, night after night. You tell me you are afraid that you will not be able to stay off drugs, and I tell you to have courage and that I'll help you. Then you say you feel much better, much stronger, and you owe it all to me. But a few nights later, we start it all over again as though we made no progress, as though the whole damn process had never happened. I can't take it any more. I'm not a therapist. That's what you need."

"My husband used to tell me that. He wouldn't help me either. I begged him not to abandon me after Gino, but the bastard wouldn't listen. All he cared about were his boats and his French mistress. Oh, what's the use!" She sighed and put her arms around Anne, but Anne shrugged away from the embrace, uncomfortable with these physical demonstrations. The proximity of an adult female made her acutely aware of the similarities in their bodies, the hidden underlying aspects.

She was still disturbed by last night's encounter. Her feelings for Elena grew more confused every day. Elena fawned on her, and then snapped at her. She had the charm to draw one in, to flatter and cajole, and then she would attack with a sharp

THE DAY AFTER TOMORROW

remark. Her volatile behavior was impossible to guard against, yet Anne felt in her debt, even though Anne was the one who had saved her life. Anne's awakening to erotic pleasures had opened her to all her feelings, and increased her desire to help Elena. But Elena took advantage of these feelings and lost no opportunity to brush her every so often, down her spine, on the side of her neck, under her knee. And embarrassingly, Anne would react with a shiver, or a nuzzle, thinking it was Carlo, feeling the same responses, and shocked to find Elena's impish grin when she turned.

Carlo came and sat down next to her and kissed her shoulder. She jumped guiltily.

"Who is Gino?" she asked him.

"A friend of mine," he answered. "I've known him for years. He is a very wonderful fellow, but he had an argument with my mother and now we don't see him any more."

"When did that happen?"

"I think it was after my parents' divorce. Gino and my mother were lovers. It was very sad for them. Gino's family has no money. He did not like it that my mother was rich and he was not. And he has a temper, Gino. So does my mother. They fought all the time. The last time they fought she called the police and he went away and never came back. But you may meet him."

"Why?"

"I understand that he is the manager of a hotel in Portofino."

"You'd better warn Elena so that she won't be upset if she sees him."

"I will." He looked at her strangely.

"Was Gino as young as you?"

"No, he is ten years older. Why all the questions?"

"I just wondered," she said. "When did your mother start taking heroin?"

He stopped to think. "Sometime after Gino left. There were many different men for a while. And then there were no more men and she started getting worse, but we were all so blind, we didn't know why. The first two times she tried to stop she went back to the drugs again. But this time she will not."

Anne prayed that he was right.

"If I knew who gave her the drugs, I would kill him!" he added vehemently.

Anne looked at him in surprise. It was not an idle threat; there was no doubt in her mind that he meant what he'd said. It was incredible to her that people of this stature and background could be involved in such sordid activities. You never know what rot lines the castle walls, she thought. No one's safe from problems. Especially Elena. And I knew what her problems were before I came here. She looked over at Elena, concentrating on her game as if she hadn't a care in the world. Knowing that Elena was an addict and seeing it firsthand was not the same thing.

"Anne." Carlo caressed her thighs, but she

brushed his hand away. "I want you, my darling," he whispered in her ear. "Let's go to my room." He stood up, pulling on her hand.

"Not now, dear," she said, turning over on the pad. "The sun feels so good." It was a flimsy excuse, but with Elena sitting there reminding her of last night, she couldn't think about sex. I must stop dwelling on Elena's behavior, she thought. But how could Elena have made an overture like that? She's Carlo's mother!

Carlo turned to see if anyone had overheard them. It was hard enough to keep anything private on this ship where everybody knew everyone else's business. Elena had noticed the exchange. He glared at his mother as he walked over to the telescope, his special Galileo Officine, 600-power. There was nothing in sight but he fiddled with it anyway, trying to control his temper. He didn't like being refused and he had never stood for it before. For the first time in his life he was in love. He wanted to be with Anne every moment, share every thought and feeling, but she was always doing something else, reading, or sunning, or exercising, or being monopolized by his mother.

Anne watched him sulk. Why did he press her so? What more did he want? She knew what he wanted; no one had ever loved her this much before. But she couldn't let go and trust him. She'd been hurt by Jeffrey and by Alessandro, and she was afraid of being hurt again, or so she told herself. But there were things about him that bothered her. He was spoiled, used to having his own way. He'd send his food back over the slightest imperfection, and only talked about two subjects, yachts and clothes. Certain fashion designers meant as much to him as if they were world leaders, yet his interest in politics was minimal, unless a terrorist group attacked any of his holdings or those of his friends. He never read a book of any kind, and he never passed a mirror that he didn't study himself, baring his teeth, smoothing his hair, inspecting his pores. Once, Anne even caught him pulling his chest hairs out of the cleavage of his open shirt in a better arrangement. She supposed he was no different from anyone else in the group. But his worst habit was telling her the plots of movies that she hadn't seen. He had no ability to synthesize a plot or tell a highlight briefly, he mixed his pronouns, never omitted a detail, and always told the ending. Even with his physical beauty, he paled by comparison to Alessandro. She didn't want to compare them but she couldn't help it. Alessandro was in her thoughts no matter what she did. And the more critical she grew of Carlo, the more he wanted her. But she couldn't have Alessandro, and that was that.

She looked at Carlo standing there, the set of his back displaying his anger. What the hell, she thought, getting up and going over to him. She put her arms around him and rubbed herself against his back. But he wouldn't capitulate immediately to her advances. She would have to appease him more. She nosed the back of his ear. "Don't be grumpy. I'm ready if you are."

Carlo leaned back against Anne and said to her, "You go first. I'll meet you below deck."

Anne kissed his back and left, crossing next to Elena and Norm.

When she had gone, Elena called out to Carlo, "Backgammon, dear?"

He came and stood behind her. She had two moves on the board to bear off, a five and a four, but she threw a three and a one. "*Merde!*"

"I'll play you later, Mother."

"Carlo! I want to talk to you!"

"In a while," he sighed.

She nodded to Norm, who vacated his seat. "Sit down, darling."

Carlo sat reluctantly, knowing what was coming.

"I hate to see you make a fool of yourself. Especially after your recent behavior." She was referring to his affair with Triana de Marcos that she had forced him to end. He could not withstand his mother's wrath, but then there was no great love between him and Triana.

"What do you mean, a fool of myself?"

"I mean that Anne will be returning to her country. I do not want you to be hurt, to expect too much."

"Say what you mean."

"She is my guest and you are my son. I would

feel responsible if it turned out badly." Her eyes begged him to understand, but he looked away.

"I'm in love with her!"

"You're always in love, Carlo."

"Not like this. I want to marry her."

"Marriage! Don't be ridiculous. She is not for you. She is a divorced woman. She's a nobody, you would be laughed at. You are heir to a title."

"Then go ahead and laugh, Mother!" he said, and left her there before he really lost his temper. What did she want from him? No one was ever good enough. Not his childhood sweethearts, not his mistresses. If this girl wasn't right for him, who was? Elena treated Anne as if she were some special goddess, but when he did the same she suddenly became judgmental. It didn't make sense. He would show her she was wrong. Anne was perfect for him.

CHAPTER 25

Alessandro pushed through the revolving door of the Sherry-Netherland Hotel and walked down the red carpet to the sidewalk. How did people function in New York in the summer? He shifted the cumbersome sample bag in his arms while he waited for a cab, and winced when a shot of pain ran across his back. Nearly four months and still his ribs hurt when he exerted himself. It was a good thing that his life was quiet at the moment. But he missed Anne. She was so much a part of his thoughts and his life, it seemed unnatural that she wasn't here with him now. But perhaps it wouldn't be too long. In the meantime she was better off with Elena, sailing, vacationing until he had arranged everything on his own. He wanted to come to her with it all completed; hand her back the business and her chance at success as she had handed over money on his behalf. He would have done it even if she hadn't paid his debt, except that he thought she didn't care about him. Learning of her unselfishness had given him new hope.

"Where to?" the cabdriver asked.

"East Fifty-seventh, between Second and Third," he replied, and sat back for the short ride from his hotel to Lydia Bannerman's apartment. This appointment was an incredible stroke of luck. Having Frederico Segri as a partner was even more valuable than the money he provided.

Lydia Bannerman was an institution in the world of couture. She had more power in the marketplace of fashion than any other single individual. For years she'd been editor of the most prestigious fashion magazine, and she was truly a pacesetter. If she liked Anne's designs, there would be no stopping them.

He was ushered into her study by an oriental houseman.

"It is an honor to meet you!" he said.

"Frederico Segri is a very dear friend." There was no beating about the bush with this woman. She got straight to the point, always.

She studied him without smiling, her gaunt body held tightly against his charm. Women in their sixties were not impervious. "Now tell me about this protégée of yours, this Scott woman."

Alessandro's face softened. "She's a remarkable person, and her accomplishments are exceptional, but of course I am here to show you her designs."

"Why hasn't she come with you?"

"At the moment she is on a much-needed vacation with friends and I have taken over the management of our line until she returns."

He opened his portfolio and took out photos of the dress collection. He'd had it modeled and photographed in New York a few days before.

"Ah, Cecily," Lydia commented, recognizing the girl. "And Astrid. Good choices for this look." She nodded as she looked at the pictures, reflecting on them quickly, perusing the shots one after the other, flip, flip, flip, without a flicker of an opinion. "Did I see a sample bag in my hallway?" She raised her thin neck in the direction of the entry and her head followed.

"Yes." He stood up. "I'll get them."

The Persian carpet at her feet served as a display table and he unzipped the nylon bag, extracting one fantasy and one hope after the other.

She kept nodding, only one glance per outfit. That was all it would take.

"The fabrics are extraordinary," she said finally. "She reminds me of Mary McFadden. How old is she? Well, never mind. They're fine!" She smiled.

"I'll call Mildred Steinberg at Bendel's, and Howard Privic at Bloomingdale's. This is definitely not for Lord & Taylor, perhaps Bonwit's. And I've a few friends you might see in Paris. When do you show at the prêt? You are showing, aren't you?"

"Yes, we're showing. The fifth day." He wanted to shout.

Again she nodded, reaching over to a pad of silver paper. In plum ink she jotted down some names for him. "Here's who I want you to see in Paris. I'm certain you don't need to use my name in Italy. And here's my address on St. Honoré. You bring this girl to meet me on the very first day of the Paris showing. I always enjoy meeting talent."

He put the samples back in the bag, wishing Anne were here to share this moment.

"I like your suit," she commented on his gray summer pinstripe.

"Thank you," he smiled. "It's my own manufacture."

"I thought as much. So you both have it, huh?" Her eyes disappeared in the folds around them when she laughed. He found her perfectly charming. "Your friend is going to be as big as any of them, my dear Duke," she said. "And your name won't hurt her either. Look what a royal title did for Diane von Furstenberg."

He took her hand in his. "I cannot tell you what gratitude I feel at the moment."

"Then why don't you take me to lunch?" she

said. "I want to hear the whole story. How you met her and what my friend Frederico Segri had to do with all of this."

"I shall be delighted," he said. "Caravelle?"

"Oh God, no!" she exclaimed. "I want to eat, not to be eaten. I'll take care of it," she said. "Do you like Szechuan food?"

"Very much," he answered.

"Then we shall dine here!" She rang for her houseman. "My chef is a genius."

Gino entered the last receipt in the ledger and closed the book sharply. The sound echoed across the lobby and the assistant manager glanced into his office curiously. Gino ignored him and yawned. It was afternoon break time, time to sleep for a while. He hated this job. Wondered again as he had countless times already if working for Visconte was worth the drudgery and decided that it was. But dealing was much more exciting, life-and-death risks. He had been lucky up to now, managing to stay just ahead of the police. But he had felt them closing in. They had picked up Martine and Lucien in Paris, that was half of his organization. Georgio managed to get word to him before he went into hiding, though he had probably fingered the other two to save his own neck. He wouldn't dare turn on me, Gino thought, because he knows I'll have one of Visconte's men take care of him. I'd even slit his throat myself if I found him pulling anything on me. Hassan could give me some pointers on technique when he arrives in Portofino. Hassan was an expert with the knife. Gino sighed, and leaned back in his chair. The sea and the sky beckoned to him from beyond his office. He just wasn't cut out for a steady job. Well, with the new shipment Hassan was bringing he'd be able to find some new customers. Very rich customers. Maybe get some of his old ones back again. Hassan had new respect for him now that he was involved with Visconte. Enough to double the amount of his shipments.

I should have asked Visconte for more than two percent of the sale to do the report on this hotel, he thought. He would have made much more than that in one week of dealing, and he'd been here two months. Of course this job had no risks, no Giorgios to worry about, and a steady income of two percent of a legitimate hotel wasn't bad. In fact it was a substantial reward for merely driving the car while Mario and Rocco roughed up some fag dress designer in Rome last spring. When you were loyal to Visconte there was no telling how far you could go. Maybe next time Mario and Rocco would let him do more than just drive the car.

If Elena had been panicky before, the prospect of seeing Gino again terrified her.

"That bastard!" she said to Anne. "That scum, that beast! Oh God, Anne, he was incredible. Stay away from him. Promise me that you will stay

away from him. Don't even meet him. You've got
to be so careful of him. I can't tell you what he's
like. Oh, I hate him. With all my heart I hate
him."

If she only had Anne's courage, she thought,
clutching the hand that was offered. Look how
extraordinary Anne was, look what she had done
with herself, what she'd carried off. And even before her change, in Paris, she'd been sweet and
sincere. It was only after meeting Anne that Elena
had begun to realize she could love a woman as
she had once loved a man. If Anne could love her,
could help her share the pain, life might be bearable. But Elena knew she was ruining her chances
with Anne behaving the way she was. And she
was filled with self-loathing for daring to compete
with her own son for Anne's favor. What a horrible predicament! Only she could devise such disgusting circumstances. And yet she had brought
Anne with her on the cruise, practically throwing
her at Carlo, and now Carlo loved her too. If he
knew what was in his mother's mind he would never
forgive her, he would never get over it. Still, happiness was within her reach. Carlo would not find out.

They arrived at Portofino in a state of hyperki-
nesis, everyone electrified by his own voltage for
his own reasons. Elena faced her nemesis, Carlo
was shopping for diamonds, Anne was curious to
meet Gino, in spite of the warnings, Norm Martinson had begun a flirtation with Triana de Marcos.

He was overwhelmed to be on the "might fuck" list of a baroness and she was interested in anyone her "best friend" Elena was interested in. Philippe de Marcos was about to purchase a villa in Portofino at a steal, and Paolo Brisson was joining them with his mother, having just left his mistress in Capri.

Their first day they lunched on the port at a café, the yacht moored majestically out in deeper water. The *Brisson* was enormous as yachts went, 185 feet with three smokestacks and ultramodern design. The appointments were elegant and couldn't have been more complete. The owners of a yacht company would hardly have less.

After lunch Carlo and Anne decided to walk up to the Hotel Splendido where his grandmother and father were staying. The hotel, a salmon-colored Mediterranean villa, was perched high on a hill overlooking the bay. The footpath leading to the hotel was bordered on both sides by luxurious ferns and the air was soft and moist as Anne and Carlo climbed hand in hand toward the hilltop.

The lobby of the hotel had dark velvet walls, interrupted occasionally by carved marble fireplaces. Flowered rose-printed cottons covered the furniture, a contrast to the antique paintings and rubbed walnut of the woodwork. Anne thought it was one of the most beautiful places she'd ever seen.

Madame Brisson was happy to see them and Carlo proudly presented Anne to his father, whose raised eyebrow gave his official seal of approval. Carlo's resemblance to his father was strong. The original and the copy, Anne thought as they both crossed their legs in the same way and tilted their chins at the same angle, eagerly discussing the sheikh of Bhitamin who was staying at the Splendido with his entourage, including eight wives. The sheikh was contemplating the purchase of a Brisson yacht.

The hotel lorry sounded its horn and Anne thought she'd take it back to the beach. She loved being with Carlo but she had to admit to herself that all this talk about yachts was boring. It was Carlo's business, but still she had expected more in the way of enlightened conversation from her new group of friends. These people knew captains and kings, and all they could talk about was who was screwing whom. They were interested only in themselves. And blasé. She remembered how eagerly Alessandro had tried to succeed. How much it meant to him. He was better off than they, even with his failures, because he had a dream. They were merely custodians of a way of life. And poor custodians at that.

"I'm going down to the beach, Carlo."

He stood up, and kissed her. "I'll join you in a while," he said.

She decided to walk down after all, following the steep mountain curves and pine-scented glades until they gave way to a small crowded beach nestled in a cove. Families lined every inch of sand and spilled out of the beachside cafés, festively dining in leisure and luxury. Domesticity reigned.

There would be no topless sunbathing here.

She walked along the tiny alley behind the restaurants lined with beach shops, and went in to try on some outrageously priced, poorly made bikinis; wandered into a shop filled with plastic inner tubes and swim fins, and another with caftans and beach togas. Then past another shop with tourist curios, and foreign papers until she came to a small beachside hotel. It was smaller than the Splendido, but certainly as elegant. She watched a group of new arrivals tumble out of a Mercedes limousine. Their pale skins would be pink by tomorrow. Tan the day after. The hotel was covered with bougainvilles and other vines trailing onto a marble-and-tile courtyard. She glanced into the lobby, tiny and exclusive. The door to the manager's office was open and a man sat at a chrome-and-glass desk. He glanced up and looked at her, and a shock of recognition poured through her. It was he! The man from Deux Magots. Elena's connection. He saw her staring at him and winked. Quickly she turned away, her heart pounding. He got up and came toward her, his radar picking up her presence, but no look of recognition on his face.

"*Buon giorno, signorina,* may I help you?"

The same curly hair, the same sinewy approach

she'd seen in Paris. She shook her head. "No thank you."

"Are you all right? It is very warm today," he said.

It was as clear this moment as it was then: this man, the package of heroin under the chair, Elena unconscious on the floor. Her mind jumped ahead but she was afraid to complete her thoughts. Just then she saw Carlo getting out of a taxi. "Excuse me," she said, "but I see my friend," and she turned and walked toward him.

But Carlo rushed past her with an excited cry, embracing the other man with a shout. "Gino! Ah, Gino, I see you have found my gorgeous girl." He grinned at Anne. "If there is a beautiful woman within a mile, you will find her right away, eh?" he teased, punching Gino in the arm, who punched him back.

"*Paisan*," Gino said, hugging Carlo in return.

Anne's heart sank. So this was Gino, Carlo's friend, Elena's seducer—a pusher! She had not put it together.

Gino studied her, wondering why she looked familiar, but then Carlo always found the best and this one was certainly the best.

Carlo introduced them and they nodded, squaring off in competition.

"How are you, my friend?" Carlo asked, oblivious to the current. "I heard you were working in Portofino."

Gino nodded. "*Sì*, but only for the season. I am

looking to buy this hotel for a group of investors. I am getting all the inside information about it."

Carlo nodded. "You are doing well, then?"

Gino shrugged. "Not bad." And then he grinned and they both laughed as if there were some private joke.

"I have a cottage here." Gino pointed to the green hillsides above them. "You must come and see it. Are you here for a while?"

"A few days," Carlo said. "We docked this morning. You'll have to come aboard and have dinner with us."

"I'm sure Gino has other plans," Anne said pointedly.

"Well then, he will break them."

Gino interrupted, "I work until eleven."

"Then you may join us later."

"Carlo," Anne pleaded. God, he was dense!

"Yes, my darling," he said, putting his arm around her, showing her off to his friend and rival, who stared at him with envy.

"Carlo," she said, "I believe that Elena might be uncomfortable! Excuse me," she said, turning to Gino, who was boring a hole through her. "But Elena told me you two were not on the best of terms."

He threw back his head and laughed. "Elena has already invited me," he said, pulling out of his pocket a note on Elena's personal stationery and putting it back again.

"You see," Carlo said to her, "you don't have to worry, everything is fine."

But Anne was furious. After all Elena had said, how could she? Everything was not fine, not fine at all! She studied Gino again, uncomfortable that she'd been protective of someone who didn't want protection. What was it about this man that made him an intimate in everyone's life?

CHAPTER 26

The situation that she feared did not materialize. In fact, everyone was so cordial she began to doubt that Gino was as bad as she'd imagined. He came on board that night and then dined on deck, superb pâté, freshly caught loup in herb-butter sauce, and raspberry soufflé. Elena had enticed a sous-chef from La Réserve de Beaulieu. Because of what Anne knew about Gino's economic situation, she was aware of how the extreme display of wealth might affect him and, ironically, how comfortable she felt in it. And yet he was accepted in their midst as an honored guest.

The evening was pleasant, orchestrated by Elena who covered her nervousness well. Anne wondered if at any moment someone might denounce Gino, but after a while it became apparent to her that no one was going to embarrass him. Besides, Gino was ignoring her and concentrating all his attention on Elena and Triana. At first she was merely surprised, and then she became annoyed. He had certainly been interested when she met him. What could have changed his mind? Did he really prefer them to her? But even as he ignored her she took his behavior as a kind of game; his glance, however brief, and his presence at the table disturbed her. That night when she and Carlo made love, she thought about Gino. That had never happened before, and though her conscience bothered her, the sex had never been better. She must tell Carlo what she knew about Gino, putting him out of her reach. But something prevented her. She remembered Carlo's words, "If I knew who supplied my mother with drugs, I would kill him!" I'll stay away from Gino, she promised herself, just forget about him.

But the next day, wherever she went she saw him. He was having coffee at the dock when she arrived for morning shopping, he was at the tailor when she went for a fitting on her new silk outfit, and he was in La Gritta when she stopped for lunch. Each time he nodded, coolly appraising her, staying back, waiting for an opening which she would not give. She began to look for him, with excitement. Her heart thumped when she found him. She kept reminding herself of his past, yet she was intensely drawn to him.

Elena noticed Anne's growing attraction and watched it with apprehension. Gino was stalking her, surely and deliberately. How well she knew his ways. But playing with fire could be deadly. She had told that to Anne. But Anne wasn't heeding her. Elena couldn't blame Anne. She too was drawn against her will. It was an extremely delicate situation and it required a lot of thinking. There were her own feelings for Anne, and her need to protect Carlo. Then there was her fascination with Gino, and her craving for all he could give her—physical and otherwise.

Philippe de Marcos's new villa came furnished. Those who were tired of the sea were invited to stay with him. Everyone accepted.

Anne waited apprehensively—and fruitlessly—for another encounter with Gino. She lay in the sun and did her exercises while her anticipation grew with every hour. But in three days at the villa she hadn't seen him once. Carlo was more solicitous than ever, though he was busy with the sheikh of Bhitamin, who had grown kittenish over his purchase of a yacht, and couldn't spend much time with her. Actually, she preferred to be alone right now to think about Gino.

The sheikh was a short, fat man with a soft pudgy face and jet-black hair, and he demanded Carlo's presence at breakfast meetings, cocktails, and for various inspections of the *Brisson*. Carlo had decided, under pressure from Elena, to take the sheikh and his entourage—eight wives, his eldest son, a boy of eighteen, and his personal adviser, Hassan—out on the *Brisson* for a few days. He had not yet consummated a sale and one didn't get an Arab client every day.

Anne was looking forward to Carlo's departure. Her passion for him had cooled, now that Gino had come on the scene, but she felt deeply tender toward him since he had awakened in her long-quiescent sexual feelings.

She ought to feel guilty. She told herself over and over that she was being dishonest with him by not telling him how she felt. She hated to hurt him, but she believed that Gino was avoiding her because of Carlo. As soon as Carlo was gone she would see what would happen. She stood on the balcony of the villa watching the ship depart until it was a small speck on the water. She knew Carlo would be watching her with his telescope.

The gorgeous group, as Anne thought of them, were all assembled for dinner at the Hotel Splendido. They had the corner table, while behind them the bay of Portofino, unobstructed by any pillars or serving carts, glistened in the moonlight. The dining patio was covered by a flowering arbor whose blossoms glowed in the candlelight. Paolo Brisson was on Elena's right and Philippe de Marcos on her left, followed by Anne and Madame Brisson. Across from Anne sat Triana and Norm Martinson.

Elena was in one of her moods. No one could touch her. She was gay and brittlely charming. She wore a gown plunging to the waist, caught there by an enormous diamond, and she regaled them with gossip about the sex life of the jet set.

When Elena finally ran out of anecdotes and energy, the company broke up into smaller groups. Norm and Triana got up to dance. Across the dance floor Anne noticed Gino ask the waiter a question, then walk directly toward her. He came forward and asked her to dance, but she felt it was too soon to try herself with him. "No thank you," she said. But Elena insisted.

"Go on darling. I shall love watching you."

Anne was amazed by this complete turnabout. But Gino didn't wait for her answer. He pulled back her chair and took her elbow. She wanted to touch him, but dared not. They began to dance. He danced smoothly, expertly, catching her waist now and then with a practiced move that brought her to him and out at exactly the right moment. They danced together, yet they were apart. He was good.

They continued to dance—the beginners' ritual, feelers extended to sensitive receptors. His eyes, green-flecked and gold-shine, drew her when his hands did not. What could possibly be so different about him, she wondered, as she turned away in her dance, but when she looked again, she felt it. He was different!

Elena watched them on the floor until she couldn't bear it any longer. Their attraction to each other was magnetic. It was obvious to anyone who looked.

The pace of the music changed. Gino drew her to him and this time she didn't resist.

"You are amazing," she said, more amazed at her own reaction than at him. He was so sure of himself.

"I've been told that."

"That wasn't a compliment. I'm not going to let you get to Elena again. I'll go to Carlo first."

"Then why haven't you already?"

Damn him, she thought. "You don't care if I tell Carlo, do you?"

"Tell him what?" His hair curled at the temples. Crazy what you notice at times like these, she thought.

"Where is Carlo?" he asked with mock innocence.

She stopped dancing in the middle of the song and stared at him; a chill of fear coursed up her back as she understood this threat. He did not react as other people did, he was indifferent to the give-and-take, the love and pain. As if to underscore her thoughts he put his finger on his tongue, wetting it, and ran it across her lips. Her mouth watered in response. Without taking his eyes from hers he returned his finger to his mouth and sucked on it.

The music came to a stop and he pulled her across the floor, out onto the terrace and adjacent to the dining area. The yachts, white and sleek, toylike, bobbed on the water while the scent of night jasmine and warm breezes engulfed her. They circled the terrace while she waited for his move—curious to see what it would be. There were two glasses of champagne awaiting them on the balustrade. He must have ordered them before. She was flattered. He handed her a glass and she sipped the champagne, avoiding him.

He brushed her shoulder with his finger. "You don't like me, do you?"

She turned to study him. She would be honest. "I'm afraid of you."

"I'm going to take you away from Carlo." His voice was deep velvet.

"Carlo doesn't have me."

"He wants to marry you."

She was surprised. "How do you know that?"

He shrugged. "I know the signs. Besides, he told Elena. But you are not going to marry Carlo, you are going away with me."

His eyes drew her and she felt that deep inside she was melting. "I would definitely not do that!" she said, almost to herself. "Though I don't know what I want to do. I know, though, that I'm not going to marry Carlo." The champagne had an un-usual flavor.

"Carlo would make a wonderful husband. But not as exciting a companion as I."

She had heard of his excitements and seen their results. "I'll pass." She finished her champagne. "Is there any more of this?" She looked around for the bottle.

"One glass is enough," he said. "Unless you want mine." He offered it too eagerly. His was still full.

"No thank you."

"Have you ever taken any drugs?"

"No!" she said. "Unless you count grass. I've tried it twice."

"You're in for a treat, then."

"Unlikely," she said, tossing her head, which suddenly felt very light. His expression was strange, watchful, and his smile seemed to grow wider as she looked at him, wider and wider until it blotted out everything. She had never been in danger before, but she felt it now.

He leaned forward to kiss her—warm sureness, delicate explorations.

She pulled away from him before he could draw her in, and shook her head again to clear it, but it wouldn't clear! He ran his fingers down her back; his touch was intoxicating. She put out her hand to stop him, but they touched instead. Her finger-tips tingled, her feet felt the solid ground beneath them often. What's wrong? she wondered. She felt as if she were expanding and diminishing at the same time.

He turned her toward the moonlight, washing her face in light, his in reflected glow, and he traced her cheek with his hands, tendons wired out of flesh.

"I should be getting back." She felt very tired, but she didn't leave.

"No one will miss you. Elena knows you're with me." Something twisted inside of her. Oh Carlo! I should not betray you. Was this what Jeffrey had felt when she waited for him, trusted him? How can I be standing here? she thought. But she simply couldn't move.

"What is wrong with me?" she asked. "Is something wrong?"

He reached into his pocket and drew out a small gold case filled with white powder. He put some to his nose and sniffed it while she stared in fascinated horror. He offered it to her and she shook her head, trying to remain calm. He dipped his finger again and placed it under her nose. She wanted to push him away, but she couldn't. His eyes held her, challenged her, gleaming in the moonlight while hers pleaded with him. Every instinct told her no! She turned her head away with great effort. She had told him she didn't take drugs.

He put the white powder and the gold case away. "It's all right. You won't need any more of this after the champagne I gave you. Are you ready?" he asked.

"I don't know," she answered, as they began to move across the terrace. She felt flushed and dizzy as he took her hand and led her to a side path through the pine and oak. It was darker there than in the moonlight and she couldn't see her conscience. Soft night sounds that would have frightened her were gentle now, new friends to guide her, darkness covering reality. He led her down a path, across another patio cut out of the hillside several tiers below the restaurant. At the end of the patio was a door. The sounds of merriment filtered down through the foliage. Her blood raced in her body. She did not know where she was, but it didn't matter. Her resistance had been put to rest long ago, along with the dregs of the champagne.

"Guest quarters," he mumbled, and held the door open for her. But she hung back, feeling that the door did not open into a room but to another door and yet another door, stretching out into an endless passage. Going where? She watched in fascination as each one opened, hoping it would reveal its secret to her. He stood at the door watching her and still she didn't move. He touched her, gentle hands now, and began to undress her. She felt him unpeeling her as skin from the fruit. Delicious nectar oozed out of her as the layers gave way.

Finally he broke the silence. "Let yourself feel it all, Anne. Let go. This is your initiation. This is

360

where we christen your new parts. You've had just enough to help you. My own blend."

She felt too dreamy to be afraid as she floated beside him. "Hold onto my arm so I don't float away," she said. And he did, leading her into the villa, a small cottage with high ceilings and marble floors. Did he carry her, she wondered, or had she floated to the four-poster bed? She lay there looking at herself in mirrors that were everywhere, saw her thickened rosebud. He came to her, kissing her wrists and ankles. She felt them being encircled and banded, but she didn't resist. Slowly the cords attached to the cuffs on her wrists and ankles tightened, pulling apart her limbs so that she lay there spread-eagled, her openings exposed. She wasn't afraid when he made love to her, though he did it for himself—touching her, using her, exciting her for his enjoyment only. An exotic butterfly on a red velvet mounting, only she was pinned to a four-poster bed, a captive, and a not-quite-unwilling one.

Now he touched her for herself, rubbing her all over with lotions that stung her flesh, tearing at it until it was raw. When she realized that he was clawing her and biting her nipples until they were burning with pain she screamed for him to stop. He struck her, hard, across the mouth, and when she shrieked with the pain he struck her again. Desperately she tried to pull her arms and legs free from their bonds. But the more she pulled the tighter the ropes became.

Despite the pain and degradation she longed to have him inside her and when she thrust up to him, begging him to enter her he cracked his hand across her face again and again.

He sucked her toes and thighs and vagina and for every sound she uttered she was rewarded with a blow. Still she cried and screamed for more until her screams became groans of pleasure and she was nearly there. When she finally quieted down he entered her, hard, strong, and cruel, carrying her to peaks of ecstasy she'd never scaled before.

CHAPTER 27

She awoke in her own room at the villa and thought it had been a nightmare. But her body ached and her wrists and ankles were brusied where she had pulled at the cuffs that bound her to his bed. There were large red marks on her body and legs and clusters of broken blood vessels here and there. She wasn't certain of what had happened, but the memories were incredible and horrifying. She sat up slowly, her head hurt more than the rest of her. She could hardly face herself. Carefully she walked to the mirror. Her makeup was smeared and her lip was swollen and blue where she had bitten it. She stared in the mirror and wept, a victim forced to look at her own de-filement. For all her beauty she was ugly. Not just the bruises and the used expression, but her own contribution to it clouded her face. He had not stopped all night, brutalizer and victim. He had opened her up. Every time she thought it was ended he began again, slowly, knowingly. In spite of herself, her fear, her rage, her terror, he knew how to do it all, exactly what would turn her on. And then when he felt her wet and ready he would hit her again, filling her inside with his hands, holding a tender steady pressure in her va-gina and slapping her body with exquisite torture, eliciting responses she longed to deny. How did it happen? she accused herself. How can I explain it? I knew he was a drug dealer, I should never have drunk that champagne. Her guilt for being where he could reach her lay heavy over her body, impairing her will, sickening her with its odor.

He was a monster! He had known exactly what weakness to arouse, exactly what would induce her reaction, especially in a novice to drugs. In a way she was more frightened now than she had been during his attack, because the drug had dulled a certain amount of her fear. Tied to his bed, she had thought she was in a state of terror, but now, the reality was worse than the altered consciousness. That any chemical could change her so, take away her control, transform her more drastically than any other change she'd ever encountered was terrifying.

Part of her was afraid that it was her own creation, that he had known what to do because she showed him, overtly or subtly, that she could be punished, her greatest pleasure, her deepest fear. But he couldn't know that. He had only assumed that whatever it was he wanted, she would comply. Most women did, he told her, especially beautiful women, somehow they never believed they were beautiful. And there was a part of her that still didn't believe it either.

She was furious at herself for that, and shaken to the depths of her beliefs. *I should have told Carlo about him before, and now it's too late!*

Elena called her on the intercom. "Darling, are you all right? We were so worried. When Gino brought you back to us nearly unconscious, I was frantic. He said you fell on the path and hit your face and that it knocked you unconscious. Is that what happened?" She could hear Elena's cat voice coming through. *Gino would not have had such a clear field without her help. The bitch!*

"I had too much to drink, Elena. I have a terrible headache."

"You must see a doctor!"

"No, I'll be all right. Let me rest today."

". . . well. If you don't feel better, you must tell me!" She sounded almost cheerful.

"I will."

"*Ciao.*"

Anne stared at the ceiling as despair swept her into its depths. She wanted to understand, but nothing was clear. The desire to do forbidden things had always been there, waiting, lurking; and it had finally been unleashed by the drug. Now she was afraid she couldn't control that desire. She envisioned Gino and Elena and herself in a *ménage à trois* and the fantasy excited her, but it upset her so to be excited by it that she cried out. Her imagination was evil! This time on Jeff's exam table it was she and her partner, who changed from Carlo to Gino to Elena. The scenes unfolded in her mind more graphic and explicit than she had ever thought possible. The difference between fantasy and experience eluded her. To think was to do, no shades of variation, no choice of refusal, excitement struggling with guilt. She'd uncovered a dark aspect she feared was there and avoided until now. Would she ever be able to have a normal relationship again, after this? Was she addicted? Oh, please no! she prayed, feeling again that helplessness of being tied and used, as if her will had been permanently subdued as well as her body. God, what a horrible thing he had done to her! How would he feel if anyone had done that to him?

She needed help, someone to advise her, to listen to her, but where to turn? She wanted Alessandro right now, with her entire being she wanted him. He would have understood, championed her, explained her to herself. But Alessandro had rejected her. Where could she turn? To Brenda! But Brenda was in Rome ecstatically happy, according to her latest letter. Now she understood why Elena had been so terrified of seeing Gino, and why she had courted him. Anne too recognized his pull, there weren't many people who could violate with such expertise. If she ever saw Gino again she didn't know what she would do. At this moment she wanted to kill him!

There was nowhere she could turn for counsel. No one she could ask for advice who would not judge her. Carlo loved her! If he were here he might understand, but that would mean revealing to him how she'd been abused, and informing on Gino as his mother's supplier. Carlo would not be able to contain himself, and then he would be in trouble. And what if Carlo didn't believe that Gino had drugged her. She saw the way they were together—their male understanding. Gino could lie and Carlo would end up blaming her! What then? Should she talk to Elena? Elena would hardly be impartial. Anne couldn't stand the thought of Elena's collusion. Had he done this to Elena too? Poor Elena! To think she might have let him. At least she, herself, had been drugged!

This was a world Anne had never seen before. A vile, disgusting world, a depravity of the senses, she might never be the same again. What right did Gino have to show it to her. What right? She wanted to destroy the maleness of him that did this. It was beyond chauvinism, it was bestial.

Finally she placed a call to Rome, but Brenda was not at work. When she reached her at home, she realized that she couldn't explain about last night over the phone. The moment she heard Brenda's voice she broke down. The connection was bad; they could barely hear each other.

"Where are you?" Brenda shouted.

"In Portofino."

"What's wrong? Are you crying?"

"Yes, I'm crying," she answered, trying to control herself. What could she say, I was drugged and defiled?

"What's happened? What is it?"

"I'm all right. I can't talk about it on the phone. I'll write you a letter."

"Did anything happen with Carlo?"

Anne calmed down a little. "No, he's all right. It's about someone I met named Gino." She stopped. "I'm sorry to call you like this."

"How long will you be in Portofino?" Brenda asked.

"I don't know. A few days, maybe."

"We're going to be there in five days."

"Here? Really?"

"Yes, Frederico has business there."

"Oh, Brenda, I need to talk to you, but five whole days is such a long time."

"We'll be able to talk when I see you. Can you wait for me?"

Anne was about to reply when the connection was broken. There was no use calling back. What else could she say under the circumstances? Brenda was too far away to help her. She was afraid that in five days it would be too late, this mood of despair would overcome her by then, or her need for revenge would. Neither possibility thrilled her. She needed something else to occupy her. But her life had become meaningless without a purpose to motivate her. She had reached her goals and they were empty victories. She was beautiful, cushioned in luxury, with no purpose beyond hedonistic pastimes. Even Carlo had an occupation, if only to sell yachts. He had a job, something that interested him. Look at what Elena had become without a purpose in her life other than frivolity and dissipation. She was frightened at how this would all end. If only her career hadn't failed, ruined before it began. She started to cry again, tears born of exhaustion, and then she laughed as she cried, realizing how hard she had worked, what she had gone through to get to this place, this bottom of the pit. What a sad commentary on improvement. Where had it all gone wrong?

She remembered Gino's voice, his murmurings of comfort as she lay in the aftermath of his passion, how he had used it to arouse, endearing noises she hungered for were fuel for his flames. Even the memory hypnotized her, his tone remembered, his promises, "That's all, my little bird, my feather," but it was never all. Until *he* was through!

Suddenly all her guilt was gone! Her will burst through, resurrected like a banner whipping away all the self-pity and self-blame. How dare he! She saw his grinning face and clenched her fists to keep from attacking his image. She hadn't felt this much hatred since Jeffrey. And she was a different person now! The last vestige of the old Anne had been exorcised last night! Now she was someone who could plan an attack!

"I'm going to get even with you, you bastard!" she said, to the walls of her room, to the victims of the world, to the gods! And even the sound of his laughter in her head didn't deter her. Revenge from a willing victim? he mocked.

Yes, she vowed. Damn you, yes!

Brenda was worried about Anne. She'd sounded terrible on the phone. Though it was nearly impossible to hear her, still the desperation came through loud and clear.

She heard Frederico's key in the door. He was carrying a huge bouquet of red roses.

She was touched. "No one's ever given me roses before!" She could smell the cigar smoke of his afternoon meeting, as she clung to him, feeling his body against hers. They would have an hour, perhaps two, to devour each other hungrily before he would have to leave. The brevity of their meetings only enhanced their quality. But she was willing to bet that she'd adore him just as much if he were all hers.

"What did Anne want?" he asked, sinking into the sofa and beckoning to her to come and sit beside him.

"Just a minute," she said, going into the kitchen for a vase. She settled for a litre wine container. "How did you know she phoned?"

"She called the bank first, looking for you. I was surprised because I'd spoken to Alessandro earlier today. He called from Paris."

Brenda came back with the flowers and set them on the table. "Anne sounded terrible. She was crying and I don't know why. The connection was awful. She's in Portofino now; she said she might still be there when we arrive. Wouldn't that be wonderful!" She sat beside him and he put his arm around her.

"Everything with you is wonderful!" he laughed.

"I'm worried about her, Frederico. She's usually so calm, even in the roughest times."

"Then she should be quite amenable to our good news from Alessandro. Would you like to go on ahead, and break it to her yourself?"

"And miss the chance to travel with you? I see you little enough as it is. Besides, Alessandro should be the one to tell her."

"Then we shall have to wait and see how she is later."

She snuggled closer to him. "Unless you can get away sooner. It will give us more time to be together."

He hugged her. "I'll see what I can do. You know, things couldn't be working out any better for Alessandro."

Yes, and for Anne, she thought, but not for me. For as soon as they made love he would leave her alone again, until the next time. And even a week with him all to herself in Portofino would not supply enough memories to fill the emptiness if he ever found it too painful or too difficult to continue their affair. Perhaps I will be the one to end it, she thought as his hands sought her breasts. Oh God, she realized, that could never happen!

Anne stayed in her room until noon the following day, and then after a swim she joined the group having lunch on the veranda. She was totally preoccupied with her thoughts about Gino, but the way to revenge eluded her. Turning him in was too easy and she really couldn't prove he was dealing. She had to wait to see what would happen. She'd work out a plan.

"I see you've really *met* Gino," Elena remarked. All of Anne's carefully applied makeup could not cover certain bruises. Elena's voice sounded shrill and loud, drawing attention to herself instead of to Anne. "I tried to tell you he wasn't nice! What will Carlo say?"

"Nobody could have told me, Elena," Anne replied. "You were right."

Elena was inwardly seething. She knew exactly what Anne meant. She ran her hands nervously over her arms, feeling her skin dry and hot. "I should have put on some body lotion," she said.

"You just did," Triana commented. "Have a glass of wine." She passed the carafe to Elena, who reached for it with a shaking hand, spilling some of it on Paolo, who sat next to her.

"Watch out!" Paolo shouted.

Elena slammed the bottle down on the table, rattling the china and spilling out some of the wine. "Don't shout at me," she said, tears running quickly down her face.

Anne had never seen her like this in public. Elena was always extraordinarily composed. "Are you all right, Elena?" she asked.

"Of course I am," she said, pulling herself together quickly, avoiding Anne's eyes.

She's still involved, Anne thought. She's still involved with that bastard, just as I am. She loathes him and fears him, just as I do, but she's caught, tied to him in a bond of depravity. And she's jealous of me. Insanely jealous. Anne watched her, feeling superior for the moment, since she felt free of Gino.

Elena got up from the table. "I'm just going inside to tidy up," she said, winking at Anne, an artificial smile stretched across her face.

Elena's calm was an act. The command that she had exhibited for the past few days was gone, and she was more troubled than ever. Gino's presence was having a terrible effect on her. He had a terrible effect on everyone.

Anne had never seen Elena in such an explosive state; she wouldn't be able to hold out against Gino much longer.

After a quarter of an hour, when Elena did not reappear, Anne left the group with a casual excuse and went to check on her. She knocked softly on the door of her room, but there was no response, and so she opened the door. The shutters were closed and Elena was lying on the bed, apparently asleep. Odd, she thought, to fall asleep so quickly after such a state of agitation. As she approached the bed she saw a hypodermic needle on the side table.

"Oh God, Elena, no!" she cried. But Elena was beyond hearing. She turned her head toward Anne. "Don't be hard on me, darling." She slurred her words. "I can stop anytime. It's only for a little while."

Anne grabbed the needle, breaking its point and tossing it into the ashtray nearby. "Why, Elena? You've been clean so long. Why did you do this to yourself?"

"Why did you?" Elena asked.

"I didn't do it, he did!"

"That's what I mean, darling. He does it all!"

Anne stood over her friend. That bastard Gino! She knelt beside the bed and took the delicate shoulders in her hands. "How long have you been shooting, Elena? How much are you taking?"

"Don't ruin it for me, Anne," she begged. "I love you so much."

Anne let go of her and she fell back on the bed. It had all been useless! All her efforts, all her caring, and still the worst had happened. Elena was hooked again. Death was too permanent to court like this, too easily gotten when you least expected it. Elena should have been better protected. She should have told Carlo. It was *her* fault. She shuddered as she was struck with her own guilt. She wanted to weep for the wasted hours, but at the same time she knew the one really at fault was Gino. She'd repay him for all he'd done. And now she knew how she would do it.

She went into Elena's bathroom and opened the medicine chest. There was a shelf full of pills, worth a fortune on the streets. She took three one-hundred-milligram Seconals and slipped them into her pocket. "Reds," Elena called them, "zonkers." Now she had to make sure that Gino would join them for dinner. Just the thought of seeing him again gave her a sick feeling inside. She wrote him a personal invitation:

> Please join me for dinner at Batis, and bring your champagne.
>
> A.

He wouldn't be able to resist!

CHAPTER 28

Carlo was bored and irritated. In his opinion the cruise was a failure. His patience was stretched to the limit by their exhausting protocol. They drank toasts, they ate meal after meal. Each time he tried to sell the features of the yacht someone would whisper, "It is not appropriate now," "The sheikh is not favorably inclined to discuss it now," or "Not before the Emir's nap," or not after his nap, or until he's crapped. They doted on his elimination. All they talked about in Arabic was how much roughage he should eat. His personal physician traveled with him, checking his diet, doling out his medicines. The sheikh's son had stayed in port with the wives. Only his personal aide Hassan and two bodyguards accompanied him.

The sheikh was actually impressed with the ship, but it was not his custom to be effusive. But on the afternoon of the third day out they hit rough water and by nightfall the protocol and digestion became secondary to *mal de mer*. The entire Arabian contingent went to their rooms.

Hassan appeared at Carlo's door. "How far from land are we, Signore Brisson?"

"We are traveling in a wide circle. Land's about twelve hours to port."

"I bring you a message from his Excellency. The sheikh is very ill. I myself am quite sick. The Emir wants you to know that he will buy two Brisson yachts if you can get us to land before morning." Hassan was pale.

Carlo went to the intercom and ordered the captain to return to port. Suddenly Hassan's eyes grew wide. Carlo recognized the look. Poor fellow, he thought. All the color drained from the man's face and he vomited all over himself. But before Hassan could apologize, another wave of nausea had hit him and he bolted across the hall to his stateroom, barely making it to the bathroom before Carlo heard him again.

Carlo called for a crew member to clean up the mess and went to assist Hassan. Hassan was draped over the head, retching violently. In spite of its excellent stabilizers the *Brisson* continued to rock in the choppy waters. Carlo helped Hassan to remove his outer clothing and went to find him something to put on. Hassan kept his face averted in shame.

There was nothing in the bureau drawers so he opened Hassan's suitcase, and took out his robe. The corner of the robe was caught in the bottom of the case. Curiosity aroused, he pulled on it, but it held tightly. The case had a false bottom. He pried it open to remove the robe, and then was struck with horror when he saw what the bottom of the case contained: glassine packets of white powder. Narcotics! And on the *Brisson*! He held one packet up to the light. It was dull and powdery, not crystalline like the cocaine he'd occasionally sniffed. Heroin! Enough to bring death and misery to hundreds of people. Fury propelled him as he grabbed the case and ran toward the door. But Hassan heard him and leaped out of the bathroom, catching him as he reached the staircase, dragging him back. Carlo fell forward holding the case. He couldn't swing it behind him in the narrow passage. Hassan was surprisingly strong after his bout with illness. He tried to drag Carlo back toward the stateroom. Carlo struggled to his feet and jammed his elbow backward, aiming for Hassan's gut, catching him in the chest. Hassan grunted as the air left his lungs, but it didn't stop him. He grabbed Carlo around the neck, catching his free arm and twisting it behind.

Turning him around, he forced him ahead into his room. Hassan kicked the door shut with his foot and pushed Carlo across the bed. Carlo jumped up and rushed at him. "You fucking bastard, you can't use my ship for your filthy dealings."

Hassan struck him across the chin, knocking him back on the bed, then he jumped on him and pinned him down. Carlo couldn't get up. Hassan's burly body towered over him, exhaling vomit breath in his face.

"It won't do you any good," Carlo said. "My crew will find me and we'll throw your crap overboard. I'll have you arrested. You and the sheikh, the whole stinking bunch of you."

Hassan placed his forearm across Carlo's throat, pressing against his windpipe as Carlo fought to get up.

"You won't do anything because I'll cut your balls off!" Hassan threatened, pressing harder, closing off all the air. Carlo felt himself panic as his heart pounded for oxygen and Hassan's knee ground into his groin. "I will kill your father and your mother and I will cut the cunt out of your girlfriend."

Hassan let up on his throat. He didn't want to kill him now, not like this. Too many things could go wrong when there was spontaneous violence, but Carlo's unexpected discovery could ruin everything. One thing he knew, he would have to kill Carlo soon, before anything worse happened. If only he didn't feel so sick. A wave of dizziness hit him. He fought to keep his hold. Carlo sensed the change in his muscle tension and rolled quickly to the right, knocking Hassan off balance. The boat pitched to starboard, throwing Hassan to the floor between the bed and the dresser. He tried to get up but Carlo grabbed the Baccarat decanter out of its bedside holder and struck Hassan on the forehead. Hassan grunted as he fell back and sank to the floor, unconscious. Gasping for air, breathing in great gulps, Carlo looked around for something to tie the Arab with, but there was no rope. He took some wire hangers from the closet and unwound them, securing Hassan's hands and feet together behind his back. He taped Hassan's mouth closed with adhesive from the first-aid kit in the bathroom. His head was pounding.

He didn't have much time. Hassan would be sure to arouse the ship when he came to. The sheikh's bodyguards were up front in the crew's quarters. But even seasick they wouldn't be pleasant to deal with. If he alerted the crew, the Emir's guards would be there immediately. They must have their share of the dealings too. It would be too much of a risk.

Carlo knew he had gotten the best of Hassan only by luck. His only hope was the sheikh. Carlo wondered if the sheikh knew about Hassan's drug dealing. He doubted that he did. Why should the Emir dabble in narcotics when his country was so rich in oil. And if Hassan was dealing in drugs without the sheikh's knowledge, then the Emir's sovereignty was being jeopardized. If the shiekh did know, and allowed the ring to operate, still he would not want anyone else to know about it. Hassan was a killer. If Carlo spoke to the Emir, forced his open acknowledgment of the narcotics ring, the Emir would have to censure Hassan to save himself, he might even renounce Hassan rather than admit his complicity. But again, it was always possible that the sheikh did not know anything about it. It was a gamble at best. Carlo thought about his mother, how she'd shot that crap into herself. In that moment he wanted to kill Hassan.

He went to his father's stateroom where the sheikh was quartered. It was also where the weapons were kept. Ever since there had been an increase in hijackings and kidnappings his father had kept guns on board.

Carlo knocked quietly on the door. There was no answer. The boat pitched and he bumped the door jamb. The unlocked door swung open. He stepped into the cabin. The red light on the intercom glowed, indicating that the sheikh's room was being monitored by the control room and the servants. The bodyguards would be there if he made a sound. The sheikh was asleep. An occasional shaft of light broke the darkness as the ship rocked, placing the porthole up to catch the moonlight, tossing it down to face dark water again. He made his way to the compartment hidden in the paneling that housed the guns. The door was electronically operated. He groped in the dark for the switch, deactivating the alarm first. He pushed the alarm button and waited for the electronic door to open. But nothing happened. The damn thing had always given them trouble! Sweat dripped down his forehead. He wiped his hands on his trousers. Silently he cursed the electronics experts, the damp sea air, the inventor of electricity. The sheikh moaned in his sleep. Carlo held his breath. He pressed the button once more. Suddenly the contacts met and the door slid open. The niche was small, but big enough to hold two revolvers. One was loaded, the other wasn't. He slid the loaded gun into his pocket.

He walked to the bed, hesitating for a moment. The sheikh would not like to be awakened, nor would he understand immediately what Carlo wanted from him. Morning would have been a better time to do this, but he couldn't wait until morning. Hassan might regain consciousness any moment.

He turned on the light. The sheikh was startled and then instantly awake. He glared at Carlo.

"What are you doing here?" he demanded.

"Forgive me, your Excellency," he began, when suddenly the door flew open and Hassan stood there holding a knife. The large welt on his forehead stood out red and ugly. Hassan raised his arm and threw the knife, just as Carlo ducked and fired at him. Carlo felt something slice through the top of his left shoulder. Hassan sank to the floor with a moan.

The Emir had rolled out of bed and was crouched behind it. He screamed. "Stop! Are you mad! Litan, Haddi!" The two bodyguards were already at the door.

Carlo stood up, pointing the revolver at the Emir. "Don't come any closer or I'll kill him."

The Emir was shaking with fear. A pool of blood spread out in front of Hassan. Litan and Haddi stood in the doorway, waiting for the moment when they could overpower Carlo.

Carlo's shoulder was cut, he could feel the blood dripping down his arm to his hand, but he felt no pain.

"Emir, listen to me! Hassan is carrying a suitcase full of heroin. If you will send someone to his room you will find it there. He threatened to kill me if I told you about it. I came to tell you anyway; that is why I was in your room. I do not want to hurt you!"

The Emir heard the sincerity in his voice and looked over the top of the bed at him. "Do you plan to fire that thing again?"

"Only if your men attack me."

The Emir motioned them to back off. Several crew members hovered in the background. Carlo's shoulder gave its first throb. He lowered his arm and sat on the bed. Haddi bent down to see about Hassan.

"He's still alive."

Litan left the room while they waited, and in a moment returned with the suitcase of narcotics. The Emir stood up to his full five feet three inches, his eyes flashing at the sight. He pulled his nightshirt around him, dignified in spite of the overwhelming events. He spoke carefully, choosing his words. "I warned Hassan not to do this. He was like a son to me. I am glad that my own boy is not here to witness the disgrace of his father by one he trusted."

Carlo sighed with relief. He had been right. "Your Excellency, I will notify the authorities to meet us on our arrival in Portofino. I don't think you'll have any difficulties."

"No, signore, your government and I understand each other."

The two bodyguards carried Hassan to his room. Carlo's legs were so weak they could hardly support him. "I have never shot anyone before in my life," he said.

"If it is Allah's will, you never shall again."

Carlo turned to go.

"You said you thought I'd have no difficulties when we arrive in port."

Carlo turned back and nodded. "Yes, Excellency."

"And I agree with you. But I suspect you may be the one with difficulties when we arrive in Portofino."

Carlo looked at the sheikh in surprise. "Your Excellency, what makes you say such a thing?"

"There is something you should know. Hassan sells his drugs to your friend, Gino Belmonte."

The 7:40 Alitalia flight from Rome arrived in Genoa at 9:20 P.M. with Frederico Segri of the Banco Moderna Italia accompanied by his assistant and dearest love, Ms. Brenda Greenstein. The plane circled south over the Mediterranean and turned north to land on runway 110. Below, the sea was gray in the twilight.

Frederico was like a child at the circus. He was new to the games of love, but he played them with enthusiasm.

"Wait until you see Portofino," he said. "It sits like an emerald above a sea of sapphires. It is quaint and seductive, and has a charm like no other resort."

"I hope you speak of me in such glowing terms," she said.

Frederico had never felt so relaxed. The worries that plagued him about doing business with the Arabs and Emir of Bhitamin were over. He had come to terms with his conscience and found his justifications.

The car and driver were waiting for them at the baggage claim. He loaded their luggage into the Mercedes.

"There are wonderful restaurants in Genoa. Where would you like to go?"

"If you don't mind, Frederico, I'd like to drive straight on to Portofino. You didn't leave Rome

385

five days early to take me to Genoa. I'm really aw-fully worried about Anne."

"Of course, my dear. I wasn't thinking." He reached over and gave her a light kiss, then nodded to the driver and they began the hour-and-a-half drive that would take them both to Anne.

Carlo sat quietly while Dr. Mhitafi sutured his shoulder, but every thrust of the ship's engines met a like pounding of his heart. As if his will were urging the ship onward. The knife had only cut him superficially. He welcomed the pain, each throb made the ache inside more bearable, a reality.

The doctor was a gentle man; sewing battle wounds was distasteful to him. These foolish young men, he thought, so full of the fires of life. Hassan lay in the other room with a bullet in his side and the doctor didn't have the equipment to help him other than to relieve his pain. Praise Allah, they would be in port soon. He sighed. Caring for the Emir was more to his liking than this. He put in the last suture, and bandaged Carlo's shoulder.

"Do you want a sling?"

Carlo shook his head. He needed the use of his hands, both of them. He flexed his fingers; the smallest motion sent a shooting flame up and down his left arm. He would ignore it. He would not be aware of any pain when the time came.

CHAPTER 29

She dressed for the occasion carefully, excitedly. It was only fitting that she wear one of her own designs, a clinging white dress tied at the waist with rows of silver and gold chains. It would give her courage. If she only had the nerve to carry it off.

They walked to Batis from the villa, and she kept her arm through Elena's, reminding herself why she was doing this. It wasn't hard to remember. Elena seemed surprisingly subdued.

They were given a patio table, Paolo, Philippe, Triana, Norm, and Elena. And Anne remained calmest of them all, until Gino arrived, looking pleased with himself. He took the chair next to her and she broke out in a sweat from nervousness. Just the sight of him was more than she could stand. Her tongue stuck to the roof of her mouth and her stomach flirted with nausea.

It wasn't difficult to drop the capsule into Gino's wineglass when he wasn't looking. In fact, she was shocked at how simple it all was. She had thought at first that she'd bribe a waiter, but that would be taking an even greater chance. Gino was very well known around Portofino now.

All during dinner she watched anxiously while Gino ate and drank, trying to concentrate on her plan and not on him. She hoped she had given him a proper dose—enough but not too much. She didn't want him to pass out here. She saw to it that he kept his wineglass full.

Gino was quiet during dinner, avoiding Elena's glances. She was becoming troublesome, playing the same games and pulling the same tricks she had before. He was furious with Hassan for leaving Portofino with the sheikh before making a delivery to him. Hassan would be back tomorrow, but every delay cost him money, lost him confidence. Norm Martinson noticed the interplay between Elena and Gino and tried to act as if he saw nothing, interesting himself in the genealogy of the former owners of Philippe's new villa. Carlo and the sheikh were expected back the next afternoon. Gino ignored Anne. She was beginning to bore him.

Elena turned to Anne, noticing that she was very cool, very composed. "Darling, you're so morose. Do you miss my Carlino so much?"

Anne shot her daggers. "Portofino is a bore, Elena. I can't wait to get out of here!" Elena flinched. Gino didn't budge.

"I never thought I'd hear sour grapes from you, Anne," Triana smirked, assuming that Anne's pique resulted from Elena's recent escapades. Secrets were not easily kept in Elena's set. "I see you bought a Franzetti necklace," she remarked.

"Yes, do you like it?"

"It's divine, but I hate the choker."

Anne was startled. "But the choker is an integral part of the design."

"Oh, they always tell you that. It would look better on a chain."

Anne glared at Triana. "I had my choice of chains."

"We all do, don't we?" Elena said. "But I like the choker, darling, it's so forceful. It suits you."

"Oh Christ, Elena!" They were stifling her with their innuendos, as if to say, We know where you've been, you bad girl. . . . Wouldn't they be amazed if they knew?

Gino's head began to droop. At first he was surprised, and tried to catch Elena's eye. He suspected he'd been drugged. This was one of Elena's tricks. As carefully as possible he excused himself from dinner. He'd be damned if he'd stay and let her laugh at him. Anne sat for a while after he left, waiting until the right moment to leave, concerned with appearances. Then, as inconspicuously as she could, she excused herself and left the restaurant. She turned toward the hills. She took her time, wanting to be certain that the pills had taken effect.

All the lights were on in the cottage. Gino was sprawled on his bed, more drunk than drugged. His body was a dead weight to move into position. It took her quite a while to undress him even though she hurried. Touching him was repulsive to her, but she forced herself to go on. Every time he flinched she was afraid he'd awaken and grab her. How often he must have done this to other people. How easy it must have been for him. She located the cuffs wound around the bedposts and untangled them. They were made with spring clamps that snapped on easily. Carefully she attached them to his hands and feet. When she closed the fourth cuff around him and wound up the cords to tighten his limbs she began to relax a little. She experimented with the crank, learning how many turns it took to tighten it and loosen it. It was a clever device, with locks in several positions. She watched her sleeping captive, her grown puppet who would willingly move his arms and legs for her. She anticipated when his part would grow. She sat down in a chair to watch him, waiting for the drug to wear off. What if I can't do it, she thought, but when she faltered, visions of

Elena kept her going. Besides, it was heady to be on top.

Moonlight shone in squares through the paned windows. He seemed as an offering to her, quite the opposite of the way it had been when she was fettered for him to use.

His sleep seemed to be more normal and he tried to turn on his side. She loosened the ties so that he could move, still keeping a watchful eye. Her excitement mounted and after an hour more she decided it was time to begin; she couldn't wait any longer. She tightened the shackles and turned on the lamp.

"Gino!" She shook him. "Wake up!"

He opened his eyes blearily, smarting from the light. He looked around, trying to acclimate himself, then with growing comprehension he saw himself in the mirrors, spread-eagled on the bed, a lion in dormant repose, breathing growls before the attack.

Slowly she touched him, curious to see what he would do, her heart pounding in anticipation. He tested each cuff. He knew this apparatus and how much it would give when the locks were in place. She had left him no room.

He began to twist and pull at the cuffs, and then he roared.

A small globule of spit hit her on her breast. She removed it and wiped it on him, any apprehension she might have felt totally gone. She knew what was coming next. She had been there.

"If you urinate, you'll lie in it," she said.

He roared at her again. "I'll kill you."

"Such a poor sport," she said sweetly.

"You ugly bitch," he growled. "You disgusting cunt." She hit him with a belt and as his fury grew she hit him again. She loved it, she absolutely loved it.

"I'll get you!" he yelled, pulling and twisting away from her. "I'll cut you to pieces. I'll pop those lead balloons of yours and dissect them under your nose."

She let him rave, touching his penis with her lips, twisting his nipple between her fingers. When the belt wasn't enough she slapped him, over and over, though it probably hurt her hands as much as it hurt him.

"You can't do it. You're too weak. You're good for nothing but a skewer up your ass."

She closed her teeth around his penis, pressing hard into his flesh.

"No, Anne, no!"

"Take it back, you bastard," she said, lifting her head for a moment and then putting it down between his legs again. He couldn't frighten her, and she thrilled with the knowledge. He was trying to hold back, fighting his excitement.

She danced for him, determined to excite him, standing above him on the bed, touching herself from her knees to her breasts, undulating over his head, squatting just out of his reach. He couldn't help himself and she gloated as she saw him growing erect. Then she hit him hard across the face and slipped down to lap his penis with her mouth, to keep it engorged. She enclosed it with her lips and with each pull of her mouth she slapped him hard, wherever she could, on his belly, butt, chest, and face.

He came fully erect and she sensed a change in him. He wanted her! Moving quickly on top of him, she rocked back and forth, careful not to arouse him enough for climax, as he had done her. She reached hers quickly, a great cry filling her throat. He watched her in fascination. A monster of his own making, matching him move for move.

She slipped off him and squatted there, panting. She felt her triumph as complete. Still, she wanted to smash his face. Damn, it was over too soon.

"I adore you!" he said.

"And I hate you!" she answered, wanting to weep. It wasn't him she hated at this moment, it was herself.

She needed touching right now, needed someone to forgive her for this crazy role she was playing. Still she wanted him to beg.

His face became sly, mistaking her look. "You want it again, don't you? Undo me, *cara, mi amore*."

"You bastard! You're going to lie there until you rot," she said, so filled with her emotions of hate that she didn't hear the creaking of the door behind her or notice the narrowing of his eyes as he glanced into the mirror above.

Suddenly she felt a hand, poking, probing, touching. Another hand reached between her legs and gently played with her clitoris. Her heart leaped to her throat. Had he gotten free? She gasped as she turned and saw Elena. "My God!" she said, trying to pull away.

"Don't stop, my precious," Elena said. "I've been here all this time. Let me help you, please, Anne. Let me," she begged, and moved her hand softly inside.

"Do it, Anne," Gino whispered. "Let me watch you. Please let me watch." His voice was hoarse with excitement. No, she thought, I can't do this, not this, and unsuccessfully tried to free herself from Elena while Gino continued to entreat her. "Let me go!" she cried, but there was no way out. Elena held fast, her grip tightening as Anne struggled to move. Her mind was screaming in protest.

"Let go!" she cried. "Elena, you're hurting me!"

But it was too late. Elena had unhooked Gino's left hand and he grabbed Anne's wrist, pulling her down on top of him. She lost her balance as he forced her mouth on his. She kicked at Elena, her leg hit the bed instead. A dull pain shot through her calf. She moaned into him.

Elena was on the other side of the bed now, releasing his right hand. Anne felt it close around her, holding her in a terrifying embrace.

She was lost now, and she knew it! They would show her no mercy.

CHAPTER 30

The launch from the *Brisson* roared up to the landing and Carlo jumped out. The police boat with Hassan and the sheikh aboard followed close behind. The police had questioned everyone from the *Brisson* and requested that they come in for formal statements in the morning. They had confiscated Carlo's gun, but before he left the yacht he'd had time to get the other gun out of its compartment and load it.

He didn't know what he was going to do about Gino, but his fury was at a high pitch. He had kept himself under control until the moment his foot hit the dock and then the molten rage overflowed. He ran across the deserted square despite the excruciating pain in his shoulder.

It was 2:15 A.M. The night clerk hadn't seen Gino since early evening. He must be at the cottage, Carlo thought, dashing out blindly, nearly colliding with two people who were coming in. He pushed past them.

"Carlo!"

He turned, not wanting to stop.

"It's me, Brenda."

"I am in a hurry." He had no time for her now.

"Wait." She grabbed his arm. "We arrived earlier tonight and I thought you weren't here. The *Brisson* was gone. Where is Anne?"

"I don't know where she is. I've been out on the *Brisson* with clients. We just got back."

"Wasn't she with you?"

"No, she's at the villa, Philippe de Marcos's."

"Is she with Gino?"

"Gino? Gino? How do you know Gino?" he demanded.

"I don't know him. Anne mentioned him to me."

"What did she say?"

Brenda realized she had said too much. She tried to back down, but she was caught.

"I must find him," Carlo said, and then ran out of the lobby. The look on his face was terrifying.

"Frederico! Something's wrong. We've got to

follow him." She ran after Carlo with Frederico close behind her. They headed up into the hills.

As soon as Elena freed Gino's legs from the restraints he wound them around Anne and forced her legs apart. Then Elena climbed on the bed behind them and Anne felt the shock of a woman's touch on her legs and on her buttocks. There was no escape. Gino's arms and legs held her and his mouth was clamped to hers. She was suffocating from fear and revulsion. Elena began to massage her from behind.

She tore her mouth away from Gino's and screamed, "Stop, Elena! No."

"Shh," Elena soothed. "It's all right. Everything's all right."

Her words vibrated up Anne's spine. Anne thrust her hips back, trying to shake loose from that nauseating touch.

Gino put his left hand around both her wrists, twisting them behind her. With his right hand he reached into a drawer in the bedside table.

"Please no," she begged. She heard a click. The corner of her eye caught a flash of metal. It was a switchblade. He was really crazy! They were both crazy. He would kill her if she fought them.

Gino stuck the point of the knife behind her ear, piercing the flesh. She was a quarter of an inch from death, steel in her brain. She didn't move.

"If you fight me, I'll slit open your breasts, one

by one. Do you understand?" His voice was gravelly, she could hear the edge of mania in his tone.

"Yes," she whispered.

Gino gave Elena a nod and she stopped her explorations. Anne's relief was exquisite.

"Get up," Gino said. She scrambled off him, avoiding Elena's gaze.

He sat up and grabbed her face, twisting her chin so that she faced Elena. "Look at her," he commanded, picking up the knife. He took her hand and placed it on Elena, guiding it over her body. Anne was sick with loathing and fear and she trembled as she felt the forbidden flesh beneath her hands. Elena leaned forward to kiss her. She stiffened but she endured it. Oh God, she prayed, help me!

"Touch her," Gino said, pushing her back on the bed and placing Elena on top of her so that they both faced him. He still had the knife.

Anne stroked Elena's body as if she were stroking her own. Elena's back pressed into her, her head was thrown back over Anne's shoulder, waiting for Gino.

Gino was fucking Elena on top of her, crushing her with every thrust. They were both so involved with each other Anne seemed to be forgotten. She desperately wanted to get out of there. She wiggled and turned and pushed until, occupied with each other, they rolled off her, and she inched over slowly, trying to get to the door. Gino noticed her movement and grabbed her by the hair, his fingers entwined in the roots. He yanked her backward onto the bed, forcing her to stay there—pulling on her scalp. She screamed with pain, crying out, "Please—no!" She couldn't reach him. He was behind her and so was the knife.

Nobody heard the noise outside, or the sound of people running, or the door until it crashed open and Carlo burst into the room.

Anne cried out, "Help! Carlo, help! He's got a knife!" Then she saw the gun.

Gino froze, with Elena still under him, Anne's head held to the bed by his hand. He saw the gun, too.

Brenda and Frederico were in the doorway behind Carlo as he took in the picture, every line scorched in acid, every sickening aspect repeated in the mirrored canopy.

Anne screamed, "No! No! Carlo . . ." just as he raised his arm toward Gino and fired. Frederico pulled at Carlo from behind and the shot missed, hitting the wall. Gino rolled over and ducked behind the bed.

Frederico was pulling at Carlo, trying to stop him. Carlo reached back and hit Frederico across the cheek with his right hand, pushing him out of the way. The butt of the gun struck bone and Frederico cried out in pain. Brenda caught Frederico as he fell, cradling him in her arms. Anne curled up on the bed away from Elena, who lay where Gino had left her.

Carlo fired at Gino again, hitting the mattress.

The bullet went through and struck the floor. Anne reached over and pulled Elena off the bed, out of range. They huddled together, two naked figures.

"Carlo, don't do this," Gino pleaded. "Carlo, you don't understand. They came to me, they wanted me, I tried to stop them, I . . ." Carlo fired in rapid succession through the edge of the mattress, still missing Gino. He was running out of ammunition. He dropped to the floor and came face to face with Gino who was on his side under the bed. Carlo took aim and fired. This time the bullet struck Gino in the groin.

Gino screamed.

Carlo aimed at Gino's head and pulled the trigger. There was a silent click. All the chambers were empty, but Gino had fainted.

Carlo dropped his gun and went to cover Elena. Anne reached for her dress, but Carlo knocked it out of her hands.

"No! You stay as we found you. Let the world see you for the whore you are!" Anne flinched as if he'd struck her.

Brenda was horrified by what she'd witnessed. Frederico's jaw was red and swollen. He was too stunned to move. She heard the gun drop to the floor and ran to help Gino. His groin was torn and bloody; the smell of urine mixed with burned flesh made her sick. She pulled him out onto the floor and covered him with a blanket.

"Somebody get the police! Call an ambulance.

Do something! He'll die!" His face was gray and he was unconscious. She knew she should stop the bleeding, but she didn't know how. She was afraid to approach Anne because Carlo stood over her clenching and unclenching his fists, breathing in frenzied gasps. He was crazy and she could see he might attack any one of them. She called to him softly, "Carlo." He didn't respond. She walked over to him and touched his arm. He winced and pulled away. She faced him calmly, but her knees were jelly. "We've got to get help. How do we notify the authorities?"

Carlo couldn't answer her. He was crying; tears ran down his face, but he made no attempt to wipe them.

"This cottage has no phone," Anne said quietly, afraid to move from where she was standing. "I'll go for the police." Carefully she picked up her dress, never moving more than a fraction at a time so as not to disturb Carlo.

Frederico recovered from his momentary shock and came over to Anne. When he saw she was all right he went over to Carlo, who appeared absolutely blank. He took him over to the chair where he had just been sitting.

"Brenda," Frederico said, "go with Anne to the Splendido. There's a phone there."

"You mustn't be found here!" Brenda said. "You go with Anne!"

He shook his head firmly. "Don't waste any more time. I'll be all right." He had already considered the consequences of his being found here—his life with his family, his business reputation could be irreparably damaged. But no matter. He had lived a circumspect life for years and any adverse results arising out of his affair with Brenda would have to be dealt with. His conscience was clean and that was really all that counted.

Carlo was in shock. He thought of Gino and the filth he had spread on everyone. He felt the slime that covered Gino coming at him from across the room. Carlo lifted his feet to keep himself from being covered by the slime, but someone's fingers were around his throat, squeezing hard, preventing him from breathing. He knew it was Hassan, pretending to be Gino, covered with the slime. He cried and pulled at those iron fingers to let him breathe. A man with a knife was stalking him, throwing knives at him, and they tore into his flesh. He dodged and twisted to get away from the knives, but they pierced him over and over again. Gino's eyes burned at him from where he lay, crouched behind the bed ready to leap at him and tear him apart. Gino. Hassan. The Devil. They were coming to take him to Hell! He screamed again, tearing at his throat, dodging the knives, kicking his feet, terrified of the advancing captors. Finally he lapsed into whimpering and crying, lost in his torment.

Frederico watched, unable to relieve the torture.

Elena huddled in a cocoon of shame until her body stopped shaking. Carlo's cries and suffering were her own. With each of his agonized sounds she felt her own inexpressible horror. Only one thing would stop that sound of suffering, that anguish she knew so well. She had thought of nothing else since the moment Carlo arrived. The way he had looked at her! She took her clothes and went into the bathroom. She dressed carefully and washed her face, but avoided looking in the mirror. There would have been nothing there if she had looked. Then she walked into the adjoining dressing room and to the closet where Gino kept his tennis racket. She knew he often made his exchanges on the tennis court. She brought the racket back with her to the bathroom, cradling it in her arms. She sat down on the toilet and twisted open the end of the racket, shaking out a packet of white powder. In her purse was a kit. In only moments the welcomed numbness was coursing through her body and the sounds of Carlo's crying grew more faint as did the beating of her heart.

Anne and Brenda hurried along the darkened path, slipping over loose stones and pushing aside branches.

"For God's sake," Brenda said, "what happened back there, Anne?"

"I can't explain it now," she replied, knowing that soon she would have to say it to someone.

"We'd better get our stories straight," Brenda said. "There are reputations at stake here. Important ones."

Anne remained silent.

"Anne, what happened?"

"What did it look like to you?"

"Like you were being sexually molested at knifepoint by a maniac! And that Carlo was coming after Gino with a gun."

"Gino's a monster!" Anne whispered, as they arrived at the hotel. There was a police car parked in front. Three officers had stayed to question the personnel after returning there with the sheikh and his party. When Anne explained about the shooting they radioed for an ambulance and hurried with her and Brenda back to the cottage. There was no more opportunity for talk.

Gino was still unconscious when they got back, though he looked worse than when they'd left. But it was the sight of Carlo that twisted the knife in Anne's heart. He was writhing, tormented in his own hell. It was pitiful.

Brenda went over to Frederico to see about his face. Then she noticed Elena was gone. "Where's Elena?" she asked.

"She went into the bathroom to get dressed."

A shock of recognition went through Anne as she stared at Brenda, shock mixed with a feeling of dread.

They both knew the moment they saw her that Elena was dead. She was slumped against the sink, the hypodermic still in her vein and she was beyond any help. The expression frozen on her face was one of utter despair.

"I can save her," Anne cried, trying to get into the bathroom. But Brenda forced her back into the other room.

Anne felt the realization slam into her; there was nothing she could do. All her emotions from this horrible night came pouring forth. She sobbed from the depths of her grief. It can't be. It can't be. If only I'd been here. If only I hadn't left she'd be alive. Why couldn't things have been different? There was no comfort, only this shattering explosion of guilt and blame. I was my brother's keeper. If I could not prevent her death, who will prevent mine?

They led Anne, crying hysterically, out of the cottage.

It was nearly dawn before Brenda and Frederico could return to their hotel. The horrible sights still whirled around in Brenda's head. She had waited at the villa until a doctor gave Anne a shot to put her to sleep, and then she told Paolo she would be back in the morning. The poor man, she thought. His whole life had been uprooted tonight.

She and Frederico didn't talk as they undressed for bed, politely passing each other in the confines of the strange room. Both of them had been so strong tonight, but she felt the need for understanding right now.

"How is your head?" she asked, sitting on the edge of the bed.

"I took something for it and it feels better now," he answered.

"What do you think really happened there tonight?" she said.

"We'll probably never know."

"I don't think I want to know."

He nodded.

"Just as I don't really want to know what is going to happen to us."

He turned from the closet, buttoning his pajamas. "I think it's too late to discuss that right now, don't you?"

"If I thought so, I wouldn't have brought it up. Tonight's tragedies have made me very frightened for my own happiness. I want to protect it, and keep it from disintegrating like the lives of those people have disintegrated tonight. My God, how Anne must feel!"

He smiled at her. "You're always thinking about others, aren't you?"

"Not always. Right now I'm thinking about me, and us."

He came and sat next to her on the bed. "All right, we'll talk about it now. But just remember, I'm not as young as you. I need my sleep!"

"I'll remember," she said, putting her arm around him.

He stood up, facing her. "If I'm going to be serious, you can't have your arm around me. It clouds my thinking."

She nodded, waiting for him to speak, feeling her heart traveling slowly up to her throat, forcing all the blood in her head to stay where it was and beat thickened pulses in her brain.

"Tonight has brought home to me some truths that I have been avoiding before this. I assume that's why you feel such an urge to talk right now?" He didn't wait for her answer. "I would have liked to give myself more time. I'm not ready for the decision that I must make . . ."

Here it comes, she thought. So long, Brenda, I love you but Elizabetta comes first.

". . . and I haven't wanted to mention it to you until I was certain. But tonight has forced the issue. Many things ran through my mind when I saw Anne on that bed with Gino and Elena. I thought, She is Brenda's friend! Will I ever walk in on Brenda and find her like this? I know that isn't fair. But I am a man, living in a society where men think that way."

"It's rather like blaming a woman for losing her breast to breast cancer," she commented, feeling tears beginning to sting her eyes.

"You are right. And before I met you I would have accepted my own judgments as valid, and condemned all the people in that room as depraved, and anyone who knew them also. But I know you, and I know how wonderful you are. And how you make me feel! And I'm ashamed to tell you that for a moment I wanted to walk away from that room and deny that I ever did know you."

"You don't have to tell me these things, Frederico. They are your private thoughts. We are not in temple now."

"Every place that I am with you is a temple to me. I know that I am too old for you, yet you seem to want me. I believe you deserve a younger man, who can give you a family, who will be with you long after I'm gone."

So this is it. He's letting me off easy, but he's letting me off.

"If you would have me, I would like us to live together. In Italy one must live for five years under legal separation and then I could be divorced from Elizabetta and we could be married."

She saw his hands shake before he put them behind his back. She rose slowly from the bed and went to put her arms around him.

"Is it what you want?" he asked.

But she couldn't talk for the heart still in her throat. She only nodded and hugged him with all her might.

Soft voices came to Anne from out of a haze. Everything was throbbing. She was in her room at the villa. Sunlight scored by the slats of the shutters burned her eyes. She lay there for a moment, getting her bearings, trying not to be frightened by the thought of Elena as she'd last seen her. She did not know how she'd gotten back or who had put her to bed. She turned toward the whispering. She could see Brenda standing in the doorway talking to Frederico, but she could not hear them, could not know what they were saying to each other.

"But will she divorce you?" Brenda asked.

"There is nothing that will stand in my way, darling. After last night I will not live apart from you. You deserve more than that. We will face the world together, you and I. Don't worry!"

"And your sons?"

"They are grown men, Brenda. Angelo will be married soon himself. You cannot deny me my happiness."

She shook her head and the blond curls bounced with the motion, then she leaned forward and kissed him, pushing him gently out of the doorway, and closed the door behind him.

"How are you?" she said to Anne, coming toward the bed.

"How long have I been asleep?"

"It's nearly noon. That sedative they gave you was strong."

The throbbing was subsiding to a dull ache. Then the events of last night hit her full force. "Oh Carlo! Poor Carlo—and Elena. Tell me it isn't true."

Brenda took her hand. "The funeral will most likely be tomorrow. Paolo Brisson is arranging everything. There's a mass for Elena today in a local church."

"How is Carlo?"

"They've taken him to a psychiatric hospital in Genoa."

"Will he be all right?"

"I don't know," Brenda said. But her expression said no. "All of us will have to go to the Questura and make our statements."

"What will happen then?" she said.

"There won't be any criminal action. Frederico's already spoken to the *commendatore*. We've both agreed to be witnesses that Gino was attacking you and Elena, and Carlo shot him in your defense. Gino's criminal record is enough to convict him."

Anne felt a terrible sense of mourning, as if an entire class of people had self-immolated before her eyes.

"Where will the funeral be?" She sat up and got out of bed. Life would go on in spite of the devastation around her and the nothingness inside.

"We're not certain yet. The Brisson family has a mausoleum in Rome, but Elena's family have their own small cemetery in their home town."

"Valdagno?"

"Yes, that's it."

So she would get to see Valdagno after all. "Has anyone notified Alessandro and his mother?"

"Alessandro is here, Anne. He arrived earlier this morning. He's waiting for you downstairs."

Alessandro here. A spark of life pulsed inside her for a brief moment, but then it died out again. What good would it do to see him? His feelings for her were plain enough the last time she saw him, and this latest disaster would only increase them. "I don't want to see him, Brenda, please! Give him my condolences. And tell him I'll come to the funeral no matter where it is."

"He's come a long way to see you, Anne. You must speak to him."

"I don't understand. I thought you were the one who hated him on my behalf. Remember how he 'took' me. What does he want, more money?"

And to Anne's surprise, Brenda smiled. "Not exactly! Why don't you get dressed and then pack? It's going to be a busy day and we'd better be ready to leave. I'll give Alessandro your message," she said, and left Anne alone.

Anne went into the bathroom and undressed. When she was in the shower she realized that she was washing away the last traces of Elena. Was she my friend? How could she have willingly destroyed me if she'd been my friend? But she knew Elena had been too troubled to be anyone's friend. And what did I do for her? Anne thought. I held out the illusion of friendship to her and then didn't follow through.

And Carlo, beautiful Carlo, made to suffer because of all of them. How could she ever make it up to him? What kind of destruction had she wrought? Searching for change had soiled her, trying to grow had sullied her; what then was left?

She was dressed and half through with her packing when there was a knock on the door.

"Come in," she said.

The door opened and Alessandro stood there. She saw his tentative smile, and his kind eyes, and she could hardly breathe.

"Hello, my darling," he said.

She was shocked by his tone. She never would have expected endearment in his voice. He took a step toward her and her heart lurched.

"Hello, Alex." Her voice trembled.

"Are you all right?" He took another step.

"No," she said, beginning to cry. All this time, all that wild searching and trying and playing at sex, and he was what she'd wanted. And the one she'd truly lost. She wiped her face. Carlo was his substitute, Jeff was his predecessor, Gino was a horrible mistake. Why couldn't she have seen it before? Before it was too late.

"I'm so sorry about Elena," she said.

"And I'm sorry, Anne." She looked back again, and this time there was no mistaking his expression. "I have a terrible pride. If I have lost you, I am only to blame."

"This is not a day to talk about blame," she said softly, trying to understand his words.

"I've brought you something," he said, handing her a manila file.

412

It contained duplicate orders, with recent dates, made out to "Anne Scott for Alessandro." Orders from Bloomingdale's, from Harrods, from Bonwit Teller, from Galerie Lafayette, and letters from *Vogue*, from *Elle*, from *Bazaar*, from *Mode International*, requesting samples for photographs. "What is this?" she asked. Some elaborate joke? But it was too authentic to be a joke, dates and signatures and style numbers and photocopies of deposits.

"It's my apology to you. And my way of showing my gratitude."

"But how?" She didn't deserve gratitude, if anything she deserved punishment. "When did this happen?"

"When Frederico Segri became our financial partner. These are advance orders. I expect them to triple after the October prêt-à-porter. And my darling, wait until you hear them sing your praises!"

"I don't understand, Alessandro, what are you saying? That we are in business again, with Frederico? And that the business is a success?" It was almost too much after last night. Somewhere she knew it was wonderful news, but she didn't feel the wonder.

"And why am I suddenly your 'darling'? Because you want my designs, because you want my money!" She saw his crestfallen look but she had to say it. "After all this time, and not a word from you? How can I be your darling if you wouldn't even let me see you in the hospital?" Some of that pain came back again, mixing with the ache already there. How much more could she take? His voice made her turn.

"I wouldn't let you? I wanted you to come!" he said. "Yours was the only name I put on the list of visitors."

"But your mother told me I was specifically denied visiting privileges. She showed me the notice. I came every day. She wouldn't let me in."

"But I knew nothing about it! Dear Lord, Anne, listen to me. I must make you understand. My mother must have wanted to hurt you very much, and she has hurt me too. I cannot forgive her for what she's done, I can still barely believe it! But I wanted you to be with me in the hospital, more than anything else. I thought that you were angry and disgusted with me for everything that had happened. The day you came to see me I knew I was right because you were going away."

"Only because you didn't want me," she whispered.

"I've always wanted you," he said. "Since our lunch together a year ago. I love you, Anne."

She heard his words but her heart was so heavy with pain that at this moment love meant very little to her.

"Somewhere inside of me, I know I love you, too, Alessandro. But it's taken me a long time to keep from feeling that love. I've been denying it

414

ever since you sent me away. I don't even know if I can ever love."

"Does it have something to do with last night?"

She nodded. "If I could only shut off my brain. Stop these incessant voices that accuse, and judge and condemn me."

"You have always been harder on yourself than anyone deserves. Why don't you listen to me for a change." He took her hand and sat her down on the bed, putting his arm around her, but she sat stiff and unyielding.

"You must remember that you are human. You are entitled to make mistakes, because you learn and grow from them. Gino Belmonte was a drug dealer. You did not turn him into one. Carlo would have shot Gino, no matter what situation he found Gino in. He took a gun from the ship for that purpose. Elena has always been addicted and she was also a lesbian. That is why Paolo divorced her. But you brought her something that no one had ever brought to her before, true friendship. Carlo was tied to her, Elena caused him terrible pain, and her other friends used her as she used them. You were unique in her life, and she treasured you. She had to love you because there was no other way she could repay you. As for me, I have been guilty of letting my pride rule my heart. I should have told you long ago how I felt, even if you didn't share my feelings. I wouldn't risk being hurt, so I hurt you instead. You'll have to be patient with me. I've spent many years living another way."

His words began to make sense to her and she relaxed in his embrace, resting her head against his shoulder. She could feel the tight bands of resistance begin to give way as his words dug their way through the debris that had been accumulating since her discovery of Jeffrey and Jill. She waited in the comfort of his arms until the deadened heart inside started to beat again, until the shame and guilt subsided enough to feel the stirrings of joy again, until the breath inside her body filled her with life.

"Will you give me some time?" she asked.

"All the time you want!" he said. "At least until the day after tomorrow."